Rome is
Where the
Heart is

Rome is Where the Heart is

TILLY TENNANT

bookouture

Published by Bookouture
An imprint of StoryFire Ltd.
23 Sussex Road, Ickenham, UB10 8PN
United Kingdom
www.bookouture.com

ISBN: 978-1-78681-117-2
eBook ISBN: 978-1-78681-116-5

For Jonny Fart Pants. You know I love you, farts and all.

One

Kate Merry had long suspected that Friday the thirteenth had it in for her. It couldn't be personal, of course, but something had brought her to its attention and each time it came around she seemed to be the default victim. There had been flat tyres, burst pipes, redundancy notices, the dreadful skirt-in-pants debacle of one particular Friday the thirteenth in 2004, along with various smaller but no less galling offences over the years. Even as a child she had been on the Friday the thirteenth bad-luck radar, falling victim to a tricycle clash in the playground of her primary school that had resulted in a broken toe. But all those past days of misfortune would be eclipsed by the Friday the thirteenth when she was thirty, a day that would change her life forever. Kate wasn't to know this when she opened her front door after a long day at work to find her husband standing in the hallway with his suitcases. But although this was by far the worst Friday the thirteenth ever, it also marked the day when lady luck had finally had enough of taunting her.

She stared at the suitcases, and then noticed the taxi with its engine idling, just outside the front door. There was an obvious explanation but it was one she didn't want to believe – couldn't believe at all.

'What's going on?'

'I'd have thought it was obvious.' Matt's reply was casual, cold even, but Kate could tell by the way he couldn't meet her eye he'd been caught red-handed in a way he wasn't prepared for.

'If it was obvious I wouldn't have asked.' Kate's tone was crisp and belied her churning stomach.

'I'm going to stay at Connor's for a bit, sort my head out.'

'Connor's? What do you mean, "sort your head out"? What's to sort?'

'Us. . . at least, what I think about us.'

'What does that mean?'

'What do you think it means? You can't say you didn't see this coming.'

Kate stared at him. 'See what coming? What are you saying, Matt?'

'I need a break.'

'What? A holiday? A week off? What the hell does that mean?'

'I need to be away from you, that's what it means.' He rubbed a hand through dark hair that was already grey at the temples. He looked tired and drawn – a far cry from the bright-eyed eighteen-year-old she had married, the man who had been in her life since they'd started high school together. If she was really honest with herself she too had felt they had been stuck in a rut and they were a long way from the bubbly couple they'd once been. But this seemed so extreme. Things weren't that bad, were they? Shouldn't they at least talk about it first? Despite what he'd just said, she hadn't seen this coming, hadn't imagined for a moment that his complaints and grumblings of discontent meant anything.

'You're leaving me?'

'It's just space – you know? It'll be good for both of us – it'll help us both to decide what we want.'

'I want you! I don't need space to decide that! At least come in and talk to me before you do anything else. Twelve years of marriage has got to be worth that, hasn't it?'

'Kate, we've done nothing but talk and it's got us nowhere.'

'No, we haven't! Not properly. You've never mentioned leaving! How is that talking?'

'You wouldn't have listened even if I had,' he replied quietly. 'And when were we supposed to get the time to talk when you're never around?'

'I have to work! I have commitments outside our marriage. Am I supposed to forget all that and be at your beck and call twenty-four hours a day, seven days a week?'

'You're always with your sisters—'

'You're saying I can't see my sisters?'

'That's not what I'm saying,' he fired back irritably. But then he checked himself, paused, and when he looked at her, Kate could see how much this was hurting him. So why was he doing it? 'It's too late,' he said finally. 'The rot is set in and I don't see a way back from here.'

'So when you said you needed a break that was a lie so that I'd let you walk out of the door without a fight? It was just so you could stop the meter running on that taxi waiting for you outside?'

'I didn't want to hurt you.'

'Oh, right. Because this way isn't hurting at all.' She narrowed her eyes. 'I suppose what you were actually hoping for was to be gone before I got in from work, so that you could take the coward's way out and not have to face me at all?'

Matt shifted awkwardly, his gaze dropping to the antique tiled floor of their hallway. Kate let out a hollow laugh.

'How inconsiderate of me to finish work early today. What would I have arrived back to? A note on the table? A text? Dinner in the oven? Nothing?'

He shook his head, but he couldn't look her in the eye.

'Is there someone else?' she asked in a low voice.

'No.'

'You expect me to believe that? This, all of a sudden? If there's nobody else then why are you leaving?'

'There has to be another woman?'

'Of course not – not if it was any other man we were talking about. But I know you, Matt, better than you know yourself, and I know that you need someone; you're not built for life alone.'

'Well maybe I changed! Maybe I'm not quite the pathetic needy man you seem to think I am.'

'I never said you were pathetic and needy, but I don't believe for a moment that you're up to life on your own. It's just not the sort of person you are.'

'Believe what you like. I'm leaving and it's down to nothing apart from the fact that you and me don't work any more. This marriage is dead in the water, and it has been for a long time now.'

'So that's it? We don't try? We don't fight for it? If there's no one else then there's no reason why we can't work it out.'

'There's no fighting to be done, and I don't want to work it out. I've grown up, Kate; I'm not the man you married. We were too young, and we thought we could survive growing up but we couldn't. That's all there is to it.'

Kate stared at him, tried to be strong and calm, but inside there was a mess of emotions that couldn't be contained. 'You selfish bastard,' she said, fighting back tears. 'We've known each other since we were eleven and that's all I'm worth? We've both grown up but I've grown up living a life that includes you. I've gone out of my way to make you happy, considered your feelings in everything I've ever done since we got together and you throw it back in my face without so much as an explanation, without one attempt to make it work when the going gets a little tough? You're bored and now you want out, and you don't give a shit about the consequences, or what it means for your wife, who has lived her life with you always at the forefront of every decision? I thought you were better than that. It just goes to show that you never really know anyone at all.'

He didn't say another word. He didn't even say goodbye. Matt picked up his suitcases and left, and he never slept under their roof again.

Two

Six months later Kate's living room was bathed in the warm morning sun cascading through the blinds. It set the deep red of her chimney-breast wall ablaze, reflecting back from the gilt of the ornate mirror that graced it, and gave the room all at once a vibrancy and cosiness that spoke volumes about the person who lived there.

'Keep still!' she chided, slapping Anna's legs. Her sister was perched precariously on a stool as Kate pinned the hem of a blue satin ball gown. Anna was taller than Kate by an inch, the same shade of red hair tumbling around her slender freckled shoulders, her eyes a deeper shade of the colour that turned from blue to grey to green depending on the light.

'I am keeping still,' Anna complained. 'Sort of anyway. It's hard to keep still on a wobbly old stool.'

Kate blew a stray lock of hair away from her forehead as she leaned back to assess her handiwork. 'It's about as straight as it's going to be with fidget-knickers wearing it.'

'Oi!'

Kate grinned. 'You can get down now and take it off – carefully!'

Anna stepped off the stool and took herself to the full-length mirror that Kate used for dress alterations to admire her reflection. 'It's gorgeous. I can't believe you made this.'

'Are you saying I'm crap?'

'Of course not,' Anna laughed. 'These bloody corporate award nights are a pain in the arse. It's all very well for those at the top of the food chain who can afford to spend five hundred quid on a ball gown to get pissed in at what amounts to a glorified work's outing, but I can do without such frivolities. That's why I'm so thankful I have you to help me out. I don't know what I'd have done if I hadn't had you. I suppose I would have had to stump up the cash or wave goodbye to any future promotions, but it would have pissed me off. I couldn't do what you do, not in a million years. I think it's amazing and you've saved me so much money!'

'That was the idea,' Kate said as she packed away some loose pins. 'I would hate for you to miss out on this awards thing, especially if you've won one and you hadn't turned up because the dress code pissed you off. . .' She looked up and caught the grin flashed by Anna. Kate's sister may have been complaining about it, but secretly she wouldn't have missed the event for the world, just in case she had won an award. 'Besides, the chance to make a ball gown – you were hardly going to stop me, were you?'

'I don't know why you keep going into that awful office when you could open a shop to make your own dresses and people would flock to you.'

'I doubt that would happen. I've got a mortgage to pay on my own too – at least until Matt and I manage to sell the house.' Her gaze swept over the living room. High ceilings, original coving, a Victorian fireplace with a wood-burning fire, beautiful bay windows that invited daylight to flood in, wooden floors and antique furniture. She and Matt had stretched themselves to buy it, sank their last pennies into it, and it was all she had ever dreamed of in a house. She had thought that she and Matt would live there together forever. Now she faced the prospect of losing not just him but the house as well. Divorce proceedings were close to being done, and she had made it all too easy for Matt to get his own way. Perhaps the fight had gone from her; perhaps a small part of her thought that he wouldn't really go through with it, and by being agreeable she might make him see what he was throwing away and he would change his mind. Perhaps she loved him too much not to let him have whatever made him happy, or perhaps she loved him so little that she no longer cared. Kate didn't even know herself how she felt any more; her emotions had been such a jumble since the bombshell had been dropped, and it was only now, as things were winding up, that she was beginning to sort things in her own head. Despite all this she had fought a little harder over the house. She loved it and she wanted it; the house represented security and familiarity, and it was all she had left to cling to in the storm of the life she had known being ripped up around her. It was tough, paying the mortgage alone, but she would have continued to do it if she had a hope of ever getting a mortgage that would lend her Matt's share too so she could buy him out. Sadly, her financial adviser had told her quite emphatically that wasn't going to happen and so she had to be prepared for the worst. Knowing that hadn't stopped her from trying to stay there for as long as possible though.

'I wish we could help,' Anna said softly. 'Lily and I talk about it all the time but we don't know what we could do, and you wouldn't take money from us anyway. . .'

Kate shook herself. 'Don't be daft. Of course I wouldn't take your money, and it's not for you and Lily to worry about; you're my sisters, not my keepers. It's not anyone's mess but mine and Matt's, and I don't expect anyone to bail me out.'

'I know but. . .'

Kate forced her brightest smile. 'Now, do you want a corsage on this? It looks a bit bare around the neckline. Or we could sit one on the waist if you'd prefer?'

'Kate. . .' Anna frowned. 'You're not fooling anyone, you know.'

'Not you as well. Lily was grumbling at me last week.'

'That's what sisters do. We may not share a room any more—'

'Thank God.'

'—but that doesn't mean we stop thinking and caring about you when you're not there.'

'I know, and I appreciate it, but I'm fine. You're both worrying over nothing.'

'Who's worrying over nothing?' Lily appeared at the doorway carrying three mugs on a tray, which she deposited on a side table before giving Anna's dress an approving once-over. The youngest of the three sisters, she shared the delicate colouring of the other two, but her eyes were an even deeper shade of blue.

'Everyone,' Kate replied, a note of irritation creeping into her tone. 'I'm thirty and I think that's old enough to look after myself.'

'No woman is an island,' Lily returned sagely as she handed out the drinks. 'I have Joel and Anna has Christian and you used to have Matt, but you were unlucky and that ended and we want to support you.'

Despite her irritation Kate had to laugh.

'I just don't need everyone mollycoddling me all the time,' she said. 'Even Matt keeps phoning, convinced that living in the house alone means I'm going to blow it up or something. He obviously only cares because he's thinking about his investment, not because he cares about me, and frankly I wish he'd stop. If Mum hadn't brought us up to be so infuriatingly polite I could tell him to piss off.'

'He's got a point,' Anna said. 'I mean, I do remember you melting my favourite Barbie on the stove when we were kids.'

'And you dropped my Hornby set down the stairs – the signals at Clapham Junction never quite worked the same after that,' Lily added.

'Then there was the time you flooded the bathroom. . .' Anna gave Lily a knowing look.

'And when you chucked warm water on the patio to melt the ice but then it froze again and Mum went flying down the garden path. . .' Lily put in.

'And—' Anna began, but Kate shushed her.

'OK. But that was when we were young. Every kid has daft accidents.'

'I didn't,' Lily said mildly.

'Well, we all know you're Miss Perfect,' Kate said tartly. 'Mum and Dad's baby – they protected you from everything.'

'I don't think either of us have had quite as many as you,' Anna put in. 'I think it comes from doing everything at a hundred miles an hour.'

'And you're the oldest so you probably had all your accidents before I was born,' Kate said, looking pointedly at Anna.

'I'm only two years older than you!' Anna laughed. 'What on earth did you think I could get into at two?'

'And I'm only two years younger than you,' Lily reminded Kate. 'Which means you were the baby for two years before I arrived so you can't use that excuse on me.'

'And get you,' Kate said, eyeing the slight bump at Lily's midriff, 'the baby of us the first to have a baby of her own.'

'I know,' Anna chimed in. 'I feel almost lazy that I haven't bothered to reproduce yet.'

Lily giggled. 'You've got the career. If I was a high-flying number cruncher I would have put it off too.' She smoothed a hand over her belly. 'We probably should have waited until Joel and I got married, but we've been together for a while now so it doesn't feel like a huge issue. It's lucky he's as excited as me, because it seems that baby will come when baby wants to come.'

'It turns out it's lucky I didn't get pregnant,' Kate said. 'All the times Matt put me off the idea I should have known . . .'

'I'm sure that wasn't the reason,' Anna said.

'Well, I suppose we'll never know,' Kate replied briskly.

Lily exchanged a worried glance with Anna before turning to Kate. 'You say you're OK every time we ask, but are you really?'

'*Yes.*'

'It's just that . . .' Anna paused. 'You seem as if you're hiding a lot of what's really going on in your head.'

Kate took the dress that Anna had wriggled out of and slipped it onto a hanger as her sister pulled on a dressing gown and clipped her hair back. 'Honestly, I'm fine, so everyone can stop worrying about me.'

'You can tell us that, but it doesn't mean it'll happen,' Anna said, and Lily nodded agreement. 'Mum is worried to death as well. She's even mentioned coming back home.'

'I don't know why. I've told her the same thing, and I most certainly don't want her to leave Scotland on my account; I know how much she loves it up there and living in the Highlands with Hamish has been the making of her since her breakdown after Dad died. Her coming home to baby me would just give me a guilt complex on top of all my other problems and would hardly do anything for her mental health either.'

'You've never really been without Matt, that's why. Mum was the first person to warn you about marrying young, but she accepted it because it was Matt and you'd been with him for so long it somehow seemed inevitable that you'd end up married. She hadn't expected it to happen so soon after college, but even though we worried, deep down we all thought it would last forever. You and Matt . . .' Anna paused.

'We were meant to be?' Kate finished with a wry smile. 'I thought so too. Why else would I have built my life around him?'

'Exactly!' Lily said. 'Which is why we're all just trying to look out for you. Nobody wants to interfere – we only want to make sure you're OK.'

Kate dropped to the sofa and reached over for her mug. 'I know. It's hard to come to terms with everything and I think I've buried my head in the sand a bit, tried to ignore it. But everyone worrying is somehow making it all real, because if you can all see the monster looming on the horizon then I have to look and see it too.'

Lily sat beside her and pulled her into a hug. 'But you have us and we'll all help you come to terms with your new life.'

Kate smiled at her. 'I know you will. I'm luckier than some in that respect. I just wish right now I could have a sneak peek of what that new life will look like – I might feel a bit easier.'

'You know what I think?' Anna said.

'What?'

'I think your new life will be fabulous.'

'Hmmmm,' Kate replied as she sipped her tea. 'So this is based on . . .?'

'A hunch,' Anna laughed. 'But if I know you, you'll make the best of the hand you've been dealt and will come out of this OK.'

'I absolutely agree,' Lily said. 'And we've got lots of exciting things coming to take your mind off all that rubbish with Matt.'

'Such as . . .?'

'You'll be an aunty for the first time! That's got to be exciting!'

'Well, yes, I suppose it is. But I'll only have a little part to play in junior's life really.'

'It's something to look forward to, though,' Anna said. 'For all of us. And you never know, the man of your dreams might be around the corner.'

'Maybe you'll bump into him when you come to antenatal classes with me,' Lily said brightly.

'I bloody hope not,' Kate said. 'If he's at antenatal classes I suspect he'll already have quite a packed relationship schedule.'

'Lily just means that you'll meet someone where you least expect it,' Anna put in.

'That would be very unexpected,' Kate said. 'But I take your point. Somehow I just don't see it happening any time soon. I think I'm just done with men, at least for the foreseeable future.'

'You say that now . . .' Lily wagged a finger at Kate as she reached into the biscuit barrel Anna had just passed to her. 'I have a feeling you'll be proved wrong. You're lovely and still young. I think there'll be a queue of men to date you when it becomes common knowledge that you're back on the market.'

'On the market – fab. Now I sound like a well-maintained semi-detached.'

'You know what I mean,' Lily laughed.

Kate tried to smile. It was comforting to think her sisters had faith in her. She only wished she could feel quite as confident herself.

* * *

The house felt too quiet and too big once Anna and Lily had bid their goodbyes and left. Kate almost wished she'd asked them to stay for supper, but even though they would have said yes, it would have been selfish. They both had early starts for work in the morning, Anna in her pressured number-crunching job for an investment firm and Lily at the PR company where she had only just begun to make a name for herself – and so had Kate when it came to it. Mr Woofy, the pet-supply warehouse where she worked as a sales executive (a posh name for an old-fashioned clerk Kate often said, though at other times she felt the word skivvy was more appropriate) was hardly as glamorous, but it was her job nonetheless, and she needed to be sitting at her desk by eight thirty if she was going to keep it. And she'd be used to the solitude of her empty house again after a couple of days.

Her gaze flicked to a pile of post on the mantelpiece, still unopened from that morning. She could try to fool herself that she hadn't opened it because she hadn't had the time, but she'd recognised the logo on the envelope and couldn't face the finality of what it contained. Perhaps she should have asked her sisters to stay after all; at least she wouldn't have been alone when her future stared her in the face – a future she hadn't asked for and didn't want.

As she tidied away her sewing box, dumped unwashed mugs in the sink, plumped up cushions in the living room and wiped down the kitchen surfaces in readiness for an early night, her mind kept going back to the letter mocking her from the mantelpiece. She could open it in the morning, and perhaps a day at work would put it all into perspective. At least she'd be too busy to dwell on it and maybe it wouldn't seem so bad when she finally got home. If she opened it now, she'd cry, and she wouldn't be able to sleep, and it would all look a hundred times worse tomorrow because she'd be tired as well.

All this was a lie, though, and lying to yourself was no kind of lie at all. There was no point in putting it off any longer, and if she was going to put her life back on track she needed to do this. If she cried herself to sleep, then so be it, but at least she'd be facing the new day knowing that it was the first day of her new life as a single woman.

Snatching the pile of post from the shelf, she flicked through it until she found the envelope bearing the logo of Lennon & Lennon Solicitors. There was a heartbeat of doubt as she stared at it, a sick feeling in her stomach, like the floor was falling away from her. But then she slid her thumb beneath the flap and ripped it open.

Decree absolute. There it was. The end, the beginning, whichever way you wanted to look at it, the *absolute* bit was what mattered. She had once seen a future where Matt would be with her forever, just as he had been with her all through her teenage years and beyond, but now all she saw were the letters of the word swimming before her. Absolute. Final, no going back, the end of the road.

Three

Kate blinked in the sunshine as she stepped off the plane and made her way across the tarmac, a lone traveller swept along with her fellow passengers on the 10.37 flight to Fiumicino Airport. Moments before the pilot had advised them in warm, friendly tones tinged with a rather sexy Italian accent that the temperature on the ground was a balmy twenty-one degrees, pleasant for early June, reminded them that they needed to set their clocks an hour forward from Greenwich Mean Time and that their flight was bang on schedule. Then he had gone silent, and the descent had begun, Kate craning to get a first glimpse of her destination, her stomach churning with both excitement and apprehension, laced with disappointment that, due to the angle of their approach, all she could see from her window was azure skies. A brisk, warm breeze greeted her as the air hostesses said their goodbyes, sweeping the stray hairs from her clip into her face, and the smell of aviation fuel rose from the ground in a shimmering heat haze. Baggage handlers shouted to one another over the steady roar of idling engines and the screech of planes taking off.

Rome. She was finally here.

On the night she had opened her decree absolute, there had been disbelief. And then sadness, followed by anger and resentment. But as the night wore on, sleep no closer at 3 a.m. than it had been at ten the previous evening, she had settled into a weary acceptance. She had given up waiting for sleep, and had got up to make herself a drink of something warm and comforting in the hope it might dull her senses and wear her out. But as she looked around her silent kitchen, the senses she had hoped to dull instead became heightened, and she began to think about what the future might hold. This life was hers now, and the decisions she took were hers alone. What had she always wanted? What paths had been denied by her marriage to Matt that she might explore now he was gone? She'd wanted children, but without a partner or a stable home environment that wasn't going to happen any time soon. She had wanted a perfect home and thought she almost had it, but that was about to be snatched away from her, and she had no idea where she might end up. On her wages it was hardly likely to be perfect. She had wanted a lifetime of happiness and contentment in a loving relationship, but that seemed a long way off now too.

That life was lost to her now, but she could salvage another one from its ashes. She had always loved to watch travel shows on TV, collected glossy holiday brochures for no reason other than to stare at the photos, and would listen to colleagues and friends talk about their adventures in foreign climes for hours, but for someone who was so interested in other countries she had been to very few. She had wanderlust in her veins, but she had suppressed the urge for the sake of an easy life, keeping Matt – who had no desire to see the world – happy. He especially hated large cities, and though he wasn't averse to the idea of holidays as such, his idea of a break was some cosy English seaside resort or a cottage in the country. While those holidays had been lovely, Kate longed to experience more of the world – new sounds, smells, languages and culture, the hustle and vibrancy of an alien landscape, a place without Tesco's or Johnny's Fish and Chips or the Rose and Crown. The one time she had cajoled and persuaded him to relent, they had spent a dismal weekend in Dublin. Kate had argued that it was so close to Britain it might as well be, and that at least everyone spoke English and he would be sure to find food similar to his old favourites. But he spent the two days sulking, despite the abundance of Guinness and chip serving establishments on every corner. The fact that it had rained continually, and that Grafton Street was so busy they were practically swimming against a tide of sales-obsessed shoppers only served to strengthen his conviction that big cities were awful places (except for Manchester, he said, because it was his home and different altogether, though Kate could never really see the logic in that argument), and the ones where the majority of residents were cursed with an accent not like his own were even more so.

So all the places Kate had wanted to visit remained unseen, and even though Anna and Lily had sometimes offered to go with her, something always got in the way. Or was that just Kate making excuses so that she wouldn't rock the boat with Matt? When she thought about those times now, she realised that she hadn't been keeping the peace in their marriage at all – she'd been a doormat. It had taken divorce to make her finally see that.

With sleep continuing to elude her and no nearer to figuring out what she wanted to do with the rest of her life, Kate took to searching for bargain flights online, putting in a range of dates to see what might come up. Before she knew it she was booking a flight to Rome. It was a place she had longed to visit above all others.

Anna and Lily had been horrified of course. As had her mum, all of them warning her of the dangers of a lone female travelling by herself.

But her mind had been made up, and she had come to an important decision. She was not going to be afraid of life, and she was not going to be afraid of it without Matt by her side. He had chosen to go his way and she was quite sure he was doing all the things he wouldn't have been able to do had they still been married (though she doubted that he was doing anything different than going to the pub and sitting in front of the telly in the flat he was now sharing with his single friend, Connor, which was what he'd mostly done when they were married) – and why should she be any different? It was time for a shake-up, to throw herself out into the world and see what it gave back.

Her boss at Mr Woofy's was hardly happy at the last-minute request for leave either, but Kate figured they owed her more than one or two favours for all the unpaid hours she'd given them, and she said as much, threatened to quit, and then basically nagged until she got a yes. It wasn't as if they were rushed off their feet. Neither was her job so demanding that the place would fall apart without her. The eventual agreement was a sign, she was sure, and she grabbed it with both hands.

Hustle and vibrancy was certainly what she was getting right now. The baggage carousel was a free-for-all, customs manned by a stern-looking woman who had simply flicked a sneering look over her passport before handing it back without a word, and she got lost in the airport for a good half an hour before she reached the taxi rank where cars waiting to take her to the city centre were lined up. Wiping a film of sweat from her brow, her cheeks already glowing as she laboured under the jacket that she had needed in Manchester but would have happily chucked into the nearest bin now, she stood and stared at the queue of people waiting. Though queue perhaps wasn't quite the right word, as it resembled a rugby scrum more than it did an orderly line.

Then she spotted a car, its driver on the pavement alongside, leaning against the door as he pulled on a cigarette. For some reason people weren't scrambling for him, though he didn't look too concerned about it. Despite her vague misgivings, Kate marched over, dragging her suitcases behind her.

'*Buongiorno*,' he greeted smoothly. 'English?'

'Yes,' Kate replied, taken aback by his immediate identification of her homeland. 'Are you going into the city centre?'

He tilted his head this way and that, as if he might or might not, but he hadn't quite decided whether the fancy had taken him yet. 'Where is the hotel?'

Kate took a scrap of paper from her jacket pocket and unfolded it to show him. He raised his eyebrows as the cigarette went back into his mouth and he took a long drag. 'It is a long way.'

'Oh. How much will that cost?'

He shrugged. 'The meter will run. I do not know until it stops.'

Hell. She'd only just got here and already she felt like a country mouse. She had the feeling she was about to get royally ripped off and there wasn't a thing she could do about it. Part of her didn't care – as long as she got safely to her hotel she'd just have to write it off and hope to get a bit savvier once she got used to being in the city. If only she'd spent a bit longer on TripAdvisor . . .

She was about to give him her luggage when she felt a tap on her shoulder.

'Excuse me.'

Kate turned to see a tall man, in his late twenties at a guess, blond hair sculpted to perfection by some kind of product, nicely tailored shirt and slacks, and a broad, apologetic smile. His American accent was unmistakable, and rather sexy.

'This might sound out of turn, but I couldn't help noticing you were alone. Might I ask if you're travelling alone or whether the rest of your party is going to pop up in a minute?'

'Oh, there's just me,' Kate replied, wondering whether she ought to be telling him this or not. But he seemed so harmless and friendly that she just had to go with her instincts. And it seemed as if he wanted to help too, which would be very welcome.

'I'm travelling alone too and I need a taxi. Would you like to share the cost?' He cast a glance at the taxi driver who was still leaning nonchalantly against his cab, inspecting a cigarette that was now almost smoked down to the filter. 'But I would recommend one of the official ones . . .' He pointed to the queue where white cars bearing the words *Roma Capitale* lined the kerb. 'Over there.'

'It'll take hours waiting in that queue,' Kate replied doubtfully.

'But you won't pay more than forty-eight euros,' the man said. 'Split between us that's even better. I promise I'll be a perfect gentleman and you can even take my photo and send it to your friends and family back home if it makes you feel better.'

'Why would I do that?'

'So you have a number-one suspect if I kidnap you,' he laughed.

'Oh.' Kate smiled. Regardless of the cost, it was a comforting prospect to share the cab with someone who appeared to know what he was doing. 'Where's your hotel, though? We might not be going anywhere near each other?'

'Don't worry about that,' he said cheerfully. 'At the very most we'll get charged forty-eight each, which is still better than not knowing how much you're going to get charged at the other end. Your hotel is within the walls, I take it?'

'The what?'

'The Aurelian Walls? Central Rome? Only these guys can get away with charging more if it's not.'

'I don't know.' Kate showed him the piece of paper. He pulled out his phone and tapped on a map, studying it for a moment.

'We're good. In fact you're just a couple of blocks away from me. That's got to be fate, right?'

'Perhaps.' Kate smiled. 'OK.'

The man looked at the driver. 'Sorry my friend, but we'll be taking one of the other cabs today.'

The driver threw him a sour look, followed by one for Kate, before reaching into his pocket and taking a new cigarette from a box.

'This way,' the American said, leading Kate back to the huge scrum for official taxis. 'First time in Rome?' he asked as they walked.

'Yes. I've always wanted to visit but I never got the chance. I get the feeling it isn't your first time.'

'God, no. I'm here far more than I want to be.'

'Oh?'

'Work trips. I make a lot of them.'

'Right. . .' Kate wanted to ask what he did for a living. Whatever it was sounded glamorous and exciting if it meant him travelling to Rome on a regular basis. But she'd only just met him and her Britishness wouldn't allow it.

'Here we are,' he said as they reached the back of the queue. 'It looks a lot worse than it is.' He held out a hand. 'I'm Jamie, by the way.'

'Kate,' she replied, shaking it. 'Thank you.'

'Don't thank me now; we're not in a cab yet.'

'But for saving me from getting ripped off.'

'Oh, I don't know that you would have been ripped off exactly, but this way is a lot safer for your euros. How long are you staying in Rome?'

'A week.'

'A week's good – plenty of time to see everything properly. Most people don't stay long enough. Anyone flying out to join you?'

'No.'

'If you don't mind me saying, that's bold.'

'You think? I hadn't really considered it that way; it was a bit of a spontaneous decision to come if I'm honest. I just wanted to get away.'

'Sounds enigmatic. What did you want to get away from?'

She shrugged. 'Home. Everything.'

'Something you'd rather not talk about?'

'It's no big deal,' she said. 'But I won't bore you with it. You know that film *Airplane!*?'

He nodded. 'Oooh, that's an oldie. I love that movie.'

'That bit where the main character is telling everyone his problems and they're all so desperately bored they're finding ways to kill themselves? That's what would happen if I told you about it.'

'You'd better not tell me then,' he laughed.

'Exactly.'

They shuffled down the line, and in ten minutes they were chatting like old friends. Kate didn't feel nearly as vulnerable as she had on her arrival and was beginning to enjoy Jamie's company immensely. She wondered what his schedule was for his stay, and whether he'd have time to spend with her. Not that she wanted to hang on his coat-tails all day, of course, and not that she wanted to come across as a desperate sap who couldn't do anything for herself, but it would be nice to get to know him and have a little company from time to time, perhaps for meals and such. Maybe then Rome wouldn't seem so scary after all.

* * *

The taxi crawled through the city. For some reason Kate had never imagined it would be so busy and so chaotic. Bikes and mopeds darted through parked and moving cars alike at terrifying speeds so that you never saw them coming until they were already upon you, and she kept jumping as they ripped past the open cab windows. Horns sounded with alarming regularity and traffic fumes intensified the soupy heat. Despite the pandemonium that seemed to characterise the roads, their driver was cheerful, unaware of the madness he worked in and humming along to something on the radio as he drummed on the steering wheel.

Jamie was happy to have Kate dropped off at her hotel first, and by the time they reached it almost an hour later, she had learned that he came from Texas originally but now lived in New York, that he worked in advertising for a swanky multinational company and visited clients all over the world, that his dad was a used-car salesman and his mum had run for mayor of their town twice but failed to get elected both times, so had decided to use her time to raise funds to feed and clothe the poor instead. Jamie's brother was also turning to politics and his career showed rather more promise than their mother's had, and Jamie himself had left a boyfriend back in New York who had recently proposed to him. At this information Kate had heaved a melodramatic sigh, lamented that all the good men were taken or batting for the other side, and they had giggled together, a sure sign that her offbeat sense of humour was something he instinctively understood. It was a good sign, but even if he had been available, and despite the fact that he was supernaturally handsome, Kate wasn't sure she was quite ready to throw herself into dating just yet. As they chatted, however, she quickly decided that she would probably have liked him better as a friend anyway, free of all the emotional traps of a full-on sexual relationship, which only ever served to complicate nice, clean, fun camaraderie in any case. You knew where you were with a man who wasn't trying to get into your knickers.

He had been so open and entertaining with the details of his life that Kate had found herself opening up too, and before long she had regaled him with the whole history of her and Matt. She told him all about the twenty-year plan they had drawn up when they first got married, about how she'd spent the whole of the inheritance left to her after her dad had died, and then how they'd scrimped and saved for the rest of the deposit so they could buy their dream house; how everyone said they'd married so young it wouldn't last and how they'd laughed at the fuss, how she'd put off having kids at his request because every year he said he didn't feel ready and how frustrated that made her. It was cathartic, healing, and despite all the lows she began to see the memories of their relationship in a far more positive light than she had before. Far from being the disaster it had felt like when the divorce finally came through, she began to remember the good times, the growing up together, how they had shaped each other for the better. The twelve years she had spent married to Matt hadn't been a waste at all; they had been an experience, and like all life experiences, they had intrinsic value for the way they helped decide who we became.

'Sounds like you had a rough time,' Jamie commented as she came to the end of the tale. 'I'm not surprised you felt like you wanted to get away.'

'It felt like it at the beginning. That day when I came home and found Matt in the hallway with his cases I thought my life had ended.'

'But you seem to be OK now.'

'I'm a lot better, but I have good friends and family around me and that helped.'

'That's lucky.' He smiled. 'The people we surround ourselves with can make a huge difference to how we deal with life.' He pulled a card from his pocket as the cab slowed to a halt outside a cream-fronted building. 'Here's my number. It's the company phone, but I answer night and day so call me if you need anything while you're here.'

Kate glanced out of the window as she took it. 'Thank you – that's so kind. It's been lovely to share a taxi with you.'

'I've enjoyed your company so it was no favour. It can get a little lonely here on your own all the time.'

She gave him another grateful smile, and then turned her gaze to the window again. They were parked outside a building of almost golden stone, wide ground-floor windows and a revolving glass door, festooned with Italian, European Union and various other flags that Kate didn't recognise hanging from poles protruding from the brickwork a few floors up. An old man in a black suit stood sentry at the entrance, greeting visitors who came to the doors.

'I think this is your hotel,' Jamie prompted.

'Oh! Yes, of course . . . I hadn't realised!'

'It's pretty nice – must have cost some . . .'

Kate shook her head, feeling rather flustered at his obvious insinuation. 'Don't imagine for a moment I'm rich or anything. This represents a huge hit on my credit card. But you know. . .' she gave a guilty little shrug, 'I'll worry about that when I get home. It's not every day you get divorced and need to let your hair down.'

'And there was me thinking I'd found myself a new millionaire friend.'

'Silly. . . I wish. . .' She fumbled in her purse and thrust a handful of notes at him. 'Is that enough to cover my half of the cab fare?'

'I'll tell you what I'll do,' he said. 'As you're not a millionaire after all, I'll put this on my expenses, and then you can meet me for dinner and a drink later. How does that sound?'

'I couldn't—'

'If I'd travelled alone I'd have been paying the full fare anyway so it makes no difference to my company.'

'But—'

'Honestly, it's nothing. I hope you don't think this forward, but what are your plans tonight?'

'I didn't really have any.'

'There's a great little place around the corner from here – Trattoria da Luigi. I'm going to eat there so why don't you meet me at around seven-thirty? Or later if that suits you better? Will that give you enough time to settle in at your hotel and freshen up? I could even come and meet you earlier. . . Show you around the immediate area a little. It's handy to know where the 7-Eleven is in case you have a desperate urge for candy.'

'They have 7-Elevens here in Rome?'

'No,' Jamie laughed. 'But I could show you the closest thing they do have.'

Kate paused. She liked Jamie but she hardly knew him. But this was her new life, wasn't it? The new Kate? And would the new Kate be scared of a friendly meal with a man who had been very kind to her and was safely engaged to the man of his dreams back in New York? And as for a friendly wander around the streets in broad daylight in full view of a thousand tourists – ditto. What possible reason was there to be scared?

'Yes,' she decided. 'I'd love that.'

'Great! You have my number, so I'll take yours too. I'll let you settle in and you can call me when you're ready to go.'

Kate's smile was rather more assured than she felt as they tinkered on their phones to exchange details. But she had committed now, and only time would tell if it was a good idea.

Four

It was a strange little convenience store, tucked away in the backstreets of an impossibly romantic city with a distinctly tired and unromantic air about it. Goods were stacked high in tight aisles with barely enough room to pass a stranger coming the other way, illuminated by flickering strip lights while a radio hummed opera in the background. But it was just what Jamie had promised – an all sorts shop where one could buy everything from pan scourers to milk.

'Well. . . this is interesting,' Kate said as she picked up a tin picturing some unidentifiable food on the front.

'This is the real Rome,' Jamie replied with a grin. 'It can't all be gelato and Gucci.'

'And you use this place a lot?'

He shrugged. 'I wouldn't say a lot. But occasionally when I need gum or a newspaper.'

'And I thought I was going to see the sights.'

'Plenty of time for that. You need to know where the important stuff is first.' He raised his eyebrows at the can she was still holding. 'You want to buy that?'

'No,' Kate laughed, putting it quickly back on the shelf. 'Or maybe I would if I knew what it was.'

'You want to walk further on? There are some other shops down this alleyway that might be more to your taste.'

'I'd rather go for a walk outside. There's loads of time for shops; I want to soak up a bit of atmosphere.'

'OK. How about we walk and find somewhere for coffee?'

'How about we walk and find gelato?' Kate asked with an impish grin. 'I'm feeling naughty.'

'Well that won't be too difficult as there's a great little place on this row. If it wasn't tucked away in such a terrible location, I swear you wouldn't be able to get near it, it would be so famous. Lucky for us it's never that busy and their flavours are to die for.'

'Now that's what I'm talking about!' Kate grinned. 'Lead on!'

'So, is your hotel as amazing as it looks?' Jamie asked as he held the shop door open for her and they emerged into the balmy air of the streets once more.

'It's nice,' Kate said as they began to walk.

'That doesn't sound very enthusiastic.'

'If I'm honest I feel a bit like a fish out of water. I sort of wish I'd picked somewhere a bit cheaper and a bit more homely now. But it's OK and I have everything I need.'

'Maybe you'll get used to a bit of luxury once you've spent a week in it.'

'Maybe, but I doubt it. I think I'm just not a luxury kind of girl.'

'Honey, isn't everyone a luxury kind of girl at heart?'

'You aren't,' Kate said, shooting him a sideways glance. 'As you're not a girl.'

'For a deep bathtub and good room service I could pretend.'

Kate giggled. 'Doesn't your boss let you stay in the good hotels?'

'Oh, they're good enough. The one I'm in at the moment is one I've used for the past year and they know me, which is always great.'

'You get looked after?'

'For sure.'

'So you've been to Rome lots of times this year?'

'Three times to Rome. Sometimes I'm in Milan, sometimes I have to go to Geneva.'

'It sounds wonderful.'

'I guess. It seems I'm lucky to others but you soon take the travelling for granted. I miss Brad when I'm away too.'

'Do you think you'll ever stop and get another job that doesn't need travelling?'

'Maybe when Brad and I get married. But that won't be for a couple of years yet.'

'Why so long?'

'He wants a huge, lavish reception, and in New York a huge, lavish reception means a huge budget. We're saving for the party of the century!'

'Ah. . . a hopeless romantic, eh? Good for you. I hope it's amazing.'

'All weddings are romantic, aren't they? Isn't that kinda the point?'

'You'd think, wouldn't you?'

'Something tells me you were short-changed when it came to the romance in your marriage. . .'

'You could say that. We were so young when we married we had hardly any money, and my parents weren't all that keen on stumping up for what they saw as a huge mistake. They were used to Matt being around because we'd been together for so long, but that didn't mean they were happy about us getting married. We had to make do with a party at the local pub and Matt got leathered because that's what eighteen-year-old lads do, isn't it?'

Jamie raised his eyebrows. 'I'd agree if I knew what that meant. What the hell is leathered?'

'Drunk,' Kate laughed. 'He got pissed.'

'He was annoyed?' Jamie frowned.

'No, pissed means drunk in Britain, not annoyed. And you can piss yourself, which sometimes means you're laughing and sometimes means you've actually urinated over yourself. . . or you can be pissed *off* at something or someone, and that means you're annoyed.'

Jamie scratched his head. 'And I thought learning Italian was hard.'

'They do say Britain and America are two nations separated by a common language.'

'And don't even get me started on the accents. What's yours?'

'Mancunian.'

'What's that?'

'From Manchester. Is it hard for you to follow? I don't think I'm as broad as some.'

'What does broad mean?'

Kate rolled her eyes. 'This is hard work. My accent isn't as strong as some people from Manchester.'

'Right. What's the weird one that even English people can't understand?'

'I have no idea!' Kate giggled. 'You could take your pick from lots of regional accents in the UK. Which one is your favourite from what you've heard?'

He shrugged. 'Irish sounds kinda hot. Scottish too.'

Kate nodded. 'I think most of the population of the UK would be in agreement with you on that. Although you might not want to tell all the people from Ireland you might meet that you think they're British. . . that's just Northern Ireland, you know.'

Jamie gave a vague smile, as if it was all the same to him. 'So you'd maybe like to score yourself an Irish guy now that you're single?' he asked.

'It's certainly an accent that would make me forgive a whole lot of ugliness,' she laughed.

Jamie shot her a grin before coming to a halt outside a tiny shop with a pastel bright window display. Kate moved closer and pressed her nose to the glass like a little kid being shown the best sweet shop in the world. Which was pretty much what it looked like to her.

'I have no idea what to choose,' she said, gazing intently at the gleaming steel pots where candy-coloured clouds of gelato called to tempt her. The flavours were written below on the shelf in both Italian and English.

'The pistachio is amazing,' Jamie said. 'So is the dark chocolate and coffee flavour – a great combo. There are no fancy, crazy flavours here like the tourist places; they stick to the traditional ones and do them well. But it's the real deal and the best you'll get in Rome.'

'Coffee sounds good. Maybe I'll get dark chocolate with it. . . you know, why not let my hair down?'

'That's what I'm talking about!' Jamie said. Holding the door open for her, he gestured for her to step in.

As they made their way to the counter, there was a customer in front, a man who looked at first glance to be somewhere around his mid-thirties and not bad looking. Kate immediately detected the accent as he spoke to the assistant, and she glanced across to Jamie and saw him grin as he registered it too.

'Irish, right?' he whispered.

Kate nodded and let out a conspiratorial giggle.

But their private joke soon became her worst nightmare as Jamie tapped the man on the shoulder.

'Hey, buddy. . . you're Irish?'

The man turned, looking surprised. A quick appraisal of Kate and Jamie and he seemed to decide that he was not being accosted from anything but friendly curiosity and he smiled. 'From Cork. You have Irish ancestors?'

'Oh, no. . . Scandinavian, though we're Texan for at least five generations now. But my friend here, Kate, is on the hunt for a hot Irish guy. . . You married, buddy? Because if you ain't, I may just have found you a future wife.'

Kate wanted to curl up with embarrassment as the man looked at her. She couldn't decipher the look on his face, but it was somewhere between amusement, pity and the same horror she was feeling herself at Jamie's blunt introduction.

'Jamie is kidding,' she said quickly. 'He's just messing around.'

Jamie looked surprised as he eyed Kate, and she raised her eyebrows in a silent warning for him not to say anything further.

'I said I liked Irish accents, that's all,' Kate added. 'We were talking about accents and I said I liked Irish. . . and Scottish too. . . 'cause, you know, most people like those accents. . .' she trailed off hopelessly.

'Thank you,' the man replied, looking as confused and flustered as Kate felt, and to her unutterable relief, he took his order and left the shop with a polite nod.

Kate spun to face Jamie, but he had already lost interest in the proceedings and was now studying the contents of the glass case at the counter.

'What the hell. . .?' she hissed.

He turned to her. 'He sounded good, and you're single. You don't get if you don't ask.' He shrugged. 'It was no use anyway; he was wearing a wedding ring.'

Kate's mouth fell open. 'Couldn't you have checked that before you said anything? Besides the fact that I would rather you said nothing full stop!'

'You're never going to see him again so I don't know why you're so hung up about it.'

'Well. . .' Kate began, but her reply faltered. Maybe Jamie had a point. She was so English, so used to keeping her opinions and feelings bottled up that she'd probably never spark up a conversation with an available man ever again. And you didn't get to meet people without taking chances. Plus the Irish man had been attractive. And Kate would probably never see him again, so all that had resulted from the encounter was a compliment on his accent for him and an anecdote to take home to Anna and Lily for her.

'These are on me,' Jamie continued, interrupting her thoughts. He tapped the glass with a grin. 'This right here. . . this is what Rome is about!'

* * *

There had been time to enjoy the gelato, which was creamy and dense, and so flavourful it was a world away from the supermarket ice cream Kate had served up every Sunday with strawberries to Matt for the past twelve years. Then Jamie had needed to get back to his hotel to make some client phone calls before he called it a day, and Kate had been eager to get back to her own room to change for dinner. Much as she had loved Jamie's company and had been looking forward to more of it, a breather was a welcome prospect; he was funny and smart, but there was no let-up, not a single moment of gravity or introspection, and the day had been a long one where a quiet moment of one of those things for herself would be enough to help her recharge her batteries to make the most of the evening. So there had been a lovely hour of peace in her air-conditioned room while she got changed and organised her belongings for the week, and then she was out on the streets again with her trusty map to meet Jamie for dinner.

* * *

The trattoria Jamie had suggested was a great recommendation. It felt cosy and authentic, without the intimidating air of luxury that some of the others she'd passed had. Those were establishments where she wouldn't have dared go in alone, let alone dine there. She had a feeling that at Trattoria da Luigi if she spilt tomato sauce on her dress, she wouldn't mind and neither would anyone else.

As she stood uncertainly at the entrance, scanning the room and hoping that she'd got the right place, she saw that Jamie was already waiting at a table that was dressed in a traditional red cloth with a candle burning in a bottle, tucked away in a secluded corner of the restaurant. Mandolin music was piped in through strategically placed speakers, but while it added to the ambience it wasn't so loud as to be distracting, and the aroma of warm bread and fresh herbs made Kate's stomach groan in anticipation. He waved her over, and as she made her way across, relief flooded through her. Going to restaurants wasn't a thing she did alone, and though she would have to get used to it if she was going to eat at all this week, she would have felt rather silly had he not been there.

'Hey.' Jamie smiled. 'I thought you'd chickened out.'

'I'm not late, am I?' Kate asked, looking at her watch. 'Oh. . . maybe a little, sorry. I got a bit side-tracked exploring. And I have to confess that I walked past this place three or four times before I decided it was the place you'd said to meet.' She took a seat across the table. 'Forgive me?'

'Of course – how could I not? The most important thing is you're here now and I'm not eating alone tonight. It makes a nice change.'

'You eat alone a lot?'

'In Rome, yes. One of the perks – or downsides – of business trips, depending on your view and how much you like the company of others. I happen to like it a lot.'

'That's got to be tough then.'

He smiled. 'Sometimes I'm lucky enough to meet great people waiting for cabs who agree to come and keep me company over dinner and who don't get too embarrassed when I try to hook them up with hot Irish guys.'

'I've forgiven you for that. . . just about.'

'But it was worth the trip for the gelato?'

'Absolutely! But I'm starving again now. If I'm this hungry every day I'm going to go home looking like a whale.'

'I'm sure you could never look like that. Your skin is the wrong colour for a start. . .'

Kate giggled. Then she raised her phone and pointed the camera at Jamie. 'Hold still.'

'Something to remember me by?' he asked.

'Something to send my sister. Remember you told me to send them a photo as insurance? I forgot to do it earlier.'

He raised his eyebrows as he broke a breadstick in half. 'You don't actually think I'm capable of kidnapping anyone, do you?'

'No, but you did suggest it, and when I called her earlier, Anna said I was a nutter for agreeing to dinner with a man I'd just met whilst staying in a city alone where I don't know anyone. I told her you seemed perfectly harmless when we went out for our walk but she said so did Hannibal Lecter to his victims just before he carved them up.'

'Well, in that case I hope you got my good side.'

'All your sides are good. Your boyfriend is a lucky man.'

'Try telling him that when we're disagreeing on. . . well, just about anything, actually.'

Kate started to laugh, but was distracted by her phone bleeping the arrival of a text. She unlocked it and read the message.

'Anna says you're hot.'

'You can tell Anna she's very kind. So she doesn't seem too worried about me taking you out to dinner now?'

'Apparently not. You must have a very inoffensive face.'

'Well it's been called a lot of things over the years but inoffensive is definitely a first.' He picked up the wine menu as Kate tapped a brief reply to Anna.

'I vote we get a nice bottle of Chianti.'

Kate raised her eyes from her phone. 'I hope you're not going to suggest fava beans with that and start making a weird slurping noise.'

'I could see why that would be a worry for you,' he said, laughing. 'On second thoughts, let's just get the house red and a nice pasta dish.'

'Good plan,' she said, locking her phone again.

They looked up at the arrival of the waiter. Jamie seemed to stiffen in his seat, and although it was a subtle action, it wasn't lost on Kate. She subjected the newcomer to closer scrutiny. He was about twenty-five with dark hair and eyes, tall and slim, and his chiselled jaw was dusted with stubble. He shot Kate a wary glance but in the same instant he smoothed his features.

'*Buonasera*. Would you like to order?'

Kate frowned slightly. How was it that everyone could automatically tell she was English? Was it that obvious just from the way she looked? She was pasty, and she was ginger haired, but surely other people in Europe had ginger hair apart from the British? But then the waiter's gaze turning on Jamie again told her everything she needed to know. This time it wasn't her who was transparent – it was Jamie. He had named the trattoria off the top of his head earlier, and she had to assume from that he was a regular. If he was, they'd likely know him and know he spoke English, although it still didn't explain the uneasy feeling she got from the loaded glances exchanged by the two men. Something was going on here and it wasn't just regular dining.

'Pietro. . .' Jamie began, 'I thought you were going to the Alps. . . What happened?'

Pietro shrugged. 'I did not go. My father needed me here. . . He is old and he could not spare his son to go and waste his time skiing in the Alps.'

Jamie offered him a tight smile. 'I'm sorry to hear that; I know how much you wanted to go.'

'I am still young; maybe next year, eh?'

Jamie nodded. 'I hope so.' He gestured to Kate. 'This is my good friend, Kate, and we'd like a nice bottle of red to celebrate her recent divorce.'

Kate felt the blush rise to her cheeks. She was learning fast that Jamie didn't think any subject was taboo and that the idea of personal information was an alien concept to him. Perhaps she shouldn't arm him with so much of it in the future if they were spending more time together.

Pietro gave her a little nod. 'If you'll permit me I know just the bottle.'

'That would be wonderful,' Kate said. 'I'm afraid I don't know much about wine so I'm happy to go with your recommendation.'

Pietro gave a stiff smile and then went off to get the wine. Kate turned to Jamie.

'I may know nothing about Rome, but I know when something isn't right. What's the deal with you two?'

'Huh?' Jamie looked up from the menu he was now perusing.

'You and that waiter? You know him?'

'Sure, I come here all the time.'

'I mean *know* him?'

'You mean have I slept with him?' Jamie looked offended and Kate immediately felt ashamed. It was a hell of an assumption, and she would have felt offended too had something similar been levelled at her by a virtual stranger.

'I'm sorry. . . I didn't mean—'

'I know,' he interrupted. His easy smile had returned. 'He's a handsome guy and I'm not too bad either. . . You know what they say: when in Rome. . . But in answer to your question, no, I haven't and I know him because, yes, we have been out to a few bars during my previous visits. But it was as friends.'

'Is he. . . you know. . .?'

'Gay?'

Kate nodded, cursing the small-town mentality that seemed to prevent her from feeling guilty for asking what Jamie obviously considered a perfectly natural and innocuous question.

He let out a small sigh at this, but it seemed to be one of sadness, not frustration at her. 'That's a question he would have to answer.'

Kate frowned as Jamie returned his attention to the menu. It was a rather cryptic reply for him, considering he seemed to be open about almost everything else. But she supposed that knowing someone for a matter of hours wasn't really knowing them at all, and what she thought Jamie might do and think about any situation wasn't necessarily right.

'The seafood linguine is really good here,' he said.

It was clear that wide-open Jamie had closed this particular discussion and there was no point in pushing it any further.

'I'm not sure I like seafood,' Kate said, turning to the menu herself and trying valiantly to make sense of it. Would Jamie think she was really stupid if she asked him what some of the dishes were?

Jamie laughed. 'How can you not be sure?'

'I just don't eat it much. Matt didn't like it so we didn't bother at home and what little I've had over the years. . . Well it's like sushi, isn't it? People who've eaten it in proper Japanese restaurants say it tastes nothing like the poor imitations on our supermarket shelves. So I might love sushi if I ate the proper stuff. The same goes for good seafood – I bet it's not a bit like my occasional boil in the bag cod in parsley sauce.'

Jamie shook his head. 'English people are weird.'

'Probably,' Kate said. 'But we think you're weird too.'

He prodded a finger at his chest. 'Me personally or all Americans?'

'All of you,' Kate giggled.

'Well that's OK then. For a moment there I was almost offended.'

* * *

By the time Jamie had ordered their second bottle of wine, Kate was finding it hard to coordinate the journey of her fork to her mouth, and to make sure that the conversation coming from that same mouth was stuff she ought to be sharing. As her *pollo pomodoro* cooled in front

of her, a great deal of her past poured out and a lot of it far more personal than the potted history she had shared so far that day, despite
her resolutions not to tell Jamie any more secrets – from sex in strange
places, to Matt's restricted diet, his stuck-up parents and his refusal to
commit to a family – it all got aired. But far from upsetting her, Kate
was finding it all funnier by the minute, and she giggled uncontrollably as Jamie joined in the fun and added anecdotes of his own from
an upbringing that sounded as colourful as hers had been secure, even
though secure had meant ultimately dull. Because she was beginning
to realise that the years with Matt had been very dull indeed. He was
a good man, he was stable and sensible, but fun was not a word she
would use to describe him, and she realised that fun was something
she'd missed, something that had been so far removed from her everyday existence with him that she'd almost forgotten what it was. Sure,
they'd had the odd DVD night with a takeaway, went to the pub
from time to time with mutual friends, even ventured out to the local
comedy club. There was the yearly trip to the seaside, birthday meals
at the Chinese buffet and the annual poring over new Dulux paint-
colour cards as they chose a new look for whichever room needed
redecorating. But it was all terribly safe and certain and if she had ever
proposed to Matt that they did something a bit out of the ordinary,
she was quite sure he'd have keeled over from the shock. Kate now
realised the only thing that had kept her sane was her dressmaking
hobby, which gave her the chance to express herself as an individual,
and not just as a perfectly sensible half of a relationship that made
Matt happy but not necessarily her.

'So. . . let me get this straight,' Jamie said as he poured Kate another glass of wine. 'You make vintage-style clothes? But that's amazing! Are you wearing one of your own creations?'

Kate beamed as she cast a quick glance over the rose-print dress she had on. The cowl neck had been a particular fiddle and the full skirt had kept her busy many evenings, something that Matt had complained about, but she was proud of her handiwork and it remained her favourite dress. 'It's just a hobby,' she said.

'You're in Italy! The Italians love fashion! You should be shouting from the rooftops about that dress and what you can do – it's amazing! Get yourself a job in the industry here, move out and start a new life.'

Despite her lack of sobriety, Kate stared at him. 'Get a job here? That's crazy – I wouldn't even know where to start! And I couldn't leave my family.'

'I bet I could find you contacts if you needed them. I have colleagues and clients who know people.'

Kate shook her head so vehemently she almost toppled off her chair.

'You already told me you hate your job,' he continued. 'What is it again?'

'Sales executive. Although that's just a posh title for warehouse clerk that they gave me to make me feel more important.' Even the sound of it made Kate feel dull and unglamorous against the dazzling individuality of Jamie. She wished dearly she had something else to offer, some other way of saying it, but there was no title she could invent that would make it sound any more exciting than it was. Which was about as exciting as watching static on the TV.

He sat back and regarded her with a wry smile. 'I can tell by the look on your face that's not your life's ambition, and therefore, I rest my case.'

Kate giggled, but her reply was cut short as she noted his attention suddenly wandering. She turned and followed the direction of his gaze, but all she could see was the rest of the trattoria buzzing with customers and waiting staff.

'Can you excuse me a moment?' Jamie asked. His grin had faded and he didn't wait for Kate's reply before leaving her alone at the table. She watched him go to a side door that looked as if it was not for public use. It certainly wasn't the toilet, which was clearly marked a few feet along the wall, and neither was it the kitchen. She could only assume it was some sort of private office/staff space, but what on earth was Jamie going in there for? Did he know the owners that well? Kate frowned as her brain worked, albeit drunkenly, to form a solution to the puzzle. Jamie was an enigma – just when she thought she had him figured out he would do something to throw her completely.

Giving the situation a mental shrug, she topped up her glass and in the process emptied their second bottle. She was quite sure she was sozzled, so how come Jamie hadn't looked drunk? Despite this, she looked around for a waiter, hoping to implore someone without having to revert to her woeful Italian (which was based almost exclusively on the menu at her local pizzeria) that she needed a fresh bottle. As luck would have it, a young and impossibly glamorous girl scooted over.

'*Per favore*,' Kate said, shaking the empty bottle at her.

The girl gave a knowing smile and took the empty as she went off to get another. She returned a few minutes later and filled up the glass that Kate had already managed to empty. It was almost as if she was drinking out of anxiety now, as she thanked the waitress with a bleary smile and then knocked back the new glass before her gaze went back to the door Jamie had disappeared through. She wanted to ask the girl what was in there, but she didn't know how. It was possible that the girl would speak English, of course, and highly likely given they were in Rome where probably half the tourists spoke English, but it wasn't just the language barrier that stopped Kate asking. What if Jamie was in there when he wasn't supposed to be? What if he was doing something he wasn't meant to be doing? Now that she came to look again, she couldn't see Pietro anywhere on duty either. What the hell was going on? She didn't want to get Jamie in trouble, whatever it was, so she simply offered the girl another grateful smile and left her to attend to the next table.

* * *

Half an hour passed with no sign of Jamie, although Kate had made quite an impressive dent in the new bottle of wine. Her gaze went to the door again. She hadn't seen anyone come out, but had she missed it? Was there another exit that she didn't know about? Something had come up and Jamie had left her in the restaurant, she was sure of it now. Had she offended him somehow? Had an emergency cropped up? Was he simply bored of her company? Perhaps he did this all the time. The more she thought about it, the more convinced she was that he had indeed gone off. But there was the meal to pay for, and though she had offered to pay it in exchange for her half of the taxi fare he had picked up earlier, she was certain that their combined bill would be higher than what she owed him for that. He had seemed so lovely – surely he wouldn't just up and leave? Or had it all been some elaborate prank for some unknown and unfathomable reason? Let's have a laugh at the sad, lonely tourist's expense. . . Perhaps he was a con man who preyed on idiotic and vulnerable lone travellers to get his meals paid for. But from what she knew of him already that didn't stack up at all. And he had settled the taxi cab earlier that day, followed by gelato which he'd paid for, so what did he have to gain by stitching her up now? Surely the few euros difference wouldn't make it worthwhile?

Draining her glass, she pulled a wad of notes from her purse and left them on the table before collecting her belongings to stagger away and out through the door. She had probably left far too much, but the end of the evening had been humiliating enough without trying to get the bill as well, and she would rather sneak away before somebody noticed.

The evening air was balmy and the skies still light as Kate stepped into the grey-cobbled alleyway, pastel-coloured terraced frontages rising high on either side dotted with lamps, moths flitting around them. As she emerged onto the wider street, people bustled to and fro, snatches of conversation on the air as she began to walk revealing more languages than she could count alongside the Italian she had been expecting to hear. She was trying desperately to dredge the location of her hotel out of the drunken recesses of her brain, but her brain was having none of it until she'd injected some coffee into it. But by degrees as she continued to walk, she became more caught up in the atmosphere of being out in the evening of the eternal city, the freedom to roam where she wanted and do what she fancied beguiling. A group of Italian women bid her good evening (at least she thought so) and she couldn't help noticing the admiring glances towards her dress. With a soppy grin on her face, she then passed an English couple arguing about where they were going to eat.

'Trattoria da Luigi. . . That way, good seafood!' she hiccupped at them as she flung an arm back the way she had come, and they stared as she smiled benignly and went on her way, certain that she had done a very good deed that, one day, they would look back on as the thing that saved their marriage.

Before she had gone two blocks, she realised that she was very lost. But lost was just another word for exploring, wasn't it? She was exploring – yes, that was what she was doing. You couldn't be lost if you were exploring because you weren't particularly trying to find anything in the first place, and you could only be lost if you couldn't find the thing you were looking for, and she wasn't looking for anything any more. That decided, the only thing to do was to stagger on, completely not lost at all.

Five

Kate stirred, batting at something tickling her face. A hair? She had no idea but she wished it would stop so she could go back to sleep. Though now that she thought about it, this bed was very uncomfortable too. . .

'*Cosa fai qui?*'

She wrinkled her nose. Was that someone speaking? What were they doing here? They weren't even speaking English – at least, she couldn't make out what they were saying if they were. If they couldn't be bothered to wake her in English then they could go away.

'*Signorina!*'

There it was again. If only she could get her eyes to open she might be able to work out what was going on. But then a prod from something cold and smooth on her arm forced her to focus.

Bloody hell, those lights are bright.

Kate slowly pushed herself up and looked around. She was outside, sitting on some huge steps, but she had no idea how she had got there or where, exactly, the steps were. What she did know was that she had the headache to end all headaches, she was shivering and her neck ached. Night had fallen now too.

'*Ti sei persa?*' There was that voice again. Kate squinted up to see a man standing before her. He had his back to the street lights and his face was in shadow, but there was no mistaking the tone of his voice. For some reason he wasn't very happy with her. All day people had been speaking English to her without being prompted, and it was typical that now when she needed someone to speak English they weren't.

'No understand,' she said, pointing to herself and shrugging as she struggled to look awake.

'You are English, madam?' the man asked.

'Yes!' Kate said, relieved to hear he had now switched to a perfect version of her native tongue.

'You are not allowed to sleep there.'

She rubbed her neck as she blinked at him.

'I wasn't asleep. . . I was just resting. I wouldn't sleep here – that would be silly.'

He grimaced. 'Perhaps you were so drunk you did not notice you were asleep.'

Kate paused, trying to take that in and recall what had led her to be there in the first place. Oh, that was it – Jamie had got her drunk and then abandoned her.

'I was asleep,' she agreed. 'But it wasn't my fault. How long have I been asleep for?'

'Five minutes, five days – it makes no difference. You are not allowed to sleep here and you must move.'

'Alright. . .' Kate muttered, glancing at her watch. It had just gone eleven. How long had it been since she'd parted from Jamie in the restaurant? 'I didn't know you were the step police. . .'

'Step police?' the man returned sharply. 'I am an officer of *Polizia di Stato* and you cannot sleep there.'

Kate groaned and, filled with a sense of alarm at his tone, she suddenly felt rather more awake. She had no idea what *Polizia di*

Stato was but she could guess from the rest of the sentence that he probably *was* the police. 'Oh God, I am SO sorry! I didn't realise!' She took a closer look and now that her vision was clearing from the alcoholic fog, she could see that he wore a blue and grey uniform, and the smooth cold thing that had prodded her awake was a baton now tucked back into his utility belt.

'I do not want to arrest you, madam, but if you do not get up I will be forced to.' He shook his head as he appeared to regard her carefully. 'How much wine have you drunk tonight, madam?'

'I'm not sure.'

'More than you should have done.'

Kate frowned.

'Kindly return to your hotel. It is dangerous out here for you alone at night.'

'Sorry,' Kate said sheepishly.

She wobbled as she pushed herself up. The policeman made a small movement towards her but then stepped back as she righted herself. 'I'm OK,' she said before beginning her slow and stiff descent down the sweeping steps. She turned to him. 'Are these the Spanish Steps?'

'Of course. You do not know where you are?'

'I think I must have done when I got here but something stole my brain when I was asleep.'

'I do not understand.'

Kate gave a wan smile. 'I must have been very drunk. Not very sensible I suppose.'

He began to follow her down the steps. 'Where is your hotel?'

'Via di Santa. . . something or other. . . Sorry, I seem to have for-gotten that too. . .' She fished her trusty note with the address from her bag. Now that she really thought about it, it was a minor miracle that her bag hadn't been stolen while she slept. But she looked around to see that a good few tourists still milled around and perhaps that was why. Although the same tourists must have thought she looked quite a sight flat out on a famous landmark, snoring like a wildebeest. Maybe one of them even fetched the policeman to move her on. He took the note from her.

'How will you get back?' he asked as he scanned the address and then gave her a look up and down that she couldn't fail to infer the meaning of, even though she couldn't see his face clearly. 'This is a long walk.'

For a stupid drunken cow, she thought, and silently she had to agree with him that she was probably far from capable in her current state. She simply shrugged.

'This way,' he said as he began to walk again. Kate stared after him. 'You must come with me now,' he insisted.

Deciding that she'd better do as she was told, she followed as he strode down the steps and made for the road.

'Where are we going?' she asked.

'I will find you a taxi, madam.'

'OK. . . am I in a lot of trouble?'

'No, madam.'

'So you won't come to the hotel and arrest me? Like, tomorrow or something?'

He stopped and turned to her. It was at this point that she saw his face clearly for the first time. There was an involuntary snatch of breath. Black wavy hair topped by a cap, film-star jawline and cheek-bones to die for. And in his dark eyes, despite his brusque manner, was a hint of amusement. 'Do you want me to arrest you, madam?'

Kate stared for a moment, unable to reply. *Yes please* was the answer that pinged around her brain, but at least her mouth had the good sense not to let it out. Her gaze wandered to the handcuffs hanging from the belt at his trim waist, and all she could think about at that moment was how she might like him to use them on her, though not necessarily in a legal capacity.

Oh God! She'd turned into one of those women who threw themselves at Chippendales and poked ten-pound notes into the thongs of male strippers! Her face burned as she mumbled, 'No. Thank you.'

'Why are you out alone with all that wine in your belly?' he asked as he started to walk again and Kate tottered after him. 'Do you have a companion?'

'I'm on holiday alone. . . well, sort of. . . unless you count Jamie who isn't really with me at all. In fact, I only just met him today. . . at the taxi rank at the airport. . . And then he took me for dinner. . . but he's gay, you know. . . And then he disappeared with the waiter so I was on my own and I thought I would do some sightseeing. . .'

She could see his profile as he marched along, and she struggled to keep pace and rambled on in a way that completely matched her unsteady steps. He raised an eyebrow and turned to her, that spark of amusement in his eyes again.

'Do you make a habit of getting into trouble?'

'Oh, Jamie isn't trouble. . . unless you count running off with the waiter and leaving me alone steaming drunk, of course. . . so I suppose that *is* trouble. . .'

'You should choose your companions with more care in future, madam.'

'Kate,' she said. And then blushed.

'*Scusi?*'

'My name is Kate. I just thought I would tell you so you didn't have to keep calling me madam. Unless it's something you have to do when you're on duty, of course. Which is fine. . . obviously.'

'Does it offend you to be called madam?'

'No. . . but I like Kate.'

He gave a slight nod.

'It's beautiful here,' Kate said.

'Yes. Is it your first time in Roma?'

'Yes. I've always wanted to come but things seemed to get in the way.'

'So you drank too much of our good Italian wine to celebrate?'

Kate looked at him. He kept his gaze straight ahead but she saw the ghost of a smile about his lips. She was about to reply when he stuck his arm out and a white cab came screeching to a halt, almost as if in panicked obedience to his command. He stuck his head in the open car window and spoke in rapid Italian to the driver, who nodded. The policeman stepped back.

'Your chariot, Kate. . .'

'Oh. . . right. . . and he knows where the hotel is?'

'Of course. Please take more care in future when you go to sleep. The Spanish Steps are beautiful, but I would rather you enjoy them with your eyes open. I am sure your hotel has a nice bed for when night comes.'

Kate found herself blushing again. Now that sobriety was beginning to bite, she was feeling more than a little foolish for what she had done. What sort of idiot took herself to a foreign city alone and then proceeded to drink herself into a stupor and fall asleep in full view of muggers and rapists – or worse? And she was also feeling stupid that this policeman (this very hot and charming policeman) had been the one to pick her up and sort her on her way. She was probably lucky it was someone as nice as him, but she was also pretty lucky she wasn't in a cell right now, sleeping off her hangover with nobody to bail her out.

'I really am sorry,' she said. 'I won't do it again.'

'I am glad to hear it.'

Kate clambered into the back of the cab. She craned her neck to look around as the car pulled away, and she could see that he watched it leave until the driver turned a corner and he was gone from sight.

* * *

The taxi proved to be a costly affair, but she supposed it was her own fault and there was nothing she could do but stump up and learn a valuable lesson from it all. But that didn't change the fact that already she had gone over her planned daily budget and she had only just arrived in Rome. At least the drive had given her the chance to appreciate the city by night as the cab had swept her down wide boulevards and cobbled piazzas flanked by delicate baroque architecture or immense stone-columned frontages, elaborately carved fountains and lively eateries where she could hear snatches of string quartets on the night air. Tomorrow she would get out and explore on her own, maybe even eat on her own. At least on her own she'd know exactly how much to drink and how much she could afford to pay. And there would be no chance of her companion suddenly abandoning her. Maybe she'd even find somewhere close to the Spanish Steps, and maybe she'd see her handsome rescuer again, although she'd be sure to admire him from a distance. She might have found him attractive but she doubted he'd have fond memories of the bleary-eyed public nuisance he'd moved on the night before.

As she stepped wearily from the taxi outside her hotel, however, all thoughts of tomorrow were banished as Jamie came rushing towards her from the shadows of her hotel doorway.

'Thank God!' he cried. 'What happened? I've been calling you for hours! I almost filed a missing-persons report!'

In all the drama, or perhaps because her brain had been too addled, Kate had forgotten to check her phone. She pulled it from her bag now and saw the missed calls. 'Oh. . . Well, I'm sorry, but I'm here now.'

'That's it?' Jamie stared at her. 'That's all you have to say? I thought something terrible had happened to you and I thought it was my fault! I didn't know who to call! I was going out of my mind!'

Kate looked at him. He did seem genuinely concerned, and perhaps he had a good explanation for where he himself had disappeared to, but she was far too tired to hear it now. She didn't even know if she wanted to hear it at all. She had wondered whether he had been a con man trying to get a free meal, but the way he spoke to her now, whether she was wrong or right to trust him again, it didn't seem that way at all. To her mind it was simple – he had gone somewhere with Pietro. If he chose to have a fling while he was away from his boyfriend, that was his business, and she liked him too much to tell him what she really thought of that sort of behaviour. Perhaps it was better that she knew nothing at all. Besides, she was a grown-up and whether he had left her on her own or not didn't really come into it. She had made the decision to leave the restaurant and she didn't need his permission to do so.

'Nothing happened to me,' she said. 'I thought you'd gone back to your hotel. I went out to see the sights and I lost track of the time, so you can relax – I'm here and I'm in one piece. I'm sorry I didn't hear my phone.'

His mouth fell open. 'I wouldn't have gone back to my hotel without saying anything and I can't believe you went off in the same way!'

She let out a sigh. 'You went off and you were ages; I thought you weren't coming back. I see now that it was a misunderstanding. I'm sorry, Jamie, but I'm tired and I don't want to have this conversation now. I'm grateful that you were worried and that you came here to make sure I was OK, but there was really no need.'

He paused. Kate had the distinct impression he had something he needed to get off his chest but after a brief moment he seemed to think better of it. 'OK,' he said. 'I'm at meetings most of tomorrow, but if you need me you'll be able to get me after three. Maybe we can try dinner again and this time actually stick together until dessert? After all, I do owe you for tonight – I know you settled up in my absence.'

She was too weary to argue this, or to engage in the sort of faff that always followed meals out with friends or work colleagues while they drunkenly tried to split the bill without World War Three breaking out. It was easier to let it go this time. 'You don't owe me. . . it doesn't matter.'

'Well if you won't let me take you out for dinner then you'll have to take the cash from me now. . .'

Kate waved his assertion away. 'Please. . . I just want to get to bed and it's really not necessary. You paid for the cab today and saved me from getting ripped off. I'd say we're even.'

'Oh. . . But it would be fun to do dinner again anyway. I do feel I owe you even if you say I don't. And I would hate tonight to be the only impression of me you take away when you leave Rome.'

Kate gave him a tight smile. Was this something she wanted to get into again? She did like Jamie, and it was nice having company for dinner. It also seemed as if he was keen for company too.

'I'm not sure what I'm doing tomorrow yet, but I'll text you.'

He looked vaguely disappointed but he nodded. 'OK. Sleep well, Kate.'

'You too.'

She watched for a moment as he made his way towards his hotel, before turning for the entrance of her own. Her bed was calling, and she was eager to fall into it.

Six

Lily had called early in the morning, far too early, though on picking up the call and hearing her voice, Kate realised just how much she missed her. Even though she'd only been gone a day, she felt so far away from the family she loved dearly, who had been her rock through the torment of Matt leaving and the divorce. But she put a smile in her voice and told Lily all about meeting Jamie and what her first day in Rome had been like, making sure to leave out all the details about falling asleep on the street and almost being arrested, which would've had her sister jumping on the first available plane in a panicked bid to sort her out. Lily and Anna had both been unable to get time off work to come with Kate on her spontaneous trip, but secretly she was glad. Being alone was scary, but it was also exciting, and if she was going to face the rest of her life without fear, she had to learn to do things on her own. Lily had filled her in on the latest pregnancy details – she still wasn't drinking coffee and the thought of an onion bhaji (which she usually loved) made her want to run for the toilet, but other than that she felt fine and not anywhere near as tired as she had done in the first few weeks. Anna was fine too, and she sent her love, and had told Lily to tell Kate that she had better behave herself because she didn't want to see her on the news embroiled in some international scandal. *No chance*, Kate had said with a self-conscious laugh and silently vowed that she could most definitely never tell Anna or Lily about her encounter with the Italian police.

Breakfast in the gold and claret restaurant at the hotel was welcome, and a few pastries washed down by hot black coffee did wonders for her hangover. She gazed around at the copies of Renaissance paintings that graced the walls, looked through the windows at passers-by and even scanned a discarded copy of *The Times*, all at once enjoying her surroundings but feeling incredibly guilty and irresponsible at the thought of her credit-card balance once she got home and had to actually pay for all of this. But as she had been travelling alone, the one luxury she would allow herself was a good hotel that felt safe and comfortable, and that was certainly what she had found. At one point during breakfast she found herself chatting to a lovely family from Kent who had brought their ninety-year-old grandma to Rome to celebrate that quite remarkable birthday – something she would never have done on holiday with Matt, who was a fiercely private man who would rather face a firing squad than make small talk with a stranger.

After going back to her room for a quick freshen up, she grabbed her brand new guidebook, handbag and jacket and headed out into the city.

It was tempting to make a beeline straight back to the Spanish Steps, though she tried to deny the reasons for this. She was highly unlikely to see the same police officer ever again, and certainly not the morning after and in the same vicinity, not in a city as busy and sprawling as Rome. Still, her attempt at logic didn't stop her from thinking about him and half hoping he would appear before her, with that delicious smile that almost mocked her and eyes that seemed constantly on the brink of laughter. Her guidebook had told her to visit landmarks that were furthest from her hotel first so that if she was left with limited time on her last few days she could stay closer to her base and fit more in. It also said that Rome needed to be enjoyed slowly, like a good wine, and to Kate that seemed like sound advice. The Colosseum looked like a good place to start. After some time studying her map and working out distances, she decided that she would walk. It would be a lot of walking and more than she would contemplate doing at home, but the sun was shining and this early in the summer the heat was still manageable. Besides, she was in no rush to get anywhere really, and at home she was almost always in a rush, which was why she rarely walked.

The main streets were alive with the hustle and bustle of tourists and residents and cars and buses tearing to and fro. Umbrellas would appear above the crowds every few yards, followed by snaking lines of young people wearing matching T-shirts from some school or tour group or other. Architectural wonders waited on every corner – magnificent colonnaded frontages in white marble, elaborate fountains and sculptures – while secluded alleyways offered respite from the sun with their gleaming cobbles and fascinating shops hidden behind faded pastel façades. Cafés lined the pavements and piazzas, calling her in with the lure of divine-smelling coffee, and gelato shops had mouth-watering displays of every colour and flavour Kate could think of, and more besides, in glass-topped freezers.

But she pressed on, resisting the lure of all the tasty treats on offer, and was rewarded by her first glimpse of the Colosseum around twenty minutes later, a sight which caused her to stop and stare and catch her breath. She had seen it on television, of course, and in more photos than she could count, but nothing could prepare her for the sheer scale and majesty of it. There was row upon row of mammoth stonework, arches built into each section and huge chunks missing from the top two layers, and Kate could only imagine how big and imposing it must have seemed all those hundreds of years ago when it first stood proud and intact against an azure sky. Even emperors must have stood where she stood now and felt tiny and insignificant in the presence of the mighty structure.

Grabbing her phone from her bag, she began to take photos.

'*Scusi!*'

She turned to see a man flash past her, an apology on his lips as he caught her arm. He was wiry, his accent slightly odd in comparison to the other Italian she had heard during her visit, and he looked as if he needed a good bath. Kate frowned and watched him disappear into the crowds, but the moment was soon forgotten as her attention turned to the building again.

After a few more photos, including a rather skew-whiff attempt at a selfie, which she immediately sent to Anna and Lily, she stowed her phone in her jacket pocket and dug in her handbag for her purse. Matt would never have paid the entrance fee to get in, as had been proved by many visits to the remains of English castles, which, he argued, looked just the same inside as out and so he couldn't see the point in getting ripped off. She'd lost count of the times they'd driven to some dramatic outcrop, stood at a distance to look at the history perched upon it, and then he'd been champing at the bit to get away again and find a decent pub for a pie and mash dinner.

It was strange, but though she distinctly recalled picking her purse up from the bed before she'd left the hotel, putting just enough euros in it for the day ahead, it wasn't in her bag now. Paying more attention, she looked again, and a sense of panic welled up from her guts.

It wasn't there. Had she dropped it? She felt sure her bag hadn't been open until. . .

Shit! She'd just opened her bag, hadn't she, to get her phone out? And then the collision with the man who had seemed in an awful rush to get somewhere. Next thing her purse was gone. Had she definitely put it in that morning? Yes, she was sure she had. So where was it? She didn't want to believe it, but the truth was staring her in the face. She'd been robbed!

More than anything she felt a numb sort of shock at the idea. And then it turned into distress. She'd never been robbed before; had never imagined it would be so upsetting. Trying not to cry, she scanned the crowds for a sign of the man but couldn't see anyone that looked like him. Not that she would have been sure anyway – she had hardly seen his face for more than a second – and she had no idea what she would do if she did see him. But across the sea of people, she could see a pair of police officers on horseback. She fought her way through the crowds as she headed towards them.

'*Mi scusi!*' she panted as she finally made it. She paused, and pulled out her guidebook, flicking to the first page where a handy list of phrases was printed. '*Parla Inglese?*' She looked up hopefully. Not only was she uncertain either of them would speak English, but her accent was so dodgy that they might not understand the question, even asked in their native tongue. One of them could well speak English, but they weren't going to if they didn't know they were supposed to.

'Yes,' one replied to her unutterable relief. 'Are you lost?'

Kate blinked at him. They were standing in front of pretty much the biggest landmark in Rome. Did he often get British people telling him they were lost while standing in front of the Colosseum? If so he must have the patience of one of the very many Catholic saints she had seen churches dedicated to on the way here. 'No,' she said. 'I think my purse has been stolen. Just now.'

He sucked in his breath and shot a glance at his colleague. 'You will have to file a report,' he said, looking at Kate again.

'A report? So you can't help me?'

'I am sorry but we are on duty here. They will help you at the *questura.*'

Kate tried not to show her exasperation, which she was sure wouldn't help her cause. 'What's that?'

'The . . .' He looked at his colleague again.

'*Questura*. . . police house,' the other man offered, before turning his attention to something that was obviously far more interesting in the crowds of visitors.

Kate presumed he meant police station, and it was easier to go with this than question it. 'Where is that? Is it far away?'

'Via di San Vitale. Not too far by taxi.'

'But I don't have any money for the taxi now – it's just been stolen!'

'Do you have a companion to help?'

Kate thought about phoning Jamie. It was lucky that she still had her phone in her pocket and she had to be thankful for small mercies. It also meant she could access her online banking and hopefully get some funds. Her credit card had been in her purse, so that would have to be cancelled, but her bank debit card was in the hotel room along with her passport. She wouldn't be destitute, but it was a mess just the same.

'Yes,' she said with an air of resignation. 'There is someone I can call.'

'That is good,' the policeman said, and then looked in the same direction his colleague was staring. Kate wondered if that was it, and

she was wishing desperately right now that the police officer on duty
here was the same one who had been so gallant last night. She was
quite sure he wouldn't have fobbed her off with vague advice to go
and walk to a police station that she had absolutely no idea of the
location of and no money to get to.

'Thanks,' she said. Not knowing what else to do and still feeling
shell-shocked, she began to walk away. After a few steps she halted and
pulled her phone from her pocket. Her finger hovered over Jamie's
number. But it wasn't yet three and he would still be in meetings.
Besides, he didn't need some helpless English woman leaning on him
every five minutes. She could do this, and she was going to prove
to herself and the world that she could cope no matter what disaster
befell her. Via di San Vitale. . . That was the address the policeman
had given her. She opened up her maps app and tapped it in, a route
appearing on the screen and a timescale for getting there. OK, it didn't
look so bad after all. And she'd wanted an adventure in Rome, hadn't
she? It wasn't quite the one she had envisaged, but adventure it was.
There was only one thing left to do, and that was to start walking.

* * *

A little over half an hour later, with her stomach now protesting that
she had skipped lunch, Kate arrived at the police station. As with everything in Rome, it was housed within an impressive stone-fronted
building, its entrance adorned by a high arch with a police officer
stationed at either side of the doorway. Feeling more than a little
apprehensive and half expecting to get stopped and told she wasn't
important enough to go in, she walked past them.

The interior was completely at odds with the grand façade, bearing
more resemblance to the council buildings at home than to anything

she'd seen so far in Italy. A tired but attractive looking woman in uniform at the reception desk gave her a tight smile. Kate couldn't help but notice her very impressive chest, barely contained by a shirt straining to stay buttoned, and the sort of cheekbones she could only dream of.

'*Buongiorno.*'

'Hello. . .' Kate reached for her guidebook, but the woman stopped her.

'Hello. Can I help you?'

'I hope so. I need to report that my purse was stolen.'

The woman nodded and turned to a computer screen, where she began to click the mouse. 'I will need some details.'

'OK.'

'Your name please.'

'Kate Merry.'

'Write please.' She pushed a blank pad and pen towards Kate, who duly noted it down and pushed it back. The woman copied it into the computer.

'Do you want me to write my address too?'

'I will take the name of your hotel at the moment. . .' the woman replied, but the rest of the sentence was drowned out by the sound of raucous laughter as a group of officers appeared from a side door. They looked as though they were downing tools for the day, some unfastening their utility belts and switching off radios. The policewoman looked up with an impatient sigh, obviously not quite as amused as they seemed to be. Then Kate glanced around, and they saw each other at the same time.

'Kate!' he said.

Kate stared. It wasn't that unlikely that she would see him at his station, but the idea just hadn't occurred to her while she had been so preoccupied with the task of reporting her robbery. But there he was, large as life and even more handsome than she remembered – her saviour from the night before.

'You are offering yourself?' he asked with a cheeky smile.

'Huh?'

'To go to jail?'

'Oh, you mean handing myself in?' Kate couldn't help but let out a breathless giggle, despite the very dodgy signals it was probably sending out. A man like him was bound to be married with at least fifteen kids. He looked like the sort of man who would be very good at making children. And they weren't exactly alone. The woman behind the desk cleared her throat in a very obvious manner.

'I can help this lady, Orazia,' he said in English, presumably out of courtesy to Kate.

The policewoman, Orazia, shrugged. It was meant to look nonchalant but Kate noted that there was another expression underneath it. It might have been jealousy, or maybe just disdain, but although she was pretending not to care that he wanted to help Kate, she obviously did. Kate looked away, not wishing to be on the receiving end of the contemptuous gaze that now turned on her and saw some of the policeman's colleagues nudge each other and grin. One of them called to him in Italian, and he laughed, but didn't offer a reply as they walked across the reception and through another door at the far side.

'Are you in trouble again?' he asked. 'I am glad to see you are not drunk this time.'

'I've had my purse stolen. At the Colosseum,' she began, and then recounted the events as briefly as she could. Somehow, it didn't seem half as scary or important as it had before she had seen him, and his presence as he listened gravely was comforting, as if he could some-how make everything better just by being there.

As she came to a finish, he took himself through a little door and around to the other side of the counter, where he began to tap details into the computer that Orazia had abandoned in favour of sipping coffee at a desk and poring over a file. Every so often she would throw a guarded glance in their direction, trying for all the world to look as if she wasn't taking any notice of their exchange but obviously listening very carefully.

'I do not know what we can do to get your purse back, but you will be able to make a claim with your holiday insurance,' he said as he typed. 'Do you have money at your hotel? A card?'

'I have some. Luckily I didn't take everything out with me and the hotel has a safe.'

'What about your friend?'

'Jamie?'

'Yes. Was he with you today when your purse was stolen?'

'Oh, no. He's in meetings today. We're not really here in Rome together, we just sort of met up for dinner last night.'

'Oh. And is he meeting you for dinner tonight?'

'Why?' Kate asked, her heart suddenly beating like a parade drum at the thought that he might be about to suggest they had dinner together tonight instead. Which would be ludicrous, of course, and would never happen, and she wasn't sure why she had even thought of it.

'I would have to tell him to keep the wine bottle away from you,' he said with that irresistibly mocking smile that Kate was beginning to know well already.

'Oh, I'm not doing that again,' Kate laughed, a curious mix of relief and disappointment flooding through her. 'I'm drinking water from now on.'

'Perhaps just a little wine.'

'Maybe a little.'

They fell silent as he began to tap some more details into the computer. She could hear raised voices from beyond closed doors and the steady whir of a fan next to Orazia.

'So,' Kate began when she could bear the silence no longer, 'you looked like you were about to end your shift?'

'*Scusi?*' he said, looking up.

'Work . . . you looked as if you had finished work for the day.'

'Ah, yes.'

'You've been on duty since last night?'

'Illness – I had to help.'

'That's a long time to work.'

He nodded.

'I bet your family don't like it.'

'My mother is happy; she has too many children and a small house,' he smiled.

'So, you live with your mother?'

'Yes. She tells me to find a wife every day,' he said, turning his gaze back to the computer. Orazia let out a cough. Kate looked at her. She seemed to be wholly absorbed in her file but Kate couldn't shake the feeling that she had some opinion on what was going on. But perhaps Kate was seeing more in the situation than there really was. Whatever, it was doubtful she was going to enlighten Kate and it probably wasn't worth worrying about. Perhaps she was just annoyed about the fact that her colleague was flirting. If that was what he was doing. . . He was certainly giving away a lot of information. And he had leapt at the chance to assist her, despite being at the end of his shift.

Unable to fathom Orazia out, Kate was silent for a moment as she digested what she knew about her policeman instead. So he was single too? It was probably highly immoral or against his professional code or something to date victims of crime, though, even if he did flirt with them. 'Are you going home now?' she asked.

'When I have done this.'

'It's very kind of you. If I'd known you'd been up all night and that you were supposed to be finished, I wouldn't have bothered you.'

'You didn't bother me. I wanted to help. It makes me sad when visitors are treated badly in my city.'

'It's the only thing that's happened so far,' she said. 'Everything else has been lovely. . . although I have only been here one day.'

'I hope you have no other misfortune.'

He pressed return, and the sound of a printer hummed and whirred from somewhere close by. He reached beneath the desk and produced a sheet of paper. 'Please read this; it is a statement of all you have told me. If you think it is correct please sign it.'

Kate read it quickly, though if anyone had asked her afterwards what it said she wouldn't have been able to tell them. She was far too busy being beguiled by the scent of his glorious aftershave as he stood across the counter from her waiting. 'It looks alright,' she said, scribbling her signature and pushing it back across the counter to him.

He picked it up, cast a glance over it, seemed satisfied and closed the window on the computer before going over to Orazia's desk.

'Would you file this?' he asked.

She looked up at him, took the paper, and slung it into a basket before turning her attention back to her work.

'*Grazie*, Orazia,' he said with a grin.

'*Prego*, Alessandro,' she replied in a tone dripping with sarcasm, before slamming her file shut and storming off into a back room.

Alessandro. So now Kate had a name. It suited him.

He made a few more notes and then looked up at Kate with a smile. 'Are you going to your hotel now?'

'I. . . I hadn't really thought that far ahead. I haven't had lunch yet so I might head back there to get some money for food. And I have to call my sister too, and the bank to cancel my card. It's a mess, isn't it?'

He shrugged. 'It is life.'

'I suppose it is. And I suppose you wouldn't have a job if things didn't get stolen.'

He nodded shortly, while Kate felt the need to punch herself in the face for such a stupid comment. But if he thought it stupid he didn't say. He simply opened the door and reappeared at her side of the counter, clicking it locked again as he did.

'I could take you,' he said.

'To the hotel? I couldn't. . .' Kate glanced across to see that Orazia was back, shaking her head, clearly listening and not approving of what she heard. Suddenly Kate felt quite belligerent about the whole thing. What had it got to do with her whether Alessandro took her back to her hotel or not? If he was off duty then it was his choice what he did and who he offered lifts to. 'That would be brilliant.'

'Follow me,' he said with a little nod, and he led her out into the sunshine.

* * *

Kate had often considered an Italian riding a moped like a nutter to be a stereotype, but as they zipped through the traffic of a busy Rome, her arms wrapped around Alessandro's torso and her hands clasped together so tight she thought she might never prise them apart again, she realised to her dismay that it was an actual thing. Not only that but her dress was in serious danger of whipping up and exposing her underwear to the world with every gust of wind, and as she couldn't get a hand free to secure things, it wasn't exactly helping her to relax. She'd wanted an adventure, but she would rather return this one to the shop and get a less scary one.

'OK?' he called behind him.

She would have answered in the affirmative, despite not being OK at all, if only she could get some words out. Instead, she nodded weakly and squeezed her eyes shut as he slalomed past a truck laden with fruit.

'Kate!' he called. 'OK?'

'Yes,' she managed to reply, if only to make certain his attention returned to the roads and not to what she was doing.

'You like?'

'No.'

She could feel the vibration of his laughter through his chest. 'It is much faster than a car.'

I'll bet it is, she thought. *Faster to the hospital too when we come off.*

If Anna could see her now, she'd be having a heart attack, and as for what her mum might do. . . Death-defying moped rides were one aspect of her holiday the folks back home were not going to hear about. The list of anecdotes that would have to be filed away in the *never talk about this* box was getting longer and longer. And it was only day two.

After what seemed like a lifetime and yet was no time at all, Alessandro skidded around a corner and Kate's hotel came into view. But as he pulled up outside and killed the engine, she suddenly didn't want to get off. Although, she did think that her reluctance to get off the moped might have had more to do with her legs and arms shaking than leaving the man whose delicious scent had been infusing her senses for the last twenty minutes. How could he have just finished an all-night shift and yet smell so good? No, there was definitely a tinge of regret. The likelihood of seeing him so randomly again was microscopic. And maybe this was the time for *carpe diem*, to grab her chance to make sure she did. At least Jamie wasn't here this time, because it was quite possible that his version of seizing the day would involve throwing a condom at her and telling them to get on with it.

'OK now?' he asked with a mischievous grin as she wobbled off the seat.

Kate gave a mute nod, and the words she wanted to say swam around her head, but they wouldn't go in the right order. When she did open her mouth, she sounded like someone who'd just won Thickville's thickest resident award.

'Will you be working again?'

He cocked an eyebrow at her. 'I hope so. I hope I won't be. . . How do you say it. . .? Fired?'

'I mean will you be working tonight?'

'Why do you ask? Are you going to get drunk again?'

'No. . .' Kate blushed. She never blushed – what was it about this man that was making her blush almost constantly? And why did she care so much about what he was up to? A week was all she had in Rome – hardly enough time to build a relationship with anyone and certainly a scenario in which getting attached to a man was very unwise. Not that her wildly beating heart was listening to her head right now.

'I am not on duty for three days now,' he said with a smile. 'I have all my time to do anything I please.'

He was playing with her – he had to be – and she was sure she could see it in his eyes. How did he have this strange but sexy way of appearing to be mocking her without making her feel as if the joke was at her expense? Instead, it made her see the joke and want to laugh at it herself. It also made her want to push him against a wall and get her hands underneath that fitted shirt he was wearing very handsomely indeed, but that was a thought she was trying hard not to have.

She shrugged, uncertain where to look for fear that if she looked in those eyes she might just do something she'd regret.

'Today I will sleep,' he added. 'Tonight I have promised my sister I will take her to the wedding-dress shop. Tomorrow, I will be doing nothing. Have you seen the Vatican yet?'

Kate looked up at him now, and he regarded her steadily with that smouldering certainty of a man who knows who he is and what he wants. Her stomach flipped and dropped, as if she'd just barrelled down the track of a rollercoaster when she'd least expected the turn. 'No, I haven't.'

'It is very beautiful. I will take you tomorrow at nine o'clock.'

In any other circumstances and with any other man, Kate might have been irked that he had assumed her answer to a request to take her out would be yes. Though this was less of a request and more of an order, she couldn't bring herself to be annoyed about it. His direct-ness made a change, and there was none of the awkwardness she had imagined would come with her first potential date since Matt.

'I'd love that,' she said.

'Good.' He kicked the engine into life. 'Tomorrow at nine,' he repeated. 'And you must cover your arms.'

Kate nodded. 'See you tomorrow then.'

'*Ciao*,' he called, and an instant later he was gone from view, swallowed up by the traffic.

* * *

Despite simply wanting to get a shower and fall onto the bed for a snooze before dinner, Kate spent the following hour making various frustrating calls to her bank, credit-card company and travel insurers. It was hassle she could have done without and not exactly the sort of activity she had hoped to be indulging in during her stay in Rome, but it needed to be done and leaving it would only make things worse. Thank God she had left some money in the hotel safe, so that although she'd been forced to tell Anna about what had happened and ask her to transfer a little money across just in case she ran out, all in all the theft wasn't half as disastrous as it could have been. It was made more palatable too by the prospect of spending the following day with Alessandro. But then, when all the phone calls had been made, and she'd showered, she stood towelling her hair in front of the mirror and a sense of misgiving began to creep over her. She didn't even know Alessandro. . . She didn't even know his second name! What were his intentions? Was this a date? A quick tourist shag? A friendly offer of company? A professional sense of duty to protect someone who was clearly going to get herself into trouble if he wasn't there? He'd told her he'd pick her up and she'd said yes – no hesitation, no questions, no consideration for motives, armed with nothing but his first name and the memory of a sexy smile that could melt the polar ice caps.

Grabbing for her hairbrush and dragging it through the tangles, she tried to shake the doubts away. This was her new life, wasn't it? This was what she'd promised herself – to step out into the world and take chances. That was why she'd come to Rome, after all. And he was a police officer – what was the worst that could happen?

He could break your heart.

But hadn't Matt already done that? There was almost no heart left to be broken, and perhaps a holiday fling was just the thing to start hers beating again, to open her up to the possibility of real love with someone new back home, something she'd refused to contemplate since Matt had left.

Her internal struggle was interrupted by her mobile ringing. She swiped to answer.

'Hey,' Jamie greeted. He sounded a lot brighter than he had done when she'd left him the previous evening, more like the man she'd met at the airport. 'Are we still on for dinner?'

Kate was pretty sure she hadn't actually agreed to dinner, but Jamie was hard to say no to, and she did feel as if she might implode if she spent the evening alone dwelling on what might happen when Alessandro picked her up tomorrow. She would feel safer with company tonight too, and nice as her hotel restaurant was, she wanted to get out and try all that Rome had to offer. Jamie's knowledge would be good for that. 'That sounds nice. Where were you thinking?'

'We can do decent tourist food with fantastic views, or not-so-good views with fantastic food most tourists don't get to know about. Your choice.'

'What a choice!' Kate laughed. 'For one reason or another, I feel a bit cheated out of the tourist thing today, so maybe we should go for the tourist option if it's OK with you.'

'How so? Didn't you have a good day?'

'It's complicated, and I should probably save the story for when I see you.'

'OK, now I'm intrigued. So how about eating somewhere in the Piazza della Rotonda? We could gaze on the Pantheon while we eat our not-so-good food and you can tell me all about your complicated day.'

'That sounds amazing.'

'I'll wait outside your hotel for you. Seven-thirty sound OK?'

'Brilliant. See you then.'

'No problem.'

Kate ended the call and tossed the phone onto her bed as she wandered over to the wardrobe. Deciding what to wear tonight was easy, but more pressing on her thoughts was what she was going to wear tomorrow. If she had known what sort of occasion it was meant to be, that might help. Should she go for sexy or demure or the quirkier style she usually gravitated towards? The one indulgence she had allowed herself on the plane ticket was a good luggage allowance so she could bring a decent selection of dresses, and right now she was glad she had. She'd made most them too, and so each one fitted her perfectly in a way that off-the-peg shop-bought dresses just couldn't do, no matter how she altered them. It was one of the things she loved about making her own clothes, and the reason why her sisters never stopped asking her for little tailoring favours for themselves too. It was something she was proud of and knew she was good at. But Italy was the home of high fashion, and she was in a completely different league here. Maybe her homespun frocks just wouldn't cut it? But then Jamie had been impressed enough to suggest she did it for a living so they couldn't be that bad. She just needed to find the right dress to wow Alessandro tomorrow.

Her thoughts were interrupted by a loud growl from her stomach. She glanced at the time on her phone. Just gone six, and Jamie wasn't meeting her until seven thirty. She'd almost forgotten she hadn't eaten since breakfast, and that she'd actually been hungry at the police station hours before. Seven thirty seemed like a long time away, especially when they probably wouldn't eat until nearer eight. Perhaps room service would bring her a sandwich to be going on with?

But as she was dialling the number on the hotel phone, her own mobile started to ring, a number she didn't recognise displayed on the screen. She reached for it.

'Hello?'

'Is this Kate Merry?' The accent was Italian, and the somewhat sultry female voice familiar, though Kate took a moment to place it.

'Yes. . . Who is this?'

'I must tell you that *polizia* are not allowed to be in love with the tourists. . .'

Kate paused, frowned. 'What the hell. . . I have no idea what you're talking about.'

'Alessandro Conti. He is taking you out? It is not permitted. This is in the rules.'

And then it clicked. 'Orazia?'

The phone went dead. Kate stared at it as the screen went black. Her heart was beating in her ears. She was certain of the voice now, and the filthy looks earlier at the station suddenly all made sense. Orazia had some connection to Alessandro, either current or previous, but phone calls containing cryptic warnings (which could be seen by some as actual threats) seemed like a hell of a risky thing to do in the circumstances. Not to mention unprofessional. On the other hand, Alessandro himself didn't seem to have anything to hide – after all, he hadn't been skulking around at the station or hiding his obvious interest in Kate from anyone, and surely he would have if he'd been up to something he shouldn't. So Orazia was the one with the problem, and perhaps whatever was going on was one-sided? Kate didn't believe for a minute that any rule existed that forbade members of the public to date police officers – if it did, who the hell were they supposed to marry? So why would Orazia make a phone call to spout some nonsense about a non-existent law? Why did she care so much about any arrangements Alessandro might have made to see her?

As Kate perched on the edge of her bed and stared at her phone, all thoughts of sandwiches firmly out of her mind, she had to wonder if agreeing to this day out had been such a good idea after all. But as she didn't have a contact phone number for Alessandro, and as the prospect of calling the police station and possibly running into Orazia again was not an appealing one, there wasn't a lot she could do to change it. For better or worse, she was off to the Vatican tomorrow with a man who already seemed rather more dangerous than he had an hour before.

Seven

It was amazing how relaxed Kate felt in Jamie's company, even though she'd been annoyed with him the night before for leaving her in the trattoria, and despite only knowing him for a little over a day. It was hard to stay mad with someone who was so funny and clever, and within ten minutes of meeting him for dinner again Kate was giggling uncontrollably. He was easy on the eye too, and she could see why he might find it difficult to stay faithful to his boyfriend back home, because he probably never went short of offers from others who might quite like to steal that title.

They found a welcoming restaurant with a fantastic vantage point for the Pantheon, and while they got comfortable at an outside table, a string quartet playing gently in the background and the babble of tourists providing the accompanying soundtrack, Kate filled Jamie in on her eventful day.

'Oh my God!' Jamie's hand flew to his mouth as Kate told him about the robbery. 'Are you OK? You seem so calm for someone who's had all their money stolen! I'll tell you what, as I do owe you – even if you say I don't – let me pay for dinner tonight—'

'At this place? You'd never be able to afford two of us!' she laughed. 'I told you not to worry about last night's misunderstanding. As for the robbery, I'm fine. Luckily I was already paranoid about being alone in a big city – probably thanks to Matt and his village-peasant mentality rubbing off on me – so I didn't take everything out with me. That means I still have a card and a little cash. It's been an absolute pain trying to sort everything out though. I ended up at the police station for ages.'

'You're sure you're OK? You don't need any help with anything?'

'The police at the station were great; helped me loads. One in particular . . .' she said, her mind wandering back to Alessandro and trying to wander very definitely away from Orazia. She shook herself. 'I don't know what I would have done without him.'

'You should have called me.'

'You were in meetings and I didn't want to disturb you. Besides, you've only just met me. It's not much of a new friend who phones you every five minutes when they need the tiniest thing.'

'I don't think a mugging is the tiniest thing.'

Kate smiled ruefully. She'd been lucky to run into Jamie on her first day. She hoped he would want to stay in touch at the end of the holiday, because she could see he would be a wonderful friend to have in the future. And maybe she'd even visit him in New York one day, on his home soil. That would be a lot of fun, she was sure, as long as he didn't make a habit of disappearing on her whenever they had dinner.

'As luck would have it,' he added, 'the meeting I had scheduled for tomorrow is cancelled, so I'm free for the day.'

'That's good. So what are you going to do with yourself?'

'I don't know. I've pretty much seen Rome over the years, but I wondered whether you wanted to do something. . . maybe catch some of the sights that first-time tourists wouldn't see? There's plenty I could show you.'

'Oh, that would have been lovely but. . .'

'But?'

'I kind of have plans.'

'Oh. Well that's cool. I was just thinking but. . . you want to spend some time on your own, I get that. It doesn't matter.'

'No! It isn't that. Ordinarily I'd love to go sightseeing with you but it's not that simple. It's. . .' Kate paused. Jamie looked so disappointed that she hated to let him down. But she'd made arrangements now that she couldn't undo, particularly as she didn't even know how to contact Alessandro to undo them, even if she'd wanted to. Which she didn't, despite Orazia's interference and even though she felt bad about Jamie. Would she sound like a crazy woman if she told Jamie the truth? Probably no worse than he already thought she was. 'I've arranged to go to the Vatican with someone.'

Jamie raised his eyebrows. 'Someone?'

'Yes. . . someone.'

As she had offered no more information, it seemed obvious that it was something more than any old companion, and Jamie seized on the idea with a grin. 'Male?'

'Maybe. . .'

'I'm impressed! That was quick work!'

'You're a male someone!' Kate laughed. 'And I met you on the first day.'

He speared an olive and popped it into his mouth with a suggestive wink that would have been skin crawling on anyone else but on him was just funny. 'You did, but I can tell by your face that this is a potential-sexual-partner kind of someone.'

'Jamie!' Kate squeaked.

'Tell me I'm wrong.'

'I don't know what he is; I've only just met him. But he asked me and I said yes.'

He leaned back again in his seat. 'Wow, you *do* work fast!'

'I don't know what he means by it. I think he was just being nice.'

'Nice because he wants to get into your panties. Guys are like that.'

'No he doesn't!' Kate giggled. 'He certainly won't be doing that at the Vatican.'

'So tell me everything. Mugging and flirting; it sounds as if you've had a very busy day.'

Kate paused as the waiter brought wine and antipasti. Then she continued as he left them again. 'There's not that much to tell. He helped me out and then took me back to my hotel this afternoon—'

'Yes, of course. . . *back to your hotel*. . .' Jamie gave her a lazy grin, looking immensely pleased with his deduction. Kate couldn't help but giggle.

'Not like that, Jamie! It was all very innocent and he just dropped me off outside. I had been a victim of crime, you know, and I was very traumatised. Then he asked if I wanted to go to the Vatican tomorrow and I said yes.'

Jamie's eyes were wide as he seemed to come to a conclusion. 'Wait! This is your helpful cop?' His grin was back, bigger than ever. 'I guess you did need personal one-to-one care from the police. Not an ugly dude, of course.'

Kate laughed. 'Shut up!' But she had almost certainly ensured that Jamie thought she was a nutter now.

'So this is a date?'

'I think so. It's hard to tell. . .'

'It *so* is!' He clapped his hands together like a little kid who'd just been shown a table full of chocolate. 'Score! You bagged yourself a cop!'

Kate shot a quick glance at the surrounding tables, all crammed with chattering customers. Jamie's outburst didn't seem to have brought as much attention to their table as she had feared, and most were happily talking away as they ate, or leaning back in their seats with a glass of wine and drinking in the scenery.

'Do you think it's a bad idea?'

'Bad idea? Are you crazy? Italian, fine sense of justice, probably looks hot in his uniform and could handle himself in a fight. I think you'll do just fine. And he's suggested taking you to the Vatican, so he's probably a good Catholic boy too.'

'I never thought about that. I'm not Catholic. Do you think it will matter?'

'Kate, you can be anything he wants for tomorrow. It's not like you're going to marry him.'

'Yeah, I suppose so. I've got myself in such a tizzy about the whole thing if I'm honest that I don't know what I'm saying half the time.' She popped a lemon-infused olive into her mouth, savouring the flavours as they burst into life on her tongue.

'I'm sure it will be just fine. I could be on standby for you if it doesn't work out. We could come up with a safe word you can call me with and I can come and meet you in an "accidental" way. . .' He crooked two fingers in the air to make speech marks. 'Or I could arrange to call you at a certain time of the day and pretend I need you for something. That way you'd have a get-out plan. In case he's boring as hell.'

Kate didn't imagine for a minute that Alessandro would be boring, but perhaps Jamie had a point. Not that she thought there would be

any issue with him, but if he turned out to be unexpectedly obnox-
ious or just started coming on too heavy, it would be good to feel she
had an escape route. After all, she didn't know him at all. She hardly
knew Jamie but at least she'd spent a little more time with him –
enough to get the measure of what sort of person he was. And despite
the episode in the trattoria the night before, she trusted him to come
to her rescue if she asked; he had come back to the hotel to check on
her, after all. 'That's probably a good idea. How about I phone you
and mention. . .' she glanced around, and her gaze fell on the antipasti plate, 'green olives if I need you?'

'Green olives, got it.'

Jamie reached over to top his wine glass up and then did the same
with Kate's. She made a mental note to drink the next glass more
slowly so she wouldn't end up in a state like she had the night before.

'So,' she began, 'now that we have that sorted, are you going to tell
me what happened to you last night? I mean, I don't want the sordid
details. . . but I get the feeling that something is going on with you
and Pietro.'

Jamie paused and took a slow sip of his wine as he held her in a
steady gaze, all merriment suddenly gone. He seemed to be weighing
up how much to tell her. Kate had been so preoccupied with whether
she could trust a man she'd only just met that she had forgotten the
same applied to him. He knew Kate as well as she knew him, and she
was probably asking him something quite personal.

'Forget it,' she said, shaking her head. 'I shouldn't have asked.'

'No, you have a right to know. I did excuse myself from the table
for a very long time, and I understand why you would have been upset and thought I'd run out on you. I wasn't intending to be so long,
and before you say anything, I'm not having an affair with him.'

'Really, if you don't want to tell me—'

'I don't mind telling you; it's just that I don't know where to begin. And really it's not my story to tell so this is in confidence. OK?'

Kate nodded. 'Of course.'

He took another swig of his wine before putting the glass down and tracing its rim with an idle finger. Kate had never seen him look so serious.

'The first time I ate at Trattoria da Luigi I was in Rome with Brad.'

'Your boyfriend?'

Jamie nodded. 'We had dinner together there, and Pietro was very attentive. I thought nothing of it, only to recall it the next time I came to Rome on business, so that when I thought about having dinner alone it seemed a no-brainer to eat at the place where I'd had great service from a friendly waiter. Sure enough he waited my table again and he was great. We got chatting, and he asked if I wanted to go to a bar when he'd finished his shift. I was alone, and I was bored.' He shrugged. 'It seemed like a good idea.'

'Did you think it was a come-on? That he wanted to take you to a bar because he fancied you?'

'Not really. He hadn't showed that sort of interest. . . he was just friendly and I was glad to be out of my hotel room for an evening.'

'So what happened?'

'Nothing. We had a few drinks, he introduced me to his friends, and we had a great time. We went out again the following night, and again the night after that. I came back to Rome three more times and each time we hooked up in the same way. I mean, it's great if you can find a friend to spend time with, otherwise these business trips can get pretty lonely.'

Kate nodded, but she didn't interrupt, sensing that he needed to stay focused on his story.

'One day we went back to his friend's apartment instead of the bar. His friend was out but he'd given Pietro a key, so we made ourselves at home. That's when he told me he'd fallen in love with me.'

He paused then knocked back the rest of his wine. Kate waited patiently while he refilled the glass. She wasn't shocked by his revelation, having already guessed that this was where the story was heading. She was only surprised that Jamie himself hadn't seen it coming at the time, as he had professed. But she didn't say so and he continued.

'We were both drunk by this point, and I thought he was messing with me. So I began messing with him, putting my arms around him, kissing his cheek. . . I told him I loved him too, but I thought it was fun – nothing more than that. I thought it was all a drunken game. It couldn't be possible that it was true – he'd never shown any signs of it before. . . hell, everything about him screamed straight to me. But then he kissed me properly and I knew. I'm not proud, but things got out of hand. I didn't sleep with him,' he added quickly, 'but things went way too far. I wasn't so drunk that I had forgotten Brad, and I stopped before I did something I might regret. Pietro was hurt, and he was ashamed, I could tell. It was hard on both of us. Anyway. . . I went to talk to him again the next night when we'd both had time to cool down, and we agreed that we could be friends, and I would even help him come out if he wanted me to. His family are pretty religious and very traditional, so he was terrified. I honestly wondered whether he would ever dare, or whether he was doomed to spend his life married to a woman he didn't love just to make them happy.'

'You said last night that you thought he was going to the Alps,' Kate reminded him.

'Ah, yes. The last time I saw him he had suddenly decided he was going to leave Rome and work as a ski instructor. I thought it was a bit random, but if it made him happy then that was cool.'

'But last night you saw he was still working at his dad's restaurant and that's why you went off with him? To find out why?'

'I could guess why. He called me away from the table to talk; there were things he needed to get off his chest and I guess the sight of me sitting there brought them all to his mind. He said he was struggling to concentrate on anything with me around.'

'He still loves you?'

Jamie nodded. 'He says he wants to come and live in New York so that he's near the only person he feels understands him. He says he doesn't care that Brad is there, and when I tried to explain to him that seeing us together all the time would be torture, he said he didn't care about that either and that he'd be able to control himself.'

'You don't think that would be the case?'

'Living near to me would be a disaster, and it wouldn't help him at all. I told him so and that it would only make things worse with temptation that close by, no matter what he said. Plus, there's the danger of him being too close to Brad. I don't think he would say anything to incriminate me, and I think Brad would trust me in the face of any accusations, but it's not something I want to risk.'

Kate blew out a long breath. 'And I thought my life was complicated. I can see why you're so worried.'

'I don't know what to do about him, but I feel responsible for him, whether I should or not. He's trusting me with something that's a huge deal for him, and he needs my support.'

'Do you think that's why he's so attached to you? Because he's latching on to someone who understands him, rather than being genuinely in love?'

Jamie nodded. 'Perhaps. If only he would come out, he could find someone who was free to love him back openly. He's a great guy, and he doesn't deserve all this hellfire and damnation shit his parents have indoctrinated in him.'

'You think they'd come round? If they're as traditional as you say, they'll take a lot of persuading.'

'It's either risk it and tell them or continue to live a lie. Neither situation is a great one, but that's the choice he's faced with. He's going to be miserable for a while whatever he chooses to do – there's no way around that. But I think if he's honest then he has a chance of happiness when the dust is settled.'

'How did you leave it last night?'

'We were interrupted by his brother, who came into the office for the safe.' Jamie paused. 'I actually think his brother suspects something is going on.'

'Isn't that a good thing? Won't it make coming out easier if they have an inkling already?'

'I don't know. His brother is a mean specimen. I think he'd be less tolerant than Pietro's parents.'

'You think he'd get violent?'

'I don't know. But I don't like the way he looked at me last night. He practically told me to get out.'

Kate's eyes widened. 'He threw you out?'

'As politely as he could. But there was no mistaking what he meant.'

Kate sat back in her seat. Her gaze went to the stone pillars of the Pantheon as she digested Jamie's story. 'I don't know what to say. Poor Pietro.'

'Exactly. I think it would be poor Jamie if Roberto had his way.'

'Roberto's his brother? He wouldn't dare surely?'

'I'm not a gambling man but. . .'

'So you can't go back to Trattoria da Luigi?'

'I don't think so. It's a shame – the seafood is the best in Rome.'

'I think that might be the least of your worries.'

He let out a sigh. 'I'm sorry to have laid all this at your door. I'm sure you have enough of your own to worry about.'

'Are you kidding? I've just done the same to you. Besides, I'm glad you've told me; at least it explains what happened. I was beginning to think it was me. I mean, I have a track record with men running out on me, but if it started to extend to virtual strangers I'd get really concerned.'

Jamie smiled. 'So it looks as if I have to find a new favourite restaurant. Care to help me? Not tomorrow, obviously. Unless your date goes so well that you don't have time to fit me in for the rest of your stay.'

'I would always have time to fit you in, Jamie. I don't think I've ever made a new best friend so quickly, but best friend is what you already are.'

He raised his glass, and Kate did the same. 'I'll drink to that!'

Eight

Kate settled on a primrose-yellow polka-dot tea dress, one of her own creations. It seemed demure enough to be suitable for a holy site, yet playful enough to be flirty. She couldn't exactly say it was perfect, but out of everything she'd brought along it fit the bill the best. Her red hair was pinned up in a cute Gibson roll finished with tiny fabric daisies. A slick of lip stain and navy-blue mascara to bring out her blue-grey eyes and she was ready. Standing in front of the mirror, she took a deep breath, sucked her tummy in, and gave herself a critical once-over. She supposed she looked a lot better than she had yesterday when she'd arrived at the police station sweating and red-faced, so it had to be an improvement.

Her phone said 8.50 a.m. Was it too early to go down and wait? What sort of impression would that give? The right one? It was the first time she'd done something like this since her first date with Matt, and that felt like a very long time ago now. Besides, things were very different these days. She had waited for Matt outside the school gates, still in her uniform, and then he had ridden alongside her on his bike as she walked and they compared insults for the head teacher they had a mutual hatred for. As first dates went it wasn't particularly sophisticated, and at the time they hadn't really even realised they were on one.

Sod it. Kate gathered her bag and a crocheted cardigan to cover up with and headed downstairs to wait on the street.

* * *

Alessandro was ten minutes late. It was quite possibly the longest ten minutes of her life as Kate considered every possible reason for this, from him deciding not to come at all to him being knocked off his moped as he sped through the streets of Rome. When he finally arrived, however, he was not on his moped at all, but stepped, smiling, from a car driven by a good-looking woman who subjected Kate to a curious study before bidding him goodbye and speeding off again. Kate wanted to ask him who it was, but something about doing that felt a bit needy and unreasonable. After all, she wouldn't be a romantic interest, surely, dropping him off for a date with another woman? But after the phone call from Orazia, which still had Kate puzzled, she was beginning to wonder if anything was possible where this man was concerned. She wouldn't be surprised to learn that he had a harem tucked away somewhere. Orazia was a question that perhaps needed to be asked of him, but Kate wasn't really sure she wanted the answer. In any case, she decided against it for the time being, until she knew where the day was heading.

'*Buongiorno!* I hope you have not waited a long time,' he greeted, kissing Kate lightly on both cheeks. It was delightfully informal, and it put her at ease straightaway. The intoxicating scent of whatever cologne he favoured was doing a pretty good job of relaxing her too, but perhaps not in a way that was quite so appropriate to the occasion. 'You look beautiful.'

Kate felt that irritating blush spread over her cheeks again. She couldn't stop it, and could only hope it gave her an English rose complexion, though she suspected with her colouring it was more likely to give her the look of a Belisha beacon.

'I haven't been waiting too long,' she lied, even though she had been at the roadside long enough to get pitying looks from the hotel doorman.

'Good,' he said. 'Are you ready?'

She nodded, and he offered his arm.

'*Va bene*. Then we will go.'

* * *

Because the walk was only half an hour or so, they decided against the metro, setting off on foot, which would give them a chance to see much more of the city. Kate had been in Rome for three days now, and she had already beaten quite a path along its streets, boulevards and piazzas, but she didn't think she'd ever get used to the beauty of the city, no matter how often she walked it. She suspected Alessandro felt the same, and the pride in his voice as he pointed out landmarks was evident. Everywhere was busy, tourists and residents alike jostling for space, skirting around them as they walked, shouting into mobile phones or at each other, giggling, chatting, kissing, or simply standing agog at some new sight, but as they drew near to the Vatican, the crowds suddenly became ten times worse. Kate stared as they approached. They were going to have to wait for a week if they wanted to get in anywhere.

'You want to go into the museum?' Alessandro asked, angling his head at a vast stone wall with a line of people snaked along it.

'Is that the queue?'

'*Sì*. But it is not as bad as it looks, and I may have some influence.'

Kate cocked an eye at him. 'Do you mean you're going to abuse your position as a police officer?'

'No,' he laughed. 'But I do have a friend I can call who will get us in.'

Kate smiled. 'What do you think? I'd like to see Saint Peter's too. Should we do that first?'

He looked at his watch. 'Would you like to be blessed by His Holiness?'

'The Pope?'

He nodded. 'This morning he will be on his balcony to bless the crowds. It is quite moving.'

Kate had never been particularly religious, and she certainly wasn't Catholic, but something about the prospect of being blessed by the Pope gave her a little kick of excitement. 'Have you been blessed before?'

'Many times.'

'Do you feel it's made your life better?'

'I am here with you now.'

Kate blushed again. It was becoming an irritatingly regular occurrence. But Alessandro did things to her that no other man had ever done, not even Matt. Not that she'd had many opportunities for other men to make her blush. But although she had loved Matt, it had been a steady, safe kind of love, one that had grown organically from a deep friendship, not the heart-stopping, stomach-churning, loin-tingling kind of love that people sang and wrote about. Matt had never made her heart stop, or made her blush or pant with excitement simply at the thought of seeing his face. But love with someone like Alessandro, she was beginning to see, could be just that. Not with *him*, of course – in very practical terms he wasn't the right man at all. Still, it wasn't a crime to enjoy a taste of it while she had the opportunity, was it? 'I'd love to see the Pope. I think it would be incredible.'

'Then we should hurry. We may not get the best place to stand now, but I hope you will be able to see a little.'

'It'll be just like seeing Take That at Wembley,' Kate said as they began to walk.

'*Scusi?*'

'A concert my sister once made me go to. We paid eighty quid each and all we saw was four ants dressed in white in the distance. We got crushed and covered in sweat into the bargain.'

'So you didn't like it?'

'I loved it!' Kate laughed. 'But I don't feel I can say I actually saw Take That at all. It could have been anyone and I wouldn't have known the difference.'

'I am sure this is the real Pope.'

'You don't think he has stunt doubles?'

Alessandro nodded slowly, as if pondering the actual possibility that the Pope might have a stunt double, and Kate giggled.

'Imagine if he did!'

'I think there would be a lot of very unhappy worshippers.'

'Would you still be blessed, even if it wasn't the Pope doing it? Or perhaps he hides behind a curtain and does the blessing thing in secret while his stunt double stands on the balcony and acts it out? That way he can be safe from assassins and still bless everyone.'

He turned to her and cocked an eyebrow. 'Do you always have such strange thoughts?'

Kate shrugged, and that burning in her cheeks returned. 'I've never really considered it like that. Perhaps I do. Does it bother you? That I might be a nutter?'

'A nutter?'

'Mad.'

'As long as it is good mad and not dangerous mad I like it on you.'

'I bet you see a lot of dangerous mad.'

'Some. But mostly I move drunken women from the Spanish Steps. . .' He turned to her with that deliciously wicked smile, and Kate almost tripped over her own feet. Her heart was beating a samba and it was a good thing they were in a holy place, otherwise she might have found it very hard not to act on her decidedly unholy impulses.

'I hope you don't ask them all out on dates—' She stopped. What she'd assumed she hadn't meant to say out loud, but that was exactly what she'd done. If this wasn't a date and he set her right now, things might get very awkward for the rest of the day. Or worse, he might think her arrogant enough to assume that any man offering some friendly company must fancy her. And until this precise moment she hadn't even considered the idea that he might be gay, just like Jamie, who had offered her lots of friendly company this week and didn't want to get into her pants at all. She stifled the groan that formed in her throat. Why did she have to make everything twenty times more complicated than it needed to be?

'No,' he said. 'They're not all as beautiful and interesting as you.'

In a strange and spontaneous reaction that she would later cringe with embarrassment at the memory of, Kate slapped him on the arm. 'Get off with you!' she giggled. He raised his eyebrows and looked at her as if he had just decided she was quite mad after all – and not in a good way – but then he relaxed into a bemused smile. 'This is Saint Peter's Square,' he said.

Kate looked across gleaming cobbles, worn smooth by centuries of footfall, towards a sweeping arc of white Doric pillars that looked

so incredible and perfect in the morning sun they just had to be the
product of some computer-generated fantasy.

'We must go through the security checks before we can enter. . .
We join the line there. . .' He pointed to the back of a wall of people
behind barriers. The Vatican ought to be called the City of Queues
because that was pretty much what they were going to be doing all
day by the looks of it. At least she had good company to queue with
so perhaps it wouldn't be such a chore.

'It's good that they check everyone,' she said.

'It is very important.'

'I suppose you must think so. . . in your line of work, I mean.'

'There are some bad people in the world and we must all be careful.'

'Do you come here a lot?'

'Sometimes.'

'On your own?'

'Sometimes with my mother. Not so much now – her legs are not
so good.'

'Do you have brothers and sisters?'

'Five sisters.'

'Wow! No brothers? You must feel outnumbered.'

'Sometimes,' he laughed. 'My sisters are all very. . .'

Kate waited patiently as he struggled for the word.

'*Prepotente*,' he said finally. 'I don't know how to say it in English.
They tell me what to do all the time.'

'Bossy,' Kate said, smiling. 'My older sister Anna can be like that,
but she means well.'

'You have sisters too?'

'Only two. There's just the three of us, no brothers.'

'Ah, so we have something in common.'

'We do. My little sister Lily is having a baby.'

'That's wonderful. I have ten nieces and nephews.'

'Ten?'

He shrugged. 'It's not so many. Maria has four children, Jolanda has three, and Isabella has three. Abelie and Lucetta are not yet married, but Lucetta will be married soon.'

'Who's the oldest?'

'Maria. Then Isabella, Jolanda, Alessandro. . .' he prodded his chest with a grin, 'Lucetta and Abelie.'

Kate smiled. She liked the way he had referred to himself in the third person as he ran down the pecking order of the family; it was cute. 'So you're a middle child?'

He nodded.

'Me too,' Kate said. 'That's another thing we have in common.'

'Then we have lots to talk about today.'

Kate beamed. 'We do!'

The sky was blue, the air was warm, her surroundings were beautiful and she had the company of a handsome, charming and courteous man. She had a feeling that today was going to be perfect, and she wasn't going to let annoying technicalities like possible bunny-boiling police girlfriends spoil it.

* * *

It wasn't often that Kate could say she'd genuinely been stunned into silence, but after a quite moving view of the Pope – made all the more poignant by how much it obviously meant to people in the crowd – Alessandro had taken her inside Saint Peter's Basilica where they had stood, awestruck at the majesty and opulence of the marble and stone interiors, priceless and iconic works of art at every turn. Together they had touched the foot of Saint Peter's statue to ask for his blessing, gone down to the Vatican grottos where Popes of old lay in eternal rest, and up again to make the 320-step climb into Saint Peter's dome where they'd emerged into the open air and gazed at the sun glinting off the rose-gold rooftops of Rome. All in all, it had been a strangely uplifting and spiritual experience, and Kate had almost been overwhelmed by it. But then they'd returned to the real world with a vengeance as they jostled through the crowds in the Vatican museums where it was hot and tiring, and she was quite glad when Alessandro suggested a quiet drink somewhere off the Via di Porta Angelica. Kate didn't know where that was, but it sounded nice and she was delighted to see that it was indeed every bit as lovely and calm as its name suggested.

Like the truest gentleman, he pulled out a seat for Kate to sit at a parasol-shaded table. Nobody had ever pulled out a chair for her to sit before, and Kate wasn't quite sure how to react. She somehow felt awkward, embarrassed even, as if she had been caught out patronising a restaurant that was far too posh for her and was afraid she'd be asked to leave. But she took the seat with a nervous smile and Alessandro sat alongside her with one that was more assured. It was a characteristic of his that she was beginning to love – that he seemed so together, so certain of himself; nothing ever seemed to fluster him. It made her feel safe.

'Are you cooler now?' he asked.

'Oh, much. This shade is lovely. It's this stupid ginger hair of mine. . . I burn so easily I have to be careful. . . It would probably cost me a small fortune in sun cream if I lived here.'

'Then it is good you live in a country with many rain clouds.'

'It is. Though we do have one or two days of sun a year.'

He raised his eyebrows. 'Really?'

'Yes!' Kate laughed. 'It's not that bad!'

He grinned.

'What do people from Italy think England is like?' Kate asked. 'I don't mean those who have visited, but those like you who haven't?'

'I know little. Sometimes I see news reports, but it is always about your prime minister or your queen. I have seen photos of London. What is it like?'

Kate was thoughtful for a moment, fiddling with the stem of a wine glass set out on the table. 'Strange,' she said finally. She looked up at his quizzical expression. 'Nice, mostly. Very different depending on what part of the country you're in. People are friendly on the streets but they don't want to talk to you on a bus or train. They'll help you when they can but they also don't really want to get involved. It can be lonely at times even when you're surrounded by people. . .' She shook herself and forced a smile.

'Your wedding ring,' he said, nodding at her hand. Kate glanced at it and then back at him.

'I don't have one.'

'I think you once did. You look for it sometimes. . . with your fingers.'

'Oh. So we're getting down to business now,' she smiled. 'I was married. Not any more, though. And there's been nobody else – no dates or anything. I didn't have an affair either and I didn't end the marriage. We married young, and I suppose we just grew up – at least Matt did. It meant that I had to grow up whether I wanted to or not. But it's OK, because I'm learning to live again and actually, so far, it's good.'

They were interrupted by the waiter, and as Alessandro ordered for them, Kate watched and wondered just how her admission of a fresh divorce might have changed his opinion of her. Was he put off? Or did he see her as prey now, someone he might easily seduce and discard? Suddenly, her position felt a lot less certain than it had at any point during their time together so far. And he had a past too – that much was certain from her run-in with Orazia – but he hadn't alluded to it yet. Although she couldn't be sure if any of it was true without asking him outright and that seemed like a conversation that was still out of bounds for now.

The waiter left with his order and Alessandro turned his attention back to Kate. 'You have been honest with me, and so I must be honest with you. I am not married. . .'

'I'm glad to hear it.' Kate gave a nervous laugh and immediately wanted to slap herself. Why couldn't she just keep her mouth shut and listen without making stupid comments? But he seemed unperturbed by her interruption.

'I was almost married.'

'To Orazia?'

His eyes narrowed for a second, and Kate cursed herself. She'd done it again.

'Not to Orazia,' he replied carefully. 'Why do you say that?'

If a trapdoor could have opened beneath her chair at that moment, Kate would have been glad of it. 'Nothing. . . I guessed. . . Something she said. . .'

'What did she say?'

'She phoned me – yesterday after I'd left the police station. At least it sounded like her but she didn't give her name, only hung up when I asked if it was her. She said you weren't allowed to date tourists. . .

It kind of sounded as if she was warning me away from you. . . You're not together?' Kate asked, feeling more flustered by the minute and wishing dearly there was some way to rewind the conversation.

His features hardened. 'We were together, for a few months only. My sister, Maria, is friends with her, and my mother was keen for us to marry. But Orazia would never be a good wife for me.'

'I think she might have a different opinion on that.'

'She does not love me – she is angry. In time she will forget about me.'

'But you work together – that has to be difficult in those circumstances.'

'Work and love are separate. Always.'

'It wasn't before,' Kate pressed, despite feeling that she was sailing in dangerous waters. 'You didn't have that rule when you started to date Orazia?'

'No. Orazia is the reason I have that rule now.'

'But what about me? Aren't I a bit close to that rule? I don't work with you but I was work yesterday, and we're here now.'

He gave her a tight smile. 'I am not perfect and sometimes I break my own rules. But you will go back to England in a week and my rule will be good again.'

Kate nodded, still uncertain where that left them but hungry to hear more. 'So you were engaged to be married?'

'Once.'

'Who was she?'

'Her name was Heidi.'

He gave a brisk nod of thanks as the waiter returned with their drinks, and Kate waited until they were alone again before she pushed the conversation further.

'It's not a very Italian name.'

'Her family are Swiss, but they lived in Rome.'

'Didn't your mum like her? Because she wasn't Italian, I mean? Is that why you didn't get married in the end?'

'She drowned in Lake Lugano.'

Kate nearly spat out the lemonade she'd just taken a sip of. He didn't flinch, but she could see in his eyes that he had left their table, and his mind was far away on the shores of a Swiss lake. 'Oh. . . I don't know what to say. I'm so sorry.'

'It was eight years ago. . . I was twenty-two.'

'Were you there?'

He shook his head. 'She had gone to visit her grandfather and they went out in his boat. She hit her head and fell in. Her grandfather tried to save her but. . .'

Kate's eyes filled with tears, but she sniffed them back. She wanted to pull him into her arms and tell him everything would be OK, but it wasn't very appropriate given the circumstances, and perhaps it was a reaction that would satisfy her needs, not his.

'You still think about her?'

'Often. But that life is no more. . .' He seemed to rally, and he came back to the table again, giving Kate his full attention now. 'My mother has tried to find me a wife since, but I have not liked any of them.'

'Perhaps she needed to let you get to the point where you were ready in your own time?'

'She said I would die alone if she did not help.'

'I'm sure she meant well and she only wanted to see you happy. But it's difficult for someone else to know exactly what will make you click with a partner – best to let them do it themselves.'

'Click?' he asked, raising one delectable eyebrow. 'What does that mean?'

'You know. . . what will make you get on well. . . have a good time. . .'

'Like you and I?'

'I suppose so,' Kate said with a small smile. 'I suppose you could say we're clicking.'

'I dated Orazia for my mother, to make her happy. It did not end well.'

Kate had to wonder at this point just what his mother might make of her if she could see them sitting together under the shade of a parasol outside the café, heads close over tall glasses of cloudy lemonade as they shared their secrets. Somehow she didn't think she'd fit the brief of suitable potential wife or even a girlfriend, but then with a divorce behind her at thirty, would she fit any mother's? Divorce meant baggage, and there was no way of getting around that.

'Does all this mean you're ready to find love again?' she asked. 'I mean you must have felt you'd moved on a bit to start dating again?'

He paused, held her in a molten gaze. 'Perhaps,' he said. 'Are you?'

She gave a self-conscious guffaw, another spontaneous and completely unbecoming reaction she would later burn crimson at the memory of. 'I think I'm having too much fun on my own to worry about another man just yet.'

'That is a shame. Perhaps you will change your mind?'

'If I find the right man. I certainly haven't seen much to change my mind in Manchester so far.'

He gave a short nod, a smile playing at the corner of his lips. Kate might have been tempted to say it was just a little on the cocky side. It should have irritated the hell out of her but, strangely, it didn't.

* * *

The conversation with Alessandro had lightened and turned to stories of his sister bossing him around, anecdotes from his police-training days and horror stories of awful women that his mother had tried to pair him up with. But all too soon it was time to go. Kate wished she could suggest somewhere else for them to go on to, but it seemed rather forward, and as he hadn't suggested anything, perhaps he'd had enough. So she left the café with him, regretful but accepting of the fact that their date was over.

As they walked the road back to Kate's hotel, Alessandro turned to her.

'Will you be meeting your friend for dinner tonight?'

'I hadn't arranged anything with him.'

'Hmmm.'

'Why do you ask?'

'I wondered. . . You have enjoyed today?'

'Of course, I've had a wonderful time. . .' She shot him a playful look. Did he want to carry on after all? Perhaps this was the moment to try and figure him out. 'Do you know a good place to eat?'

'I know many.'

'Aren't you going to offer to take me to one of them? I am a stranger to Rome, after all. . .'

He broke into a slow smile. 'I would like that very much.' He looked at his watch. 'You would like to go back to your hotel first?'

'I could do with freshening up. But I don't want you to go off in case you don't come back for me – I want the dinner I've been promised. It might be a little forward, but would you like to come up to my room to wait? I won't be long and you can get a drink from the minibar.'

'I would always come back for you, but if you prefer me to wait in your room then I will.'

'I would,' Kate said. 'It seems silly to send you away when you'd be coming back in less than an hour anyway.'

* * *

Jamie had sent a very irreverent text in reply to Kate's news that she was going to have dinner with Alessandro and she hoped he wouldn't mind. It said something along the lines of how he would be most disappointed to hear that she hadn't seduced Alessandro, and that he wanted to hear all about her date when he saw her again. She was glad and relieved to see he didn't seem to be offended that she had effectively ditched him for dinner that night, and it crossed her mind to ask what he was going to do with himself instead. But her thoughts were distracted by the sight of Alessandro sitting on her bed and the question soon slipped from her mind. While she wasn't going to take Jamie's advice completely, she had made up her mind to get closer and to get a taste of the one thing she had been gasping to do all day.

Emerging from the bathroom with her teeth cleaned, hair un-clipped and brushed, make-up touched up and perfume spritzed, she strode over to where he sat and perched next to him.

'I've had a fantastic day,' she said, holding his gaze. 'Thank you.'

He said nothing in reply, simply wrapped her thoughts in those dark eyes until they were filled with nothing but how much she wanted him.

And then they moved as one. It was obvious he wanted it as much as she did, and as their lips met it was like a jolt of electricity running through her. She had never felt anything so intense, not in all the hundreds of times she had kissed Matt, and it was all she could do to stop herself digging her hands straight into his shirt and ripping it off.

She couldn't breathe, could barely speak as they broke off, could only stare at him dreamily, hungry for more. And then he obliged, pulling her closer still, one hand in her hair and the other on her cheek. She could feel his chest pressing against hers, and she could imagine her heart beating right out of it. Back onto the bed they fell, and she rolled on top of him, his groin springing to life as her tongue searched his mouth. He groaned as her hands ran down his flanks and pulled his shirt from his trousers. He went for the zip of her dress and she heard it slide open. She wanted him – she wanted him so badly it was an ache that consumed her.

'Kate. . .' he panted, breaking off. 'This. . .'

'What's wrong?' She pulled away, looked at him. With the lust in his eyes, there was uncertainty. The sight jolted her to her senses. How could she have misread the situation so badly?

'I'm so sorry. . .' she mumbled as she climbed off him and re-zipped her dress. 'You must think I'm such a whore.'

'No,' he said, sitting up and reaching for her arm to guide her gently back to the bed. She sat beside him, deflated now and feeling very stupid. But he smiled and stroked a lock of hair from her face. 'I think you are a beautiful and sexy woman. . . very passionate. And I think that no man has been passionate with you for some time. I would love to show you that passion. . . But you are in Rome for days, not years, and I must live with only memories when you are gone.'

'I don't understand.'

He leaned in to kiss her, softly this time. 'I do not want just a taste of what I can never have again. It is too cruel.'

What was he saying? That he didn't do one night stands? Didn't all men do one-night stands? But then it hit her – she didn't do one-night stands and maybe he knew that. Could he tell she would regret it? Was he saving her from herself?

'I feel so embarrassed,' she said.

'There is no need. If you lived in Rome, I would want this with all my heart because I would know we would meet again.'

'Why ask me out for the day then?'

He seemed confused by her question for a moment. 'Because I like you and I wanted to show you my city.'

'But you didn't know this would happen?'

'Yesterday, no. Today, I thought maybe yes. But I decided I would be strong if it did.'

'Unlike me, who was about as strong as a jelly,' she replied with a rueful smile.

'You are stronger than you think, Kate.'

She tugged a hand through the tangle of her hair. 'So, I don't suppose you want to have dinner now?' She had asked the question, and in light of what had just happened and been said, she wasn't sure what she wanted the answer to be. It would be awkward as hell for both of them, but a tiny part of her wasn't ready to let him go yet, despite this.

'Why not?' he asked with an encouraging smile. 'I am hungry. You must be hungry too.'

'A bit,' she admitted.

'Then we will have dinner.'

Nine

Kate was woken by Anna's call. She reached over to pluck the phone from her bedside cabinet and clamped it to her ear.

'Hey. . .' she mumbled, rubbing sleep from her eyes and trying to shove her brain into gear. 'This is early – what's up?'

'I have to call early because apparently you're too busy to talk to me at any normal hour.'

Kate sat up in bed, suddenly wide awake. 'OK, I get the impression you're pissed off with me.'

'Of course I'm not.'

'That's definitely your pissed-off voice. I've heard it enough times over the years to know it by now.'

'Oh, alright then, I am. But I've phoned you about twenty times since you got to Rome and you either don't pick up or you're with *someone* and you can't talk.' Anna made certain to emphasise the word *someone*, as if she didn't approve of it one bit. 'I mean, how many someones are there?'

'I've been spending quite a bit of time with Jamie, which you know about. . .' Kate hesitated. She had never kept secrets from her sisters and she didn't want to start now, but she wasn't sure how Anna would take the news of her day out with Alessandro. It wasn't that Anna was a prude, or that she pretended to know what was best for Kate, but she would worry about the emotional implications of getting involved with someone while the ink on her divorce wasn't yet dry, and if Kate was perfectly honest with herself, she had started to wonder about those too. Dinner had been surprisingly good-humoured after her brief and ultimately embarrassing encounter with Alessandro on the bed, and she had even begun to relax in his company as he went out of his way to let her know, without actually spelling it out, that she had no need to feel awkward. He was gallant, witty, charming, and oh so much sexier for trying not to be. Alarm bells had started to ring in the back of Kate's mind somewhere towards the end of the evening, and she had almost fancied herself falling for him in a real, actual true-love kind of way. It was not good at all, and yet the thought of not seeing him again, despite how sensible that plan would be, had left her feeling hollow. Then, for reasons only he knew, before they'd parted he'd asked her to join him again for a second trip to the Colosseum, ostensibly so he could make up for the visit she'd had to abort when her purse was stolen. Without hesitation, she'd said yes. Now, as she recalled that decision, she wondered how wise it had been. And what Anna would say if she knew the half of it.

'You would have said if it was Jamie,' Anna cut into her thoughts. 'I already know about Jamie. Have you hooked up with someone else? I only want to know what you've been up to, and only because I'm jealous as hell because you're in Rome having a fantastic time and I'm stuck at work in rainy old England.'

'Sort of.'

'What does that mean?'

'I met a man and he took me out yesterday. To the Vatican. And then to dinner.'

'A man!' Anna squeaked. 'Oooh! How exciting! Where's he from, is he staying in your hotel, how did you meet him, is it a date situation or just friends, are you going to get his number when you get back home—?'

'Whoa! It's not all that. We're just friends. He's actually a policeman.'

'A policeman? Is he on holiday on his own too?'

'He's a Roman policeman.'

There was silence at the other end of the line.

'Anna?' Kate prompted. Silence wasn't good when it was coming from Anna. It meant she had something to say that she knew Kate wouldn't like.

'He's local?'

'Yes.'

'Oh. You'll find it hard to keep in touch then. Was it a date?'

'No.'

'Liar. Men don't just take you out for no reason.'

'Jamie did.'

'Jamie was different. Unless this Alessandro is gay too?'

'Not that I know of,' Kate replied, blushing as she recalled the evidence of his absolute heterosexuality.

'He's not one of these men who shag a new tourist every week? Like that one in *Shirley Valentine*?'

'*Shirley Valentine*? What the hell—'

'Is he?'

'We haven't had sex. And it would be nothing to do with anyone else if we had.'

'But he might want to. I bet he's taking you out again.'

'Actually he's—'

'I knew it! Have you told him you're newly divorced?'

'Yes but—'

'Then he totally thinks you're ripe for the plucking! Jeez, Kate!'

'Anna! Calm down. I'm not completely stupid you know. I'm thirty, and I think I can handle a date with a man at this point in my life.'

'You're not stupid, but you are in a vulnerable place right now. . .' Anna's tone softened. 'I know you can look after yourself and I don't think you're stupid. I don't want to see you hurt, that's all. You've literally just received your decree absolute and. . . Well, I can't pretend to know how that feels but I think my emotions might be a mess if it were me. A bit of flattery from a local would go a long way to making me feel better and before you knew it. . .'

'I'm not going to fall in love with him if that's what you mean,' Kate said haughtily. 'I'm not that needy.'

Even as she said it, she pushed the thoughts of kissing Alessandro on the very bed she now sat on firmly from her mind. Anna's interference wasn't welcome, but perhaps she had a point. She just hated it when Anna was right, which was most of the time.

'I know,' Anna said. 'Just promise you'll be careful.'

Kate pulled at a loose thread on the hem of her pyjama top. 'I'm having a bit of fun, that's all. That's what I came on holiday to do and you said I should get out more. . .'

'I would have felt easier if you'd been having your fun with a fella there might be a future with.'

'An Englishman you mean? There's no guarantees for that to last longer than the holiday either. Don't you remember what happened when you had a little holiday fling with. . . what was his name. . .? Craig in St Ives in 2003?'

Anna laughed lightly. 'OK, you got me – I was an idiot to expect that boy to phone me when he got back to Skegness. Point taken.'

'But it did lead to you getting together with Christian, who is the best husband anyone could have. So you never know what can come of something that might not seem good at the time.'

'True. But remember that Christian and I were friends already at that point. Although I'm still not sure that crying all over him because of another boy could be recommended as a come-on tactic for anyone else.'

'I agree. I'll try to avoid that myself. But I also want to make my own mistakes, and you have to let me. Maybe the thing that seems like a mistake at the time won't turn out to be a mistake after all.'

She heard Anna let out a sigh. 'OK, so tell me more about this Alessandro. Maybe I won't think he's so bad after all.'

* * *

The first hour of the day had felt thundery, but the clouds burnt away as the sun climbed to reveal a sky as blue and clear as the day before. Alessandro arrived in the same car, driven by the same woman, who subjected Kate to an even steelier stare this time before driving off.

'I don't think your friend is keen on me,' Kate said as he kissed her on both cheeks.

'My friend?'

'The woman who dropped you off.'

'Ah! Lucetta!' He laughed. 'My sister. She is curious about you. She says she likes your orange hair.'

Kate's brow furrowed. The icy look she'd got from Lucetta didn't exactly scream approval but she let the comment pass. At least it wasn't his other sister, Maria, who was apparently friends with a certain Orazia, who seemed to hate Kate with a passion and had probably filled her head with all sorts of nonsense about how awful she was. She had to wonder whether the news of their dates had got to either of those women yet. Kate could leave it all behind her at the end of the holiday, of course, but it still made her uncomfortable to think of them slagging her off, even just for the week. From the look on Lucetta's face, perhaps they had all been discussing her, hunched over a cauldron with a voodoo doll and some pins.

Alessandro offered his arm. 'Would you like to walk again?'

Kate nodded and linked with him, marvelling at the easiness between them despite all that had gone on the day before. As she'd dressed that morning she'd wondered whether, in the cold light of day, he would change his mind about coming to meet her today, or whether it would be awkward and uncomfortable between them, but he seemed as relaxed and jovial as he had at the Vatican. It made her feel easier too. Perhaps she was just seeing problems where there weren't any.

'Your dress is nice,' he said.

'Thank you. I made it myself.'

'You made it?'

She nodded. 'It's a hobby. I make most of what I wear. I like that I can have different clothes than what's in the shops that way, and it means I never turn up to a party in the same dress as someone else.'

He gave her another once-over and a nod of approval. 'You are very good. I think Lucetta would like you even more if she knew that.'

'Would she?' Kate asked, still unconvinced that what she had seen on Lucetta's face was anything but contempt.

'She would ask you to fix her wedding dress.'

'Is there something wrong with it?'

'Big arguments with the shop. They say it fits, Lucetta is not happy but we have no money to buy another one now.'

'That's where you took her the other night, to ask them to look at it?'

'Yes. . . you remembered.'

'I take notice where dresses are concerned. And the shop won't fix what's wrong?'

'They have fixed it five times. No more, they say.'

Kate was thoughtful for a moment as they walked. 'What does Lucetta think is wrong with it?'

He shrugged. 'I hear her shouting at Mamma, but I do not know.'

Kate had never taken on anything as complicated as a wedding dress, but she wondered whether offering her services might be something she could do to repay Alessandro for his kindness over the past couple of days. But then the thought of possibly making it worse and upsetting Lucetta even more wasn't an appealing one and her gesture might just backfire in the most spectacular fashion.

'How long does she have until the wedding?' she asked.

'Five months.'

'That's not long to get a new dress.'

'She does not want a new dress.'

'What is she going to do? Can she take it to another shop?'

'Another shop will want more euros to fix it.'

'I suppose so. But if she wants it to be right then it looks as if she'll have to pay a little more.'

'My mother is proud and she will not take money from her other children to help pay for the wedding, but I know she has no more left for Lucetta now. Lucetta knows it too. If my mother pays any more. . .' He shrugged. 'She will be in trouble. No rent. But she wants to make Lucetta happy. She doesn't know what to do.'

'Is your mother trying to manage on her own? I mean, is your father. . . you haven't ever mentioned him.'

'He has been dead a long time. Since I was a boy. . . thirteen.'

'I'm sorry. My dad is dead too. I was twenty – not so young but I still miss him every day.'

'Another thing the same between us,' he said and smiled.

Another thing. It should have made her happy but Kate's heart sank. Alessandro seemed more perfect for her every minute she spent with him. It was just her luck that he lived hundreds of miles away from the place she called home.

'I could look at your sister's dress,' she said. She had made the offer almost by way of an apology, half in the hope he would politely decline it. So she was horrified when a huge grin spread across his face.

'Tonight!' he said. 'I will take you to my house tonight! Lucetta will be so happy!'

'I'm not saying I can definitely make it right,' Kate replied, trying to inject some measure of caution into the promise, 'but I'll see if I can tell what's wrong with it and if I can fix it I will. I'll probably need a sewing machine, though. Does your mother have one?'

He shook his head.

'Oh. Do you know where I can get access to one?'

'I will phone my mother and she can ask the neighbours.'

Before Kate could stop him, he had dialled the number and was speaking rapidly to someone. It was at times like these when she wished she could speak a little Italian so she could tell what he was saying. What she did hear was a squeal on the other end of the line, even above the noise of the traffic and tourists on the street around

them, so she guessed that whichever female member of his family
he was talking to was unfeasibly excited about the prospect of her
sorting Lucetta's dress out. That was assuming she could fix it at all.
Ball gowns for her sisters and little summer dresses for herself were
one thing, but a full-blown wedding dress – that was a different skill
set entirely and Kate just hoped she was up to the challenge. The last
thing she wanted to do was disappoint Alessandro and his family now.

* * *

They'd had a wonderful time at the Colosseum, but all Kate could
think about was the prospect of meeting Alessandro's family later
that day. Why couldn't she have kept her big mouth shut? And why
couldn't he have had the sense to turn her offer down? She was certain
he wasn't being pushy assuming that she would do it that very night,
but in the same way that he had assumed she would want to go to the
Vatican with him, and to dinner, and the Colosseum the next day, it
seemed it was just his way of looking at the world – someone could
do something, so why wouldn't they want to? And he appeared to
be excited about the prospect of introducing his family to her. Kate
could only wish she shared some of that enthusiasm.

Jamie had phoned as she perused a rack of gladiator-themed sou-
venirs, and he had sounded a little more disappointed this time that
she couldn't meet him for dinner again. This made her feel even worse
about the situation, because she was starting to feel like the girl who
ditched her friends the moment a boyfriend appeared on the scene,
and Alessandro wasn't even that. Despite all this, they had been easy
and familiar with each other, just like they had been at the Vatican,
and at one point she had even found herself unconsciously reaching
for his hand as they weaved in and out of the ancient stones that

marked the gladiatorial arena. He had held it just the same, and it was a whole minute before she realised what she'd done and pulled away. He simply marked the action with a faint smile. If only she could know what he was thinking. Was he finding it all as fraught as she was? Judging by the way he had been happy to leave her hand in his, maybe not. Or had he resigned himself to keeping her friendship and put other complications to the back of his mind? Whatever the reason, he didn't seem to be fazed at all by the uncertainty of their relationship status. If she had been the type of person to flag it up on Facebook, it most definitely would have been categorised as 'complicated'. But did he see it as complicated? He kept requesting her company, so what did he want from it?

So she'd promised Jamie that she would definitely meet him for dinner the following evening, and decided that it would probably be a relief to spend time with a man that didn't lead to some sort of emotional turmoil. But first she had the dreaded family visit to get through.

* * *

It was as they were leaving the Colosseum that Kate saw him in the crowds. He was wiry, needing a wash, and at first glance looked chillingly familiar. He was also acting suspiciously, eyeing up visitors and paying no attention to the landmark looming behind him at all.

'Alessandro. . .' she said quietly. 'I think that's the man who stole my purse.'

There was no reply. Perhaps he hadn't heard over the bustle of the lines of people pouring out from the ancient ruins. She looked around to speak again and saw that he was scanning the crowds. Then his gaze settled, focusing intently on a figure. 'The man in the hat?' he asked finally.

'I think it's him,' Kate said, now uncertain and slightly worried by the stony expression on Alessandro's face. She had pointed the man out on an impulse, the sentence uttered before she'd really had time to think it through. But she wasn't with any old man – he was a policeman, and one who had already expressed the greatest disgust at people who gave his beloved city a bad name. Right now he looked as if he wanted more than a stern word with the suspect. 'I can't be sure because it was such a fleeting glance but—'

'I know him,' Alessandro cut in. 'He is known to the police. He is in jail many times for stealing but this is not his usual area. . .'

Before Kate could stop him, he was striding towards the man, the crowds almost seeming to part for him as if instinctively understanding his authority.

'But you're not on duty!' Kate squeaked as she jogged to catch up. 'What are you going to do?'

'Talk to him,' Alessandro said.

She wasn't sure she liked the way he said *Talk to him*. She'd never heard talking described so ominously before. It looked as if an angry, righteous Alessandro might be a formidable force. She wasn't sure if it made him sexier than ever, or terrifying, or a thrilling combination of both.

Kate's gaze flicked to the man. She watched as he bumped into an elderly woman. Anyone else might have missed the intent, but to her it looked as if he had launched himself at the lady almost deliberately. '*Mi scusi!*' she heard him say, and then he changed direction and began to walk back towards the shadow of the Colosseum. Had he just struck again? Kate glanced back at Alessandro as she struggled to keep up with his increasingly long strides, and she watched as his jaw tightened. He muttered something under his breath, and then he broke into a run, as fast as the heaving mass of tourists would allow him. Kate gave chase, her heels hampering her efforts to keep up.

The man in the cap looked up, and it was immediately clear he'd spotted Alessandro, and that he recognised him too. Kate had never actually seen someone turn ashen in an instant, but she saw it now, and the man turned tail and began to barge people out of the way in a bid to escape. Alessandro shouted across the space, but the man took no heed, and although a few people in the crowds turned in some surprise to look at Alessandro, there was very little reaction to his warnings. He had to move people aside too as he tried to gain on the man who was quite obviously guilty of something, even if he wasn't the man who had stolen from Kate, and it hampered Alessandro's pursuit that he was far politer about it than his quarry.

'Wait!' Kate squeaked, but Alessandro was now intent and didn't even turn to acknowledge her plea. It was likely he hadn't heard it anyway. She tried to quicken her pace, but he got further and further away.

She stopped, panting and red-faced, no hope of keeping up. She watched in defeat as Alessandro disappeared from her sight.

Ten

She had spent twenty minutes waiting and wondering if Alessandro would be able to find her again. There were so many people around, even as the Colosseum got ready to close for the day, that there didn't seem much hope he'd be able to spot a tiny English woman amongst all that confusion, particularly as he wouldn't have noticed where she was when they finally lost sight of each other. Now she wished that she'd asked for his mobile number. It had been stupid, this shyness she had developed over it, particularly as she hadn't been quite so shy over trying to instigate sex, which was a far more dramatic statement of commitment than a stupid old phone number. But she had felt as if asking him was implying an assumption on her part – that their few dates would turn into something more permanent – and she felt it would look like an arrogant assumption in his eyes, so the question had remained unasked. Perhaps he'd done the same, as he hadn't asked for hers either, or perhaps he'd simply thought that if he wanted her at any time during her stay in Rome, knowing the location of her hotel, he'd know where she was. And she supposed he had her particulars on the police records of the robbery too.

But now she worried that because she'd had to move from the spot where he'd left her to get out of people's way, he wouldn't be able to find her again. She would be able to get back to the hotel, of course, but it was what the complication would do to their day out that bothered her. Even more of a worry was what Alessandro might do if he did catch up with the thief. At best he'd arrest him and have to take him to the station or something equally time-consuming, which would eat into their day together and possibly put a premature end to it altogether. It was a selfish thought, but one that she couldn't help having. At worst, judging from the look on his face, he might well give him a good thumping, which probably wasn't what a police officer should be doing, particularly an off-duty one.

There was one thing about her time in Rome – it had certainly been eventful.

She wandered around for a while, keeping a sharp lookout for Alessandro. But it started to seem a bit hopeless, and perhaps it might be more sensible to stay in one place and watch for him. So she found a bench where she could sit with the sun on her face and pulled out her phone. It seemed a good idea to use the time sitting around wisely, and it wasn't as if she was going anywhere soon, so she sent two text messages: one to Lily and one to Anna, both asking if everything was OK.

Anna didn't reply, so Kate guessed she was working. Lily did after a couple of minutes.

All good here. Heartburn but not sick now, yay! How's everything with you?
Good. Seen the Colosseum again today, it's amazing.

Amazing in ways you couldn't possibly imagine, Kate thought, but it was easier to keep the whole drama still unfolding here to herself for now.

Jealous, Lily replied. *Stuck at stupid work. Phone me after six so I can hear all about it.*

Can't after six, going out. Will call you tomorrow.

Rubbing it in now, eh? I have no social life, only heartburn and obsessive baby shopping. OK, talk to me tomorrow. Love you. X

Love you too. X

Kate smiled to herself as she locked the phone. Of all the sisters, Lily was probably the sweetest, most easy-going, and she would be the most natural and perfect mum. All she'd ever wanted was kids, and Kate recalled vividly her grabbing any opportunity to fuss over a doll at school – or a real baby whenever she could get hold of one. When she had first got together with Joel, she had told him right from the start she wanted kids galore and he seemed happy to say yes to any demand, clearly head over heels in love with her. They were almost a fairy tale couple, perfectly suited in every way and a world away from what she and Matt had had, although she never saw that for what it was until it was over.

As she put her phone back in her handbag, a shadow fell across her and she looked up to see Alessandro.

'I am sorry I was away for so long,' he said.

'It's fine.' Kate stood and scanned his face anxiously. No signs of a scuffle or any kind of violence, which was good, and she was relieved that he had managed to find his way back to her after all. 'Did you get him?'

He pushed damp hair back from his forehead and mopped a sleeve across his brow. 'No. He escaped. He knows doors to go through where his friends live.'

'There's a ring?' Kate asked.

He frowned. 'A ring?'

'A lot of them. . .' she elaborated, 'many thieves working together.'

'In this area, not before. Maybe now if he is here.'

'What will you do?'

'I will make a phone call and tell someone about it.'

'Now?'

'If you are happy to let me.'

'Of course. . . I don't want to stand in the way of justice,' she said, grimacing slightly as she realised how ludicrous her reply probably sounded.

He gave a short nod and then walked a few paces on. She heard him begin a conversation, phone clamped to his ear and his brow furrowed, gesticulating in jerky movements. It was strange to see him in full-on police mode again, and even this was different because both times she had seen him on duty before he had been relaxed, the most pressing concern the fate of a ditsy English woman who kept getting herself into trouble. It was hardly the thin blue line. But this was real policing and it made him different, altogether more serious.

After a couple of minutes he came back to her. 'We will get more men to patrol here,' he said. 'Perhaps if we catch them we can get your purse back.'

'I doubt whether there's any money left in it now and I cancelled the card. But thank you,' she added, not wanting to sound ungrateful for his efforts. 'I'm still not sure it was my man that we saw today either.'

'It may not have been, but he is a criminal so it is good you showed me his face. I am sorry I left you alone to run after him.'

Kate shrugged. 'You were doing your job. . . even though you weren't at work today. I suppose once you're a policeman you never really stop being a policeman.'

'It is difficult. When you see bad things, it is in your blood to stop them, even if you do not wear your uniform.'

Kate was thoughtful. It was a hell of a life for a partner to compete with and she imagined that it would be one of constant worry. And in the back of her mind was the thought that perhaps only another police officer would be able to understand it and live with the threats he faced daily. Someone like Orazia. But she tried to push the woman's scornful face from her mind. He'd assured her that his relationship with Orazia was over, despite Orazia herself intimating otherwise, and that should have been enough, shouldn't it?

'But you'd never do a different job?'

'I love my job. I could never do anything different. It is like showing my love for Roma when I watch her streets.'

They walked slowly, and absently she reached for his hand. It was warm and strong and he didn't pull away. Then Kate realised with a jolt she'd done it again. But it felt good and he didn't seem to mind. It didn't mean anything, did it? It was just handholding and it didn't mean sex or marriage or anything that complicated, right? Just this once, she'd allow herself to enjoy it.

* * *

Lucetta was waiting in her car for them when they arrived back at Kate's hotel. It had just gone six. Kate had no idea how long she'd been there, but she had her dark glasses on, leaning out of the open window with her face turned to the sun and the radio blasting. She looked unconcerned about the irritated glances of passers-by who commented on the volume of the music, and it seemed that, however long she'd been waiting, she'd managed to make herself pretty comfortable.

'My sister will drive us,' Alessandro said, gesturing towards the car as Lucetta gave them a casual wave.

Kate blinked at him. There he was again, assuming the situation. She had hoped for an hour to freshen up and phone home before she went to his house, but it looked as though she wasn't going to get it. But then it seemed he read it in her face, and for the first time he faltered.

'You don't want to come?'

'No. . . of course I do. I was just going to call my family back home first. Maybe get changed into some fresh clothes.'

'But you look beautiful; Mamma will love your dress.'

The fact that she had been sweating in it and felt sticky as hell seemed to escape him. On the other hand, despite his *Sweeney*-style chase earlier, he looked as fresh as if he had only just got out of the shower. She gave her brightest smile. 'I'd really like to call my sister.'

He nodded. 'Of course. What time would you like me to come back?'

'Could you give me an hour?'

'One hour. OK.' He climbed into the car.

Lucetta leaned across and called out of the window before pulling away from the kerb. '*Arrivederci!*'

It was the first time she had spoken to Kate, and Kate hoped it wouldn't be the last. But she'd count herself lucky if she didn't get a punch in the face if she cocked this wedding dress up. How on earth did she get herself into these situations?

* * *

The moped had returned, and by the time Alessandro killed the engine outside an apartment block in the suburbs of the city, Kate was wishing she had accepted the offer of a lift in his sister's car earlier. Lucetta might have driven like a maniac too, but at least there would have been four steel walls to keep her safe instead of fresh air.

'Is this where you live?' she asked, looking up at the terracotta building as he helped her off the bike. It was flat roofed, lined by elaborate balconies that looked like frills around a dress. Every balcony had plants, chimes or washing hanging from it, and some had vegetables and fruits growing in pots that covered tables, while the building itself was shaded by tall cypress trees. The neighbourhood was far more unremarkable than the centre of Rome, but it had a homey atmosphere and a certain urban charm that Kate warmed to immediately.

'Do you like it?'

'Yes, very much.'

'I will take you to meet Mamma now. She is excited.'

'Is she?' Kate asked doubtfully as she followed him into the lobby, unsure what to make of that information.

He led her up two flights of stairs and along a corridor to an unassuming wooden door. As his key went into the lock, Kate wondered if it was too late to run away, but she took a deep breath and followed him into the apartment.

The main living space was a strange but comforting mix of old and new. It was evident that everyone who lived here or who had lived here before had left their mark on the décor. Sleek lamps sat alongside faded prints of saints, a state-of-the-art TV jostled for space with a dusty old record player, while white walls and warm honeyed wood adorned with crocheted doilies contrasted sharply with chrome and glass shelves. In a strange way, it worked. Evening light poured in through the huge windows that led out onto the balcony, while a clunky old air-conditioning unit whirred and cranked in the background to keep everywhere a pleasant temperature. It smelt of rosemary and freshly baked bread, and it was a world away from her posh but frankly soulless hotel room.

A tiny woman, steel grey hair cropped into a bob and held back from her face by a patterned headband, came through from what Kate presumed to be the kitchen, wiping her hands on an apron. She broke into a broad smile as she saw Kate and Alessandro standing in the living room.

'Hello, hello!' She nodded, beaming at Kate as she stepped forward to shake her by the hand. Alessandro kissed his mother and then spoke to her in Italian. She nodded and grinned again at Kate. 'Hello, Kate!'

'Her English is not so good,' Alessandro said in a low voice.

'Probably better than my Italian,' Kate said. '*Buongiorno,*' she added, smiling at Alessandro's mother. The woman gestured to the window.

'*Buonasera!*'

'Oh,' Kate said, glancing uncertainly at Alessandro, who nodded encouragement. '*Buonasera, Signora Conti,*' she corrected herself, addressing Alessandro's mother in the way she had been practising in her head the whole way over. 'Of course, it's evening.'

'See, you will learn Italian quickly with my mother,' Alessandro said with a grin.

Kate thought, not for the first time, she might quite like to learn Italian. At least she wouldn't feel so ignorant right now if she could have just a tiny conversation with his mother. It would most certainly go on her list of things to do when she got home and started that brand new single life she had promised herself.

Lucetta came through from another doorway off the living room, struggling under the weight of a huge swathe of white silk and lace.

'*Ciao*, Kate!' she called.

Alessandro frowned but Lucetta merely smiled sweetly.

'Kate and I are friends already,' she said to him, and Kate silently marvelled at how the promise of a free favour could change someone's attitude entirely. That morning she had fired death stares at Kate mean enough to fell a man at twenty paces, and now it was all *ciao* and best friends. But perhaps she was being unfair, and perhaps Lucetta was only suspicious of Kate in the same way Anna had been suspicious of Alessandro that morning on the phone.

Lucetta dumped the dress on the sofa and began to undo the plastic cover protecting it.

'Not now,' Alessandro scolded. 'We will eat and then Kate will look at the dress.'

Lucetta pouted, but she dragged the dress from the sofa and hung it from a doorframe. Signora Conti gestured for Kate to sit at a table already dressed in a lace cloth and set for a meal. She hadn't expected to be fed and had snacked on crisps from the hotel vending machine as she got ready for Alessandro to pick her up. She was glad now that she hadn't asked room service to bring a sandwich up to her because it looked as though Signora Conti had gone to a lot of trouble to make a meal. She hoped it wasn't in her honour or anything silly like that, and that it was just the regular family meal she was being asked to sit in on. If anything, she quite liked the idea of being asked to sit in on the regular family meal – it felt more personal, more special – that they were accepting her as more than a visitor. Why did that matter so much?

As Alessandro pulled out a chair for her, she glanced up and caught his eye and her heart did a little jig. *That* was why – because despite her best efforts not to acknowledge the swooping of her stomach every time he looked her way, her heart couldn't lie. She was falling for him, whether it was sensible or not, and if anything, this strange state of friends but not quite anything else was making it worse. Like being on a diet, when usually she couldn't care less if there was chocolate in the house, the minute she was forbidden to eat it she craved it like nothing else. That was the feeling she had for Alessandro now – he was forbidden and she wanted him more for it. This couldn't end well, and she had to get it out of her system before it got any worse.

As these thoughts whirled through her mind and she got settled at the table, another girl came in. She was younger than Alessandro and Lucetta, perhaps in her early twenties, softer featured with the prettiest green eyes, which were all the more startling against her olive skin.

'Ah,' Alessandro said, beaming. 'Kate, this is my favourite sister, Abelie.'

Lucetta cuffed him around the head as he sat, but he merely laughed and patted a chair for his youngest sister to sit next to him. Kate was at his other side, and she smiled and greeted Abelie who gave a shy hello in return.

'Kate will be our saint,' Alessandro said to his sister. 'When she has fixed Lucetta's dress we will have peace in the house at last.'

'When you find a wife we will have peace in the house,' Lucetta fired back. Kate felt herself blush, and dipped her head in the hope that nobody would notice until it had gone. She couldn't help but wonder at the insensitivity of the comment too, in light of his one doomed engagement, but it seemed he was used to no pulled punches from his sisters, as he merely grinned.

'You will be married first,' he said nonchalantly. 'And your poor husband will send you back after a week.'

'At least I have found a husband.'

'I don't want a husband,' Alessandro said.

'You will have to have a husband because you will never find a wife.'

Oh please make it stop! Kate knew it was only banter, but she wished the conversation would turn to something less embarrassing. Every time Lucetta said the word wife, Kate was sure she was looking directly at her. She wasn't, of course. It just felt that way, because why would anyone do that when she'd only met Alessandro a matter of days before?

* * *

Signora Conti had a humble home and a tiny kitchen, but her food was better than anything Kate had tasted in any restaurant since she'd arrived in Rome. A first course of small tortellini pasta in a light broth was followed by some kind of delicious Italian sausage she'd not heard of before, served with lentils. Never in a million years would she have cooked lentils at home for any meal, and if she'd served them up to Matt she'd have been asked why she was giving him hippy food, but whatever Alessandro's mother had done to them, they were delicious. There was a divine dessert she'd never had before that Alessandro informed her was called *affogato*.

'It's all amazing,' Kate said. She turned to Signora Conti. '*Grazie!*' Alessandro's mum beamed. '*Prego.*'

'I can't believe how much work your mum has done to cook all this,' Kate said to Alessandro.

'Because Alessandro didn't return home for lunch today, Mamma has made the day back to front and we are eating lunch now,' Lucetta said. 'This is how we eat every day for lunch.'

Kate frowned. 'Really? I would just have a sandwich for lunch at home, sometimes not even that.'

'Not in Italy. Lunch is our big meal, and our small meal is in the evening.'

'Oh, so is she annoyed that she's had to make the day back to front?'

'No,' Alessandro cut in with a smile. 'She is happy you could come and we do this often when one of us cannot be here for lunch.'

'Oh,' Kate said, relieved but not certain that he wasn't telling her a little white lie to make her feel better about messing up his family's day.

As Abelie and Signora Conti cleared away the remains of dinner, Kate turned to Lucetta. She was feeling a little sleepy already, pleasantly full from the good food, but if she didn't make a start on the task she had promised to undertake she'd be here all night.

'Would you like me to look at your dress now?'

'Thank you!' Lucetta leapt up from the table in a way Kate was quite sure she wouldn't manage with the amount of food she'd just packed away. 'I will get it now!'

'Do you need some help getting into it?' Kate said as Lucetta made her way to where she'd left the dress hanging. 'Perhaps we should go into one of the bedrooms and try it there?'

'*Sì*,' Lucetta said, and beckoned Kate to follow.

* * *

'You are very kind,' Lucetta said as Kate helped her into the dress. 'I can see why my brother likes you.'

Kate was glad Lucetta was facing forward while she zipped up the dress, because she was certain her expression would have given away emotions that she didn't particularly want Lucetta to be aware of. 'I like him too,' she replied carefully. 'He's been kind to me this week, and I'm sure I wouldn't have seen such a lot of Rome without him.'

'He is a good man,' Lucetta agreed, 'and life has been unkind to him, which makes us all sad.'

'Hmm,' Kate said, and she didn't dare elaborate any more on that point. 'Let's have a look at you properly.'

Lucetta turned around and Kate studied her thoughtfully. The dress was pure white, lace-embellished, with a demure scooped neck, full skirt, structured corset and a sweeping train. But she could see straightaway why Lucetta wasn't happy with it. 'It's beautiful, but there's something not quite right.'

'I am glad you agree,' Lucetta said. 'The dress shop does not.'

'I don't necessarily think it's a fault in their alterations, though,' Kate replied. 'I mean, it wouldn't hurt to nip it in a little at the waist because it's not showing off how tiny yours is. . . but I think the sleeves are what's making it look odd. See here. . .' She stepped forward to inspect a sleeve and then manipulated it into a few different shapes until she was happy. 'That's a much more flattering length. Or you could go full sleeve but we'd have to somehow get matching lace from somewhere. But the length they are now is neither here nor there and makes you look wider than you are. They need to be shorter or longer.'

'Can you do it?'

Kate looked up. 'Are you sure you want me to? Once I've cut there's no way back if you don't like the result.'

Lucetta nodded. 'I do not like it now so it will be no worse.'

'You might think it looks a lot worse afterwards. At least you have a dress you could wear now if it really came to it, but if I alter it and you think it looks horrible. . .'

'You will not make it look worse. Did you make the dress you are wearing?'

Kate nodded as she glanced down at the fifties-inspired rose-print number she had picked out for her visit.

'It is beautiful. You will make a good job of my wedding dress – I know it.'

Kate took a deep breath. She wasn't happy about this despite Lucetta's confidence. She could make it look very much worse working on a borrowed sewing machine without her own tools and on a type of fabric she had never sewn before. 'I don't know whether you ought to ask the dress shop to do it for you,' she said. 'They're used to working on wedding dresses and I only make everyday wear for myself.'

'Alessandro said you made a beautiful big dress for your sister. He saw the photo.'

'Yes, but—'

'This is not so different.'

Kate let out a sigh. She had said she would help and it didn't seem as if she was going to be able to wriggle out of it now. She didn't want to wriggle out of it, and she was happy to help anyone where she could, but this felt like a huge responsibility. She sincerely hoped she would be forgiven if it all went horribly wrong, but from what she knew of Lucetta so far, she wasn't sure she was the forgiving kind.

* * *

It was 11.30 p.m. by the time Kate turned off the sewing machine. Her fingers ached from handling such heavy material and her brain and eyes were tired from the concentration. It probably wasn't at all how a professional wedding shop would have done the alterations and she wasn't that happy with what she'd done (nor did she feel confident that it was in any way good enough) but as Lucetta had been so insistent that she couldn't possibly make the dress any worse, she'd done what she could. Lucetta was asleep on the sofa where she had got tired of watching Kate work, Abelie had gone to bed, while Alessandro and his mother were talking in low voices in the kitchen. Kate wondered whether she ought to wake Lucetta to try the gown on, or if it would be better to sneak back to her hotel now and let her try it on alone in the morning. At least that way Kate wouldn't be able to see the disappointment in her face when she decided it still wasn't right.

But the sudden contrast of the silence from the whirring of the machine seemed to rouse Lucetta, and she sat up, rubbing her eyes and looking expectant as Kate stood and shook out the dress.

'Can I try it now?' she asked.

'I suppose you should. If it's still wrong I'd rather try and sort it before I leave tonight.'

Lucetta snatched it from her and headed for the bedroom. 'It will be perfect.'

Let's hope, Kate thought as she followed.

Once again Kate helped Lucetta into the dress and zipped it up. Then Lucetta went over to the full-length mirror at the corner of the room and immediately began to smile. She studied her reflection for a moment, while Kate waited anxiously, and her smile began to grow. She spun around and grabbed Kate to kiss her on both cheeks.

'You have done a miracle!' she cried.

'It's OK?' Kate asked feeling slightly shell-shocked.

'*Sì!*'

Lucetta dashed out of the room and called Signora Conti. Kate saw the old lady's face light up as she laid eyes on Lucetta in the dress.

'*Molto bella!*' she cried. She turned to Kate. '*Molto bella! Grazie!*'
And then she rushed over to hug Kate too, who was beginning to feel
distinctly overwhelmed by the reaction. Alessandro stood behind his
mother with a broad smile.

'Thank you,' he said. 'It looks wonderful.'

Kate shrugged. 'It was nothing. I'm just glad you're all happy.'

Signora Conti began to speak rapidly, gesticulating between Alessandro and Kate.

'My mother says she would like you to be our guest for a proper
family lunch tomorrow. I think she will be very hurt if you say no; she
wants to repay you for your kindness.'

'There's no need,' Kate said, half wishing she could slip away now
and avoid any more fuss. 'You've been so good to me already that I've
been repaid in full, if I needed repaying at all, which I didn't really. It
was honestly nothing that I wouldn't have done for anyone.'

'And that is why you should come. You would have done that for
anyone, and that makes you a kind person. Let us honour that.'

'But. . . I did say I would meet Jamie tomorrow and he'll be sad if
I let him down again,' Kate replied, more for an excuse to get out of
the offer than for anything else.

'Your American friend?' Alessandro turned to his mum and they
had a brief conversation. Then he turned back to Kate.

'Mamma says Jamie should come with you. She says a friend of
yours is a friend of ours. She says if he is handsome he might be a
husband for Abelie.'

'He certainly won't be that,' Kate smiled. 'I think he'd rather have
you than your sister.' She checked her watch. It was certainly too late
to message Jamie now, so she would have to ask him in the morning.
It was a hell of a change of plan to drop on him too. She had thought

that the best thing from now until she went home was to avoid another day out with Alessandro and spend it alone exploring or with Jamie – both of those options would be ultimately less painful. Every second she spent in Alessandro's company would make things harder when she eventually had to leave him and head back to England. A broken heart was one souvenir of Rome she didn't want to take home with her. But as Signora Conti, Lucetta and Alessandro all looked at her hopefully, she realised that it was going to be much harder to let them down than to break it off now. And she supposed that if Jamie was with them it would dilute the tension between her and Alessandro too. 'I'll have to ask him tomorrow morning,' she said. 'But he loves company so I think he'll say yes.'

'*Va bene,*' Lucetta said. 'That is that. I will take off my dress and I will drive you back to your hotel now. In the morning I will come for you and your friend.'

* * *

Lucetta was almost as crazy a driver as her brother, but Kate had seen enough of the traffic in Rome over the past few days to realise that this was pretty much standard for the roads here. Rome looked beautiful at night – grand buildings lit up from the streets below, fairy lights strung outside restaurants and the pavements still filled with tourists even at this hour. It really was the eternal city – eternally present and eternally busy. Too soon Kate was going to have to leave it, and for the first time since her arrival, the thought pricked at her heart.

'Will you come back to Rome one day?' Lucetta asked as she drove.

'It's funny; I was just thinking about that,' Kate replied. 'I'd like to. I don't think I'll be ready to leave at all. I think it's helped that I've met such wonderful people here.'

'I would not live anywhere else.'

'I don't blame you. Do all your sisters still live in Rome?'

She nodded as she screeched around a corner so precariously that Kate grabbed for the door handle and held on tight. 'We all stay close to Mamma.'

'I can understand that,' Kate said, her mind going back to her own mother who'd remarried after the death of Kate's dad and moved up to Scotland, and whom she didn't see nearly enough of. She and her sisters all made excuses, though the truth was that seeing their nervy mother was a strain on their nerves too and hard work, but their mother she was and they loved her just the same. It was probably time for a visit, and she made a promise to herself that she would drive up there at the first opportunity once she got home.

'Does it worry her that Alessandro is in the police?' Kate asked. 'Does she think it's a dangerous job?'

Lucetta laughed. 'She is very proud of him. We all are. Papa was a policeman too.'

'He died, didn't he? What happened to him?'

'A hole in his heart. Nobody knew. One day – boom. Dead.'

'Oh, that's awful.'

Lucetta shrugged. 'I was very young and I remember little of it.'

'My dad is dead too.'

'I know; Alessandro told me. I am sad for you.'

'That's life; we carry on, don't we? I miss him every day though.'

'Of course.'

They were silent for a moment. Kate wondered what else Alessandro had told Lucetta about her. Had they discussed her at any length? If so, why? What conclusions would they have come to?

'My brother is fond of you,' Lucetta said into the silence. Kate whipped around to look at her, but Lucetta stared straight ahead and her expression gave nothing away.

Fond? What did that mean? He liked her friendly company? He wanted it to be more? He was fond of her in the way an uncle was fond of a favourite niece or she was fond of carrot cake? 'I like him too,' she replied carefully.

'I see that when you look at him. He knows people's hearts very quickly. He told me the first time you came to the *questura* he knew you were a good woman. I think he would marry you one day if you were Italian.'

Kate wondered what not being Italian meant for the possibility of that scenario. And why on earth was she even thinking about that? 'Does Alessandro know you're telling me all this?'

'No,' Lucetta said.

'Would he be angry if he knew?'

'I do not know. Perhaps.'

'Then. . . I don't understand why you're telling me.'

'Because I think you love him.'

Kate stared at her. 'That's crazy. . . And I couldn't do anything about it even if I did.' But even as she said it, the realisation hit her. When she had feared earlier that evening that she was falling for him. . . there was no *falling*; she'd already fallen. Her thoughts exploded, like someone had just thrown a grenade amongst them. And it hurt. She'd fallen for him, like a stupid, inexperienced teen clutches for the first boy who will kiss her, and Alessandro was simply *fond* of her. Whatever that meant.

'Why not?'

'I live in England! I'm only on holiday. . .' Kate let out a sigh. Why was she even having this conversation with Alessandro's sister? Aside from being crazy it was none of her business, and she was quite sure Alessandro wouldn't thank her if he knew.

Lucetta shrugged. 'What are you willing to do for love?'

'Alessandro doesn't love me – he doesn't know me.'

Lucetta shrugged again. It was infuriating. 'I think he would.'

'So I'm supposed to do what?'

'I do not know. If I loved a man I would go anywhere to be with him.'

What was Lucetta trying to say? That Kate should give up England for a man she'd only just met? Or that Alessandro would come to England, something she would never ask or expect him to do? What was the point? What was Lucetta trying to achieve by telling her any of this? It was obvious to anyone with half a brain that this was a situation with no happy ending for anyone, and torturing herself with the promise of anything else was not going to do Kate, or Alessandro for that matter, any good. When she'd first booked her flights to Rome, if she had foreseen any of this, would Kate still have booked them? She couldn't honestly say what the answer to that question was right now. While the trip had been more than she could have possibly hoped for, the complications had been beyond anything she could have imagined.

'But that would be foolish unless he loved you back.'

'I will speak to Alessandro, and I will find out what is in his heart.'

'Don't you dare!' Kate squeaked. 'Please don't do that.' She grappled for something to throw Lucetta off the scent. Why did the girl have to be so bloody persistent about it anyway? Was the whole family simply obsessed with marrying Alessandro off to the nearest available woman? 'Tell me about your fiancé. Is he from nearby?' she said, trying to level her voice.

'Gian is Roman. My sisters married Romans too.'

There was silence for a moment, and Kate couldn't tell whether Lucetta was bored of the conversation, had admitted defeat, or whether she was offended at Kate's refusal to discuss her feelings. But then she spoke again, and Kate wished any of those things had been true.

'Do you love Alessandro?' Lucetta's question was blunt and forward. She could have been asking whether it was raining outside.

'I don't think I should come tomorrow,' Kate said slowly. 'It's not a very good idea.'

'Do you love him?' Lucetta repeated.

'Even if I do there's no point in saying it because nothing can come of it. Please apologise to your mother and your sisters; tell them I'm sorry I can't come to lunch after all.'

'Forgive me,' Lucetta said. 'I did not mean to make you unhappy. Please, come tomorrow. Mamma will be sad if you don't. I will be sad too, and I would like to meet your friend Jamie.'

Kate didn't reply. Instead, she gazed out of the window and the car was silent until they pulled up outside Kate's hotel.

'Thanks for bringing me back,' Kate said.

'You will come tomorrow? I will be here at midday.'

Kate paused. God, Alessandro and his family could be so irritating, and they were all as bad as each other for assuming that their plans were agreeable to everyone regardless of any other factors. Hadn't Kate made it perfectly clear that it wasn't a good idea? Despite that, she still liked them all immensely and part of her did want to go for lunch, even if the sudden truth of her feelings for Alessandro did threaten to break her heart – particularly as he didn't feel the same way. When she returned to England, she would think of him all the time, and he would forget her quickly until she became just a jumble of fond memories of a girl he'd flirted with for a week. Perhaps Jamie being there would help take her mind off that, though, and she would persuade him to come even if she had to pay him a million dollars. And she'd wanted the authentic Italian experience – it didn't get more authentic than spending the day with an Italian family. Against her better judgement, she nodded. 'Twelve. I'll be ready.'

Just as she had promised herself earlier, it would be the last time she'd see Alessandro, and she could spend the rest of her time being a normal tourist, whose only worry was where the next stop for gelato was or how to find the nearest toilet – just like all the other visitors to the eternal city.

Eleven

'I'm so excited to meet this family!' Jamie said as they stood on the pavement outside her hotel waiting for Lucetta, who was proving to be fashionably late.

Kate threw him a sideways look. He was like a little boy waiting for his birthday party and, despite the churning of her stomach, she had to laugh. When she'd asked him that morning if he fancied lunch with a family he'd never met she'd expected some hesitation, some concern about the eleventh-hourness of the request or the social awkwardness of the situation, but his reply had been a very excited and immediate yes. His work could wait, he'd said, and he could be ready in plenty of time. True to his word, he had reported for duty an hour later with a grin stretching his face that had lit up her morning. One thing was very true – it was impossible not to feel happy around her new friend. She would take many precious memories back home from this trip, and meeting Jamie was one of the best.

'You must have seriously impressed them to earn lunch,' he continued. 'It sounds like they've practically adopted you. And you look stunning again today. Your cop won't be able to take his eyes off you.'

'I doubt that,' Kate said, trying to calm the ferocious beating of her heart at the mention of Alessandro. She had barely slept, turning the night's events over and over in her mind and ending up back at the conversation with Lucetta in the car on the return to the hotel, each time its meaning perplexing her more. What did Lucetta think she was going to do? What did she mean by opening up this whole can of worms? Why couldn't she have kept her big mouth shut? And why hadn't Kate had the balls to do the sensible thing and refuse this lunch offer?

'You're always trying to be humble,' Jamie scolded. 'Take a bit of praise and enjoy it. You have a talent for creating fabulous clothes, and you look lovely in them and I won't hear you argue anything else.'

'Sorry.'

'And please stop saying you're sorry for everything! How many times have you told me that this morning? Sorry for making me come out on a date, sorry for making me skip a boring day of work, sorry for being great company. . . just stop it already!'

'Sorry. . . For saying sorry, that is.' She shot him a sheepish smile.

'That's the last one,' he said, wagging his finger like a pantomime dame.

'That's the first time I've seen you look actually camp,' Kate said, unable to prevent herself from laughing.

'I reserve my full rainbow glory for very special occasions.'

'I feel privileged, then, that you let it out for me today.'

He smiled and nudged her. 'See, that's better. I like it better when you're happy.'

'I've been happy all morning.'

'Not as happy as when I saw you last. Do I have to get tough with Alessandro? Has he broken your poor heart already?'

Jamie was joking, of course, but Kate wondered what he would say if she told him he wasn't so far from the truth. 'No, I'm fine. I suppose I'm just tired; I didn't sleep all that well.'

'Missing home a little now?' Jamie asked.

'I suppose I must be a bit.'

'I did too the first time I travelled away on my own, but it gets easier. And next time you're planning to come to Rome you can check in with me first and I'll see if I can get any business trips to coincide.'

'That's very presumptuous of you,' Kate said.

He laughed. 'It's what I do best.'

'I don't even know if I'll ever come back to Rome. There's such a lot of world to see.'

'You'll always come back to Rome in the end; it's like an irresistible force. Why do you think all the Roman roads lead here?'

'Silly,' Kate said. But then her smile faded. He was right – she loved Rome and she wanted to come back one day. But it might not end up being that simple. 'Maybe I'll come and see you in New York.'

'I'd love that. I just know that Brad will adore you as much as I do, and I could show you the sights. . . You'd need weeks to see everything but you'd be more than welcome to stay at our apartment.'

'Thank you; that's so sweet of you. I'd feel better if I got a hotel, though. Tell you what – you get to take me for dinner instead, you and Brad. And I know that if he's anything like as funny as you I'll adore him too.'

'You could bring your sisters.'

'I could, though I'm not quite sure what their partners would have to say about it. Plus, Lily will have her baby by then I imagine; I'm not sure she'll be going anywhere for at least eighteen years after it's born.'

'She could bring the baby too – we like babies.'

'In principle I like babies too. I'm not sure about the stinky reality, though. I don't suppose I'll be finding out any time soon either, at least, not for myself. I'll just have to make the most of Lily's and spoil him or her rotten.'

'Doesn't she know which she's having yet?'

'She's not far enough along for that scan yet. She's past the danger zone – about fourteen weeks I think – but the gender scan isn't until you're twenty weeks gone. I don't think she wants to know even if they offer to tell her; she'd rather have the surprise.'

'That's cute,' Jamie said. He turned to her and suddenly looked earnest. 'You're OK, though?'

'Me?' Kate laughed. 'Of course.'

'I just know that when we first met you told me you'd wanted children before Matt left you.'

'Well,' Kate replied, her smile fixed even though inside it had died, 'that was before. That was my old life and it's gone now. I'm happy, I'm moving on and whatever will be will be.'

'*Que sera sera*, huh?'

'Exactly.' She stared into the distance as she mused on her own words. Whatever will be will be. Did she mean that? If she did, then why did she suddenly feel so wretched?

In the distance she saw Lucetta's car. From here Kate couldn't see her face, but she could imagine the look of impatience on it just from the way she was driving. She didn't know what was worse – Alessandro's crazy moped or being thrown around Lucetta's passenger seats.

'Here's our lift,' she said. 'Get ready for a white-knuckle ride.'

'My favourite kind,' Jamie said and grinned.

* * *

If Kate had thought the dinner prepared by Signora Conti the day before was sublime, the spread she'd put on in anticipation of a new guest was in a whole other league. It seemed she had gone full out and what was on offer was far more than an ordinary family lunch. There was antipasti of artichokes, olives, cheese and various meats, bread, a simple but delicious pasta dish in tomato sauce, succulent pork cooked with vegetables followed by lemon and ricotta cheese-cake. Signora Conti and Abelie were still preparing it when Lucetta arrived with Kate and Jamie, and through the course of the next half hour the rest of Alessandro's family began to arrive. Kate had not been prepared for this, although now it seemed obvious that they would all come, and meeting everyone was a little overwhelming. First Maria with her husband and four children, who subjected her to the type of scrutiny that made Kate feel she'd been undressed and examined by customs. Next came Jolanda without her husband (who was working) and her three children (a friendlier greeting), then Isabella, also hus-bandless, with her trio. Last to arrive was Gian, Lucetta's fiancé, who greeted Kate warmly and thanked her for the work on Lucetta's dress. They all went through to the kitchen for a while to speak to their mother and youngest sister before returning to the main living area to inspect Kate *en masse*. . . or at least that was how it felt. She had to wonder just how much they knew about her friendship with Ales-sandro, but it seemed that Maria, at least, knew quite a lot. It wasn't a huge leap of the imagination that Lucetta might have told all her sisters exactly what she had told Kate the night before, too, and they might have discussed it at great length. It was less of a leap and more of a skip to assume that Orazia had filled Maria in on her encounters with Kate too. If she had, then it was no wonder they were looking at Kate like a prize specimen in a zoo.

Jamie seemed to take it all in his stride, however, breaking into sporadic bits of Italian every now and again even though all Signora

Conti's offspring spoke very good English, which gained him huge smiles. This was despite telling Kate he knew hardly any at all. He might have thought it was hardly any, but it was a great deal more than she knew, and it made Kate even more determined that when she got home she was going to learn some, so if she did come back she could gain the favour that Jamie seemed to from trying to speak a little of his hosts' native language. It helped that Jamie was charming and funny as well, two qualities Kate felt very lacking in. Before long he was the absolute life and soul of the party, regaling everyone with funny stories about his travels, life in New York and his work, and taking the heat off Kate – something she was very grateful for.

The children, ranging in age from fourteen to two, were all incredibly well behaved and polite, the smaller ones sitting on laps around the table while the older ones squeezed into whatever space they could find. And it was a squeeze around Signora Conti's dinner table for sure, and Kate couldn't imagine how on earth she managed it every week (apparently she called the family together for a meal at least once a week) but somehow she had found enough chairs and they all just about fit. They were close to their neighbours, however, and Kate felt the heat of Alessandro's body pressed against one shoulder, Jamie at her other. Jamie she didn't mind so much, but she desperately wished Alessandro would move, because the contact was causing strange and inappropriate feelings that were hard to ignore.

'Lucetta's wedding dress is perfect now,' Isabella said, smiling across at Kate as she helped herself to some cured meat. 'She says you worked all night.'

'Not quite all night. . .' Kate said.

'It was very kind,' she replied. 'It was lucky for us Alessandro met you.'

'How did you meet Alessandro?' Maria chipped in from the far end, looking very pointedly at Kate. It was obvious that she knew exactly how they had met, but she was waiting for Kate to enlighten them and make herself look pretty bad into the bargain.

'Well, I, um. . .'

'She had her purse stolen and came to report it,' Alessandro cut in, sparing her the need to tell the story of their actual first meeting on the Spanish Steps. It wasn't a story she was keen to tell and she was grateful for his gallant rescue. His version sounded a lot better, and he had probably guessed that Maria and Orazia had spoken at length about Kate.

Maria shook her head and tutted loudly. 'It's terrible. People like that make everyone look bad. There are many things that give our city a bad name. Just like all the tourists who get drunk and misbehave. . .'

Kate grabbed a glass of water from next to the wine that had just been poured for her and took a huge gulp. So Alessandro *had* mentioned the incident on the steps to someone. . . maybe one of his closer colleagues, perhaps even before he'd realised that he and Kate would end up out on a date? Kate hoped so, because the alternative – that he had told Orazia, who had then told Maria – was rather disconcerting. It meant she couldn't be sure that what he'd told her about his relationship, or lack of, with Orazia was true.

'Did they take all your euros?' Jolanda asked.

'Luckily I didn't take everything out with me and left some in the hotel safe. I'll have to try and claim it back on my holiday insurance.'

'How long do you have left in Rome?' Isabella asked.

'Two more days. It's flown by.'

'I'll sure miss her,' Jamie put in. 'I've got to stay another week.'

'You must come to eat with us again,' Lucetta said. 'Whenever you are in Rome you must come to see us.'

There were noises of agreement, even from Signora Conti, who seemed to get the gist of the conversation and smiled broadly at Jamie.

'I'd love that,' he said. 'I do get lonely sometimes when I'm here on business. It's OK when I have clients to take out but that's not all the time. That's why it's been so great having Kate around.'

Kate smiled. Jamie was like a brilliant, eye-catching social butterfly, and he probably made a new friend every time he went anywhere. He probably had a whole address book full of people from all over the world he'd picked up on his travels. It was no wonder the impressionable Pietro had been dazzled by his charm, because he had the whole Conti family eating out of his hand right now, and it was easy to see why.

'I'll give you my address,' Jamie continued to Lucetta. 'You can come to see me any time you're in New York.'

'I've never been to America,' Lucetta said. She looked across at Gian. 'Perhaps we will go before we have our children.'

'You will not be able to go when you have your children,' Isabella laughed. 'They will have all your money.'

'Gian has a good job,' Lucetta sniffed. 'He will bring me lots of money.'

'It is not too bad,' Gian said, looking rather embarrassed about the boast.

'It will never be enough,' Maria said, wiping a bogey from the nose of her youngest on her lap and not seeming to care one jot who was looking. She scrunched it in a tissue and then shoved it into a pocket.

'Not for Lucetta,' Alessandro said, and the Conti family, apart from Lucetta, laughed. Gian looked as though he didn't dare laugh, and it was easy to see who would wear the trousers in that marriage. Kate saw Lucetta stick her nose in the air, but she didn't look overly upset. She was probably used to getting ribbed by her siblings, and in a family that big it was going to happen a lot.

'So, where do you think I should visit tomorrow?' Kate asked in an effort to change the subject.

'Wherever it is, make sure you hold onto your purse,' Jamie said with a grin.

'Yes,' Alessandro agreed. 'You must be more careful when you are alone.'

'Will you be on duty tomorrow?' Jamie asked him.

'Yes. I will rest in the day and start in the afternoon.'

Kate knew this and she should have been relieved to hear him say it, but she just felt empty. She would miss his company for the rest of her time in Rome. She had Jamie, of course, but it wasn't just about being alone. It was him, Alessandro, that she'd miss. The smile that gently mocked her, the eyes that showed every tiny shift of emotion, the kindness and goodness in his soul, his downright turbocharged sex appeal. . . Her mind went back to her musings of earlier, when she had been waiting for Lucetta to pick them up. *Que sera sera. . .* Whatever will be will be. Over the course of the last few days she'd fallen in love. Not just with Alessandro, but with Italy itself, and that was a love which was far more certain. Sitting here today with this remarkable family had only proved it to her. This was a way of life she wanted now that she had tasted it. She loved her own family, of course, but they were the only thing keeping her in Britain. She hated her job, owned a house that now gave her only painful memories where she had once loved it, along with a deep sense of humiliation that it wouldn't be hers for much longer anyway, and then she would have to watch as Matt moved on with his life and found someone else to take her place. As Lily had her family and Anna eventually did the same, their priorities would change too, and Kate would become less important in their lives in the face of new bonds, and, as much as she'd be happy for them, it would break her heart. Her mum was in Scotland, forever on the brink of another breakdown, and barely ever made the journey down to visit. Besides, she had her husband, Hamish, to look out for her now and he did a great job. What was left in Britain for her? More importantly, did any of it matter enough to stop her from leaving?

Alessandro looked at her and smiled as he filled up her wine glass. 'Are you happy?' he asked. 'You have enjoyed the meal?'

Kate tried to smile back, though her thoughts had sobered her mood. 'Yes, thank you.'

'I am glad. We are a big family and very noisy.'

'I've had a lovely day, and I really haven't noticed the noise. It makes a nice change from a big empty house.'

He replaced the wine bottle on the table and as she picked up her glass to take a sip she couldn't help but notice that he was still watching her. Was he thinking about how he would miss her when he was back at work? Was he wondering if she would ever come back to Rome? Was he falling for her as she had fallen for him? It didn't seem likely, and Kate resolved at that moment to put this silly notion out of her mind once and for all. She might well decide to come back to Rome, perhaps for good, but the reason had to be a better one than a relationship with absolutely no certainty to it whatsoever.

Twelve

Hangovers weren't something that Kate often suffered with, but this was a humdinger. It probably meant she'd had a very good night with the Conti family as lunch had turned into the evening meal, which had then turned into night, although God only knew what awful, embarrassing things she might have said as she slipped steadily under the influence. It was probably very lucky that Jamie had been there to take the attention from her; he had entertained like a pro and had everyone in stitches with his jokes and stories, even Signora Conti, whose laughter was always delayed by a few seconds as someone translated for her, but laughed heartily just the same. Kate had to wonder how Alessandro was faring – she wasn't sure he had drunk as much as her or that he had been affected by what he had drunk quite as much, but it was still undoubtedly a good thing that he didn't have to report for duty early. As for her own memories of the evening, things were hazy, but she recalled many moments with perfect clarity: her hand brushing against Alessandro's as she tried to help clear the table; the looks she caught from him when he thought she hadn't noticed, the feeling of belonging with his family, even though she barely knew them, the warm hugs and goodbyes at the end of the night, Rome sparkling as Lucetta drove them through the city back to her hotel, the words of friendship from her and Jamie as they'd bid each other goodnight before she staggered back to her room. She had collapsed, spark out on her bed in her clothes, and had woken in exactly the same position this morning but with a drum and bass convention in her head, though she had woken happy. What it might mean was confusing, but she had once heard it said that if a decision was tough and scary and hard to make, the best thing to do was pretend you'd made it and live with that thought for a day. At the end of the day, if the choice you had made felt right, then it probably was right.

So this morning, despite not really having a clue where to start and knowing that it was just about the maddest thing she had ever done, Kate was going flat hunting. It was only pretend, of course, and there was a lot to consider before she took such a huge leap, but she was curious, and she wanted to find out what her chances of success were – how much rent was likely to be, what sort of area she could hope to be able to afford, whether there were other English people living nearby and whether she'd be able to get work. But she could enjoy the dream for a while, and indulge in a little fantasy house shopping, and perhaps it would give her something other than Alessandro to focus on.

A modest breakfast was needed, and she felt more human once she had some pastry and coffee inside her to mop up the excess alcohol still clogging her system and fogging her brain. After filling her new purse with as much money as she thought she'd need for the day and locking her room safe again, she picked up her phone to make a quick call to Lily. Being with Alessandro's family last night had also reminded her that she hadn't phoned her own sisters nearly as often as she ought to while she'd been in Rome, and it was no wonder Anna had been annoyed with her when she last spoke to her. Sooner or later she'd have to tell them the plans she was mulling over too, and she knew that their reaction would be shock, worry, perhaps even a little hurt, but maybe it was something that would wait until she was certain herself.

'Hey,' Lily said, picking up on the first ring, 'I was just on my way to work. Is it something urgent?'

Kate looked at her watch. 'You're going in early.'

'I know. We have this presentation today for the directors. Angela cocked it up and I've had to step in and give her a hand. She owes me a night out for this – when I can drink alcohol again, that is. So you're still having a nice time in Rome? You're enjoying yourself? You don't need to talk about anything? A certain date?'

'No, I was only going to check in. . . see how you and baby are,' Kate said, ignoring the reference to Alessandro, though it was obvious Anna was always going to tell Lily and there would be some sharing of views. Kate was only glad she hadn't been there to witness it.

'Oh, we're both good; nothing to report except a lot of heartburn and an already expanding waistline. I'm going to be the size of Wembley Stadium by the time I get to nine months.' There was a pause. 'So you're not going to tell me what happened with this Italian fella you had a day out with? Don't tell me you're running off with him to get married.'

The remark was flippant, and Lily probably would have forgotten it almost as soon as she'd said it if Kate had lied about the plans she was considering, which didn't involve running off with a man, but quite possibly did involve running off. But it wasn't that easy and perhaps it would have been worse to let her sister find out later down the line. Kate didn't know what was going to happen, but she knew what she wanted.

'Actually. . .' Lily cut into her thoughts. 'You'd better tell me later. I'm running late for work as it is. I'll call you tonight if that's OK – about seven?'

'I might be out – I'll phone you.'

'Right!' Lily laughed. 'Out again? Phone me when you can fit me into your packed schedule then. Love you.'

'Love you too,' Kate replied before ending the call. She had been ready to say it, but the moment had been and gone. It was going to be that much tougher later on when she'd had time to digest the enormity herself of what she was actually planning to do.

* * *

Feeling quite full of food, culture and history, not to mention her dalliance with the locals, the only thing left in Rome that Kate hadn't sampled was the shopping. Window shopping, of course, and Via Condotti, Via Borgognona and Via Frattina had been recommended at the hotel reception as the streets to visit if you wanted to stare into the windows of the high fashion houses that Italy was famous for. It was a far cry from Kate's own home-made clothes, but she had been keen to see their glitzy shops, if only for ideas she could admire and perhaps adapt for her own creations. It wouldn't be a trip to Rome without seeing some of the glamour, and before Kate had left for her break, Anna had insisted she try a dress on in the most expensive store and take a selfie to send home. Kate hadn't dared, of course – she hadn't even dared step inside one of those hallowed premises in the fear that they might want a thousand euros from her just for doing so – but she had enjoyed mingling with the crowds, lost in a world of crocodile handbags, diamante-detailed evening gowns and razor-sharp suits. She'd also been keeping an eye out for estate agent windows, in the hope she might get a handle on property and rental prices in the city, but hadn't come across any. By the time her stomach had started to groan to remind her that lunch was well overdue, her thoughts had turned back to the issue in earnest.

Finding a pleasant roadside café, she settled at a table under a large parasol and ordered lunch, rather enjoying the novelty of dining alone. She'd expected to do a lot of that when she'd first arrived in the city, but now having an hour by herself was practically a non-existent occurrence. As she waited for the food to arrive, she connected to the Wi-Fi on her phone. After a few minutes of searching, she came across a handful of websites that offered help to expatriates wanting properties nearby.

One thing was clear as she scrolled down the listings – almost everything that looked nice enough to live in was out of her price range or, at least, out of a price range that would make for sensible budgeting of an as yet unknown income. It would need a search further afield, and she would need to feel a lot more confident in her knowledge of the suburbs before making such a commitment. She could ask Jamie if he knew, though she suspected his knowledge of anything outside central Rome might be as limited as her own. There was one person who would know – the most obvious candidate – but she wasn't sure it was a good idea to ask him. She hardly knew herself what she wanted yet and any sort of hint to Alessandro that she was thinking of staying in Rome would complicate things hugely. Lucetta had told Kate her brother was fond of her, but how could she know what that meant? Had Alessandro said it in passing, flippantly, knowing that Kate would be on a plane back to England soon? Was it that he simply fancied her but knew that she wasn't marriage material? Did he like her as a companion? Or did he actually think he was falling for her, in which case, why hadn't he told Kate this himself?

The more she puzzled it over, the less certain she was of the truth and of what her own heart was telling her to do. Anna and Lily would think her foolish and immature to move across Europe on a whim, and even more foolish to do it just to live in a city she'd spent only a week in as a tourist. But something was pulling her here, even if she couldn't get a handle on exactly what it was herself. And the more she thought about the possibilities of a future in Italy, the more excited she got, even though the idea was truly terrifying. What if it was simpler than it sounded, simpler than she was making it? What if she just never got on the plane home? Matt could put the house up for sale, and perhaps it was about time he took some responsibility for all that he had walked away from. She hated her job, so it would be no hardship to tell her boss where to stick it, and maybe she could rent a place right out in the suburbs of Rome where it was cheaper, find some work and build herself a little sewing business in her spare time. She was certain Lucetta would spread the word for her and that she could make her own friends and contacts along the way. There had to be other English people living here too, surely? They'd give help and advice, wouldn't they? They couldn't be that hard to find if she knew the right places to look.

As the waiter brought her iced lemonade, she checked her watch. Perhaps Jamie would be free for a chat.

He picked up on the third ring. 'How's your head?' she asked.

'Like a marching band is walking through it. How's yours?'

'It was bad first thing but shopping has blown away the cobwebs.'

'Lucky you. Have you bought much?'

'Nothing. I couldn't afford any of it.'

'That's too bad.'

Kate heard him stifle a yawn at the other end of the line. She could have felt guilty about waking him but it was lunchtime and his suffering was as self-inflicted as hers was, so she didn't. 'Where are you?' she asked instead.

'In my room. I feel like death.'

Kate frowned. 'You're OK?'

'Sure. If someone could cut my head off and put it in some ice I'd be even better.'

Kate giggled. 'You have nobody to blame but yourself.'

'I can blame you, can't I? Please tell me I can blame you because I was kinda counting on it.'

'Afraid not. Listen, can you come and meet me for lunch?'

'Like lunch as in now?'

'Uh huh.'

'Sorry, no can do. I have a meeting at three and I need to pull myself together. But it shouldn't be longer than an hour, so I could meet you afterwards for dinner. Unless you have plans with hot cop, that is.'

'No,' Kate said. 'He's working and we hadn't really arranged to see each other again.'

'You're kidding me! You're not going to see him again? He was panting after you like a dog last night!'

Kate grimaced. 'Thanks for that lovely image.'

'Seriously, Kate! What's wrong with you? You have his number, right? You'd better call him and make sure you see him again before you go home.'

'I don't have his number and that's exactly why. There hasn't been a need to get it up until now and there didn't seem any point because

I would be going home but. . . I don't know. I'm so confused and it would be great to chat to you later. I've got some stuff to talk about, and I don't feel ready to share it with anyone but you yet. So dinner would be great if you could spare the time.'

'That sounds very serious but OK.'

'It's nothing bad, I promise. I'll meet you at seven-thirty – the usual place.'

'Sure, catch you later.'

Jamie hung up. Some might think it odd that he was the go-to person when she needed to pour her heart out, but throughout her visit to Rome he had been the one constant. And perhaps it didn't matter what he knew or didn't about her feelings; because he was a stranger, it was somehow easier to share it all with him. There was no emotional baggage, no guilt, no preconceptions based on what he knew about her or her life before Rome, and he wouldn't judge her in the way her sisters or her mother might. It didn't matter to him where her life went after this week, and maybe she would never see him again after all this, so she and her angst would be nothing more than an interesting anecdote he'd trot out during his next dinner party. She sincerely hoped that wouldn't be the case, but she was getting used to the idea these days that life didn't always go how you thought it was going to and that people you thought would always be there were not.

Thirteen

'I found this great place for dinner,' Jamie said as he kissed Kate on the cheek. 'And by the way you look incredible again – is that another of your self-made dresses?'

Kate nodded and smoothed a hand over the skirt of the black dress she was wearing. It had a sweetheart neckline, and she'd teamed it with a red belt and shoes. The cut of it gave her a definite wiggle when she walked. While she waved away the compliment, inside she was bursting with pride. 'Where's this new restaurant? Is it far?'

'It's near the Spanish Steps,' Jamie said carelessly as he offered Kate his arm. She shot him a sideways glance as they began to walk. Alessandro had mentioned that his beat would take him around that area again. Was Jamie up to something? Kate didn't mind running into Alessandro, of course, but she didn't need Jamie's help to do it, and Jamie already knew that Kate had decided not to see him again while she was in Rome. At least, that was the last version of her thoughts that Jamie had been privy to, because she hadn't yet told him about her new decision to spend a lot more time in Rome than just her week's holiday. It still didn't give Jamie an excuse to cause mischief, though.

'I thought we might go somewhere else,' Kate said. 'I've already seen the Steps and I'd like to go somewhere I haven't seen yet.'

'But you haven't seen this restaurant yet. It's divine – you have *got* to try it. I promise you won't regret it.'

'Hmm, well it had better be good.'

'My taste is impeccable – you know this.'

'Well, you did make friends with me,' Kate said.

Jamie grinned. 'Exactly.'

As the sky was overcast, they caught a bus, something which Kate hadn't done much since she'd arrived. There had been a lot of walking, and quite a lot of hair-raising lifts in cars and on the back of mopeds, but public transport, busy and noisy as it was, was another fun way of experiencing the real Rome.

'So, do you want to tell me about this big secret?' Jamie asked as they settled on the seat together.

'It's not so much of a secret really, more of a dilemma.'

'You're staying in Rome and having thirty kids with Alessandro?'

Kate stared at him. 'How. . .? You're only half right, so you can stop looking smug.'

Jamie grinned, looking very pleased with himself indeed.

'Am I that obvious?' she added.

'I'm just that good. So, which bit am I right about?'

Kate took a deep breath. 'I'm going to stay in Rome. I don't know how long for, what I'm going to do here or where I'm going to live, but I want to stay.'

'Now that's what I call a life-changing decision. What do your sisters have to say about this?'

'I haven't actually told them yet. . .'

'Do you think they'll be pleased for you?'

'Eventually, maybe. Until they get used to the idea they'll be worried to death, and I suppose I can understand that. I'd probably feel the same way if it was one of them, but we're adults now and we can't have someone holding our hand all the time, can we? I've come to realise that the life I was living with Matt. . . well, that was the easy path, but it was the slow path too, and it was leading to a dead end.'

'That's a lot of analogy in one sentence. I'll be careful not to take that path if I see it signposted.'

Kate let out a giggle. It was encouraging that Jamie didn't seem to be dismissing her idea out of hand and that he didn't seem to think she was crazy.

'What I mean to say is I was coasting because I was just so comfortable with it all. I didn't push myself to do anything new and I know that Matt and I were bored with each other partly because we were just bored with our lives. It doesn't matter now, and there's no going back to fix it because since our separation we've both become different people – at least I know I have – so I should use this opportunity to shake things up. I should go out and find the life I didn't even know I wanted until now, and I only wish I'd had this epiphany sooner. Matt and I might still have been together.'

'Do you think that?'

'Who knows?'

'But would you really want that? It seems to me that you're moving on pretty quickly. Maybe you weren't as in love as you thought you were.'

'I think you're probably right, though it's hard to admit it to myself, because then I feel the waste of those years even more keenly. In many ways Matt walking out was the biggest gift he's ever given me; I just couldn't see it at the time.'

'It's a shame more people don't spin these things into something more positive, like you've done.'

'Believe me, I didn't at the time. If you'd seen me over the last few months you wouldn't have recognised me.'

'Ice cream from the tub?'

'Uh huh. On the sofa, every night. Gallons of it.'

'Shoot; it was bad.'

'You don't know the half of it.'

'So what's next? You just up and leave? You'll go home, surely?'

'Do you know what, it's half crossed my mind not to get on that plane at all on Monday. But I should, if only to start putting things in order. My sensible brain tells me it's going to be hard to organise things from here, but. . .'

'You're afraid that if you go home your courage will fail you and you won't come back at all?'

She gave him a rueful smile.

'Honey, I went through exactly the same thing when I left Texas to live in New York. I was terrified. But I did it, and I have faith that you can too.'

'I feel guilty too. I mean, my sisters have stuck by me through the separation and the divorce, and I repay them by buggering off at the first opportunity.'

'They won't see it like that. They'll be happy for you once they get used to the idea. It's only you holding you back now.'

Kate leaned over and kissed him on the cheek. 'You're amazing, do you know that?'

'Kinda,' he laughed. Then his gaze went to the window. 'OK, looks like we need to get off here.'

* * *

Whatever his reasons for taking her there, the seared sea bass alone made it worth the trip to Jamie's new restaurant discovery. It was a bit grander and stuffier inside than the cosy Trattoria da Luigi, where he had taken her the first night, with wall friezes in the style of the Renaissance painters and opera piped in through the sound system, but the staff were friendly and the ambience was relaxing. The house wine wasn't too bad either, and it might have been that Kate had underestimated its potency as, after only the second glass, she was becoming pleasantly tipsy. If she was going to move to Rome, her wine intake was one thing she'd have to address or she'd either be bankrupt or alcoholic, or possibly both. For now, there seemed no reason to worry, and the drink only helped loosen her tongue in a most cathartic way, so that she and Jamie were able to discuss her future plans without her feeling awkward or silly.

'So there was me, knee deep in live crickets. . .' Kate said, recalling an incident at Mr Woofy with a damaged shipment of reptile food. 'They're in my hair, in my bra. . . they're bloody everywhere. . .'

'Crickets? Oh my Lord! I would have been screaming!'

'I would have been too, but if I'd opened my mouth I'd have eaten half of them. So my colleague, Deidre, the one I told you about with glasses so big they look like two car windscreens strapped to her face, she just walks into the warehouse with her copy of *Hello!* magazine, takes one look at me, shrugs, and walks out again.'

'She didn't help you?'

'Not a bit. And there are so many of them I end up stamping on them by accident, you know, they're under my feet and I'm trying to get away from them, but they're following me around like a little chirruping cloud.'

Jamie snorted as he took a mouthful of wine. 'So gross. But weirdly cute too.'

'Not when they're chirruping around your head it's not.'

'So what did you do?'

'Eventually some of the warehouse boys came and scraped them off me. When the boss got back the only thing he cared about was how many of them I'd killed. That's how underappreciated I am there.'

'I can see why you want to quit!' he laughed. 'That's so gross!'

'It's not just that. I can put up with the weird and wonderful stock, but God, it's boring! That's about the most exciting thing that's ever happened there.'

Kate reached over and filled up her wine glass. 'Ten years of a dead-end job in the most boring business imaginable, looking at those same boring faces every day – it's no wonder I want to emigrate! I'm going to email the boss on Monday morning and tell him I'm not coming in ever again.'

'Really? You don't want to think about that for a moment?'

'Nope,' Kate said. 'I do not. I never want to go into that damp, smelly, dull office, not for as long as I live. I'm going to have a little dress shop in the backstreets of Rome and I'm going to do exactly what I please. Maybe I'll even get as famous as one of those swanky shops I saw today.'

'And you're going to marry Alessandro and have beautiful children.'

'Maybe. . .' Kate giggled, the wine blurring the edges of her uncertainty with Alessandro and letting her fantasies run riot. 'Stranger things have happened.'

'I knew it!' Jamie said, clicking his fingers. 'I'm going to be invited to the wedding, right?'

'Guest of honour, obviously.'

He clapped his hands together. 'I'm so excited for you! I almost want to relocate to Rome too, just so I don't get left out!'

'You would never get left out. And you're always welcome to stay once I'm settled, so at least you'll always have a friendly face when you're over here on business.'

'And that invitation still extends to you coming to New York. I'll be pretty pissed if you don't come and visit me at least once a year with your gorgeous husband and beautiful children.'

'Steady on!' Kate laughed. 'I haven't even moved here yet!'

'But you will and you'll be fabulous.' Jamie raised his glass. 'To a fabulous future!'

Kate clinked with a giggle. It was the drink talking, of course, and they both knew that she'd be back at her desk the following week – at least to work her month's notice if nothing else. And as for marrying Alessandro, if that day was ever coming it was a long way off. But it was a nice fantasy, and Kate was happy to enjoy it for a while.

'I think it all sounds perfect,' Jamie said.

Kate was about to reply, something flippant about her being destined for greatness, but she stopped short as he took his phone from his pocket and frowned at the display.

'Shoot. . . I'm sorry,' he said, not taking his eyes from the screen, 'but I have to reply to this text.'

Suddenly he seemed preoccupied, and the bantering mood they'd just shared dried up. She watched as he finished tapping on his screen and locked the phone, finally looking up at her again. 'Um. . . OK, so where were we?'

'I was telling you about my dress shop and you were telling me what a terrible idea it is.'

'I think it's a great idea—' He was interrupted by the phone bleeping the arrival of another message. 'Sorry.'

'It's fine,' Kate said. 'If you need to get it. . .'

She glanced over and saw Pietro's name flashing on the screen. Jamie's frown deepened as he read the second message. He quickly sent another reply and laid the phone down on the table again. He'd barely resumed the conversation when it went off a third time. He swiped the screen and then began to get up from the table. 'I'm so sorry. I have to go outside and sort something, but I promise I'll be back, so don't go wandering off again.'

'Pietro, by any chance?'

Jamie nodded.

'He's outside now?' Kate asked.

'I'm sorry, but I had to tell him where we were; he said he was desperate to tell me something. I won't be long.'

'Shall I come with you?'

'No, keep our seats warm.' Jamie gave her a tight smile, a world away from his usual easy grin.

As Kate watched him go, she couldn't help but feel that something didn't stack up. She wasn't entirely happy about the prospect of a repeat of her first dinner in Rome with Jamie – that she would end up ditched in favour of Pietro – but it wasn't just that bugging her. Aspects of the situation didn't make sense. How had Pietro got here so fast if he didn't know where Jamie was? Why couldn't he talk to Jamie over the phone, or even wait, presuming that Jamie had told him he and Kate were eating together? Perhaps he hadn't – it wasn't completely outside the realms of possibility. Maybe Jamie had told him in advance where he would be, had even chosen the venue with a plan in place that Pietro would come to find him later, but why would he have gone to the trouble of taking Kate there if that was the case? Why not simply put Kate off for another night and meet Pietro? After all, Jamie must know Kate well enough by now to know that she wouldn't have minded. She decided quickly that Jamie wouldn't do that, but still, the whole thing made her feel uneasy. Her mind automatically went to Alessandro, and although there was something comforting about the idea that he was on duty nearby, it was lucky she didn't have his phone number or she'd be sorely tempted to call him right now. He'd probably come running, and it might well be for nothing. Then again, Jamie was too quick to trust, and too eager to help, and she couldn't escape the feeling that he was heading for trouble.

* * *

Fifteen minutes had passed and Kate was growing increasingly anxious as Jamie failed to return. The waiter cleared their plates and returned with coffee for Kate. She'd ordered it mainly to stall the dessert menu, or even the bill, neither of which she wanted while Jamie was still missing. Perhaps fifteen minutes wasn't that long though; she'd had much longer conversations than that with the owner of her local shop while popping in for a loaf, so maybe she was overreacting.

But then fifteen minutes turned into half an hour and still no Jamie. She pulled her phone from her bag and sent him a text. There was no reply. After another minute of procrastination she decided to phone him, but it rang out. She drained the last of her coffee and looked hopelessly towards the door of the restaurant.

Come on, Jamie, where the hell are you?

'Would you like anything else?' The waiter's voice came from behind her. She spun around, almost losing her balance on the chair.

'No thank you.'

He took her coffee cup without a word. She dialled Jamie's number again. Still no reply. Pushing her chair away from the table, she

got up, deciding to go and peek out of the door to see if he was anywhere to be seen.

'Madam, you have not paid the bill!' The waiter was there again, a
slip of paper on a tiny tray in his hand.

'Oh. . . I'm not leaving. . . I'm just looking to see where my friend
is. . .'

The waiter stared at her, and it was obvious that it looked very
much like she was trying to leave without paying. She took the tray
from him and scanned the total with a sharp intake of breath before
depositing the right amount of euros into his hand.

'*Grazie,*' he said.

Kate nodded and headed out into the evening air. Whether Jamie
wanted to or not, there was no coming back in now. If he wanted to
continue the meal, they'd have to go elsewhere. But as she searched
the street, there was no sign of him.

'Bloody typical,' she muttered.

She'd been an idiot. Jamie was quite obviously having an affair
with Pietro, despite what he'd told her, and he was obviously with
him now. She'd fallen for the same bloody con twice, and twice she'd
ended up abandoned to pay for both their dinners. She didn't think
he'd done it on purpose, but she did think it was an almighty piss-take
to leave her alone in a restaurant again when they were supposed to be
having dinner together. If he couldn't control his libido then perhaps
he shouldn't be asking people to come to dinner with him; perhaps
he ought to just hang around Trattoria da Luigi like a lovesick puppy
so that he'd be on tap whenever Pietro called him.

She stamped her feet like a petulant child, a growing feeling of
annoyance coming over her. What she wanted to do was give him a
piece of her mind. It was tempting to phone again and leave a mes-

sage to do just that. Anna would have told her that a friend who kept letting her down was no sort of friend at all, no matter how fun and charming they were, and she'd probably be right. Kate hated it when Anna was right, even an Anna who wasn't here and had no idea what she might be right about. The thought of it made Kate even more vexed.

But what was the use of being angry? She was getting used to people letting her down and this was a valuable lesson. It was time to start relying on herself a lot more and others a lot less; that way the chances of being disappointed were a lot slimmer and if it happened she had only herself to blame. Jamie was just being Jamie, and she couldn't expect him to be anything else. She took a deep breath and counted to ten. Anger was a waste of time and no good to anyone.

The evening air was cooler now, and Kate shivered slightly. She pulled a feather-light cardigan from her bag and swung it around her shoulders as she began to walk away from the restaurant. It wasn't a great deal better, but it was something at least. An ambulance flashed past on the road, its blue lights giving the buildings a fleeting eerie glow. It looked as if someone else's night had been ruined too. She looked at her watch. It was gone ten, and it probably wasn't the best idea to walk back to the hotel alone at this hour. Turning around, she had just made the decision to return to the restaurant and order a taxi when she heard her name being called.

A man was striding towards her. He was wearing full police uniform, but it wasn't Alessandro. This man was stockier, a little shorter; he had the sort of laughter lines earned from a life well lived, but he wasn't laughing now.

'You are Kate?' he asked.

'Yes, but how do you know. . .?'

'No time to explain,' he said. 'I remember you from the *questura* when you came to report your robbery.'

'Is it Alessandro?' Kate said, suddenly gripped by a sense of panic. 'Has something happened to him?'

'He has gone to your hotel to find you.'

'Have I done something wrong? I don't understand. . .'

'Do not be scared when I tell you this. It is bad news for your friend.'

Fourteen

The man led her to a waiting police car. She had not asked for his ID, had no idea whether he was a real policeman and hadn't even asked his name, but she got in anyway, too distracted to think about the danger she might be in. Anna and Lily would have been horrified to see it, but there wasn't time to think about that now. All she could think about was Jamie, and how she had harshly misjudged him. If anything happened to him she would never be able to forgive herself. If only she'd gone to look sooner, insisted she went with him to meet Pietro in the first place, done something. . . anything. But wishing was not fixing, and there was no magic time-travelling box to take her back.

There was another officer in the car when they got there, and Kate sat in the back while the first one contacted someone on his radio. Then he turned and spoke to Kate.

'I will take you to your hotel now.'

'OK.'

She sat in silence as the lights of Rome sped by, the tourists and revellers a blur on the pavements. The roads were still busy, but clearer than during the day, meaning the snail's pace she'd travelled at before had been swapped for a brisker journey and they were back at her hotel surprisingly quickly. When the car pulled up, she thanked the officers and turned to the hotel. Through the vast windows she could already see Alessandro in his uniform at reception. He looked strained and solemn, and her heart sank at the sight. But there was no point in delaying. She pushed open the doors and went inside.

'Kate. . .' Alessandro's tone was brisk as he strode towards her. She wanted to bury herself in his arms, but this wasn't the time or place. He kept his distance and his tone was guarded. She understood: he was on duty and he had to maintain a professional manner. But it still stung. 'Has my colleague told you what happened?'

'Not everything. Only that Jamie is injured. Is it bad?'

'I do not think it is too bad, but he was attacked, which is a very serious thing. A tourist found him. . . lying on the street. . . eyes closed. . . sleeping. . .' He paused, frowned, reaching for the English.

'Unconscious?' Kate asked.

'Yes. The doctor is looking at him now. I need you to tell me what happened, all that you know. Can you do that?'

'I don't know that much,' Kate began, but Alessandro put a gentle hand to her elbow and guided her to a chair in the lobby where it was quieter. He pulled out a tablet and began to type.

'Your friend woke in the ambulance. He said he did not know who attacked him, but I do not think that is true. He wants to protect someone?'

'I don't know. . .' Kate paused. What could she tell him? How much would Jamie want her to tell him? He might not appreciate her potentially complicating an already difficult situation. Was Alessandro acting now in the capacity of law enforcement or as a concerned friend? And did it matter which? 'We were having dinner together, and then he had a message. . . on his phone. He went outside to talk to someone and said he'd be right back, but he didn't come back. I paid the bill and started to walk to my hotel. I thought. . .'

'What did you think, Kate? Who did he meet? This is very serious.'

'I don't know him. A sort of friend. Can I see Jamie? Can I speak to him?'

Alessandro shook his head. 'Not now. Tomorrow.'

Kate's gaze went to the floor. She hated this Alessandro. Not because he was horrible, but because she felt like a terrible person keeping secrets from him. He was doing his job to the best of his ability and she was making it a hundred times more difficult. But until she had spoken to Jamie she didn't want to tell him anything at all. The more she turned things over in her mind, the more confused she was. Pietro didn't seem like the type of man to attack someone, especially a man he considered a friend, a man he claimed to be in love with. But the evidence all pointed that way. Pietro had sent Jamie a text asking him to come outside, and then Jamie had been knocked unconscious. Kate just didn't want to believe it could be true. Was this a crime of passion? She had always considered that term rather melodramatic, and she had never met anyone who was victim or perpetrator before, but she supposed that didn't mean crimes of passion didn't exist. Or had something else happened?

She didn't want to, but she began to cry. Silently, holding onto her tears as hard as she could, but still they fell. She couldn't look at Alessandro.

'Kate,' he said, 'Jamie will get well. He is young and strong.'

'I'm not crying because of that,' she said. But she couldn't say why she was crying, and when she dared glance up she could see that he looked pained at her distress. 'I'm so sorry.'

'You have not done anything wrong.'

'But I. . .' Her attention was caught by the sight of another police-man coming into the hotel lobby and making his way towards them.

Alessandro followed her gaze and stood to greet his colleague, talking rapidly in low tones. But whereas he usually spoke English in her presence as a courtesy, this time he used Italian. It made her feel even more wretched. What was he saying? Didn't he trust her now? Did he suspect her of keeping information from him? She was, of course, although she didn't want to, and it was only out of loyalty to Jamie and to give Pietro, who didn't strike her as the criminal type, the benefit of the doubt until she knew more. How could she make Alessandro understand that without actually telling him the whole story?

'I must go,' he said, turning to her.

Kate stared dolefully at him. Was that it? Would he come back to take an official statement? Was he done with her as a witness? Letting her off the hook? Or was he just done with her full stop? She'd blown it, hadn't she? He didn't trust her now, and he didn't think she was a good person for being so awkward, and he knew that she was holding back for sure. She was no trained officer but even she'd recognise it if the tables had been turned.

'Go to bed,' he added, his tone softer now. 'Bad things will look better with the new day.'

There was no promise to meet her again, no offers of days out, no invites to his house. There was barely an acknowledgement of the time they had shared at all. He didn't even tell her what to do about Jamie or how she'd be able to find him in the morning. He simply stowed the tablet he had been working on into a wallet on his belt and followed his colleague out of the hotel. She glanced across at the reception desk, where the two members of staff on duty were watching her with some curiosity. Beyond that she could see the sleek glass and chrome of the hotel bar. They were still serving, and she could go and get a stiff drink. God knew she needed one right now. But what was the point? It wouldn't help anyone to get more pissed and she'd need a clear head in the morning. She didn't know what she was going to do about Jamie, but she was going to have to try and contact him, if only to reassure herself that he was alright. As for Alessandro, it looked as though that ship had sailed.

Out of habit, she checked her mobile. There was a text from Anna asking how things were and a missed call from Lily. *Shit!* She'd promised to phone Lily, hadn't she? And while Lily would probably let the oversight slide, Anna would be fuming at what she would perceive as a selfish lack of consideration for how they might be worrying about her being alone in a foreign country, and would think they were owed a check-in once in a while. She'd be bang on too, of course, but no matter how much Kate wanted to put it right, she wasn't sure now was the time for that either. Emotional turmoil and a calm demeanour didn't go well together, and she wasn't sure she'd be able to keep it together if she heard either of their voices. It would have to go on the list of things to do in the morning, which was growing bigger and more complicated by the second.

Fifteen

'Dear God, Kate, why didn't you tell us any of this before!' Anna cried.

Kate held the phone away from her ear as she sat on the bed in her hotel room, daylight streaming through the windows and warming her back. Anna was doing that thing she did when she got worked up, where her voice gradually got higher and louder until it became a sound that humans ought not to be able to make, and Kate rather liked her eardrums in one piece.

'I didn't want to worry you. . . besides, there wasn't that much to tell before. I didn't know it was going to end up in a punch-up, did I? As far as I knew Jamie was just offering a friendly shoulder to cry on.'

'Typical you, though,' Anna shot back. 'Can't wait to go wading into the danger zone, always hooking up with the losers, the waifs and strays, the people who will bring trouble to your door. It's like they can sniff you out.'

'Hardly,' Kate said, straining to keep her tone civil. 'Jamie went out alone and left me in the restaurant because he received a text from someone asking him to. I wouldn't call that the behaviour of someone who will bring trouble to my door and, actually, he went out of his way to make sure I stayed out of it by leaving me inside.'

'But you could have been with him. If he'd been attacked on the way to the restaurant, you could have got caught up in it.'

'I didn't and I'm safe.'

'Use your brain. . .' Anna gave an impatient sigh. 'Whoever it was obviously knew where Jamie was going to be and was lying in wait. That's the only explanation. If they'd been less than kindly disposed to you, they might have attacked you both. There might have been more than one attacker for all you know, and you'd have been in hospital with your friend. . . maybe even dead.'

Kate flinched at her sister's melodramatic assessment of the situation. Anna had a way of bringing out the worst in her and usually managed to drag her into an argument, but she refused to be drawn this time. 'But how would they know?' she insisted. 'Jamie was with me and he had no reason to tell anyone else where we would be eating.'

'Then it was an unprovoked attack, which is worse.'

'But he went outside because of a text from someone he knew. It doesn't make any sense. Why would that lead to an unprovoked attack? How could it?'

'That's a question you need to ask Jamie. Have you had any sort of explanation from him yet?'

'I phoned you first,' Kate said. 'I didn't want you to be annoyed with me,' she added, with obvious sarcastic emphasis on the fact that Anna was being unreasonably irritated. Kate was a grown woman, after all, and she was beginning to wish she hadn't come clean with her sister about the events of the previous night. But she'd needed a good excuse for not calling her or Lily, and she was sick of lying, or withholding the truth, or whatever you wanted to call it. Eventually it would trip her up and that would make things worse. Besides, they weren't a family that kept secrets, and she had kept far too many already this week. 'I don't even know if he's out of the hospital yet. Come to think of it, I don't even know which hospital he's in.'

'Didn't the police tell you?'

Kate was thoughtful for a moment. She hadn't told Anna that Alessandro had been the one to come and see her about Jamie, and she wasn't sure why not. But he hadn't volunteered the information about where Jamie was, and now that she thought about the way they'd parted last night, she was certain it was because he'd lost all respect for her. The thought made her squirm with shame, her heart heavy, but there was nothing she could do now. 'I suppose because I'm not really family they couldn't tell me. But I would imagine they've informed his family back home.'

'That's hardly useful to you, is it? That won't get you an explanation for what the hell he was playing at.'

'Oh, give it a rest, Anna. He didn't ask to get beaten up, did he? I'm sure he wasn't playing at anything.'

'Sounds like he was poking his nose – or something else – where it wasn't wanted.'

'I just don't believe it was Pietro who hit him. He doesn't seem like that sort of person at all.'

'I suppose if he was in love with him it does seem quite a strange thing to do,' Anna conceded, her voice more level now. 'Perhaps he was jealous because he thought you were having it away with Jamie too?'

'I doubt it!' Kate couldn't help a little laugh. 'I don't think there's any confusion that Jamie is exclusively about the men. He's engaged to be married to a man for a start.'

'But he could be bisexual. It's not impossible, you know.'

Kate had never actually considered this possibility before, and Jamie had never volunteered any information about his relationships other than his current boyfriend. Had Anna struck on the reason Pietro may have lost it? But that was ridiculous, surely? They didn't look one bit like a couple, did they? Jamie didn't have a thing for her, did he? A secret thing that Pietro had guessed? If he had, he'd done a bloody good job of hiding it from her. Either that or she'd been ridiculously short-sighted about the whole thing. But then she'd been so wrapped up in Alessandro that maybe. . .

She shook herself. 'No chance. Jamie is in love with Brad and that's it.'

'So in love he's having an affair with an Italian waiter whenever he hits Rome?'

'I don't know that for sure.'

'Sounds like you do to me. It sounds very much like you're back-tracking now to defend him. It doesn't matter how much you like him, Kate, but the man is what he is, even if he's nice with it.'

'I'll admit that's how it looks. But I need to talk to him first.'

There was a pause. 'I'll be glad when you're home,' Anna said. 'I don't like all this going on while you're so far away from us that we can't help and we can't look out for you.'

'You can't always look out for me,' Kate said. 'I'm thirty, not thirteen. I love that you care so much but it's time I stood on my own two feet.' At any other time, this would have been the moment to tell Anna about her plans to move to Rome, which, despite what had happened overnight, were still very much at the fore of her mind. After the Jamie incident, however, Anna would go nuts at the idea. It was lucky that Kate hadn't told her about a lot of the other things that had happened to her or Anna would be chartering a private jet to drag her back to England even if she had to lasso her and put a sack over her head to do it. 'I'll be home before you know it, and there's no need to worry about me. How's Lily?'

'She's fine. Actually she had a bit of a funny turn yesterday, but she seems herself again now.'

'What sort of turn?'

'I don't know. She just felt off and a bit odd. Weepy. Hormones probably. Not that I'd know.'

'Not that I'm likely to ever know,' Kate said.

'So this bloke you had a date with. . .'

'Alessandro.'

'Him. Have you seen him since?'

'Yes. . .' Kate said carefully, sensing a new topic for Anna to lose her cool over. 'I met his family actually. They're lovely.'

'You met his family! Is this serious then? Are you a *thing*?'

'Of course not. He's just being friendly.'

'Very friendly if you ask me. Taking you home to meet mother – that sounds serious in my book.'

'I doubt it.'

'Why?'

'I'm from England and he's from Italy. We live in different worlds. I'm not even Catholic.'

'That doesn't make it impossible. I don't think non-Catholic fraternising is totally forbidden you know.'

'I know. It's just. . . well, it doesn't matter now.'

'Kate. . .' Anna began, but then she stopped.

'What is it?'

There was another pause. 'I don't know if this will make any difference to your thinking, but I might as well tell you because you'll find out soon enough anyway. . . Matt is moving in with someone. And she's pregnant.'

Kate blinked. Was she hearing this right?

'Kate?' Anna said. 'Are you still there?'

'Yes,' Kate replied, the ground seeming to fall away from her. Perhaps it was the fact that she hadn't yet had breakfast, but she suddenly felt weak and sick.

'I didn't want to tell you until you got back but then Lily said you might see it on Facebook, even though I know you don't use it all that much, or someone else might tell you before we got a chance to and that really wouldn't be on. So I thought it was better to just get it out in the open. So you can have time to process it before you come home. And while you're still chilled and happy on holiday where things won't seem so bad, even though it might not be that chilled right now. But, you know, you have had a date. . . actually, possibly two dates. . . and you met Jamie, of course. . . So it doesn't seem as if Matt is having all the new life and you're not. . . Kate? Please say something because you're making me worried here.'

'Who is she?'

'I don't know her. . .'

'But you know who she is?'

'I think she's younger than us. . . about twenty-five.'

'That makes me feel better,' Kate said, unable to clip the sarcasm in her tone. 'I love hearing he's swapped me for a younger model that he wants to have babies with. What's her name?'

'Tamara. That's all I know.'

'She's local?'

'I'm not sure but I think Stockport – at least, somewhere that way.'

'Hmm. And how long has he been seeing her?'

'I don't know. I'm sorry, Kate. . . I wish I hadn't told you now.'

'Forget it; I was just being curious, but what difference does it make to my life who she is?' she replied in as level a voice as she could muster. 'Matt can do whatever he wants.'

'I know but the baby—'

'It doesn't matter. If we'd had kids then I'd be stuck as a single mother, which would be horrible.'

'You don't mean that,' Anna said.

She was right; Kate didn't mean it at all. She had longed for kids, just as Lily had, and Anna knew that. Matt knew it too. Had he valued their marriage so little that he'd refused to give her the one thing she felt would make her complete, and yet within six months of their separation had got another woman pregnant and moved in with her?

'Do you think he was having an affair with her?' Kate asked quietly. 'Before we split up?'

'Does it matter? The end result is the same whether he was or wasn't.'

'I don't know. Maybe not, but it feels like it does. The way I trust another man might be different. . . Oh, Anna! Was I that stupid not to see it going on under my nose?'

'Of course not! Besides, you don't know that it was going on at all. It only takes one illicit shag against a nightclub wall and hey presto – baby. . .'

Kate shook her head. 'That's not Matt's style; it must have been an affair. Either that or he's a quick worker. How far gone is she?'

'I honestly don't know. This is all from the grapevine – somebody telling somebody else and you know how that is. Please, don't let it ruin the rest of your holiday. God, I really shouldn't have told you. . .'

'It's OK,' Kate said, doing her best to sound as if she didn't care. 'You're right – it doesn't matter now. Whoever she is she's welcome to him. He was a boring bastard anyway.'

'And clearly you don't do boring any more, judging by your first holiday without him,' Anna said, sounding relieved.

'Exactly. Listen, don't worry about me. I'm going to ring off now so I can speak to Jamie and I'll let you know later how that goes.'

'OK. Love you. Please take care for the rest of this trip.'

'Love you too. And I will.'

Kate ended the call and tossed the phone onto the bed. She lay down next to it and curled into a ball, staring at the perfect sunlight pouring in through the window as the tears began to fall.

Sixteen

There hadn't been time to cry for long. Jamie called ten minutes after Kate had finished speaking to Anna.

'Hey,' he said, sounding sheepish. 'I guess you know all about what happened last night.'

'Yes,' Kate said stiffly, drying her eyes as she sat up. Since the news about Matt, she wasn't in the mood to be messed around by anyone, especially a man. 'Are you out of hospital?'

'Yeah, they just let me go. There's nothing wrong with me but a few bruises and a big bump on my head. I guess I owe you an explanation.'

'It would be nice. And forty euros for dinner too.'

'That too,' he said. 'Have you eaten breakfast yet?'

'No.'

'Want to have breakfast with me? I can tell you everything and pay you back at the same time.'

Kate shrugged, even though he couldn't see it. Why not? She had nothing better to do.

* * *

The grey skies of the previous evening had given way to the blazing sunshine Kate had been more used to seeing. The cream façades of grand buildings, wide boulevards flanked with colourful café awnings and cobbled piazzas looked bright and dazzling again, and it was incredible what it could do to lift one's mood. Despite the news about Matt, her regrets over Alessandro and her conflicted sense of worry and yet annoyance at Jamie, Kate felt more positive for the sun on her face as she stepped from her hotel and out onto the street. It was early, and she was too exhausted to make an effort, so she had slipped on a pair of linen trousers and a vest top, scraped her hair back into a bun and was barefaced other than her sun cream and a layer of tinted moisturiser over the top. She took out her phone as she walked to meet Jamie, dialling Lily's number. She owed her sister an apology, and just before she set out for work was probably the best time to catch her; if not it would have to be much later. But Kate felt as though she would be in bed by eight tonight, the week's events slowly and unexpectedly catching up with her, and Lily might not get her call again if she accidentally fell asleep before then. Not only that, but she still had to pack for her flight home the next day.

Drinking in her surroundings, she listened to the dialling tone and waited for Lily to pick up. Though she was ready to see her family again, to have some semblance of calm in her life while she regrouped and reassessed where it was going, the sight of the city she now loved caused a pang of regret that she was leaving it. Would she ever come back? The fears that Jamie had guessed at the night before were all too real for her, even if they hadn't been for him. Once she arrived home and ordinary life took hold again, would her dream of starting a new one in Italy become just that – a wonderful, magical, fantastical dream? People would talk her out of it, and she would listen, and the old, safe routine of work and nights out at the pub and days spent with her sisters would return, and rejecting all that would feel so much more terrifying. Then Lily would have her baby and Kate would feel guilty for leaving. There were a thousand more reasons why she feared her courage would fail her, and apart from the city itself, almost none to find the strength to come back alone.

'Hi, it's Lily. I can't get to the phone right now but if you leave me a message I'll get right back to you. . . Joel. . . is that it—?'

Kate smiled as she ended the call. Lily had obviously never listened to the message she recorded six months ago, and every time Kate heard it the same broken sentence was tagged onto the end, where Lily had presumably turned to her boyfriend to ask if she'd done it right and caught that bit on the recording. It was so Lily that Kate loved it and she didn't want to tell her because she'd change it. Everyone else who knew her had probably thought the same. As for now, it was easier for Kate to try her sister later than to leave a huge complicated message, and she supposed that Anna would fill her in on Kate's adventures long before Kate could anyway.

Still, it was odd for Lily not to pick up at this time of the day. She usually had her phone to hand when she was getting ready for work – often her boss phoned her in the mornings to ask her to pick something up on the way in, or to let her know that she herself would not be in the office for one reason or another and Lily would have to hold the fort. Lily had joked on many occasions since she became pregnant that she had no idea how her boss was going to cope without her when she went on maternity leave and would probably ask her to come in for presentations with the baby strapped to her front.

Ten minutes later she spotted Jamie outside his hotel. He was wearing dark glasses, and it would have looked a bit cheesy at this time of the morning had she not known the reason why. He walked a few paces to greet her.

'Let's have a look then,' Kate said.

He gave her a small smile and took off his sunglasses to reveal a bloodshot eye, the skin around it purpling nicely.

'That's going to be some shiner,' she said, sucking in her breath.

'A shiner?'

'Black eye. God, you're so American.'

He grinned ruefully. 'This is nothing. It's the bump on my head from when I went down that was the worry.'

'But you're OK now?'

'They kept me in for obs – my boss is going to go nuts when I put the medical bill on my expenses – and they let me out this morning. They said they were happy I wasn't going to go into a coma or anything and that I'd be OK to fly.'

'You don't need to worry about that for another week anyway,' Kate said briskly as they began to walk towards the entrance of his hotel, still not in the mood to offer sympathy. 'I'm sure you'll be fine by then.'

'Actually, I'm going later today.'

Kate stopped in her tracks. 'Today?'

He shrugged slightly. 'I just feel home is the best place for me right now. I need people I love around me. . .'

He needed Brad. Kate could understand that only too well. Jamie pretended nothing bothered him but being attacked on the street, far from home, would shake the most confident and fearless of travellers. She felt desperately sorry for him at that moment and even sorrier that she'd been annoyed with him. No matter the circumstances of the incident, he didn't deserve what he had suffered.

'What time's your flight?' she asked as they walked again, and he opened the doors for her.

'Two-fifteen. When we've had breakfast I'll pack and head out.'

'Your boss is OK with that?'

'She's been great. I called her from the hospital last night. She said to take as much time as I need to get back on my feet so I'm going to do just that. . . This way. . .' he added, leading her through the lobby towards a restaurant cordoned off by vast swathes of giant pot plants. She followed him to a table, but then her heart almost stopped as she saw who else was sitting at it. She stared at Jamie but he simply offered an apologetic smile. 'He came to pick me up after his shift had finished this morning and brought me back here. He was first on the scene last night, apparently. I owed you both an explanation so it seemed like a good idea to stand breakfast for both of you.'

Alessandro rose from the table.

'*Ciao*, Kate,' he said softly, his gaze searching her face. He kissed her lightly on the cheek. 'Did you sleep well?'

'Fine,' she lied, her pulse beating out of time, her legs suddenly weak. He had been up all night, and he looked tired and strained, but the power of his dark eyes to swallow her was undiminished. She couldn't deny that, despite this, she felt awkward seeing him there. How was she supposed to have that candid conversation with Jamie now? Unless Jamie was planning on spilling the beans about everything for Alessandro too?

He nodded and let go of his gentle grip on her shoulders, pulling a seat out for her to sit before retaking his own.

'I've already told Alessandro what happened,' Jamie said. 'So you don't have to worry about putting your foot in it now.'

'As I don't know all that happened myself I can hardly put my foot in it,' Kate said as Jamie sat down and poured coffee into an extra cup at the table, which he pushed across to her.

'I understand now,' Alessandro said. 'You were afraid to tell me the truth last night because you wanted to protect your friend. It was brave and honourable.'

Kate blinked at him. 'It was? But I thought you were angry with me?'

'I was angry last night because I was trying to be a police officer. I needed information. This morning, Jamie has explained and I am not angry any more.'

'Because you're not a police officer this morning?'

'I am always a police officer. But I am a man too. Life is complicated and I understand that.'

'I'm sorry for being so awkward,' she said. 'I didn't know what to do.'

'I'm sorry that you had to cover up for me,' Jamie put in, giving her hand a squeeze over the table. 'I should never have put you in that position.'

'I don't suppose you could have explained it to anyone last night anyway if you were unconscious,' Kate said, giving him an encouraging smile.

'True,' Jamie replied. 'But it's far more complicated than that.'

'You didn't want to get Pietro into trouble? You must care for him a great deal.'

Jamie frowned. 'It wasn't Pietro's fault.'

'Then. . . who did you meet last night? I thought—'

'Sure, I got the text message from his phone. I thought it was him too, and that's why I told him where I was and why I went out and left you in the restaurant. I thought he needed help, but it wasn't Pietro waiting for me when I went outside.'

'Then who was it?'

'Roberto.'

Kate's hand flew to her mouth. 'His brother?'

'He'd got hold of Pietro's phone and pretended to be him to get me to reveal where I was and lure me out.'

Jamie pushed a basket of pastries towards her, but suddenly Kate's appetite had disappeared. She shook her head. 'His brother planned to ambush you? That's awful!'

'It's pretty nasty,' Jamie conceded. 'But then I'd always known he could cause a whole heap of trouble if he felt like it. I guess he felt like it.'

'He should be in jail,' Alessandro said, reaching for the coffee pot.

'We talked about that and you gave your word. . .' Jamie began, but Alessandro held a hand up.

'I did. I understand your reasons.'

'Could someone please explain them to me because I don't,' Kate said, looking from one to the other.

Jamie took a gulp of his coffee and set the cup carefully back in the saucer. Kate heard the rattle of the china as his hand shook slightly. 'Yesterday afternoon Pietro himself did message me. He wanted to talk and I went to see him.'

'Your three o'clock meeting?' Kate said with a wry smile.

'Yes. He was at the end of the road, feeling really down again about his life, and to be honest I was kinda sick of hearing about it. So I told him that if he didn't come out to his parents, his life would be a lie. Nothing would ever change and he'd be miserable forever. I told him that even if there was no Brad, even if I'd been free to love him, I still wouldn't have done because no lover wants to be a guilty secret. I told him he would spend his life alone if he didn't finally admit to the person he truly was. He broke down, said it would kill his parents, but we talked some more and I finally got through to him; he said he was going to do it.'

'Which was a good thing. . .' Kate said.

'I thought so too,' Jamie replied.

'But I suppose it didn't exactly go well?'

'You could say that.' Jamie picked up his coffee cup, stared into it for a moment and then put it down again. Kate had never seen him look so distracted. 'His parents didn't take it well, or so Roberto told me just before his fist connected with my face. He said it was all my fault, that I'd destroyed their family and that, basically, it was my fault that Pietro was gay, that I'd done something to him. He said that Pietro was just fine until I turned up.'

Kate's mouth fell open. 'Seriously?'

Jamie shrugged. 'I've encountered homophobia before, but this was on a whole new level of ignorant.'

'You're not kidding. You don't want to press charges? Surely Roberto can't be allowed to get away with this.'

'I think Pietro's family have been through enough.'

'What about you!' Kate squeaked. 'Haven't you been through enough too? And what's to stop Roberto beating every man who gets close to Pietro to a pulp?'

'Because I will talk to him,' Alessandro said.

Kate turned to him. 'And you think that will stop him?'

'If he misbehaves, Jamie will come back and prosecute.'

'You will?' Kate asked Jamie.

'No. . .' Jamie smiled faintly. 'But he doesn't need to know that. I think Alessandro simply warning him off will be enough. At least, I hope so.'

'Does Pietro know about any of this?'

'He called me this morning,' Jamie said. 'I guess when he realised that Roberto had been missing along with his phone, he must have figured out something was wrong. He told me that his mother was in a state of shock and his father was just about ready to disown him.'

'Did he know what Roberto had done?'

'Roberto confessed when he confronted him.'

'What about his parents? Do they know what Roberto has done? Whatever their feelings about Pietro they surely can't condone that?'

'I honestly don't know the answer to that,' Jamie said. 'I guess neither of the boys will want to share that dirty little secret with their beloved Mamma and Papa.'

'Do you think they'll work it out? The family, I mean? Do you think they can get back on track, fix their relationships?'

Jamie nodded. 'I think when Alessandro visits, they'll realise just how serious this all is and that they really need to address it. His parents are good people and they love their sons. I hope that means they'll be able to overcome their disappointment and accept Pietro for who he is. My own folks were pretty shocked when I came out, and it was tough for a while, but they're fine now.'

Kate sipped at her coffee before turning to Alessandro. 'When will you go to see them?'

'Soon. Before I go home.'

'I'll come with you.'

'There is no need—'

'I think it would help. A woman would be less threatening and I could talk to his mother.'

'You don't speak Italian,' Alessandro reminded her.

'Oh. . .' Kate said.

He gave her a warm smile, the first sign of the Alessandro she had got to know over the last few days that she'd seen that morning. 'I judged you badly and for that I am sorry. You are good and kind and I will not forget that.'

Kate blushed. 'Oh, I don't know about that. I'm doing a rubbish job of trying to help.'

'But you are trying to help,' Jamie said. 'And that's what counts.'

'If you wish to come then please do,' Alessandro said. 'But it may be better to stay with your friend until he goes home. I will come back to see you both after I have spoken to Pietro's family and tell you what happened there.'

Kate glanced at Jamie. He looked like someone who needed a friend right now. 'OK,' she said. 'But you'll definitely come back?'

'Of course.'

'And then maybe we should let you get to your bed,' Jamie said with a smile that spoke to Kate of his relief and faith in Alessandro to sort the whole mess out. It was strange, because although she barely knew him, Kate had faith that he would too. She was already beginning to see that he was a man of his word, and if he said he would do something he would move heaven and earth to do it.

'I *am* getting hungry,' Kate said. 'And those pastries do look good. Maybe it wouldn't be such a hardship to stay for a while and polish the rest of the breakfast off.'

Jamie gave her a broad smile. 'I was hoping you'd say that. I'd appreciate your company.'

Alessandro drained his cup. '*Va bene*. Then I will go now.'

* * *

Breakfast at Jamie's hotel was good – better than the breakfasts Kate had been taking at her own hotel. She supposed when you travelled to Rome as much as Jamie did then you got to know the best places to stay. She wondered vaguely, as she demolished her third pastry and washed it down with a second cup of excellent coffee, whether one day she'd be a seasoned almost Roman, just like him. It seemed like such an impossible idea – at least it was one that she would have laughed at a year, even six months ago – but it was within her grasp now, if she could be brave enough to take the chance.

'It's funny,' she said as Jamie pushed his plate away and declared he'd finished, 'I'll miss you when you go back home.'

'I'll miss you too. I've loved getting to know you these past few days and you've been such a support. But you'll have Alessandro. . .'

Kate gave him a rueful smile. 'Who knows? I can't be sure of where I stand with him.'

'You're going then? Do you think you'll do what you said yesterday?'

'Move here?' She shrugged. 'Things felt different yesterday. . . I don't honestly know. My head is in a whirl over it all. Maybe it was just silly dreaming.'

'It sounded like more than dreaming to me. And I think Alessandro is crazy about you, if that helps make up your mind.'

'It's funny, because I don't see that. His sister said he was fond of me. . . fond? What the hell does that mean?'

'That he's being cautious where his feelings are concerned and he doesn't want to tell anyone the truth?'

'Unlike me – bull in a china shop?'

'What does that even mean?'

Kate laughed. 'I don't know. It's another of those British things. But I think we need a happy medium somewhere.'

'What the hell is a happy medium?'

'You don't know much, do you?' Kate giggled. 'It means Alessandro and I need to meet somewhere in the middle. If we could both take a healthy and calm approach it might be perfect.'

'I don't think love is often found in happy mediums.'

'I'm sure there's some sensible accountant sitting on Tinder that would take me on.'

'I'd marry you myself before I saw that happen. You deserve way better than that. You deserve adventure and excitement and romance. I see the way Alessandro looks at you – he could be the man to give you all that and more.'

'Everyone seems to see that but me. I don't know why that is.'

'Because you're full of doubts and you're scared after the way things ended with Matt. It's totally understandable for you to be like that but you shouldn't be. A bit of you must think you can make Rome work for you? Why don't you try it out for six months and see how you feel after that? I know plenty of people who could help you set up with some work and I could talk to them. You can start small, just like you said, work from your apartment until you start making enough money to hire people and a workspace.'

'Ah, I don't know. I can't help but feel it was a silly, impulsive daydream – pie in the sky. Just like my fashion business idea. Who would want to buy my clothes when they have Gucci and Prada and all those other amazing shops here?'

'Plenty of people hate those labels and plenty more can't afford them. There's always a place for niche stuff. I think you'd be crazy not to try it. What have you got to lose?'

'Apart from my job, my house, my savings, the goodwill of my sisters and my sanity? Nothing,' Kate laughed. 'Put it that way and it's a no-brainer.'

Jamie grinned. 'That's the spirit. It's what America was built on and look how that turned out.'

She smiled in return but then it faded. 'Are you really OK? What will you do now?'

'Me? Sure I'm OK. I'll go home, get some TLC from Brad and in a few days I'll have forgotten all about the assault. It will never put me off coming to my favourite city in the world, if that's what you mean, so when you live here I'll be visiting all the time.'

Kate didn't think for a minute that he was telling the truth about being OK, but she let it slide. If he wanted to believe it, then such a positive outlook was half the battle. He wasn't OK now, but he would be in time, she was sure.

'And if I live here you'll always be welcome. But if I end up staying in England, you'll come to see me there too?'

He furrowed his brow and scrunched his nose. 'England. . . hmm. . . remind me where that is again. . .'

'Cheeky!' She smiled. 'We're not that tiny and insignificant.'

'You're like the size of Central Park or something, aren't you?'

'Central Park is bloody massive though, isn't it?'

'True. Probably a lot more dangerous to cross too.'

'You've obviously never been to Manchester on New Year's Eve,' Kate said darkly and Jamie laughed.

'Of course I'll come to England. I want to meet these amazing sisters I keep hearing about.'

'I want you to meet them too. I think you'll get on famously.'

'And you have to take me to see Manchester United.'

Kate raised her eyebrows. 'Man United? You want to see a match or the grounds?'

'I don't know. Any of it.'

'I didn't have you down as a soccer fan.'

'I'm a David Beckham fan. . . big difference.'

Kate giggled. 'And I bet it's not about his free kicks, is it?'

'What's a free kick?'

'Oh my God!' Kate's giggles rang around the restaurant, causing a waiter and several other patrons to stare. 'You know David Beckham doesn't actually live in Manchester? And he doesn't play for United any more?'

'I know, but some of his sweat might be in the walls, and that's close enough for me. . .'

'Jamie, you are a tart!' Kate snorted. 'Yes, I'll take you to Old Trafford and I'll even get you a souvenir shirt. How about that?'

'Deal.'

* * *

It was just as Jamie was giving up on Alessandro returning, and had announced to Kate that if he didn't come back in the next ten minutes he would have to go and pack for his flight, that Alessandro strode into the restaurant and made his way to their table. He looked calm and determined, and Kate wondered at his stamina – he'd been working all night and was still racing back and forth way after his shift had ended. She'd have been barely able to stay on her feet, let alone play peace envoy in a warring family. He pulled out a seat at their table and dropped into it. Jamie signalled to a watching waiter that they needed more coffee as Alessandro began to speak.

'All is well,' he said. 'I have spoken to Pietro's mother and father. They did not know about Roberto's actions last night; Roberto had not told them and Pietro has been too afraid to go home since he told them his secret.'

'So where has he been all night?' Jamie asked anxiously.

'At a friend's apartment. His mother phoned him while I was there and told him to come home. She will talk to him, but I think they will make friends.'

'What about, Luigi. . . Pietro's dad?' Kate asked. 'What did he have to say?'

'He is sorry for Roberto's actions and he is ashamed of his oldest son,' Alessandro said, accepting the new coffee pot from the waiter with a nod. 'He wanted me to tell Jamie that. He would like to make amends.'

'What about Pietro?' Jamie asked, clearly not enthralled by the idea of Pietro's father making amends and what that might entail. 'Shouldn't he be his number one priority?'

'We must be patient. It is not easy for him to accept this news and he will take a long time to get used to it. He feels he now has two sons to bring him shame. He understands that it was not your doing and he will have to talk to Pietro when he comes home. I do not know what they will say to each other, but they understand that if word of any more trouble comes to me I will visit again as a police officer and things will be bad for them. He has worry for Pietro and for Roberto now.'

'I think a good smack in the face is what Roberto needs,' Kate said. 'So that's one sorted. As far as Pietro is concerned a hug and a bit of acceptance would go a long way to solving that situation too.'

'It's not that easy for some people,' Jamie said. 'And maybe Roberto needs a little bit of patient tolerance too. He's a product of his upbringing, and if his family have always had such traditional values and have always voiced their opposition to homosexuality, then it's only natural Roberto would freak out. What he sees is a challenge to the order of their little world, and the breakdown of his family. I can totally understand why he would lash out against that, and I don't think more violence is the answer.'

Kate gave a wondering smile. 'You're amazing. How many other people would see it like that when they'd been at the receiving end of that lashing out?'

'Perhaps Jamie is right, however,' Alessandro said. 'They need time. Pietro will not work in his father's restaurant for a few days while he decides what he is going to do next, and Roberto will take his work as punishment for his insult of Jamie. I feel happy that they will resolve things now in the family. It may not be perfect, but it will be peaceful.'

'I hope so,' Kate said. She turned to Jamie. 'But from now on promise me you'll try to stay out of trouble. You've given me more than enough headaches this week.'

'Nope, I can't do that,' Jamie said. 'Trouble is in my blood so I might promise it but I'd break the promise no matter how hard I tried not to. Best not to make the promise at all so nobody is disappointed.'

Kate rolled her eyes. 'At least next time don't keep everyone in the dark and take someone with you when you get invited out to a dodgy alleyway by an angry brother.'

Jamie laughed. 'Sure will. I can do that much, but you'd better bring your boxing gloves.' He turned to Alessandro. 'I can't thank you enough for all you've done, except to extend the invitation I've already made to Kate that you should absolutely come and stay with Brad and I next time you're in New York.'

Alessandro inclined his head. 'That is very kind. I will do that.'

'You never know,' Jamie added, an impish look now creeping over his face, 'you might want to come over together. . .'

Alessandro smiled at Kate and her cheeks burned crimson again. The old feelings were back to plague her, and she wished that she could have heard Lucetta say something other than he was fond of her. Fond didn't even begin to cover the emotions engulfing her right now.

'I'm glad that Pietro is going to be OK,' Jamie added. 'I guess I really need to get packed now for my flight home. What are you guys going to do for the rest of your day?'

'I still haven't seen the Trevi Fountain – at least not properly yet,' Kate said. 'I suppose I might do that as it'll probably be my last opportunity.' She looked hopefully at Alessandro.

'Would you like me to accompany you?' he asked.

Kate glanced at Jamie, and she caught the hint of a smile. He gave her a tiny nod.

'You must be exhausted,' Kate said, turning back to Alessandro, her heart pounding, hoping that her flimsy platitude would be ignored and that he would insist on taking her out. It might not end the way she wanted it to, but despite all that she had said before, she wasn't ready to let him go. 'I bet you're heading home to bed.'

'I have to work this evening,' he said. 'But I am not tired yet.'

Seventeen

When she was a little girl her mother used to warn Kate about the old cellar of their house. She'd tell her it was unsafe and cold and dark, that she shouldn't go poking around down there because there were all kinds of dangerous things stored there. The warnings only served to inflame her curiosity, and one day when nobody was looking she unlocked the old door and went in. It was dark, and the steps were slippery with years of damp and mould, and Kate fell down them and broke her wrist.

Her mother's warning was very much like the sorts of warnings her brain was issuing about Alessandro right now, warnings that she was cheerfully ignoring as she revelled in what she had forbidden herself only a few hours ago. This time the risks included a broken heart rather than a broken wrist, but she was willing to take them. She had leapt at his offer to accompany her to the Trevi Fountain, and the only misgiving she was allowing herself to acknowledge was the fact that she wasn't exactly looking her best and if she'd had the time she would have gone back to her own hotel to change first. She was also aware that Alessandro, despite his assurances to the contrary, must be getting tired, and that he had to work again later, and she didn't want to keep him up all day. But guilt wasn't going to put her off – she was greedy for his company, and she wanted to spend as much time with him as she could get.

He had reached for her hand as they stood and gazed over the crystal water of the fountain and the imposing colonnaded backdrop, adorned with sculptures of gleaming travertine stone that dominated the skyline. It felt like a theatre, the way a long seat curved around the stage of the sweeping pool, already filled with tourists rapt at the view. She left her hand clasped in his as the sun warmed their necks, enjoyed the thrill of the contact as he shared his knowledge of the fountain, explaining the figures of the god of the waters, the seahorses, about how the cascading water arrived from an ancient Roman aqueduct, and how the fountain had just been renovated so that it was now even greater than the wonder it had once been. He was so knowledgeable and so obviously bursting with pride, so patient and willing to answer all her questions, she could have listened all day. Just the sound of his voice gave her chills, the delectable accent and idiosyncrasies of his pronunciations when he spoke English, the slipping between that and his perfect native Italian, and Kate didn't think she had ever been so entranced by a man before. Perhaps this could all be hers if she would only take the leap. Now more than ever before she yearned to stay, if only to be near him, to be able to see him every day. But it was still an impossible dream, wasn't it? Though his actions now whispered feelings stronger than fondness, she couldn't be certain, not until he said it. And perhaps he never would. Romance like this happened, but not to people like her.

'What are you thinking about?' He looked down at her, noting a brief, pensive silence as she watched the sparkling waters race over the stones. 'You are tired? Hot? Would you like to sit down?'

'I should imagine you're the one who's tired,' Kate said. 'You've been up all night.'

He waved away the comment. 'I can sleep later, an hour or two will be enough.'

'I'll remind you of that when you're on duty at midnight,' she smiled. It was probably true, and anyone nicer than her would insist that he went home to get some rest, but she didn't feel nice right now. 'I was just thinking how beautiful everything is here and how dull home will seem tomorrow. Do you ever get so used to Rome that it all looks very ordinary?'

'How could I think this looks ordinary?' He swept a hand towards the magnificent structure in front of them. 'I love my city; it is my heart.'

'That's what I thought,' she said quietly. 'If you lived somewhere like this you'd never want to leave it, would you?'

'Where else would I live that would make me feel so happy?' He turned to her. 'You are sad to leave tomorrow?'

She nodded.

'I am sad too,' he said. He pulled her around by the shoulders to face him squarely and took both her hands. 'Kate. . . this is difficult for me to say but I must tell you what is in my heart. Like Pietro, I must not lie to myself any longer.'

There was a pause, and Kate held her breath as he continued.

'I feel things for you,' he said.

She stared at him, not knowing how to respond and hungry to hear more, to hear the words she longed to hear and yet dreaded at the same time, because finally hearing it from him would make her soar today but her departure tomorrow all the more painful.

'I am confused,' he continued. 'But I know one thing that is clear – I do not want you to leave Rome tomorrow. I know you must but I do not want it.'

Kate's eyes filled with tears. He couldn't say those three little words, just as she couldn't say them either. As soon as they were out things would shift and change, and every action would have seismic implications, and it was a terrifying thought. She wanted to come back, but what if she didn't or couldn't? What then? Love didn't deserve to be treated that way, abandoned and left to die. And yet there were so many barriers, so much else to think and worry about that would stand in the way of it. She took a deep breath and stepped into the void. Only time would tell if she would fly or fall, but the decision was made.

'There's so much to do at home before I can think about anything else,' she began.

He gently thumbed away a tear. 'I understand,' he said.

'No. . .' She shook her head. 'You don't. I've been thinking a lot about my future, and I'm going to try to come back to Rome.'

'When?' His face lit up. 'If I know when I will try to take leave and we will be together all the time you are here!'

Kate smiled, sniffing away her tears. 'That'll be a lot of leave then. Because I want to move here.'

He frowned.

'I want to live here,' she clarified. 'In Rome. When I come back again it'll be for good.'

He broke into a grin and pulled her into a kiss that melted her in his arms. 'I am so happy,' he whispered. '*Ti amo troppo.*'

There was some Italian that Kate didn't need interpreting. Her heart soared at his declaration as he kissed her again.

'This is true, a promise?' he asked as their lips parted. 'You will come back?'

'I'll do my very best,' Kate said, though already reality and uncertainty were setting in. He rifled in his pocket and produced a coin.

'We must make a wish in the fountain,' he said, leading her through the crowds to get closer to the waters. They stopped at the lip of the fountain's basin. 'We turn our backs, like so. . .' He turned away from the water and she copied him before he handed her the coin. 'You throw it behind you, and if it lands in the water then you will return to Rome.'

'I would think it's pretty hard to miss,' Kate laughed, but then her laughter died as she saw the earnest look on his face.

'It will make me trust your promise,' he said. 'If you do this I can be sure you will always come back.'

He wanted reassurance, and after losing someone dear once before, she understood how desperately he must need it. She closed her eyes, uttered the prayer under her breath, and tossed the coin over her shoulder. The crowds were too noisy to hear the splash above them, but she opened her eyes and saw that he was smiling.

'*Va bene.* I am happy now.'

'Me too,' Kate said.

At that moment her phone buzzed in her bag. For a second she considered ignoring it, but then she wondered if it might be Lily, who had been on her mind in one way or another all day, so she pulled it out and checked.

'Jamie.' She smiled up at Alessandro's questioning look.

Have you told him yet?

Kate locked the phone and dropped it back into her bag. There would be time to talk to Jamie later, and when she filled him in he would understand that right now it was all about Alessandro. He was probably at the airport, bored and wanting to talk to someone, but it would have to be one of the other many friends he had. She reached for Alessandro's hand.

'I think we've seen the fountain.'

'You do not like it?'

'I love it. I just think we've seen it.'

'You would like to see something else?'

'Not really.'

He frowned. 'You would like to go back to your hotel?'

'Yes.'

'Oh. . .' His expression was one of disappointment. She smiled. Perhaps she had a cure for that.

'Are you tired yet?' she asked.

'No,' he said.

'Good. I was hoping you'd say that.'

* * *

She'd never understood how functional the years of sex with Matt had been until Alessandro made love to her that afternoon. It wasn't even that she'd only ever been with one man, but she knew instinctively from the way he touched her that he could do things few other men could or would. It was about her pleasure and her desires, and only when he was happy that she was floating on a cloud of ecstasy, unable to take any more, did he allow himself his own. There was no fear, no anxiety, no hang-ups, only trust and contentment as she dozed naked in his arms in the afterglow, the city breeze whispering over their bodies as if casting an enchantment of love as it blew in through the open window. There was no going back; she was completely and irretrievably lost to this man no matter what else happened from now on.

* * *

From the length of the shadows as she opened her eyes, it was early evening. Alessandro was dressing.

'You're going?' she asked in a groggy voice.

'I must,' he said. 'It is late and I must be on duty in one hour.'

Kate shot up. 'We've been asleep that long?'

'Yes.' He grinned. 'You were very tired.'

'I'm not surprised,' Kate said with a sly, flirty look, the instant tingle in her loins making her wish she could pull him back into bed and do it all again. 'You should be tired too.'

'Not me,' he said, his grin widening. 'I am like a horse.'

Kate laughed. 'My Italian Stallion. Now I can't get that image out of my head!'

He pulled on his shoes before grabbing a notebook from the bed-side cabinet, where he wrote a number and gave the page to her. 'You will need this. My phone number.'

Kate looked at it before tearing off a blank section at the bottom of the page and writing hers.

'And you'll need this. I don't know why I didn't give it to you before, but. . .'

'*Va bene*. It does not matter.' He took a seat next to her on the bed and cupped her face in his hands, kissing her gently. 'I will not see you again before your flight?'

Kate shook her head, the awful reality of their imminent parting sapping the happiness from the air around them until the room felt a little colder and a little greyer than it had done a moment before.

'You must hurry back to me,' he said. 'I will not be happy until then.'

'I will.'

There was time for one more passionate kiss, whispered promises, and then he was gone.

Eighteen

Lily still wasn't answering her phone. It was strange and very worrying. Kate tried once Alessandro had gone, and then again after dinner, and once more as she packed for what she hoped would be a return flight. She sent a brief text expressing her now mounting concern and a wish for Lily to get back to her as soon as she could, and the only other thing she could do was call Anna.

'Have you heard from Lily today?' Kate sat on her bed, her gaze drawn to the filled suitcases now standing in the corner of the room. 'I tried her this morning and a few times since but there's no reply.'

'Have you tried Joel?'

'I sent him a text but he hasn't replied either. He is a bit crap at checking his phone, though.'

'He is but it's unlike Lily. I can try her if you like.'

'I doubt you'll get any further than me but you never know. Will you let me know if you hear back?'

'She's probably just working late on some big project or other. I wouldn't worry too much.'

Kate was silent for a moment. Perhaps she was worrying too much. 'I suppose it's being so far away that makes me more worried. . . I feel a bit helpless to do anything if something was actually wrong, you know?'

'Well, you'll be home tomorrow so if there's a state of national emergency declared you'll be right on hand to sort it out, won't you?'

Kate smiled.

'I can't wait to see you,' Anna added. 'Do you want me to come to the airport to pick you up?'

'That would be brilliant; thanks.'

There was another silence. Kate could break her news about Alessandro now, and her decision to relocate, and she desperately wanted to. She felt she could burst with it, and she hated keeping secrets from her sisters, especially one this big. But was it fair to do it over the phone? And was it the time when there were other things to think about, like where Lily was and why she hadn't replied to her messages?

Kate chewed her lip, and as Anna spoke again she knew the moment had passed. It would have to wait until she got home, but perhaps that was for the best.

'Are you all packed? I bet you're ready for a cup of English tea, aren't you? That's what I miss most when I'm abroad, a good, proper cup of English tea.'

'Sounds lovely,' Kate replied absently.

'Are you OK?'

'Yes. Of course. . .' Kate shook herself. 'I was just thinking about things I have to do when I get back.'

'Only. . . I wondered if you were still upset about Matt. . .'

'Matt?'

'You know. . . the baby business. I wondered. . . well, I didn't want it to ruin your holiday and I was worried that it might have done. I've been thinking all day that I shouldn't have told you until you got back and it was a stupid thing to do and—'

'It's fine. She's welcome to him and I couldn't care less if they have ten babies.'

'Really?' Anna's tone was one of disbelief and Kate could understand why. But the landscape of her future had changed beyond recognition since Anna had broken that news to Kate, and her words now were heartfelt. Matt was in her past, and she had no desire to see him feature in what was to come.

'Absolutely. He's nothing to me now. I don't wish him ill but I don't particularly care what he does either.'

'Wow. . . what's brought this on?'

'I've moved on. It's not that strange; people do it all the time.'

'I know, I just thought. . . never mind. I'm glad you're putting it all behind you now. Text me when you get on your plane tomorrow so I'll know when to be at the airport.'

'Thanks, I will. And don't forget to let me know if you hear from Lily.'

'OK. But I'm sure she'll be fine. See you tomorrow. Love you.'

'Love you too.'

Kate tossed the phone onto the bed beside her and stared at the suitcases packed and waiting. If someone had predicted for her the week she would have she would have laughed in their face. But she was leaving the eternal city a different person, for better or for worse.

She got up and went over to the window, throwing it wide and leaning over the narrow balcony to get a better view of the streets below. They were still warm and teeming with people, despite the hour, still vibrant and exciting and full of possibilities. Somewhere out there Alessandro walked his beat, keeping those same streets – the ones he loved so dearly – safe. How was it possible that such a man could love her too? He was everything she could have dreamed of but never dared hope for, and yet he had promised himself to her, told her he would wait however long it took for her to get back. She was the luckiest woman alive, so why did she feel like crying? What she wanted to do was run and find him right now, just to see his face once more before she left, even if he was working and she couldn't talk to him. It was late, and everyone who cared for her would be unhappy at the idea of her wandering the streets to look for him, but none of them were here. Before she could think about it long enough to talk herself out of it, she had grabbed her phone and keys and was heading for the door.

Almost as if he was psychic, her phone bleeped the arrival of a message from Jamie. He'd just landed at JFK airport and was waiting for his luggage at the carousel. Kate smiled as she read it.

You never told me – did you get your man?
Yes. He's all mine.
Did you seal the deal?
Kate's smile grew. *My secret*, she replied.
You go, girl. I never thanked you properly for being an awesome friend.
No need to thank me, it was my pleasure. I loved having you show me around Rome. Thanks for taking good care of me.
Not that good! You owe me a visit in New York. Don't forget about me.
As if I could!
Damn straight! Have a safe trip home tomorrow. X

Kate dropped the phone back into her bag. Not only had she fallen in love with a man and a city, she had fallen in love with a brand new best friend. And who knew what other possibilities life held, because right now it felt like everything was out there, just waiting for her. The world felt fresh, like the first page of a new book, and it was a wonderful thing. She'd emerged from the shadow of Matt's betrayal and rejection and she'd become stronger, more dazzling, ready for anything. She was capable of so much more than she ever thought possible. And she couldn't wait to see what life threw at her next.

* * *

Her walk took her to the Spanish Steps, and although she saw a couple of pairs of policemen, she didn't see Alessandro. Making her way to the Piazza Navona she scoured the streets, but there was no sign of him there either. She'd never actually asked him where he would be tonight – perhaps he was in a brand-new area, or even working at the station.

Another half hour and she had to admit defeat. She could spend all night looking and never find him. He was working too, and despite her temptation to phone him now that she had finally obtained his number, it probably wasn't a good idea. Along with all that, she had a flight to catch in the morning, so it was probably time to make her way back to bed. A slow walk back took her past the Trattoria da Luigi. She glanced through the wide windows, the warm interior of the restaurant almost deserted apart from a couple kissing at an intimate corner table, and a man who looked so startlingly like an older version of Pietro that it could only be Luigi himself manning the bar. She was struck by a sudden wild urge to go in and talk to him, wanting to know for herself that everything had worked out OK for the family. The old Kate would have hurried back to her hotel, ignoring such silly impulses. But this wasn't the old Kate. She pushed open the restaurant doors and went in.

'*Buonasera*,' he said, looking up from the till.

'Hello.'

'A table?'

'No, thank you. . . a drink might be nice. Do you have limoncello?'

He nodded and reached for a glass. Clearly he didn't recognise her from the evening she'd been there with Jamie, despite the unusual circumstances of her departure.

'I wondered if Pietro was here tonight. . .' she asked, and he stopped dead, holding the bottle over the glass as he stared at her.

'My son?'

'Yes. I. . .' Kate was suddenly aware that perhaps she shouldn't be poking her nose in after all, but she was here now and she had already raked the mess up. She felt herself colour as she quickly changed tack. 'I don't suppose you remember me but I dined here earlier in the week. I met Pietro. . . he was very nice. I just wondered if he was here tonight. Just to say hello.'

Luigi looked her up and down as he continued to pour the liqueur. 'You are wasting your time,' he said gruffly. 'He would not be interested.'

Oh shit! Now it looked as though she was trying to cop off with him! Shit, shit! Could she have given a worse impression? This wasn't how it was supposed to go at all! 'I'm not trying to get a date or anything,' she said, her face burning even redder. 'I just wanted to thank him, for good service and being friendly. It was my first night in Rome. That's all. It doesn't matter.'

Luigi looked her up and down again. 'He is not working tonight. I will tell him.'

If he meant that, then at least he was in contact with Pietro, which had to be good. Kate had to satisfy herself with knowing at least that much; it looked as though it was all she was going to get out of Luigi and, in the absence of other family members in the restaurant, all she was going to get from anyone. She paid for her drink, downed it quickly, and left.

So much for sticking your nose in, she thought as she emerged back on the lamp-lit street to return to her hotel. She'd barely gone ten steps when her phone rang. Immediately, she thought of Jamie, bored again as he waited for a cab or something. Better not to tell him about her embarrassing episode at the trattoria. But when she pulled the phone from the depths of her bag, it wasn't Jamie but Anna.

'Hey. . . what's up?'

'Kate, it's me. . . I managed to get hold of Joel. He's been at the hospital with Lily all day and he's only just managed to get free. Oh, Kate, it's bad news. . . she's lost the baby!'

Nineteen

Kate stared at the phone.

'Did you hear me?' Anna asked.

'Yes. Oh God, poor Lily. What happened?'

'The details are a bit sketchy – Joel's in bits and he's not making much sense. From what I can gather she started to bleed this morning. She stayed in bed, hoped it would go away, but it didn't and the midwife told her to go straight to hospital. She'd already miscarried when she got there.'

'I'll come straight back, see if I can get a plane tonight—' Kate began but Anna stopped her.

'Don't be daft. What can you do? It'll cost you a fortune and the damage is done now. Stick to your original flight – Lily wouldn't want you to go to all that trouble on her account.'

'She needs me there!'

'Mum is on her way down from Scotland and I'm on my way over to the hospital now so she's got plenty of support and probably more than she wants. There's honestly no point and she'll be back at home tomorrow; it will really hit home then what's happened and she'll probably need you around a lot more than she does right now.'

Kate chewed her lip. 'OK,' she said. 'But you stay with her and I'll make my own way back from the airport. I'll be straight over as soon as I'm home.'

* * *

Ordinarily, Kate would have dumped her suitcases in the hallway and gone straight for the kettle on arriving home. But this time she had dumped her suitcases in the hallway and hopped straight into her car for Lily's house. The skies were leaden, a fine drizzle peppering the windscreen as she drove through suburbs that looked grubby and un-inspired against the stunning architecture of the city she had just come from. Everything was so different and everything seemed duller – the atmosphere as soon as she stepped off the plane; the attitude of the cab-bie taking her home, the ordered and steady pace of the traffic that was a world away from the exuberant driving of the Italians, the chill of the streets where she lived, the angular, functional houses lacking in beauty or charm, the looks of boredom on the faces of her neighbours as they greeted her in a way that suggested they didn't really care at all whether she was well or not. Perhaps it was the circumstances of her return – Lily in the darkest hour of her life and Kate herself leaving behind the man who might become the love of hers just when she'd found him, and, with him on duty until after her flight, not even time for a proper goodbye – but there were few more depressing prospects than this.

Her mood wasn't any easier or more positive when she pulled up outside the house Lily shared with her boyfriend, Joel, who answered the door looking ten years older than his twenty-eight, his usually playful blue eyes ringed by dark shadows, matched by the uncharac-teristic shadow of black stubble around his chin.

Kate stared at him as she stood on the doorstep. What did anyone even say in a situation like this? There were no words that would make it better, nothing that wouldn't sound trite and hollow and meaningless. But his face told her everything she needed to know and she didn't need the words; a quick, dull greeting was followed by a flat invitation in. All she could do was follow him into a house that felt as if every brick had absorbed the mood of its occupants so that it was bleak and unwelcoming, and nothing like the happy place it normally was.

Lily was lying on the sofa clutching a pillow to her chest, duvet tangled around her feet. Her hair was lank around a chalk-white complexion and puffy red eyes. Anna sat close by, looking tense, and their mother, newly arrived from Scotland, was weeping quietly on the opposite chair. On Kate's arrival, her mum leapt up and threw her arms around her.

'Oh, Kate! What a mess, what a terrible mess. . .' she cried.

Lily forced the weakest smile as Kate pulled away, kissed her mum on the cheek, and then turned to her youngest sister.

'How are you feeling?' Kate asked.

'Like you'd expect,' Lily replied. 'How was your flight back?'

'Like you'd expect.' Kate forced a smile of her own. She could tell that Lily was barely holding it together and the thing that would help most was that everyone else held it together for her. It didn't look as if much of that had gone on, with their mum still crying and Joel looking as though his world had come to an end as he stood silently at the living-room doorway with his hands dug in his pockets, watching them with a blank, empty expression. The only person who looked calm and determined was Anna, but Anna had always been the rock of the family, even as a youngster.

Kate bent to kiss Lily. 'I don't know what to say. I'm so sorry.'

'There's nothing to say.' Lily's eyes filled with tears. 'It wasn't meant to be, that's all.'

'That doesn't make it any easier to bear, though.'

'No. But nothing will make it easier. All we can do is grieve and look to the future.'

'I'm sorry I wasn't here sooner.'

'Why are you sorry for that? You were in Rome, and nobody was to know this was coming. I wouldn't have called you back and cut your holiday short for anything.'

'I know. But I would have wanted to be here if I could.'

Lily squeezed her hand, like she was the one having to give comfort and not the other way around. 'You're here now and so it's OK. I had Joel and Anna and that was enough of us to be going on with.'

'Are you OK in yourself?' Kate asked. 'I mean. . . It hasn't damaged you in any way?'

'Oh, the doctors sorted me out and I'm fine. It wasn't pleasant but these things never are.'

'So what now?'

'They asked if we wanted to have a funeral and we said yes. We wanted to name the baby too. We called her Stella, because she's going to be a star now. So at least there's going to be a grave with a name we can visit. After that. . . I can't even think that far ahead.'

'You look exhausted.'

'I am. But I'll be OK in a couple of days. I've got sleeping tablets so I can get some rest later. I bet you're tired too.'

Kate shrugged. 'I'll survive.'

'So Rome was beautiful? And you had a good time?'

Kate smiled thinly. It was just like Lily to make everything about someone else, not to wallow in self-pity but to put those around her first. And at the back of her mind Kate also realised that she had a lot to tell her family about her time in Rome, and some news that they may not like to hear, but this wasn't the time. Right now it didn't feel as if it would ever be the time. How did she break this to her sisters, who needed her now more than ever? They'd been there all through her break-up with Matt, so how could she abandon them now? She would have to make a call to Alessandro that she was dreading, to explain her situation, that she now didn't know when she could return, and hope he understood. 'Rome was great,' she said.

'You've actually got a tan,' Lily said. 'I don't think I've ever seen any of us gingers with a tan before.'

'I hadn't really noticed. I was out a lot, but it wasn't so hot I got burnt.'

Anna stood up. 'I'll make some tea,' she announced. 'I think we could all do with one.'

'Want me to help?' Kate asked, straightening up. Anna nodded.

'That would be good.'

Kate followed her to the kitchen, where Anna gently closed the door behind them.

'How is she really holding up?' Kate asked.

'I'm not sure the full enormity of it has hit home yet,' Anna said, filling the kettle from the tap. 'She's distraught, obviously, but I think she's still in shock a bit as well. As for Joel, I don't think he knows what to do with himself. These things are all a bit much for blokes, aren't they?'

'Most of them, yes.'

'Just to make things even more complicated for your arrival home, I had a visit from Matt last night.'

Kate turned to her sister and raised her eyebrows in a silent question as she reached for some mugs from a cupboard.

'He'd been round to the house and you weren't there.'

'Does he expect me to be holed up like a hermit all the time now that he's gone?'

'He said he'd been round a few times last week and you weren't there, so he wanted to know where you were. I hope you don't mind that I told him you were in Rome. I wanted to see the look on his face.'

Kate smiled faintly. 'And was it worth it?'

'I think you could have blown him over. I told him he didn't need to worry about you and he didn't need to keep checking up because you were totally over him and having the time of your life now you were divorced.'

'I bet he loved hearing that.'

'Serves him right.'

'I don't wish him any ill. I just don't want to think about him any more. But actually I do need to talk to him at some point, because I really need to get this house sale sorted sooner rather than later.'

Anna turned to her. 'I thought you weren't in any hurry to leave the house? I thought you loved living there and didn't want to move out?'

'I've had a lot of time to think in Rome and I've concluded that the only way I'm going to move on is to throw out all the reminders of my old life. The sooner the house is gone the sooner I can start afresh somewhere else. Matt has made his choices and he needs to accept the responsibilities that come with them. I want him out of my life and that won't happen if I'm tied to him emotionally, financially or any other way.'

Anna nodded. 'Good for you. I knew you'd come through this eventually. You're stronger than you think you are.'

'Maybe. But we have another worry now – Lily. She's going to need all the support we can give her over the next few months, and my problems pale in comparison to what she's going through.'

'I don't know. I suppose in a way you were mourning. The loss of a life, of a future you thought you were going to have. It must have been hard.'

It had been hard, but the truth for Kate was she now had the opportunity of a future that was like a blazing sun compared to the candle Matt had been offering. She was almost there, but Lily had a long way to go before her own situation would seem positive again.

'It's all water under the bridge now,' Kate said briskly as she dropped teabags into a pot. 'How do you think Mum seems to be coping with the news? Has it helped Lily, her being here?'

'She's been about as useful as that teapot if it was made from chocolate,' Anna smiled. 'She never was very good in a crisis and everyone is conscious of her own unpredictable mental state. In some ways I wish she hadn't come, because as well as looking after Lily, I feel as if I have to watch Mum like a hawk in case this tips her over the edge again like Dad's death did. But I think Lily is just happy to have her around. After all, don't we all just want our mummies in the end, no matter how old we are?'

'Probably,' Kate said and smiled, thinking about how Alessandro clearly adored his own mother. 'Right. . .' she exclaimed, dusting off her hands, 'we should get this tea brewed. I can't tell you how desperate I am for a cuppa right now, and if we don't go back through soon Lily will send out a search party.'

'Good old tea, eh?' Anna said ruefully. 'Sorts out everything, doesn't it?'

Twenty

Nothing brought you down to earth with a bump like a morning of cleaning, but it was needed after the house had been empty for a week, and Kate had to get on with it. She had already booked an estate agent to come and value the place too, and it was hardly going to look enticing to prospective buyers if the sales photos showed half an inch of dust over everything. Tomorrow she was supposed to be back at her desk, and despite her resolve to quit as soon as she landed back on home soil, she would undoubtedly chicken out and report for duty as usual. With that in mind, her last day of leave might be the last chance she got to go through the house properly.

She had reluctantly left Lily the night before with Joel and her mum, who was staying with them, and Lily had assured her and Anna that it was quite enough family members to make sure she was OK. This morning, a quick call to her mum, who told her that Lily had been fine overnight and had slept like a log due to her tablets, was followed by one to Matt where she briefly informed him they needed to meet up to sort out the loose ends of their relationship once and for all. He sounded genuinely shocked by her tone, and she supposed it was her own fault for letting him mess around and do things at a pace that suited his situation but not hers for all this time, but despite his surprise he'd agreed to meet on neutral territory to go over the necessary. There was a Costa in town that would fit the bill – not exactly cappuccino overlooking the Pantheon but it would have to do. She'd had a text from Jamie asking how she was, which had made her smile a lot and shone a brief light over her gloomy morning, and one from Alessandro to let her know he was thinking of her. She would have smiled at that too, but she knew she would have to phone him later and the thought of the conversation they needed to have tied her stomach in knots. He would think the worst, that she had strung him along and wasn't going to return to Rome, and Kate had to admit, had the tables been turned, she would have thought the same. Anna would say that she had the home situation all in hand, but Kate knew that she would need her support in seeing Lily through her troubled time, no matter what any of them said to the contrary, so there was no way she could leave in the next few weeks at least, and she couldn't really say when it was going to be a possibility. Away from the sparkling fountains and bright streets of the eternal city, reality was beginning to bite. What seemed possible there now seemed unreachable here when things like house sales, secure jobs and family ties came into the equation. Could love overcome all those obstacles, and a love that was brand new and untested at that?

Her gaze went to the suitcases as she passed them on her way to the windows with her ladders and bucket in hand, still unopened and unpacked in the hallway. Somehow, she hadn't had the heart to do it, as if emptying them and throwing their contents into the laundry would somehow wash away the wonderful dream of her holiday, as if once the residue of Rome had gone from them it would mean it had never happened at all. It was silly, of course, and the sooner she got it done the sooner she could put the cases away and, besides, she had a much bigger packing job to embark on soon if she was going to sell the house and remove one more obstacle between her and the future she longed for.

With an impatient sigh, annoyed at herself for being so impractical about the things she needed to do, she stood the ladders against the wall and put down her bucket, grabbing the biggest suitcase to lug it upstairs to the bedroom. She did the same with the second, and once they were both up there proceeded to empty them, tossing the dirty clothes into the wash basket and replacing toiletries and make-up in the cabinets she had removed them from before she left. One last sweep of the pockets inside the case to make sure she hadn't left anything in there, and her hand brushed against a folded piece of paper. With a frown she pulled it out and opened it up.

The page bore the mark of the hotel she'd been staying at; she recognised the paper from the notepad on the bedside table during her stay. On it in exquisite handwriting was a note.

> *Dear Kate*
> *Know that as you read this you are in my heart. You are in my heart when I sleep and when I wake, in every minute of every hour, and I count the days until you return. I will be only half alive until you come back to Rome and to my arms.*
> *Alessandro.*

Kate clutched the note to her chest, overwhelmed by a surge of emotions that reduced her to instant tears. He must have written it when she was asleep, during that last afternoon they had spent together, and slipped it in her suitcase to find when she got home. Nobody had ever done something so romantic for her. She was filled with love for him and with sadness too. Already she missed him so much it hurt in a way that was physical, and her gut twisted at the thought of the weeks, even months, that she might have to spend away from him. He had promised he would be patient, but how long would he wait? She couldn't expect him to hang around forever, could she? What if he gave up on her, thought she was moving on without him and did the same? What if he began to think she wasn't coming back and was stringing him along? What if he lost faith? She could call him every day, tell him that things were moving along and that she would be back soon, but words without actions meant nothing in the end. Rome was full of beautiful women, ones that were probably a great deal more suited to him and his family. His mother was keen for him to marry – what if her efforts to find the right woman for him came good? There were perfect candidates right under her nose, after all, including the very persistent Orazia, who seemed intent on winning Alessandro back despite what he said to the contrary. If only that damn woman hadn't made her feelings known, perhaps Kate wouldn't find herself obsessing over the threat she posed, even if it wasn't a real one, which it probably wasn't.

She sat on the bed and stared at the note. What had she done? This was a crazy, doomed romance, and she had instigated it, encouraged it, made it an impossible thing that neither could live without but might yet break both their hearts. She should have listened to the voice in her head that told her to leave well alone, should have walked away while she had the chance and filed Alessandro away as a brief, fun flirtation on her first holiday as a single woman. She was an idiot, because this couldn't work, could it?

Tucking the note away in her jewellery box, she tried to shake her negative thoughts. Her future with Alessandro might be uncertain, but she had a future regardless and she had to stay positive if it was going to be worth anything at all. There were windows downstairs waiting to be washed. Not exactly lunch on the Piazza Navona, but it was a start.

* * *

Accompanied by the chug of the coffee machine and the low hum of conversation, the smell of roasted beans and sweet syrups on the air, Kate put down her own drink and took a seat across from Matt, who already had a latte on the table in front of him, half of it gone, and an empty biscotti packet.

'Just to keep me going until tea,' he said by way of an explanation as Kate's gaze settled on the litter. 'Tamara's cooking spag bol for when I get back.'

'You've trained her up quick,' Kate commented, shrugging her jacket off. 'Does she know Tuesday night is spag bol night or is it just a coincidence?'

He fingered the handle of his cup but didn't reply. He looked uncomfortable, but Kate didn't care. She hadn't come here to make friends, she had come here to make him get on with the things he should have been doing at the start of their break-up.

'How is she?' Kate asked. 'Blooming?'

'She's good.'

'Lovely. Give her my best won't you?' The sarcasm in her tone was unmistakable, though her expression was neutral.

'Don't be like that, Kate, please. I thought we might be past that now. Tamara is a great girl and none of this is her fault. And I think you'd like her if you got to know her.'

'Very probably. But as it would be a bit weird, a sociable night out is hardly likely to happen, is it? So I'll have to take your word for that.'

'So we're dispensing with the niceties, are we?' Matt asked, his tone hardening to match hers.

'What did you expect from me?'

'I don't know, but you asked to meet up.'

'I'm fed up of messing around with the house. I'm paying a mortgage that still has your name on it and I can't afford to keep doing that. I can't afford to buy you out, either, which you know, so we need to put it on the market, sell it quick, get what we can for it.'

'There's no rush, is there? I don't want rock bottom price for it just because you're feeling impatient.'

'And I don't want to keep paying the mortgage so that you can make more money in the end.'

'You're living in it. You'd make more money too if we bide our time.'

'I'm not sure how you work that out but if you think so then perhaps you'd like to contribute to the payments I'm making. I'm not living there through choice right now but necessity. You know that.'

'I would, Kate, honest. . .'

'But?'

'I can't afford it, not on top of the rent Tamara and I are paying for our new place.'

'You could buy your old place from me and then you'd be killing two birds with one stone.'

'Tamara would never do that.' He stirred his latte with a finger and licked it. Kate shuddered. It was just another one of the gross and irritating things she'd learned to ignore over the years, but to see it now she wondered how she'd managed to keep her mouth shut. 'I mean, would you live in a house with a new fella that he'd shared with his ex-wife?'

'I don't know; it's never come up in conversation with him.'

He looked sharply at her. 'You're seeing someone?'

'I don't see what that has to do with anything.'

'Is that who you went to Rome with?'

'He was there, yes.'

'So this is the reason you're suddenly in a hurry to sell the house?'

'Matt. . .' Kate straightened to her full height. 'You left me – remember? You can hardly claim to be the injured party now.'

'I'm not, I just want to know.'

'Why?'

He stared at her. 'What happened? Why so shitty all of a sudden? I thought we'd agreed that the split would be amicable?'

'So that you wouldn't have to feel guilty about it? We did but I changed my mind. Why should you get it all your own way? And while we're on the subject of the split, how about you give me a bit of honesty? We're divorced now, so it doesn't matter. . . but were you having an affair with Tamara before we parted?'

'No,' he said. But the reply was a bit too hasty and a bit too guilty and Kate didn't need to ask him again. If he hadn't already been having the affair then he had been on the verge of it. She wanted to believe he'd done the honourable thing and waited until she and him were definitely over before he started banging his current girlfriend, but you didn't know someone for nineteen years without learning what their face looked like when they lied. But they were divorced now, and just as she'd said, it didn't really matter. Except that it did, and Kate couldn't help the feeling of utter betrayal that swept over her. Right now she didn't even want to look at him.

There was painful silence as she stirred her coffee, staring into it.

'You have a tan,' he said, breaking it. She looked up.

'It was hot.'

'We've had hot summers and I've never seen you tan before.'

'Maybe the Italian sun suits my skin.'

'You look well. Good. . . It does suit you.'

What was this? He'd practically admitted to adultery and now he was trying to compliment her?

'Thanks. I feel well,' she said. 'Never better in fact.' It wasn't strictly true, of course, but he didn't need to know that. In fact, the better he thought she was doing without him the more satisfying the feeling of making him believe that would be. Childish, yes, but satisfying. It was tempting to tell him about the fantastic sex she'd enjoyed in Rome too, but maybe that was taking it too far.

'Maybe I should check out Rome if it's that good for your health.'

'I think you might be a bit busy for holidays in a few months.'

His gaze went to his latte. 'Oh. So you know.'

'About the baby? Yes.'

He looked up. 'I suppose that was what the sarky comment about her blooming was for. It wasn't planned,' he added, his expression earnest. 'We didn't plan it.'

'But you got it. Something went very wrong for you somewhere along the line, didn't it? Unless she's the sort of woman who you would like to have kids with, unlike me, who simply got lied to about it for years.'

'Kate—'

'I don't want to hear it. You reap what you sow. Apparently, quite literally in your case. And don't talk to me about unwanted pregnancies because right now it'll only make me want to throw this coffee in your face.'

'But if you think about it, us not having any was a good decision.'

'That's not what I'm talking about. I couldn't care less about that now.'

'Right. . . so what do you need from me today? Is this just about the house?'

'Yes. I need you to be on board with the efforts to sell it. There are jobs that need doing – bits of DIY to get it in a saleable state. I want you to do them or get someone else to. And I want you to stump up the cost. I've already arranged for an estate agent to come and do a valuation and I can take care of the admin side of things until it's time for you to sign paperwork.'

'Got it all worked out, haven't you?'

'One of us has to.'

'I thought you liked the house. Now you're desperate to get away.'

'Matt. . .' She clicked her tongue, tried to bite back her impatience. 'I'm not going over it again. I want rid, and that's all you need to know.'

'Where will you move to? You won't get much of a place around here on your salary. . . Surely it would be better to stay put for a while.'

'And build up a nice little nest egg for you, so that when you and Tamara decide to buy your own you can sell this house for more money with every right to kick me out? I don't think so.'

'You haven't answered my question.'

He was trying to twist it, trying to manipulate her into making things as easy for him as possible. It was one of the many traits she'd come to recognise since their split, and the fact that she'd never seen them before amazed her. She'd been a doormat all her married life. Not any more.

'It doesn't matter where I'm going.'

'So you haven't thought it through,' he said. 'Typical. . .' And in his words was the hint of a sneer. Kate could take no more.

'Italy! Alright? I'm moving to Italy!' Kate held him in a defiant stare, her pulse roaring in her ears. It was not information she had wanted to give him and it could signal a whole heap of trouble over the next few days, but he'd made her so angry she had wanted to lash out, shock him, make him see her in a different light as the new person she was. . .

He blinked, finger dipped in his latte again as he froze. 'What?'

'You heard me. So are we going to sell this house or not?'

'You can't move to Italy!'

'Says who?'

'Are you crazy?'

'I know *you* think so because you think Skegness is an alien landscape. But there's a big wide world out there, Matt. If you opened your eyes, you might see it.'

'What do Anna and Lily say about it?'

'They're happy for me,' she lied, knowing that if she didn't his next phone call would be to one of them to stir up trouble. 'They think it's a brilliant idea.'

'You'll be back in a month,' he said, taking a sip of his latte and raising his eyebrows in disbelief.

'And Tamara will be a single mother in less,' Kate fired back. 'You think I'm not capable of making a new life without you, that I'm too immature and inexperienced to do it? I've got news for you it's you who's the immature one and you who was holding me back! I've got as much chance of making it in Rome as you do as a father, so let's see who throws in the towel first. I know who my money is on.'

'That's out of order.'

'Yeah? Well I feel out of order right now! You made this mess, Matt. You left me and I had to grow up quick. If you don't like the way that turned out, well, it's too late now.'

He offered no reply. After a pause, he turned in his seat and dragged his jacket from the back of it.

'Wait,' Kate said, struggling to even out her tone. 'I didn't come to have a fight and I'll admit that it just got out of hand. But you have to understand my situation. I didn't choose this change of direction but now it's been foisted upon me I have to make it work.'

He dropped his coat again and turned to face her. 'But Rome? Seriously? Aren't you terrified? Is that really what you want?'

'Yes.'

He let out a long breath. 'What's the new boyfriend got to say about it?'

'He's happy.'

'It can't be serious then. . .'

'Oh, it is. He lives there.'

If Matt's eyes could have got any bigger they might have gained their own gravitational pull. 'What the actual. . .' His sentence petered out and he simply continued to stare at her.

'It's not that weird. People from different nationalities get married all the time.'

'You're *marrying* him?'

'God, no! What I'm trying to say is that it's my choice now and you have to respect that. You've moved on and shouldn't I be allowed to move on too?'

'But with an Italian? In Italy?'

'It's where many of them are often found,' she replied with a faint smile.

The corners of his mouth twitched too. He drained the last of his latte and held her in a measured gaze. 'Jesus, Kate. I never saw this coming. It'll be weird not seeing you around.'

'You could have seen me around, all the time. It was your choices that made this, not mine. Besides, you have Tamara and a baby to think about now. I know at the beginning we said we'd stay friends, but it's proving difficult in reality, isn't it? Too many crushed dreams and hard feelings can sour the best intentions to stay friends pretty quickly. The best we can hope for is civility, and maybe we should just aim for that. You go off and have your life, and I'll go and have mine. We had a good run but it's over. There's no need to keep torturing each other by keeping alive a relationship that deserves a decent send-off and we'd both be happier if we didn't see much more of each other.'

'Tamara would be,' he said.

'Exactly. So I'm asking for a chance to be happy, and I only wish that for you in return.'

'And selling the house now will make you happy?'

'Of course. I can hardly go to Italy without doing that.'

He shook his head. 'I still can't believe this is the girl I was married to for all those years. Taking off to Italy just like that.'

'I'm not the girl you were married to. Not any more.'

'Right. . . I suppose not. So, you want to let me know about this estate agent business? I'll see if I can book some time off work to come and get those jobs done.'

'Thanks. I think you know which ones they are. . .' She raised her eyebrows and he gave a self-conscious laugh.

'The bathroom door handle, the damp patch in the kitchen and the faulty wiring in the landing light. . . I would have thought this new independent Kate would have been able to sort those things out herself.'

'She could,' Kate said, 'but why should she when she can get someone else to do it?'

'OK,' he laughed. 'I'd better go.' He pulled his jacket from the back of the chair. 'I'm glad we cleared the air, sort of, even if that's not what we came here to do.'

'Me too, actually.' And despite her anger and her misgivings, she did feel lighter for this meeting with Matt, a chance to finally air the feelings she had kept bottled up to spare his guilt, and for the chance to make him understand what he'd done. She didn't think he would dwell on it, not for a minute, or that it would cast a shadow over his new life, but she did feel that it was some kind of closure for her, and that had to be healthier for both of them.

'Right. . . well give my best to Anna and Lily. . . I never asked, how's Lily getting on? You know, with the baby and all. . . I suppose she'll be due just after Tamara.'

'She lost it,' Kate said. There was no point in telling him anything else and he would hear about it on the grapevine soon enough.

His expression was one of genuine shock. 'Oh, God. . . I'm so sorry. Is she OK?'

'Not really, but we'll stick by her until she pulls through it.'

'Of course. . . sorry,' he said again. 'Tell her I send my condolences. She was like a sister as we grew up and I hate to think of her going through this.'

Kate nodded. 'I will, and she'll appreciate that.'

'Right. . .' he said. 'I'll call you. . . about the DIY stuff. . .'

Kate watched as he left the coffee shop. Her own drink was hardly touched, cooling in front of her. But she'd done what she'd come to do and now she just wanted the solitude of her house, time to think over what came next. She grabbed her coat and headed for the exit too.

Twenty-one

The windowless box that passed for an office at Mr Woofy Pet Supplies had always made Kate feel depressed about going to work. Today it felt like a prison cell. A walled-off corner of the main warehouse, it was dark and smelly and perpetually freezing, even at the height of summer. The radio whined in the corner all day at the insistence of Deidre, a colleague who was so beige it was hard to see her when she sat in front of the magnolia walls, and it never quite managed to latch onto a wavelength, so that every terrible old song was accompanied by a static hiss that waxed and waned in volume whenever anyone walked past it. The desks were grubby, no matter how many times Kate got the polish out from the supplies cupboard and cleaned them, and in summer ants roamed the floors in organised patrols, woodlice taking their place in winter. Any food left out for more than an hour developed instant mould, and there were jars in the back of the rusting fridge that almost certainly had been filled during the First World War. But she had knuckled down for the sake of a wage that would keep the roof over their heads, turned up for work week in and week out, convinced by Matt to stay in a secure job in the belief that the devil she knew was a lot safer than the ones she didn't, ones that she secretly suspected might be more fun, even if they weren't safer. It was just another way in which Matt had continually shrunk her world during their marriage, until she had almost become as short-sighted and inward-looking as he was.

On her return, Deidre had wished her a good morning, asked her how her holiday was, and then promptly turned back to her computer screen as Kate began a reply. Chantelle, the office junior, was texting on her phone, and her boss, Gavin, was apparently out dealing with a fracas in the main warehouse. Presumably the ants had finally staged a major military coup and were threatening to stop the supply lorries from coming in and out of the warehouse compound until their demands were met. Whatever it was, Kate was relieved to note his absence. She was hardly in the mood to talk to him at the best of times, but today even less so. All she could think of as she logged on and saw the two hundred unopened emails in the shared inbox that both she and Deidre were supposed to deal with (but that her colleague had clearly not even bothered to look at in the week Kate was away) was how long she had to endure this torture until home time.

Why was she doing this to herself? The old Kate worked here, but the new Kate didn't have to, did she? Didn't the new Kate have big plans for a bright future, a ship that she was now captain of? But the new Kate also still had a mortgage to pay and needed money to make that future happen.

Her mobile sat on the desk. As she began to work through the mountain of emails complaining about overcharged accounts, wrongly delivered items and damaged stock, it pinged a notification from Facebook. She wasn't exactly the most active user and it wasn't often that she got them, so curiosity got the better of her and she took a look. Jamie had sent her a friend request. She accepted quickly and scrolled down his page, smiling to herself as she saw all the images of his life, things that he had described but she had only been able to imagine before. Brad was gorgeous, of course, and there was a huge collection of selfies and other photos of them together at various cafés, parks and other landmarks. They looked deliriously happy, and so very right for each other. No wonder Jamie had tried so hard to safeguard that precious love in the face of Pietro's threats to go to New York and cause trouble. There were pictures of parties galore, of family members, funny GIFs and video clips, jokey status updates and heartfelt wall messages. It looked like a wonderful life, and she was suddenly struck by how dull her own timeline must look in comparison. She hadn't even posted any photos of Rome, hadn't taken one single snap of Jamie or Alessandro during her time with them apart from the one of Jamie on the first night to send to Anna. There was no story for her, barely a status update. She hadn't even changed her relationship status from married to single.

She couldn't go back and get those photos, but she did upload the few she had taken in Italy and then changed her relationship status. Her finger hovered over the rest of her personal information.

Works at Mr Woofy Pet Supplies

That ought to have read: *Works at Kate's Classic Creations*, or *The Vintage Vixen*, or one of the other numerous names she had toyed with whenever the dream of owning her own dressmaking business had floated through her head. On Jamie's Facebook wall she had just read a meme. There was a photo of a ship floating on a bleak, vast ocean, and the text over it said: *Nothing will change until something changes.*

As she looked up for a moment, she caught Deidre watching her with owlish disapproval through her huge glasses.

'You've only just walked back in,' she tutted. 'I've been snowed under while you were sunning yourself abroad and now you're messing around on your phone.' She angled her head at Chantelle. 'It's bad enough that one doing it without you starting. I don't see the fascination with it all. A phone is for phoning people, end of.'

'Nothing will change until something changes,' Kate murmured.

'What was that? I couldn't hear over the radio.'

'I'm going.' Kate pushed her chair away from the desk and stood. She brushed down her skirt. Her heart was beating twice as fast as usual, and she was light-headed. But she also felt incredible.

'Going where?' Deidre asked with a sniff. 'If you're going to the vending machine you can get me a Twix.'

'Home,' Kate said.

'But you've only just got here!'

'And now I'm going.' She smiled at Chantelle, who had now looked up from her phone at the first sign of a drama worth watching instead. 'Chantelle – get out of here. Go to college, do something that really moves you, because it sure as hell can't be this. And Deidre. . .' She turned to the woman whose mouth was now hanging open like a basking shark waiting for a meal to swim in, 'I'd like to say it's been nice working with you but that would be a big fat lie. But if you want the lie then you can have it. Would you like me to lie about it right now to your face? I thought I'd give you the choice.'

Deidre simply stared at Kate as if she had gone quite mad. Maybe she had, but it was the first time since Rome that she had felt properly alive, properly in control of her destiny. If this was madness then she wanted more.

'No?' Kate asked. 'OK, well, I'll be seeing you. Or not. Probably not, to be honest, and there's no point in lying to you about that either.'

She took one last look around at the drab, windowless room that had blighted so many years of her life. However could she have been content with this? Then she grabbed her coat and bag and marched out before she had time to change her mind.

* * *

Lily opened the front door on the third ring of the bell. Kate had almost given up and gone home, confused about where her sister could be when she'd already messaged ahead to say she was coming. Kate briefly appraised her. Still in her pyjamas and hair unwashed, she didn't look much better than she had the day before.

'Where's Mum?' Kate asked as she followed Lily down the hallway. She wondered why her mum hadn't answered the door. She was supposed to be helping out once Joel went back to work, shielding Lily from life for a while until she got back on her feet, but there seemed to be no sign of her.

'Headache,' Lily said. 'She's asleep in the spare room.'

Kate frowned.

'She'll probably have to go home tomorrow anyway,' Lily added.

'So soon?'

'Apparently the cat has gone missing.'

Kate let out an exasperated sigh as Lily collapsed back onto the sofa and pulled the duvet around her chin.

'I'm alright anyway,' Lily said.

'That's why you're still on the sofa.' Kate took a seat across from her.

'I'm tired, that's all. My body has to recover. That's what the doctor says.'

'What about your brain? How do you feel?'

'Numb. I don't know how to feel. I keep wondering if I could have done something to prevent it, or if I did something that caused it. Everyone keeps saying it's just a thing, a fact of life, it happens for no reason, but I can't make sense of that. There has to be a reason, and the more I try to figure it out, the more it's driving me mad. And then I feel guilty that I'm not sad enough. I mean, I'm sad, but it's not *enough*. . . I can't explain it.'

'You're probably still coming to terms with it all. It's only just happened and you're in a state of shock. There's no wrong or right way to feel, only the way you feel, and everyone must feel it differently. How's Joel holding up?'

'Terrible,' Lily said. 'He can't talk about it, but he looks so pale and sad and not himself at all. I almost think he'd feel better if he could talk about it. That makes me feel like I have to be the strong one too, so I mustn't cry.'

'You must do whatever comes naturally. If you want to cry you bloody well cry, no matter who says what about how you should feel and behave. And if you don't cry nobody will think any worse of you, or that you care any less about what happened. This is your grief, and only you know what to do with it.'

Lily gave her a thin smile. 'You got wise all of a sudden. You sound like Anna now.'

'I'm not sure that's a compliment,' Kate said with a small smile of her own.

'Me neither,' Lily said. She looked up at the clock and seemed to check herself. 'Wait. . . aren't you supposed to be at work?'

'Not today,' Kate replied. She would tell Lily about the grand departure, but now wasn't the time to add to her worries.

'Oh. I must be confused. I was sure you said Wednesday.'

'Change of plan.' Kate forced a bright smile. She needed to change the subject, and fast. 'How about a cup of tea?'

'I've been drinking tea all day. I've drunk so much tea these last couple of days I could drown in it from the inside out. Everybody keeps making me tea. It's very British, I suppose.'

'I've hardly had any at all for a week, so I'm quite enjoying guzzling loads at the moment,' Kate said.

Lily waved her towards the kitchen door. 'Help yourself if you want one. Just please don't make me drink another cup.'

Kate went into Lily's kitchen and filled the kettle. It was as she was waiting for it to boil that her gaze fell on a cork noticeboard. Nothing special pinned to it, just leaflets they'd wanted to save, phone numbers and important bills that needed to be sorted. Kate suddenly felt the breath catch in her throat. *Bills.* She didn't know where it had come from but she was gripped by a slowly growing sense of panic. She'd just quit her job, and she had a stack of bills exactly like this at home. How was she going to pay them now? What had she done?

You can't think like this. . . get it together.

She pulled in deep breaths, tried to get a handle on her anxiety. She could type, right? So she could get agency work. But what was the point of leaving her job at the warehouse if she was just going to walk right back into another office that she'd very likely hate just as much? But she couldn't get the dressmaking off the ground and making money that quickly, could she? The house needed to go, and fast – it was as simple as that. And then what? Take off for Rome? Was that even possible? What about Lily and Anna and her mum?

Her head was spinning by the time the kettle clicked off. It was all so confusing. The new life she wanted wasn't quite as straightforward as she'd first thought.

As she went back into the living room, Lily was holding out her phone for her. 'It was ringing in your bag. Deidre from Mr Woofy. . .' She shot her sister a quizzical look as Kate took the phone.

'Hello?' Kate took the call into the kitchen, feeling Lily's eyes on her back as she went. She shut the door behind her as she listened to Deidre.

'Yes I meant it,' Kate replied in answer to the first and most obvious question. 'No I won't change my mind,' she added in reply to the second one. 'You're sorry to hear it? I'm sorry that you're sorry but the answer is still the same. But thank you, for calling me and checking I hadn't gone mad.'

Kate ended the call. Despite her earlier panic, going back to Mr Woofy would be like ripping out her soul and shoving it into the nearest bin. She needed money, yes, but there had to be another way to get it that didn't involve her slowly dissolving into the magnolia walls of Mr Woofy's warehouse office, until she was as indistinguishable from her surroundings as Deidre was. And from the way she'd been feeling for the last few years, that day wasn't far away.

Switching the phone to mute, she went back into the living room and shoved it into her bag. She grabbed her tea and took a seat with Lily, who was looking at her expectantly.

'I may be an invalid with a lot on my mind but that doesn't make me stupid,' she said.

'Huh?'

'What did Deidre want?'

'Something and nothing. Wanted to ask me about an overdue account. . . you know how it is there – I have to do bloody everything. The place would fall apart without me.'

Lily made no reply, but eyed Kate keenly. Eventually she seemed to decide that dropping the interrogation was the best policy.

'Maybe I should check on Mum, see if she wants anything.'

'Shouldn't she be doing that for you?' Kate asked, peering over the rim of her mug.

'She did look pale earlier. And you know how her headaches knock her off her feet.'

'You're knocked off your feet.' Kate put her mug down on a side table. 'If you're really worried I'll go and look in on her.'

Lily nodded. She seemed happy with the arrangement. Kate held in a sigh as she pushed herself up from the chair. Everyone in this family was perfectly capable of looking after themselves, but they all felt they had to look after each other nonetheless. It had always been the way, and that sense of duty carried with it a sense of guilt too. She might not be needed as much as she thought she was, but it was still going to be hard to leave her sisters and her mum – even Matt to some degree – when the time came.

* * *

She'd had a feeling this was coming. Kate had barely closed her front door behind her when she heard a familiar engine and looked through the window to see Anna's car pull up outside. Seeing no point in waiting for her to knock, she opened the front door and stood on the step.

'It's a lovely surprise but what brings you over at this time of the day?' Kate said brightly as Anna locked her car and walked towards her. 'It's a bit early, isn't it? Finished work already?'

'I took some time owed to me,' Anna said.

'To see me? I know you missed me last week but I didn't realise you'd got it that bad.'

Anna didn't smile at Kate's joke. Not that it was hilarious but she had expected some kind of good-natured reaction, however subtle.

'Lily called me,' Anna said as she followed Kate down the hall and into the kitchen, where Kate filled the kettle. 'She told me you went to see her today, but I recall you told us that you were back at work today. She said she thought so too. You definitely told us you were back at work today and I'm sure both of us didn't get it wrong. Then she says Deidre phoned you. And you made some vague excuse about it that Lily didn't buy for a second. Christian also had a weird phone call from Matt.'

'Christian?' Kate frowned. 'Why would Matt be calling him?'

'They're still on the same Sunday league footie team, don't forget, so he calls him about fixtures all the time. But that's not the point. He says you've told him you're moving to Italy, that you have a boyfriend there. . . but that's ridiculous, isn't it? What's going on? Kate, please tell me you haven't done crazy things.'

Kate leaned against the worktop and stared into space, grappling for a reply. Trust Matt to revert to type and stir things up at the first opportunity. She had thought she'd got through, that they'd finally come to an understanding, and she thought that maybe he'd swallowed her lie about Anna and Lily already knowing her plans to emigrate. Apparently not. And as for Lily, well. . . Lily was always going to be straight on the phone to Anna at the first sign of trouble. But the panic in Anna's voice was also stirring up the panic in Kate too. She *was* doing crazy things and even she could see there was no other way of looking at it. But it was like she had no control any more – as if life was leading her and not the other way around. How could she explain that to Anna, though? Anna, the pragmatic, practical sister who had a life plan and days that ran like clockwork?

'I think I might be doing some crazy things,' she said, turning her gaze to her sister.

'Go on. . .'

'I quit my job.'

'OK, so that's not totally unexpected. What are you going to do instead? I assume you have a plan. . . right?'

'I haven't thought that far ahead, not really. I know I want to start my dressmaking business, but I don't know the ins and outs of that yet.'

Anna was silent for a moment. 'You have a plan B then? Something to tide you over until it gets off the ground?'

'There's sort of no point in getting another job. . . at least not a long-term one.'

'What does that mean? Is this something to do with what Matt said? Please tell me this isn't something to do with what Matt said. Tell me he got it wrong.'

'Not exactly wrong. I do want to move to Italy. Alessandro. . . the guy who took me out in Rome. . . he told me he loves me—'

'Christ on a bike, Kate! And you believe him! He probably says that to a new girl every week, but I bet most of them aren't gullible enough to swallow it! He's told you he wants you to move to Italy?'

'Not exactly but—'

'What the hell are you thinking of then?'

'I love him too!' Kate cried. 'I love him and I love Rome and I know you don't understand or approve, but it's what I want, and I thought you might be happy that for the first time in my life I want something that isn't the same as what Matt wants! You kept telling me I needed to start again, find myself, and that's what I'm doing!'

'I meant a new job and a bit of decorating, not buggering off to Italy!'

'I'm single and I'm an adult; I can do what I want.'

'Of course you can. . .' Anna's tone softened. 'God, of course you can do what you want. But doing what you want isn't always doing what's best for you. Surely you can see how mad this all is? I get it – you're in a weird place right now, cast adrift, and you're looking for answers, but running away to Rome with a man you've just met isn't going to give you those answers.'

'You don't know Alessandro. If you did you'd think differently. He's not at all like you say he is.'

'Well I'm not likely to meet him any time soon so I'll have to take your word for it.'

'Come with me to Rome then. For a holiday. I'll introduce you to him and his family and you'll see!'

'Would you listen to yourself? Have you any idea how this sounds?'

'What's wrong with a holiday? We can go back together; you'll love it there. What have you got to lose?'

'I can't get the time off work for a start. Then there's Christian; what's he supposed to do while I'm chasing around Italy with you?'

'He can come too. Why wouldn't he want to come? Think about it, Anna – this is the perfect opportunity. You always said you wanted to go to Rome.'

'That was before all this. And am I supposed to leave you there with this man at the end of the holiday? Is that how this works? I wave at you from the plane as I take off without you? Do you even know what you're asking me to do?'

'I'm not asking you to do anything but trust that I can find my own way.'

'It sounds like it, but I'm not sure I can when you're making decisions this massive on a whim.'

Kate turned her back and busied herself making tea. Anna hadn't asked for it and Kate didn't want it, but it was a viable excuse not to look at her sister and not to reply. At least not until she had a reply that made sense. Because when she looked at it from Anna's point of view, infuriatingly, Kate could see perfectly why Anna was freaking out. It was the conversation she would probably be having with Anna if the tables were turned.

A jingling tune sounded from the direction of the handbag Kate had abandoned on the table. She crossed over and pulled her phone out. Alessandro's name lit up the screen. He was probably on a break at work and decided to call, as she hadn't yet called him. She glanced at Anna, who watched her carefully. She couldn't answer this now but she didn't want him to think she was avoiding him now that she was home.

'Aren't you going to answer it?' Anna asked. 'Perhaps your exciting future is calling.'

'Funny,' Kate said, cutting off the call. It pained her to do it, and she desperately wanted to hear his voice, but she couldn't answer it now. Before she could put the phone back in her bag, though, Anna grabbed it from her.

'There must be some photos on here,' she said. 'Let's have a look, see what all the fuss is about.'

'If you're going to be like that I don't want to talk about it,' Kate replied, snatching it back. 'And I certainly don't want to show you photos so you can scoff at them.' She stuffed the phone back in her bag and tucked the bag itself into a cupboard.

'So do we get to talk this through or have you already decided?' Anna asked, accepting the mug of tea Kate handed to her.

'Honestly? Whenever I think I've decided something comes along to make me doubt myself. Your visit today hasn't exactly helped there.'

'Taking it steady is not a bad thing. This is a big leap.'

'I know that. I've thought about almost nothing else since I got back. Apart from Lily, of course.'

'How did she seem today?' Anna asked.

Kate shrugged, but she was glad to be changing the subject, even if it was to something more painful. 'She seemed OK. That's what worries me. We both know how desperate for kids she is, how excited they were about this baby. It means the world to her and although she's tired and low, she isn't devastated. Not that I want her to be devastated, of course, but this isn't the reaction I was expecting. In fact, I think it's a bit weird.'

'I was thinking the same thing. I think it's delayed. If I know Lily it will come and it's going to be horrible when it does.'

Kate sipped at her tea. 'I hope you're wrong.'

'So do I. For all our sakes.'

Kate raised her eyebrows. There was nothing to say to that and she had a feeling Anna was right, yet again. She hated it when Anna was right, but this time it was for very different reasons than it normally was.

Twenty-two

She had tried to return Alessandro's call as soon as Anna had gone, but it went straight to voicemail. He was probably back on duty and she would have to get up early to catch him just off his shift before he headed home to bed. Whether he had broken the news of their relationship to his mother yet was one thing she didn't know and she wasn't sure how Signora Conti would react to it, so she didn't want to phone him at a time when it might be awkward at home. His mother had been pushing him to find a wife, of course, but Kate imagined that she had a very different set of criteria than what Kate herself represented – namely Italian, Catholic, and not newly divorced. Kate and Signora Conti had got along famously as friends, but as anything more significant. . . it was too early to tell and Kate didn't want to dwell on yet another potential hurdle to her happiness with Alessandro – she could find quite enough of those at home.

There was no need to set the alarm to ensure she was up to make the call in the morning – she woke with the sunrise after a restless night filled with dreams of lost babies, bailiffs and loved ones who kept evading her grasp every time she reached for them. She was finally pulled from sleep at the climax of the last and worst dream, where Alessandro's mother locked her in a jail cell and swallowed the key with a piece of gorgonzola, laughing loudly, Alessandro standing with his arm around Orazia and laughing along with her as they watched Kate plead to be let out. Quite how she knew it was gorgonzola Kate wasn't sure, but the important bit of the picture was the key. And possibly the laughing. She opened her eyes with a squeal, almost hyperventilating until she focused on the familiar layout of her own bedroom and fell back onto the pillows with a relieved sigh.

Once she'd pulled herself together, she grabbed her phone from the bedside cabinet.

'Good morning,' he said, in that voice that turned her into a puddle of molten lust, and instantly, every worry and fear was banished.

'How was your night?' she asked. 'Busy?'

'Quiet,' he said. 'I thought of you often.'

'I thought of you too,' she replied, trying to shake the images from her last dream as she said it. 'I miss you like crazy.'

'Then we are the same. Is all well? How is your sister?'

'Lily? She's bearing up. I mean, she's sad and everything but she's not as bad as I feared she would be.'

'And Anna?'

'Hmm. Anna's worried about me. She's making things difficult at the moment.'

'You have told her about me?'

'Yes. And my plans to come to Rome for good.'

'She will worry for you. My sisters would worry for me too.'

'And also. . . I quit my job yesterday.'

'You have no work?'

'Not at the moment.'

There was silence at the other end of the line. Then: 'How will you come to Rome if you have no money?'

'I would've had to quit anyway. This is just sooner than I had anticipated. Besides, it means that I'll have to do everything here that bit quicker so, actually, I'll be back there sooner than I'd hoped. Which is a good thing. . .'

'You must sell your house? Have you spoken to your husband?'

'Ex-husband,' Kate reminded him, though she suspected it was a language thing. 'Not my husband. . . not anything now really. But he's going to do the jobs around the house that are needed to get it ready to sell and he's agreed we can do that straightaway. At least there'll be some money in that to get me on my way, though perhaps not enough to do any more than put a deposit on an apartment somewhere and cover the moving costs. I may need your help to look for one as I'm stuck here. I mean, I can see them online, though it's not the same as viewing them in person, but perhaps you could do that for me – make sure they're as nice as they look on the photos.'

She could tell by his voice that he was smiling at the other end of the line – that slightly sardonic, sexy smile that on anyone else might have been offensive or infuriating but on him she loved. 'Lucetta is excited to help; she is already looking for the perfect apartment.'

'So you've told her? About my plans?'

'Yes. She's very happy. She likes you very much.'

'I like her too. And it's kind of her to look for an apartment.'

'She is clever; she will strike the best price for your rent.'

Kate didn't imagine for one minute that Lucetta would do anything but get the best price. She was a formidable force of nature, and Kate certainly wouldn't want to be on the receiving end of her assertiveness. Although assertiveness might be putting it mildly, like saying that Thor was quite good with a hammer. 'Then there's the matter of getting work, or at least a business up and running. Whatever cash

I have left over from the apartment deposit won't last long, if there's anything left at all.'

'You are worried? Do you think it is a mistake to come here?'

There was genuine concern in his voice now. He thought she was going to change her mind and give up, that it would all be too much to achieve in the end. And often, when she looked at the task she had set herself, it felt like that to her too.

'It's going to be hard,' she said. 'I can't pretend it won't be. . .' She wanted to ask him if he loved her enough, if he was sure of their future before she leapt into the abyss for him, but how could she? He could say that he was sure, that their love would last forever, but how could he know? Matt didn't know, even though they had both thought so as they took their marriage vows. Nothing was ever certain and almost nothing was forever. It was a lesson Kate was learning fast.

'We will help,' he said. 'I will ask everyone I know.'

And there was another question, just begging to be asked, one that she wasn't sure she wanted the answer to.

'Have you told your mother about us?'

There was a pause. 'I am waiting,' he said.

She didn't ask more and there was no point. He was waiting to see if their dream became a reality and she couldn't blame him. Why rock the boat if there was no need? If she hadn't blurted her plans out to Matt then she would very likely have been doing the same. She wanted to ask what he thought his mother's reaction might be, but she was too scared and she didn't want to sour the first conversation they'd shared since she got home. 'Where are you now?' she asked instead. 'Still at the police station?'

'In the locker room.'

'Alone?' she said, thinking about the personal nature of their call and his openness.

'Yes, alone. I am in the toilet block.'

'Ugh! Not on the toilet?'

'No.' He gave a warm laugh. 'I am going to take a shower before I go home.'

'So… you're naked right now. . .'

'Do you wish me to be naked?' he asked in a mischievous voice.

That delicious thrill ripped through her, her loins tingling and suddenly she was desperate to have him near. She pictured his perfect tanned torso, his trim waist, his pert bottom, imagined the last time her hands had explored him, and it was all she could do not to explode at the images that invaded her thoughts. 'I'd be unhappy to know you were naked right now,' she said.

'Why?' He sounded confused.

'Because it would be a waste if I wasn't there to kiss every inch of your nakedness.'

'Perhaps we can pretend you are here. I will imagine your nakedness and you can imagine mine.'

'Well. . .' Kate said lazily, lying back on the bed, 'it's not going to be the same at all but I'll see what I can do. . .'

* * *

Kate dreaded to think how much her early morning call to Alessandro had cost, but she had been on the line for a very long time. As she tried to get her head around the rest of the day, her mind wandered back to the sound of his voice, things they had said, things they had done. . . The memory of it made her blush more violently than any time she'd actually been with him, but she was happy and, despite all the misgivings that still jostled for pole position in her thoughts, she felt positive. If you had love, anything was possible, wasn't it? And she was becoming increasingly certain that what they had was the real thing.

But then the call came.

'Kate. . .' Anna's voice was shaking. 'I'm at Lily's. Can you come over right now?'

Twenty-three

Kate's mum had this strange habit of appearing to wash her hands in mid-air whenever she was stressed. It had been the one abiding image that had accompanied her near-breakdown in the weeks after Kate's father had died, but Kate hadn't seen it for a long time. As she walked into Lily's kitchen following the call from Anna, her mum's hands were going like crazy. That was the first clue that things were every bit as bad as Anna's voice on the phone had suggested.

Then her gaze travelled the room, taking in the scene of devastation as smashed crockery, glass, ripped food packets – their contents spilled across worktops – and things so broken up they were no longer even recognisable littered the surfaces, coming to rest on Lily herself, head in her arms, bits of food in her hair and over her pyjamas, squashed up in a corner, sobbing and shaking uncontrollably. Joel was there, doing his best to hold her and comfort her, but he looked close to breaking point himself.

'I was in bed,' Kate's mum said. 'Then I heard this almighty crashing. I thought we were being burgled or something. I rushed downstairs and. . .'

'Lily was going mad, tearing the place up,' Anna finished for her quietly. Not that it would have mattered if she'd said it loudly, because

Lily herself didn't seem to be aware of anything but what was in her head. And it broke Kate's heart to see it, because it looked as if the thing filling Lily's head was grief – all-engulfing and sharp and desperately painful. A delayed reaction – both she and Anna had predicted it, and both had hoped to be wrong. Being right was almost more than she could bear.

'Lily. . .' Kate said gently, stooping down to her on the floor. 'It's me. . . you want to talk to me?'

Lily looked up, but her expression didn't seem to register Kate at all. Kate turned to Anna. 'Help me get her away from all this mess – she'll cut herself on something.'

Anna rushed over and together they took an arm each, leading their sister into the living room where they sat her on the duvet-covered sofa. She was still shaking, still crying, though she seemed a little more responsive to their presence now.

'It's alright,' Kate said. 'We're here now.' It was a pointless and stupid thing to say, and Kate was quite sure that Lily didn't care who was there at that precise moment, but it was all she had to offer.

Joel came to sit next to Lily and tried to put his arm around her, but she shook him off violently. Confusion on his face, he leapt up from the sofa again, casting a glance at Kate and Anna in turn that pleaded for help. This was unfamiliar emotional territory for him, his happy little bubble of life with Lily suddenly burst, and he looked lost and close to breaking himself. Then their mum filed in from the kitchen, still wringing her hands and looking helpless. It looked as if everyone was falling apart other than Kate and her eldest sister. Anna took Kate to one side.

'I really have to get to work,' she said in a low voice. 'I feel terrible for asking but—'

'I know. I don't have to go to work and you do. It's OK; don't feel bad. Of course I'll stay with her.'

'I'll finish as quickly as I can and come straight back.'

'Go home first and have some tea. You'll be no good to anyone exhausted and hungry, and you don't want to put stress on you and Christian as well as all this. I've got nowhere else to be.'

'Apart from Italy,' Anna said with a faint smile. 'I'm glad you haven't gone yet – I don't know what I would have done without you today.'

'You'd have coped,' Kate said, but the damage was done and the guilt instantly set in. Anna would have coped, but it wouldn't have been fair that the responsibility would have fallen on her shoulders alone.

Anna kissed her briefly on the cheek and then bent down to hug Lily, Joel and her mum in turn. 'I'll be back shortly,' she said, and then hurried from the room. Kate turned to Joel.

'Can you phone your doctor to come out to make a house call?'

'I've done that,' her mum cut in. 'They said it would have to wait until the end of morning surgery but they'd send someone over.' Kate gave a tense smile. At least that was something. 'I can go and make a start on cleaning up the mess too,' she added, and after a last uncertain glance at Lily she left the room.

'That's brilliant, thanks, Mum,' Kate called after her. She turned back to her sister, whose head was buried in her arms again. There wasn't much else they could do but wait for professional help now, but she realised that Lily was going to need her a lot while she got better, more than she'd ever done before, and Anna was going to need support too if she was going to keep her own home life afloat in the face of so much outside pressure. For how long was anyone's guess.

She was just about to say so to Joel, but as she turned to him, he was already across the room, rushing for the exit. She heard the sound of the front door slamming. Her mum came back into the living room.

'What was that?'

Kate gave a slight shrug. 'Joel's gone out. I suppose he needed some air.'

'The poor boy is in such a state. I don't know how much more he can take.'

Three words sprang to mind as Kate studied her mother's strained expression – pot, kettle and black. It wasn't a huge stretch to imagine that she was feeling the stress of her daughter's loss too, and she had a track record where that was concerned. Kate would have to watch not only Lily carefully, but Joel and her mum into the bargain. She had a feeling it was going to be a very long day – and it promised to be the first of many.

'Why don't you go and finish cleaning up? I'll get Lily settled and then come to help.'

Her mum nodded with a thin smile, the hand wringing resuming as she left the room, and Kate sat down next to Lily with a heavy sigh.

* * *

Kate had thought the first week of her separation from Matt had been bad, but it paled in comparison to the pain of seeing her sweet, happy little sister turn into a hollow shell of the woman she had been. The first days had been the worst, although now, a week on, Lily seemed more communicative whenever Kate was there, which was as often as she could manage without interfering too much with the grieving process that Joel and Lily also had to go through together as a couple. Her mum had wanted to stay but Anna, Kate and Lily had insisted they could cope and had seen her back on a train to Scotland, where her husband, Hamish, waited, and it had been something of a relief. They loved her dearly, of course, but just by being there in the house where she needed meals and clean bedding and all manner of other everyday things – not to mention their worries about her mental state as well as Lily's – she was an extra burden on a family network already at breaking point. Harsh as it was, she was better away from them at a time when Lily needed to be the priority. Joel wasn't faring much better when it came to it, and he needed almost as much support as Lily. Left to their own devices, the pair of them might well be sucked into a void of misery, so far down that they would never return. If Kate was determined to do one thing, it was prevent her sister's relationship going the same way hers and Matt's had, especially when they were so perfect for each other in the first place (far more perfect than she and Matt had ever been) and if she had to be there to support them so that they stayed together, then she would.

Telling Alessandro had been the hardest thing for Kate. His complete understanding, his lack of complaint when she told him that every plan to return to Rome was now on hold indefinitely, his concern for her well-being without mentioning his own disappointment once, made her all the more desperate to get back to his arms. And yet there was this, hanging over her, and it was impossible to say when, if ever, that would happen.

When she had the time she drew up plans for her sewing business, and though she still looked at the real-estate sites online for properties in Rome, it was in a half-hearted way. What was the point when everything was so uncertain? But she had done her best to carry on regardless with the things that she could do in the short term – the for-sale sign had gone up outside the house and Matt had kept his promise, arranging to come and do the little repair jobs around the place as he'd said he would.

It was a bright Sunday morning when she opened the front door, the kind of morning where, if she closed her eyes and stood in the sunshine, she could almost imagine herself standing by the Trevi Fountain, Alessandro by her side. Matt greeted her cheerfully, a toolbox looking ridiculously out of place in the hands of a man Kate knew to have about as much natural affinity with DIY as she did with genetic engineering.

'Morning! Reporting for duty!'

Kate raised her eyebrows as she let him in. It had been a long time since she had seen him so cheerful. 'Great. Do you want a drink or something before you start?'

'I'll just crack on. Tamara wants to go shopping for a pram this afternoon so we're obviously on a deadline to catch the store before it closes.'

'Does it have to be today? She knows you've got things to do.'

He glanced up the stairs, scratching his head. 'Why? Do you think this stuff is going to take longer than a morning?'

'No,' Kate said, 'I mean, doesn't she have ages before the baby is due?'

'Oh, right. . .' Matt sniffed. 'She's excited, I suppose. And I suppose it'll be on us quicker than we think.'

It didn't sound as if Matt shared Tamara's enthusiasm but it was hardly a surprise to Kate. Perhaps he would come round as the birth drew nearer. He would have to; there wasn't a lot of choice.

'How's Lily?' he asked. 'Bearing up?'

'She's been better. In fact, I may have to leave you to get on with things here and go over to see if she's OK. You'll be alright for an hour, won't you?'

'It's not like I don't know where everything is.' He gave a rueful smile as he gazed around the hallway. 'You know, I do sort of miss this house. We picked a good one, didn't we?'

'I've told you before you can buy me out with pleasure. You like the place and we know everything is sound – it makes sense to me.'

'Not to Tamara it doesn't.'

Kate couldn't really blame her replacement for being reluctant to nest in the home her boyfriend had shared with his ex-wife but it was worth a shot – Matt taking the house on would save a lot of time and money selling it. She gave a shrug. 'Have a drink before you start; you might as well.'

'OK then; that sounds good.'

He followed her down the hall into the kitchen, where the morning sun slanted through the blinds, painting the walls with slices of light. She busied herself making drinks in silence. Whenever she looked around Matt was tapping on his phone.

'She messages you a lot more than I used to,' Kate said.

'How do you know it's Tamara?' he asked, looking up.

'Unless you've suddenly become party central then it's got to be her – you're not exactly a social butterfly.'

'Got me,' he smiled.

'In fact, I'm quite amazed that you went far enough from your sofa to meet a girl at all. You never did tell me how you met her. . .'

'Oh. . . just a friend of a friend – works do, I think,' he replied vaguely.

It was a bit too vague. Was he really trying to convince Kate that he couldn't recall the exact circumstances in which he met the mother of his unborn child? Kate could have pushed him to be more specific, and undoubtedly holes would have started to appear in his story, but it wasn't worth the effort any more. She placed a mug in front of him.

'You're still having sugar in your tea, I take it?'

He nodded.

'Good,' she said. Sometimes, it was comforting to see that not everything in her new life was unrecognisable.

* * *

Leaving Matt with some damp-treatment paint that was stinking the whole house out, Kate had gone over to see how Lily was faring. On arrival she was concerned to see that, despite Joel managing to extend a period of compassionate leave by another week to look after Lily, he wasn't there. Lily had no idea where he was. But Kate needed him to be there, she needed him to take some responsibility, to be able to square up to the challenges of their situation so that he and Lily could face the future together, so that when Kate did finally leave them – a hope she still clung to despite the obstacles – there would be someone to talk Lily down on the days when her grief ripped through her. It felt as if those days were less frequent now, and she always perked up with Kate around, but she was still a long way from normal.

Kate put some washing in for them, wiped the surfaces of the kitchen and bathroom, and made sure that the fridge was stocked as Lily shuffled around after her, chastising her for every job she did, insisting she and Joel could do it, though Kate could tell she was grateful just the same. They had a quick drink and some lunch together, where Kate chatted about this and that and Lily seemed content to listen. Joel turned up, briefly acknowledged Kate, and then went upstairs.

'I expect he's playing on the Xbox,' Lily said in a dull voice.

'But he's OK?' Kate asked.

Lily gave a vague shake of her head.

'You two haven't talked about any of this?'

'Yes,' Lily said, but Kate remained unconvinced. They might have mentioned it in passing, and they could hardly ignore the huge hole in their lives, but acknowledging its presence and actually having a meaningful discussion about it were two very different things.

'Promise me you'll try,' Kate said.

Lily stared at her blankly for a moment, but then nodded slightly. Kate had no idea whether that meant a solid yes, or was simply a platitude to get Kate off her back, but it looked as though it was the best she would get for now.

* * *

Once she was happy that Lily and Joel were as OK as they could be, Kate headed back home to see how Matt was getting on. As she let herself in, she couldn't help noticing that the house was unexpectedly quiet.

'Matt?' she called, half-expecting to find that he'd taken himself off to the pub and abandoned his jobs, or that Tamara had turned up demanding he drop everything to go pram shopping immediately. But then his voice came back.

'Upstairs. In our room.'

In my room, she was tempted to reply, but what was the point in being so facetious? Old habits died hard, especially for someone like Matt.

He was sitting on the bed, photo albums spread out before him.

'You can take some of those if you want them,' Kate said as he looked up. 'Choose the ones you want to keep and I'll make an album for you.'

'I don't think Tamara would like that very much.'

'Why, doesn't she have a past? Was she hatched fully formed from an egg six months ago?'

'Don't be daft.'

'Then why should she deny yours? Whether she likes it or not you had a whole other life with another woman, and a good deal of that was during your teenage years. Our relationship is written in our history – yours and mine – and we can't erase that without erasing all those formative years that make us who we both are now. And why should we? They were good times, weren't they? Good memories?'

'They were.' He sighed. 'I suppose it's just hard for her to understand. She feels as if she can't compete with all that.'

'She doesn't have to compete. She's already won.'

'You know what I mean.'

'Not really.' Kate cleared a space next to him and picked up an album. 'But if life is easier for you indulging her silly insecurities then go for it.'

'That's harsh.'

'True, I think. Once you would have thought so too. I seem to recall you didn't indulge me in the same way.'

He stared at her. 'You've changed, Kate.'

'I didn't have a lot of choice.'

'I wish you wouldn't.'

It was Kate's turn to stare. 'What's that supposed to mean?'

He shook his head. 'Remember this?' he said, holding a page open for her.

'Oh, God!' Kate laughed, the strange moment gone in an instant. 'That hideous tracksuit you thought was the bee's knees! Where's that. . . oh, the Year Ten geography trip to the reservoir! That was the day you fell in from that jetty, wasn't it?'

'Half an hour after this was taken, my amazing tracksuit stank of pondweed.'

Kate smiled. 'I don't think the reservoir was that dirty.'

'It wasn't exactly filled with Persil, was it?'

'No, I suppose not,' Kate said, laughing. 'If it was, I'm sure Mrs Arterton would have dunked Brendan Copperwhite and his BO in there. Do you remember the bus smelt like soup all the way back to school? And Mrs Arterton kept retching. Jane Forester had to empty her leftover dinner out of the window so there was a carrier bag in case she was sick, and her Dairylea triangle splatted all over the windscreen of that old man's car. He was shaking his fist at us for ten miles until we got off the motorway.'

Matt was roaring with laughter as he looked again at the photo. Then it seemed to quiet. 'You looked fit that day.'

'Thank you,' Kate said. 'Was that a compliment?'

'I remember thinking it as soon as you rocked up in that crop top and those low-slung jeans, and I had a little trouser issue at the sight of it. . . I can only say that it's a good job the tracksuit trousers were baggy. Even Shawn said you looked hot and he was dead fussy about girls – rarely gave over a five.'

'What was I that day on Shawn's scoreboard?'

'Seven, I think.'

'Wow. . . If only you'd told me. It might have changed my life knowing Shawn Hutson had rated me a seven.'

'You might have gone out with him instead of me.'

'His teeth were a funny colour, so I doubt it.'

'I thought all the girls fancied him.'

'Not me.'

Matt was silent again, turning his attention back to the book. 'Look,' he said after a moment. 'Our engagement party. That was a night and a half too.'

'That's because most engagement parties aren't full of underage drinkers. We were only seventeen ourselves and some of our mates were younger than that. As I recall there was a lot of puking, and I'm sure someone got pregnant under the coat pile in the spare bedroom.'

'Cassie Wareham,' Matt said. 'That was Shawn's doing too.'

'Bloody hell,' Kate said. 'Some poor child has inherited his oddly coloured teeth now.'

'Unlucky bugger,' Matt agreed, and Kate giggled. 'What happened?' he asked, sombre now. 'We should have been rock solid, with all this behind us. How could we have shared all this history, gone this far back and yet still end up apart?'

'I don't know.' Kate held him in a frank gaze. 'You tell me.'

'I wish I knew. But looking at these. . .'

'What?'

'I just wonder if it was a mistake.'

'Us?'

'No. . . us breaking up. I wonder if I've made the mistake.'

'Well. . .' Kate slammed the album she was holding shut. 'It's too late now.'

'Is it?'

'We're divorced – remember?'

'People remarry.'

'And leave their pregnant girlfriends in the lurch?'

'She got herself pregnant. . . it all happened so fast.'

'With the turkey baster, I suppose. . . Get real, Matt. For once in your life take responsibility for a mess of your making.'

'That's what I'm trying to do. . . Kate. . . I would miss you if you went to Rome. I didn't realise how much until you told me it was really going to happen. It's made me think a lot about what I've done, the thought of you not being in my life any more, not just around the corner. I. . . it doesn't matter.'

'If you're saying what I think you're saying then you'd better stop right there.'

'I need to tell you. Don't go to Italy. It's not right for you.'

'There's nothing here for me, Matt. Why shouldn't I go?'

'I'm here.'

'With Tamara! I'm hardly going to be coming over for Sunday lunch, or babysitting or watching the tennis with you both. You have a new life now and I need one too.'

'I don't love Tamara!' he cried.

Kate stared at him. He was telling her this now? Why? She had a horrible feeling she knew why, and if he dared to say it she wasn't sure she would be able to contain her anger. She stood up and backed away from the bed. 'It's a bit late for that now, isn't it? I hope you're not telling me this while keeping her in the dark, because I don't think that's very fair.'

'I can't tell her. I can't talk to her about anything. . . not like I can with you.'

'That's not what you said when you left me. Then you didn't want to talk or listen.'

'But. . . a man can make a mistake, can't he?'

'Yes. But then he has to be man enough to live with the consequences. We can't go back.'

'Why not?' Matt leapt up from the bed and strode across to her. He tried to take her into his arms and she dodged his embrace.

'Because I don't want to!'

'You're happier like this?' His tone had an edge again, hardened just a little. 'Is that why you're running away to Italy?'

'I'm not running away from anything – I'm running towards something. There's a world of difference.'

'To this man? Whatever his name is. . .?'

Kate ignored the jibe. 'Yes.' There was a moment's silence, during which neither could look at the other. Kate struggled to hold in her rage. It wasn't the fact that he wanted her back, or that he'd admitted he didn't love Tamara – it was the selfishness that made her want to punch him. His girlfriend was pregnant, and he was about to be a dad – the most important, the most precious job in the world. Across town Lily and Joel mourned the loss of their hopes and dreams to start a family, and yet Matt was happy to walk away from his before it had even begun, on a whim or a fit of jealousy, or just plain fear. Whatever it was, her blood boiled at the thought of it.

'I think you should go,' she said quietly. 'I expect Tamara is waiting for you.'

'But—'

'Before you say anything worse than you have already.'

'What about the jobs?'

'I'll get a handyman in to do them. Please. . . just go. I'll phone you if there's any movement on the house sale. Otherwise we have no need to talk to each other again.'

'That seems harsh.'

'Does it? It seems perfectly reasonable to me, but if you want to see me being harsh I can arrange that.'

He opened his mouth to speak, but then he closed it again. Without another word, he left the room, and Kate listened to his footsteps on the stairs, the rustles and clanks of him gathering his belongings, and then the slam of the front door as it shut behind him.

Twenty-four

Kate knew that Anna or Christian would be straight round to Matt's new place to give him a roasting, and she had no desire to drag what had happened between them that afternoon out any longer or for it to become more complicated. Lily had enough to worry about with her own relationship teetering on the brink and still dealing with her grief, and so Kate had decided against telling Anna or Lily about Matt's admissions. She certainly couldn't tell Alessandro. Other friends were mutual, or too close to Matt, or possibly knew Tamara, or knew too much about the whole affair already, and so there was nobody close to confide in. She did desperately need to get it off her chest, though, to talk it through and make some sense of a situation that made no sense at all. That left Jamie. A brand new and relatively untested best friend, but still a brilliant choice when you needed to get something off your chest – happy to listen and too far away to cause problems.

It was late when she sent the text, but he'd probably be just home from work.

Hey, got time to talk?

It was another half hour before he replied.

I have corn chips and beer and I'm all set. Want to FaceTime? Then you can see me in all my post-work glory.

Kate smiled to herself as she dialled the number. Post-work glory for her would have been bags under the eyes and a vacant stare, possibly some drool leaking from the corner of her mouth where it had been hanging open all day. Jamie would probably look like a golden-skinned Adonis.

Her heart did a little dance as his face appeared on the screen. The bruises he'd sustained from his altercation with Roberto had faded now, and he looked happy, healthy and extremely handsome – just like when she'd first met him at the taxi rank at Fiumicino airport.

'Well, hello there!' he said. Kate grinned.

'Hello yourself. You look really well.'

'So do you.'

'No, I don't think so. I'm getting pasty already now I'm back at home.'

'Pale and interesting.'

'Something like that.'

'Hey, I was sorry to hear about your sister. I didn't want to call or interfere or anything, but if you feel like talking now I'm all ears.'

Kate smiled. 'Thanks. It's really Lily's suffering and her who needs the help. I just stand by and watch and be a bit useless.'

'I'm sure that's not true but I do understand what you mean. You may not realise it but you're probably going through a significant amount of stress too.'

'Perhaps,' Kate agreed. 'Though it's not all from Lily.'

'You're missing Alessandro?'

'Like crazy.'

'But you're still going ahead with your plans to get back to Rome permanently?'

Kate sighed. 'That's just it – I don't know. It feels like two steps forward and three back at the moment. Maybe it's not meant to be.'

'You can't back down now! What happened to following your dreams, taking a leap of faith and all that other bullshit you spouted when we spoke last?'

'Maybe it was just that – bullshit.'

'Hey. . . I can't believe I'm hearing this. You pull yourself together right now.'

'Thanks, Jamie,' Kate said, smiling. 'See, I feel better already having spoken to you.'

'But you still don't feel brave enough?'

Kate shook her head, tears filling her eyes. She sniffed them away. She'd been strong so far, for the sake of everyone else, but she didn't feel like being strong any more – at least not right now. She deserved a little weakness sometimes, didn't she? It wasn't a crime to show that you weren't quite in charge of everything, was it?

'You want to tell Uncle Jamie all about it?' he asked. He held up a green bottle. 'I have plenty of beer to hand.'

'We don't want our *Airplane!* moment, though. I warned you before how it might go if I started offloading my problems.'

'You did,' he laughed, 'but I think I'll be able to hold out for a while. Is this about your sister? You feel bad about leaving her?'

'Partly that. Joel isn't doing much better and I'm worried that losing the baby will split them up. You have no idea how perfect they are for each other and what a terrible waste that would be, and I have to at least try to help them get through it without destroying each other. And I know Lily has Anna too, but I still feel as if I'm abandoning them when they need me most. We're a close family, and we've always helped each other through everything; it wouldn't be right for me to leave them in the lurch this time.'

'So delay things. It doesn't mean you have to give up your dreams altogether and I'm sure they wouldn't want you to.'

'But what if it's a huge mistake?'

'Why this negativity suddenly? I thought you had this. When I spoke to you last—'

'I don't know. . . something Matt said, my own doubts, a feeling that I'm shirking my real responsibilities, that I'm running away from things I don't feel capable of dealing with. But those things will still be there even if I live in Rome. They might come in different packaging but they'll still be there.'

'What did Matt say? Or can I guess this?'

'You can probably guess it. I told him about Alessandro. I didn't see any point in hiding it and he's got Tamara now. He said that I was running away and I belong here in England. Perhaps he's right.'

'It has nothing to do with Matt. What does he care where you go? He gave up all rights to have an opinion when he walked out on you.'

'We have a history together. He's just looking out for me.'

'It doesn't sound that way to me. Are you sure he's not just jealous?'

Kate paused. 'I don't know. He said. . .'

Jamie rolled his eyes. 'He wants you back, can't stop thinking about you, he's made a terrible mistake. . . All the rest of it.'

Kate raised her eyebrows. 'How did you know?'

'Honey, I've been round the block a few times, even though this youthful face would say otherwise. Of course he wants you back because now he can see that you're having more fun than he is. He wants what you have, or what he thinks he can't have, and he'll never be happy with what he's got because someone else's life will always look better.'

'I don't think it's that. . .'

'Think about it – he didn't want you until someone else wanted you. Now Alessandro finds you desirable he does too. But if you were his again, he'd take you for granted like he did before. Like the little kid who doesn't like apples until his best friends are all telling him that apples are the greatest thing in the world, then he wants apples. But when he gets an apple it's not what he thought it would be. You understand?'

'I'm an apple?'

'You're an apple, and a cute one at that. So screw Matt. He had his chance of apples and he blew it. Let someone else who'll enjoy it have the apple.'

Kate laughed lightly, but then she frowned. 'Say you're right, I still don't know if that's the answer. It doesn't mean I have to take him back – and believe me that is the last thing on my mind – but it doesn't mean Rome is the right choice either.'

'What about Alessandro? I thought you were crazy in love.'

'But when it comes down to it, I've only known him for a week.'

'You love him?'

'I feel as if I do, but it's complicated, isn't it? I don't know him at all so how can I be certain?'

'Maybe you know enough. It's not like you can't go home if it doesn't work out.'

'That's true, but I don't know if I'm emotionally solid enough to deal with the fall-out if it doesn't.'

He was silent for a moment as he sipped his beer. 'I think that's your issue right there. Only you can get past that and move on and only you know if you're strong enough to try. But I wouldn't spend too much longer working it out, because from what I've seen of your hot cop, those ladies must be forming a line around the block bigger than the one to get into the Vatican museums for a piece of him.'

'He wouldn't go with another woman, would he?' Kate asked, filled with a sudden sense of alarm as her thoughts went back to the wilful and very available Orazia, who was ready and waiting to take her place at a moment's notice and would be only too happy to erase Kate from Alessandro's thoughts. Was he the unfaithful type? Would he go off with someone else that quickly in her absence? He was attractive and charming, and he was only human. Perhaps Jamie had unwittingly provided her with the answer to the problem of whether she should go or not, but not the one he wanted to. 'I mean, he'd wait?'

'Nobody is going to wait forever. It may be tough, but you need to make a decision or you'll lose him.'

* * *

Jamie's words stayed with Kate until the lights had gone out and she was lying in bed, still wrestling with them as she tried to sleep. She had wanted to speak to Alessandro, just to hear his voice and feel reassured that he wasn't going to give up on her, but he wasn't answering his phone. He was probably on duty, but it didn't help to allay her fears.

Things hadn't exactly got any easier when she woke the next morning to a long email from Lucetta. It was no surprise to hear from her, as she'd promised to search for an apartment for Kate and was updating her on what she'd found, sending over the details for one in particular that she thought was great – in a prime location, reasonable rent, a landlord with a good reputation, wonderful views and the most beautiful clematis trailing from the balcony. It sounded perfect and Kate felt a flutter of excitement just looking at the photos, though she had to check herself on noting that the rent wasn't quite as reasonable as Lucetta seemed to think. Trying not to choke on her wake-up coffee, Kate read on, and if she had spluttered at the sight of the rent on the proposed apartment, what came next was sure to send a spray of coffee right across her living room had she not been half expecting it.

Alessandro has spoken to Mamma. He has told her about your love for each other. I was in the kitchen with Abelie, and we ran in to see what the matter was. Mamma was shrieking and crying. She said she would not have invited you into our home if she had known. Alessandro said she was overreacting but Mamma thinks it is a huge disaster. Mamma thinks that you will not come back as you have said you would and Alessandro will have his heart broken again, and he will never try to find a wife after that. I told her that we have been trying to find an apartment for you. Mamma says that even if you do return to Rome you will want to go home to England eventually and you and Alessandro will get a divorce. Mamma says that would put her in a grave (we have not dared to tell her that you are already divorced). Alessandro says you and he are not getting married yet so she does not need to worry, but that made her crying worse! She says there is no point in you coming to Italy to be with Alessandro if you are not going to get married. But you will marry Alessandro, won't you? Mamma will not be happy until you do. I am leaving home, of course, but poor Abelie will have to listen to her complaints every day, and she begged me to ask you if you would consider marrying Alessandro very soon.

I asked Mamma if she liked you and she said yes, you were a very kind and good woman but not for Alessandro. He told her again that he loves you, and she said that was worse because if you wanted to go back to England he would want to return with you and live there and her only son might as well be dead as living in Manchester. She says that she would probably die on the spot anyway, so I said it wouldn't matter if Alessandro was dead to her or not because she wouldn't know about it. She did not like that and chased me from the kitchen with a broom. She has not done that since I was fifteen.

I am sorry to tell you, dear Kate, that my mother has decided to try very hard to find Alessandro an Italian girl to marry. She likes you very much, and I do not want you to be offended by this, but she says you belong in England with an English man. If you love Alessandro as I know he loves you, you must return soon or Mamma may find someone he likes just as well in your absence. She is so desperate I think she would even consider Orazia, which would make Maria happy, although I think the rest of us may consider leaping out of the window. But when Mamma says she will do something, she is very determined. She has already spoken to Federigo Valvona about his daughter, but I do not care for her because she once said my nose was big. I went to see Federigo and told him that my mother was going crazy in her old age and Alessandro did not need to meet with his daughter because he was spoken for, but I will not be able to do this every time Mamma tries to find a match.

I hope it is not raining too much in England. Rome is sunny and hot, and we miss you.

Lucetta.

Kate had to assume that when Lucetta said they missed her, she was referring to herself and Alessandro and possibly Abelie. It certainly didn't sound as if Signora Conti did. Lucetta was probably aiming for sparky conversation rather than all-out threats, and Kate was sure she had meant well in sending the email to keep Kate abreast of all that was happening in the Conti household, but in reality all it had done was feed the doubts Kate had already been growing rather nicely herself. If his mother didn't really believe in a relationship with Kate, and had more or less told Alessandro that she didn't want Kate in their family, however highly she had regarded her as a friend (she was not even that, but only a brief visitor really), then was there any point in going back to Rome? If the matriarch wouldn't accept Kate, then would Alessandro end up bending to her will? And all those beautiful, suitable, favoured Italian girls would be there to step into Kate's shoes in a heartbeat, just as Jamie had said. Despite Lucetta's insistence that she was not suitable or wanted either, images of Orazia sitting next to Alessandro at the family dinner table, taking the place Kate should have occupied instead, filled her thoughts. It seemed that bloody woman refused to leave them, and her face popped up more and more the longer she spent away from Alessandro, which was worrying in itself and suggested to Kate that she might soon be just as much a bunny boiler as her adversary. And although she had no idea what Federigo Valvona's daughter looked like, she couldn't trust that the girl wasn't lovely enough to turn Alessandro's head in her absence either. It was frustrating that she couldn't be in Rome to smooth everything out, but then would she have made things better, even if she had been there? For now she had to trust that Alessandro and Lucetta could fight her corner and talk their mother round.

After breakfast she had tried to call Alessandro again, but once again his phone was unanswered, and so there was nothing more she could do but dwell on what a mess it was all becoming.

* * *

Kate cheered herself up the only way she knew how – she made a dress. And it seemed a good idea to try and cheer someone else up in the process, so after breakfast, once she had decided that she wouldn't be able to speak to Alessandro for a while without interrupting his shift, and that it was pointless to mope about it, she set about making a dress for Lily. It was a copy of her rose-print number, a dress that Lily had always admired, using a swathe of fabric patterned in a forget-me-not motif she'd picked out and bought with Lily a few weeks before but hadn't got around to using yet. The sizing would have to be approximate because she wanted it to be a surprise for Lily, but she could alter it once her sister had tried it on to make it the perfect fit. It wasn't exactly going to lift her from her grief – Kate wasn't silly enough to think it would come anywhere near – but at least it might be a symbol, something to show Lily that Kate was thinking of her.

* * *

It was early evening by the time Kate had got the dress in a state she felt happy enough to show Lily, and during that time she had pushed all other thoughts but the creation of it from her head. So by the time she turned off the sewing machine, she felt calm and pleasantly empty of her recent angst. A quick text to Lily confirmed that she was up to a visitor, and rather than sit around moping by herself, Kate was in the car and on her way over.

Joel answered the door. He looked exhausted, and almost over-whelmed with relief to see Kate, but at least he was there and that was progress considering his absence at her last few visits. Perhaps he and Lily had had that talk after all, she wondered as she followed him down the hallway.

'You two don't need me, do you?' he asked as Kate bent to the sofa to give Lily a kiss.

'We'll be alright for an hour,' Kate said.

'OK. I'll get out of your way. . . have an hour on the Xbox.'

Kate smiled and he disappeared. 'How are you feeling today?' she asked Lily.

'Pointless,' Lily replied.

'And Joel? You two are OK?'

'He's still here. . .'

Lily looked spaced out but calm enough. Kate supposed that was down to the drugs she was taking. She didn't have an answer for her sister's critical appraisal of the situation, so she simply sat down next to her and pulled the dress from a bag. 'What do you think?'

'It's gorgeous,' Lily said in a dull voice.

'It's the same pattern as the rose one you like so much.'

'Oh, I see that now. Did you just make that?'

'Yes. For you. Remember this fabric? We picked it out but you said. . .' The sentence tailed off as Kate recalled the conversation. Lily had chosen the fabric and Kate had said she would use it to make her a dress. But Lily hadn't wanted Kate to do it until after the baby was born, in case she had changed shape or size. 'Well. . . the point is you chose it so I'm hoping the dress isn't too far off what you wanted.'

'It's beautiful,' Lily said. 'Thank you.'

Kate laid the dress across the duvet that Lily had pulled up around her shoulders like a shield. Lily didn't reach for it; she simply stared at it.

'Do you want to try it on?' Kate asked. 'Then I can see if it needs altering.'

'I haven't had a shower today – I'll probably make it dirty.'

'It'll wash.'

Lily shook her head. 'Later. I'll have a shower when you've gone and then try it on. If it needs altering I'll let you know.'

Kate chewed her lip. She had hoped to get more of a response than this – not that she expected undying gratitude, but she had wanted to shake Lily into a more receptive state. Her sister loved clothes, and especially loved the fact that Kate could make them for her so that nobody else had the same, and Kate had been convinced that she would be a little more engaged with her surprise gift than this.

Lily pulled her duvet further up around her neck and turned onto her side. She looked up at Kate. 'Have you got another job yet?'

'No. I don't intend to. . . at least, not at the moment. I'm going to get some business cards done, put some advertising out, see if I can get some orders for sewing in. I thought I'd have a look for some premises maybe too, if the rents are cheap enough.'

'Is there any point in finding premises if you're moving away?'

Kate blinked. So Anna had told Lily about her plans? But this was the first Lily had said about it. Did that mean she didn't care? Or that she simply had so much of her own pain and worry she didn't have room to fit any more in?

'What's Anna told you?'

'That you want to live in Rome.'

'That's it?'

'And about your boyfriend there.'

Kate opened her mouth to speak, but they were interrupted by a knock at the door.

'That'll be Anna now,' Lily said, though she made no attempt to get up.

Kate stood and went to the door to let her other sister in.

* * *

'I just don't think it's a wise move, at least not without a bit of time to think it over,' Anna said. She was curled up in the armchair across from Kate, while Lily was tucked up in her duvet, watching the exchange. The conversation had turned pretty quickly to Kate's plans, particularly as it was the topic they had been discussing on Anna's arrival. 'What's the rush?' Anna continued. 'Leave it for six months and if you still feel strongly that Rome is where you want to be then see about going. But you're fresh back from a fantastic holiday where you met a fella and probably had some steamy sex. . .' she held a hand up to silence Kate's protest, 'and so you're bound to be viewing it through rose-tinted glasses. The reality of trying to set up home won't be anything like that.'

'I'm not twelve,' Kate said, failing to keep the note of irritation from her voice. 'I know the reality won't be like that. I know it will be tough. . . The thing that's bothering me most is not going there and starting anew, it's leaving things here. . .' She glanced at Lily, who was staring into space. Her gaze turned back to Anna, who gave a slight nod. It would be difficult for any of them to leave the other two in normal circumstances – they had become so close in the years their mother had been living in Scotland, had come to rely on each other – and now that Lily's need was greater than ever, it would be even more difficult to contemplate leaving. But didn't Kate deserve some happiness too? Was she being selfish to ask for it?

There was silence for a moment, punctuated only by the sound of muffled footsteps on the floor above as Joel moved around.

'If it makes you happy, you should go,' Lily suddenly said into the void. It was her first input into the debate since Anna had arrived.

'I'm not saying she shouldn't, but only after a decent period of careful consideration,' Anna said.

'If she's free and eager, she should just go. What's the point in waiting around?'

'Because that would be the sensible thing to do.'

'What's the point in sensible? Tomorrow everything could be shit – best to grab some happiness while you can.'

'You're supposed to back me up!' Anna squeaked.

'I changed my mind. I think Kate should go if she wants to.'

Kate looked from one to the other. So, despite Lily's problems, they had discussed this at some point. And though Anna had thought she had Lily's backing, it seemed Lily had now decided to voice a conflicting opinion. It was rare – often Anna had the final word with both of them – but she was particularly influential where Lily was concerned. Lily had always looked up to her, admired her, wanted to be just like their eldest sister in a way that Kate hadn't done quite so much. She had often wondered whether that was a lot to do with the influence Matt had exerted over her formative years, whereas Lily hadn't had her first proper boyfriend until she was seventeen and had spent a lot more time with Anna as a result.

'If you've decided to go then go,' Anna said, turning to Kate. 'But it won't be with my blessing.'

'What does that mean? You won't give your blessing? Don't you want me to be happy?'

'I can't, Kate. How can I give my blessing to something that I think is crazy and will end in disaster? If I did I'd be lying and doing you a disservice. I'd be failing you as a sister and a friend. Surely you can understand what I'm saying? Would you give it if things were the other way around; if it was me going off half-cocked?'

'It's hardly half-cocked. I came home, I'm wrapping things up here, putting other things in place before I go—'

'You walked out of your job! That's half-cocked to me.'

'You've been telling me for years to get out of that job!'

'Not like that. You find another one first – it's what everyone else does.'

Kate let out a long sigh. It felt as if they were going round in circles with this discussion, and she was beginning to realise that Anna would never see her point of view no matter how many times they went over it. She wondered if Alessandro was having as much trouble at his end. Possibly, if Lucetta's email was anything to go by. The notion didn't exactly fill her with confidence that this future she dreamed and hoped for could ever get any further than dreaming and hoping.

'I can't just carry on as if nothing has changed. Everything has changed. . . I've changed because of it. I'm not the same person any more.'

'But you're still our sister. We're still a rock-solid team, aren't we?'

'Of course. . .' Kate chewed her lip as she glanced at Lily again, no longer following the conversation after her brief moment of lucidity but staring out the window. 'Of course we are. We'll always look out for each other, just like we all promised when Mum left. But. . .'

It was selfish to leave. Anna would see it that way even if Lily didn't. Anna would be left with not only Lily to worry about, but Kate too.

'I can't tell you what to do and I understand that you feel you want something big to happen, to make changes in your life.' Anna reached for her arm and gave it a gentle squeeze. 'I just don't think this is the right way to go.'

'That's you *and* Matt then,' Kate said. 'You both think I'm mental.'

'Not mental, just tired and eager for something else. I get that. I'm not saying don't go; I'm just asking that you give it some time. And not just the time it would take you to sell up and go anyway, but some real time to reflect and think about it and be sure it's the right thing for you. Surely if you're determined to do it then another six months won't make any difference. And if that six-month delay does make a difference to how you feel, then maybe it wasn't quite the plan you thought it was.'

Kate looked at her. It mattered to Anna a great deal, she could tell. And six months wasn't so long really, was it? Long enough to see Lily get well, sell her house, set up a business that could make her a little money and make Anna happy. She wouldn't change her mind, no matter what Anna thought, but she would have proved her point and Anna would back down, give her blessing to the venture. Whether Alessandro could or would wait for six months was a different matter, but Kate supposed she could visit, just to remind him of what he was missing in case he got impatient enough for his affections to stray. And if she lost him. . . she didn't want to dwell on that, but maybe Anna had a point. Perhaps if she lost him it was never meant to be in the first place. But if he loved her he'd wait, wouldn't he? If they were meant to be then no time would be too long to wait. . .

Twenty-five

When she called him the next morning, Alessandro said nothing of his mother's plans, and Kate said nothing of Anna's disapproval and request for her to wait a while before deciding about moving. It was probably a bad sign that both were keeping secrets but, for Kate, it felt like a subject too difficult to broach and she supposed Alessandro felt that way too. Kate had contented herself to hear his words of love, how much he was looking forward to seeing her again, and she had promised that as soon as she was able she would visit for a weekend, even if she couldn't stay for good right away. He told her about work, about Lucetta's progress with the organising of her impending nuptials, about a new boyfriend Abelie had brought home who he was watching very carefully before he decided whether he liked him or not, and about how he'd checked on Pietro and his family at the trattoria to find that they seemed to have come to an acceptance of Pietro's coming out and that Pietro himself was back working in the restaurant with Luigi and Roberto. Pietro's mother had instigated the truce, and had threatened to disown Roberto if he resorted to violence again and, in Alessandro's opinion, the mother having the last word was the most sensible resolution to their problems.

Meanwhile, Matt had been back to finish the jobs he needed to do on the house while Kate was out and had left his keys on the table in a gesture of closure. He'd finally relinquished his hold on her life, and it seemed he was telling her to move forward with his blessing. She didn't know what had caused this epiphany, and she didn't need to; she was just glad he'd seen sense. It was a shame if what he'd said about his relationship with Tamara was true, but he would have to deal with it by himself now. With everything neat and tidy, the house had gone on the market and within a week Kate had accepted an offer for the asking price; Matt in agreement that they should take it. So things were moving along at a brisk pace now, but it only made Kate anxious that it was a pace she'd struggle to keep up with. She didn't have anywhere else to live, didn't have her dress business up and running yet, had no temporary job to tide her over and even her plans to move to Italy were on hold. Lily had offered her the spare room at their place, but Kate had been loath to accept, despite being touched by the gesture. The last thing they needed was the stress of a permanent guest, and the last thing she needed was to be sucked into the atmosphere of negativity and sadness that still smothered their house like a blanket. Kate had enough stress of her own, without adding Lily and Joel's to it.

She was packing when the knock came. The sun streamed into her bedroom, illuminating the buttercup yellow of the walls, the honeyed tones of the woodwork, but also showing up the dust on the skirting boards. Kate had let out a sigh, made a mental note to clean them later on, and had started to sort a lifetime of hoarded books into piles that she would definitely take to wherever she was going, ones that she would give away and ones that would otherwise flit back and forth between the two piles because she couldn't make up her mind. It was a job that she found therapeutic, and she smiled at the memories each book elicited as she found herself flicking through the pages, old bookmarks, bits of letters, handwritten notes falling from them. There was an old book of nonsense rhymes her dad had bought for her on a trip to Chester when she was ten, a vampire novel – the first book she had ever bought for herself with her first wages from a Saturday job at the local hairdressers – a book about decorating gifted from Anna when Kate had first moved into this house with Matt, and the complete Brontë collection, leather-bound and gold-embossed, that Lily had bought her for her twenty-first birthday. Kate wiped a tear from her eye. It was strange how objects manufactured for mass consumption could have such personal meanings for the person at the end of the chain, who treasured them like real memories alive in their heads.

She'd just sat down with the decorating book, idly glancing over the pages at all the tips and techniques she'd tried out on the bricks and mortar now surrounding her with varying degrees of success. And then she heard the rap at the front door. It wasn't Anna's knock, which was always a single assertive boom, nor was it Lily's jaunty little rhythm. Three raps of a knuckle, separated by distinct pauses.

Putting the book to one side, Kate wiped the dust from her hands on the old jeans she was wearing and chanced a quick glance in the mirror before heading down to get the door. Her hair was scraped back into a ponytail, and apart from a thin layer of foundation she hadn't bothered with her make-up; a big shirt with the sleeves rolled up covered a strappy top beneath. She hoped it wasn't the buyers for the house, who had promised to come back and measure up for soft furnishings at some point. If they had come unannounced it would be difficult not to be annoyed despite the fact they were taking a huge millstone from around her neck.

With a sigh, she made her way downstairs. Through the small square of frosted glass she could see a shadow, a profile that looked familiar, and suddenly her heart was beating like a steam hammer. It couldn't be. . .

Flinging the door open wide, Kate's hand flew to her mouth as she saw Alessandro smiling on the doorstep.

'Hello, Kate,' he said.

'What. . . what are you doing here?' she stammered.

His face fell. 'I should not have come?'

'God, yes!' she squealed, throwing herself at him. He caught her in his arms and held her close. It felt so good, so right, and she was suddenly overwhelmed with a fierce love. It wasn't until this moment that she had let herself think about how much she was missing him, because if she had she would have crumbled, unable to function. But now he was here, it was like the stopper was yanked from the bottle of emotions she'd been struggling to keep shut, and she began to cry. 'I missed you so much!' she whispered. 'So, so much. . . I thought about you every minute of every day.' She rubbed her eyes and stared up at him. 'I can't believe you're really here!'

'I am here,' he smiled. 'I missed you too. I wanted to see you, and I had permission to take time from my job to come.'

'You came all the way to England for me?'

'Why else?'

Kate's eyes filled with tears again, even as she beamed through them. 'Nobody has ever done anything so romantic for me before.'

'Then nobody has loved you as I do.'

She pulled away to stare at him, as if she took her eyes off him for a second he would disappear in a puff of smoke.

'I can't believe you're here,' she repeated.

He lifted a bouquet bearing the signs of crush damage. Clearly damage she'd caused in her haste to get into his arms. 'These are for you.'

They were beautiful despite the odd casualty – a bounty of delicate pink and white roses embellished with tiny beads that looked like water droplets. They must have cost a fortune. The only flowers she'd ever been given were ones Anna or Lily had picked up for her at the end of market day as they were being sold off or ones that Matt had hastily collected from the supermarket or petrol station when he'd done something to upset her and needed to get back in the good books. Not that she had been unhappy to receive any of those gifts, but Alessandro's were something else.

'They're gorgeous! Thank you!'

She took the flowers from him and breathed in the sweet perfume. She had never imagined that roses could smell so divine. Surely they must have been engineered somehow, because the scent was intoxicating. Or perhaps it was just Alessandro being on her doorstep making her giddy, because she couldn't seem to think straight and she was almost convinced that if she looked away she'd find he'd never actually been there at all.

They gazed at each other, silent and grinning, until Alessandro spoke and broke the spell.

'Perhaps you would like me to come back later?'

'Why?'

He arched an eyebrow, and that playful, teasing smile she had missed so much came out to taunt her. 'I have surprised you and perhaps you are not ready for guests?'

Kate yanked the band from her ponytail and mussed her hair to let it fall around her shoulders. There wasn't a lot she could do about the clothes right now, except sit him down and make him wait while she did her best to improve things. But even as she was thinking this, he pulled her into his arms and planted a passionate kiss on her lips that faded the world around her. 'You look beautiful,' he breathed. 'More beautiful to these eyes that have not seen you for so long.'

Oh God. . . his scent. . . the heat of his body against hers. . . the feel of his hands on her waist. . . the voice like velvet. . . that accent. . . He had come for her, thousands of miles just for her. Nothing else mattered. 'You'd better come in,' she replied in a teasing whisper. 'We have a lot of catching up to do. . .'

Twenty-six

The sun dipped into the room, and as it hit Alessandro's skin, he seemed to glow. It was silly, of course, but Kate was mesmerised by the way it kissed his tanned arms, made him look almost godlike. He had certainly been as godlike in bed as she remembered, and as she lay in his embrace now, the thrum of his steadily beating heart in her ears, she basked in the afterglow, content and sleepy and yet more alive and exhilarated than she had ever been.

'I missed you so much,' she said into the silence.

'I missed you too.'

'I'm so happy to see you, although I wish I'd known you were coming.'

'I am sorry. . . I should have warned you. I wanted to surprise you. I thought you would be glad and amused.'

'Not that,' Kate replied quickly. 'Of course I'm glad! I think what we just did should have told you that. . . But I would have got food and cleaned the house and stuff. I'm halfway ready to move out so I'm in a bit of a mess.'

'I can help while I'm here,' he said. 'I have a hotel so you don't need to worry about where I will sleep.'

'You don't have to go back to the hotel tonight. . .'

'I should go to the hotel. I do not think your sister will like it if I stay here.'

'Sister?' Kate frowned. 'What's it got to do with my sisters? I don't understand. . .'

'Anna. I have spoken to her.'

Kate shot up and stared at him. 'You've spoken to Anna? When? How?'

He sat and took her hand. 'Don't be angry with her. She phoned the *questura* and found me. She wanted to know what I was like, if I am good for you, if I am honest. It is only what I would do for my sisters. . .'

'That's completely different!' Kate squeaked. 'She has no right to stick her nose in!' She started to get off the bed, intent on fetching her phone and giving Anna a piece of her mind. How dare she call Alessandro to spy on him and check him out! How dare she assume Kate was so useless and docile that she couldn't even choose a man for herself without him being a complete charlatan! How dare she take up the mantle of protector or guardian, or whatever it was she thought she was doing, without Kate's knowledge! Kate was an adult and she would make her own choices. She might discuss them with her sisters and she might even take on board their opinions but that did not give them the right to interfere. 'I think I can make up my own mind about whether you're good for me! Is that why you've come? Did she ask you to come to somehow prove yourself to her?'

He shook his head. 'She did not ask me to come, but after I had spoken to her I understood that she is afraid for you. I came to make it easier for you. If she speaks with me in person perhaps she will be happier.'

'Oh. . .' Kate's anger evaporated. So he didn't come because he couldn't bear to be apart from her – he came because he felt he needed to straighten things out with Anna? It was a noble sentiment, of course, but somehow she felt deflated by the idea.

'And I wanted to see you.' He laughed lightly, as if reading her thoughts. 'Of course I wanted to see you.'

'I'm going to have to speak to her,' Kate said, relaxing back into his arms again. 'She has no right to call you. . . and she didn't even say a word to me. If you hadn't told me I wouldn't have known. Imagine if it had scared you away and we'd split up.'

'Nothing would scare me away from you.'

'Not even Anna? You must be brave.'

He grinned and kissed her. 'Even Anna could not keep me away from you. But I do want your sisters to be happy about me. I know you love them very much and I will do anything to make you happy.'

'That's so sweet of you. I'm still going to give her a good slap though, and then you can set about being charming to win her over. Not too charming, mind. I don't want you to win her over in quite the way you've won me over.'

He laughed. 'I will be careful. Please don't be angry with her.'

'Angry? You don't know what angry means until you've seen me in action with Anna. She seems to have this knack of bringing out my very angry side.'

'Are you angry with me?'

'Why would I be angry with you?'

'My surprise.'

'I don't mind your surprise. . . it's a very nice surprise. . .' Kate giggled as he pressed his lips to the back of her neck. 'That tickles.'

'Tickles?' He frowned.

'Makes me laugh.'

'Oh. . .' He pulled her round to face him. 'I do not want to make you laugh.'

'What do you want then?' she asked, unable to tear her gaze away from the darkness of his eyes. 'Because if you look at me like that for much longer I won't be laughing anyway. . . I'll be very horny.'

'Horny?' He raised an eyebrow at her.

Kate laughed. She would have to remember that he didn't know a lot of slang. Or she would have to learn Italian. Lord, how she'd hated modern language lessons at school – she'd been so terrible at French and German. Perhaps Italian lessons with Alessandro wouldn't be too bad. Although she could see the potential for almost every attempt to descend into a scene from a *Carry On* film. 'Horny means to want to make love.'

'You want to make love?' He grinned. 'We could do that now if it would please you.'

'Oh, it would please me,' Kate replied with a slow smile, all thoughts of Anna and her underhand scheming forgotten. 'You have no idea how much.'

* * *

Despite the bursting boxes stacked in corners and her kitchen utensils and pots in a state of disarray, Kate made a valiant attempt at Sunday lunch. In fact, it was possibly the most important Sunday lunch she had ever cooked, and she wanted desperately to impress Alessandro. The stodgy Yorkshire puddings and chunky roast beef were a world away from the delicate cooked meats and olives that she'd been served by Signora Conti, but he'd said he wanted to try a traditional British roast and if Kate was perfectly honest, it was just about as advanced as her culinary skills got. He had wanted to arrive from his hotel early to help, but she'd forbidden it, knowing that Anna wouldn't be able to resist doing just that – the stress of them meeting at lunch itself was enough without having them both present as she worked in the kitchen where she couldn't keep a close eye on the conversation. Worse still was the prospect of them both trying to help her to cook, where they might get under her feet, disagree on cooking methods or just stress her out so much that she ruined all the food. That they'd got to this point was a minor miracle in itself – Anna and Christian, Lily and Joel, her and Alessandro finally about to sit around a table together and share a meal for the first time. It felt hugely exciting and yet terrifying at the same time, although the fact that Lily felt able to leave her sofa to come to dinner was encouraging and perhaps the most exciting outcome of the day. It meant a lot to Kate that she was willing to make the effort, and perhaps she was now on the path to a recovery that, if not full, was a good start. She hoped that Joel would find it equally as encouraging and that they might start to mend their fractured relationship from this point on.

It had taken a stern phone call to Anna, during which they had both said things they'd instantly regretted, for them to finally call a truce. Anna was as shocked to hear that Alessandro had felt the need to come over to England to reassure her as Kate had been to see him standing on her doorstep, but she didn't offer an apology, only stood by her assertion that what he had done was not noble, only the most basic courtesy that he owed them all. It made Kate's blood boil, and she had to keep reminding herself of what Alessandro had said – that she shouldn't be angry with a sister who was only looking out for her. There had been a phone call from Lily an hour later, who had heard about Alessandro's arrival, and it was Lily who'd suggested they all share a meal to get to know one another. That had taken Kate by surprise too, but she was happy to hear Lily felt up to it and that she wanted to meet Alessandro properly. Lily had made the call to Anna – Kate was still feeling stubborn about the whole Anna calling Alessandro situation – and the date had been agreed. Kate had a feeling that Anna might give Alessandro a much harder time than Lily would, but she felt sure that he could win her over eventually. And if he didn't. . . well, Kate was a grown woman and it was nobody else's business what she did with her life. She wanted Anna's blessing, but her heels were digging further and further in with each altercation, and if she had to do it without, she was certain now that she would.

Lunch was scheduled for one, and just as Kate had predicted, Anna and Christian arrived at midday, the former armed with pots and extra food of her own and an apron, the latter banished to the living room to watch TV or read the papers – anything to stay out from under their feet until the food was ready. It was a cautious hug that Anna offered Kate; she seemed uncertain whether she was back in the good books or not, and Kate in turn was uncertain whether she could trust Anna to be polite and tolerant towards Alessandro.

Kate smiled. 'I knew you wouldn't be able to resist coming to help. I *can* cope, you know.'

'I know,' Anna said as she unpacked the bags of organic carrots, parsnips and cabbage she'd just picked up from the local farm shop and put them by the sink to be washed. 'But you have a lot of people coming over and I thought as well as helping, it would be a good idea to get here early and catch up.'

'Catch up?' Kate took the very expensive looking jar of horseradish sauce that Anna handed to her from the depths of her carrier bag. 'The kind of catch up where you warn me that you're not going to promise you'll like Alessandro or that this dinner will suddenly make everything hunky-dory?'

'Don't be like that.' Anna frowned and planted her hands on her hips. 'Can't you see I'm trying?'

'You're trying alright,' Kate muttered.

'It's hard for me to understand, that's all. But I will do my best to like him. After all, I want to feel confident that the man you're going off to Italy with is the right man for you, so why put barriers in the way of that? I'm going to be happier if I think you're OK; I'd have thought that much was obvious.'

'I'm not exactly going off to Italy with him; I was going to go to Italy anyway. It just so happens that we'll be a couple when I get there. My life won't revolve around him.'

'I didn't say that. But support will be further away if it goes wrong.'

'It won't go wrong,' Kate said, though she wished the conviction in her voice was what she truly felt in her heart.

'You can't know for sure,' Anna said, airing Kate's fears for her. 'Look what happened with Matt.'

'I was trying not to.'

Anna pulled a colander from a unit and began to tear the leaves from the cabbage to wash. 'I have to say I am quite impressed that Alessandro has come to England just to meet your family.'

'Well, I've met his, so I suppose it makes sense,' Kate said, choosing not to remind her of the real reason he had come, which was almost exclusively Anna's doing. It wouldn't serve any purpose to bring up that argument again, and Kate could see that Anna really was trying to put a positive spin on things, even if that was only to convince herself rather than anyone else. 'I wish you wouldn't worry quite so much. Is my character judgement really that bad?'

Anna paused and turned to her. 'No. But some people are really good at pulling the wool over everyone's eyes. You read about these things all the time – lonely women being conned by suave rogues.'

'Lovely,' Kate huffed. 'So that's what you think of me, is it? A sad, lonely, desperate divorcee who will throw herself at the first man who takes an interest?'

'Of course not!' Anna turned back to the cabbage and began to rip at it. 'I'm just saying I have some right to be suspicious. You'd thank me if he did turn out to be a bad one, and I would never forgive myself for not intervening.'

'You think you'd be a better judge than me? How come you'd be able to spot a con man but I couldn't?'

'Because you're emotionally involved and I'm not. They say love is blind and I think that can be quite true.'

'Besides,' Kate sniffed as she filled a pan with water, 'you're talking about rich old spinsters being courted by men who want British passports or money. As Alessandro needs neither of those I don't see how he could possibly be a danger.'

'I don't know what other reasons might be out there. Some men just get a kick out of screwing people over.'

'Anna, he's a policeman. What more proof do you want of his integrity?'

'That doesn't mean anything. He might not do anything to break the law but he might still be emotionally stunted. In fact—'

'Whatever horror story you're about to tell me, you can save it!'

'Alright. . . no need to get shirty.'

'I'm not shirty! It's just that we seem to be going round in circles. Please, can you get these ideas out of your head and give him the benefit of the doubt? Just try, for me?'

Anna was silent for a moment. She tore the last of the leaves from the cabbage and tossed the stalk into the bin. 'Only because I know it means a lot to you,' she said finally.

Kate pulled her into a hug. 'Thank you. It does mean a lot to me and if you give him a chance I know you'll love him.'

'I can't promise but I will try. I won't hold back if I see something I don't like, though.'

Kate smiled. 'I know you won't be capable of holding back. But I honestly don't think that will happen.'

Anna sniffed the air. 'Does your meat need checking?'

'It's fine, I just checked it before you came.'

'What's the joint?'

Kate shrugged. 'I don't know. . . it's just beef, I didn't really look.'

'So how do you know the correct way to cook it?'

'I looked at the instructions on the label.'

Anna frowned. 'Nobody uses the instructions to cook meat.'

'What are they there for then?'

'For people who don't know how to cook.'

'That's me then. So it's lucky there are instructions for me to follow or we'd be eating raw meat.'

Anna rolled her eyes. 'It's a good job I'm here.'

'I have cooked Sunday dinner before – many times.'

'Yes, but you've never had an Italian over for Sunday dinner before – they know about food.'

'And you're saying I don't?'

'Clearly not judging by the way you've tackled your roast. . .'

Kate opened her mouth to reply, but then she grinned.

'What?' Anna asked.

'Nothing,' Kate replied, but her grin spread. Anna would never admit it, but Kate had a feeling she was warming to the idea of Alessandro already. Otherwise, why would she care so much that he approved of their cooking?

'Where's your veg scraper?' Anna asked, her tone brusque.

Yep, she was definitely more bothered about the success of this afternoon than she was letting on. At least Kate hoped so, because it would make life a lot easier.

* * *

Kate had never seen Alessandro look scared of anything, not even when he'd been hunting down a known felon at the Colosseum, but he looked something close to scared now, sitting at the dinner table, surrounded by her sisters and their partners, all regarding him with curious eyes. A huge slab of roast beef took centre stage on the table, a little charcoaled around the edges but under the circumstances, Kate reflected, it could have been a lot worse. It wasn't as if she'd been short of distractions in the kitchen, and Anna's well-intentioned help had ended up as more of a hindrance by the time she'd finished either trying to take over Kate's kitchen or talking her ears off. The joint was flanked by her best serving dishes – usually reserved for Christmas Day so they looked incongruously festive right now – containing as many vegetables as she could think of to accompany the meat. The collection was finished off by a steaming pile of golden roast potatoes and a plate of Yorkshire puddings standing next to a holly-and-ivy decorated gravy boat.

'It smells wonderful,' Alessandro said. His smile was fixed, as if someone had stapled it to his face. Kate tried to give him a reassuring one of her own, but it felt a bit the same if she was honest.

'Thank you,' she said. 'It won't match up to your mother's cooking but I hope you'll like it.'

'I am sure it will be delicious,' he replied. 'What is it called?'

'Roast beef with all the trimmings. The trimmings just means it has veg and potatoes with it.'

He nodded. 'Ah. I do not eat this at home.'

'We have it every Sunday. . . well, most Sundays anyway.'

'*You* don't,' Anna said, raising her eyebrows at Kate.

'Sometimes I do,' she replied defensively.

'It must be a great deal of work to prepare,' Alessandro cut in.

Kate glanced at him. Conversation had never been so stilted between them, and she wondered vaguely if someone had sent a cardboard cut-out in the real Alessandro's place. She hoped things would improve, because she didn't like this new and boring Alessandro; she wanted the teasing, witty version back, and she wanted Anna and Lily to meet that version too.

'So, Alessandro,' Anna turned to him, 'Kate says you're a policeman.'

'Yes.'

'Do you like your job?'

'Yes.'

'And are there a lot of criminals in Rome?' she asked, throwing a pointed look at Kate as she did.

He shrugged. 'It is a large city. In every large city there are criminals. But I am proud that we keep Rome as safe as we are able.'

'Christian,' Kate cut in. 'Would you mind carving for me?' She threw a pointed look of her own at Anna. Another comment like that and she would have to take her sister in the kitchen and give her a good slap.

'No problem,' Christian said cheerfully. He seemed to be the only person in the room unaffected by the odd atmosphere, and he whistled softly as he began hacking at the meat in a way that was like no carving Kate had ever seen before, although she was quite sure she had seen something similar being done to a victim during a horror movie once. But it was easier to let him get on with it and he seemed to be happy enough with his little chore. It was clear that Anna never let him anywhere near a job as important as carving at home.

'I think law enforcement must be a very difficult job,' Joel said, and Lily nodded agreement. 'Anyone who does it has my respect.'

'I think so too,' Kate said, grateful beyond words that her youngest sister was there to lend some support.

'Especially with all that Mafia wandering around Italy,' Joel added, and Kate almost choked on the wine she had just taken a gulp of.

'I'm pretty sure there aren't Mafia bosses on every street corner,' she said, glancing quickly at Alessandro and hoping he wasn't offended. Suddenly this dinner didn't seem like a good idea after all. At the very least she should have briefed not only Anna, but everyone else on what not to say. Next he'd be asking how many Cornettos a day Alessandro ate.

Alessandro, to her relief, smiled patiently. 'Most of what I deal with is simple. Lost tourists and stolen purses and other such things.' He looked at Kate, and for the first time that afternoon she saw a little of the old Alessandro in his eyes.

'But that's how you met, isn't it?' Lily asked. 'Kate's stolen purse?'

Alessandro looked to Kate for guidance. He must have guessed that she wouldn't tell her sisters about the actual first time they'd met, when she'd been drunk and ridiculously vulnerable on the Spanish Steps and he'd had to pick her up and see her back to her hotel.

'That's how we met,' Kate replied for him.

'I think it sounds romantic,' Lily said. She turned to Joel. 'Doesn't it?'

'I suppose,' Joel said, looking as though he wouldn't know romantic if it slapped him around the goolies.

'I expect you get a lot of women coming to you reporting stolen things,' Anna said.

Kate frowned. Anna had promised to behave, and this wasn't Kate's idea of behaving.

'Some,' Alessandro said. 'I do what I can to help make it better so it does not spoil their trip to Rome.'

'I'll bet you do,' Anna said.

Kate kicked out, and her foot connected with a shin under the table.

'Ow!' Christian cried, almost dropping the carving knife. He stared at Kate. 'What. . .?'

'Oh God, I'm so sorry,' Kate said. 'I must have slipped crossing my legs.' She glanced at Anna and could see the ghost of a smile. Kate glowered at her. Was she doing this on purpose? Did she find it funny?

'Pass the plates,' Christian said, gathering up the carving utensils again.

One by one everyone held theirs out as he served the meat.

'Help yourself to everything else,' Kate said. There was a flurry of activity, and Kate was gratified to see Lily help herself to a pile of potatoes. Her little sister had lost so much weight over the previous couple of weeks that Kate was almost convinced she would end up in hospital. Kate saw Anna look too and noted the approving smile.

'You might always burn the meat, despite reading the cooking instructions,' Anna said to Kate, 'but you do know how to cook roast potatoes.'

'What do you mean I always burn the meat? Cheeky cow! I always burn the meat because you always insist on trying to help me and get under my feet instead!'

'You'd burn the meat anyway. Matt said you did it every time. . .' Anna stopped. 'Oh, I'm sorry,' she said, glancing between Kate and Alessandro.

Kate shook her head. 'Could you pass the peas?'

At least Anna had the decency to look embarrassed this time. She had probably not meant that comment as a jibe in the way she'd been trying to wind Kate up with the others, but this one had cut in a way the others hadn't. Alessandro didn't need reminding that Kate had had a life before him, with a man who was firmly entrenched into her family in a way he could never be. Kate didn't need reminding of it either. Perhaps he hadn't noticed the comment at all, but it was hard to tell what was going through his mind as he concentrated on spooning some of Anna's organic spring cabbage onto his plate.

'Would you like the carrots, Alessandro?' Anna asked him with uncharacteristic shyness. He looked up.

'Yes, please.'

She reached across the table and handed him the dish with a small smile. 'They're good,' she said. 'I get them from a local farm shop and he grows them without any chemicals at all.'

'You should try the parsnips too,' Lily said. 'Anna's honey-roasted parsnips are amazing.'

'You cooked them?' Alessandro asked Anna.

'I only helped today. Kate's done most of it.'

'You've helped a lot,' Kate said. 'With more than the cooking.'

Anna smiled. It seemed that things were moving in the right direction at last.

'I'm starving,' Lily said. 'I've been saving myself all day for this.'

'Well there's plenty,' Kate said. 'And I don't want to have to freeze any of this as I'm supposed to be emptying the thing, so you'd all better eat up.'

'I think we can assist with that,' Christian said, scooping a mound of potatoes onto his plate. He went for the Yorkshire puddings next, and after helping himself to one, handed the dish to Alessandro, who took one.

'What is it?' he asked.

'A Yorkie,' Christian said. 'The best bit of the dinner.'

'Yorkshire pudding,' Kate said in reply to Alessandro's slight frown of confusion.

'Oh, I have heard of these but I have never eaten one,' he replied.

'There's not much to them really,' Kate said. 'I don't know why everyone gets so excited about them but they do. Sunday dinner's not really Sunday dinner without one.'

'Or two or three,' Joel said, and Christian grinned at him.

'At least,' he agreed. 'Filled with gravy so it's nice and squishy.'

'No, mate,' Joel said looking horrified. 'Gravy? Keep them separate so they stay crisp – that's the way to eat one properly!'

Alessandro looked slightly bewildered as the debate between the two men got underway, and Lily giggled.

'You'd hardly think that they're getting passionate about what's essentially just batter,' she said.

Kate turned to her. It was the first time she had heard Lily laugh since she'd got back from Rome, and it was a sound that made her heart swell. If nothing else came from this dinner, that one sound would be enough on its own to make it all worth the effort.

'Apparently, batter is a very serious subject,' Kate replied. She glanced across at Anna, who was smiling at Lily too.

'Personally I can take or leave Yorkshire puddings,' Lily said. 'But your potatoes. . . Pass the gravy, would you?'

Kate, her eyes still trained on Lily, reached across the table. At the same time Alessandro shot up and reached for it too, so that instead of the thing she was trying to retrieve, Kate found her arm connecting with his, and the gravy boat he'd just grabbed in a bid to be helpful flew into the air and exploded all over the table and them both. The room was silent as everyone stared at the carnage.

'Oh, I'm so sorry!' Kate cried. 'Are you OK? You're not burnt, are you?'

Alessandro shook his head. 'I am sorry. It was my fault; I was trying to reach it for you. I have ruined your food.'

Lily stood up. She reached for the bowl of roast potatoes, now drenched in gravy, and spooned a few more onto her plate. 'Saves me a job,' she said.

Everyone else looked at one another.

'Although,' Lily added, glancing up at Joel and Christian, 'whether or not gravy works on Yorkshire puddings is a bit of a moot point now, isn't it? You're getting gravy whether you want it or not.'

Kate stared at Alessandro. His pristine white shirtsleeve was covered, and there was a good deal on his torso. There were even flecks of gravy in his hair. She supposed she hadn't fared much better, though everyone and everything else apart from the food seemed to have escaped.

'I'll get you a cloth to clean up,' she said, making to leave the table.

Alessandro licked at his hand. 'It's good,' he said, the smile that Kate knew so well now playing about his lips. 'Maybe I will eat it and there will be no need of a cloth.' He licked some more from his sleeve.

Kate stared at him. But then she heard a guffaw from Anna, followed by a high-pitched giggle from Lily and laughter from the boys.

'A man after my own heart,' Joel said. 'Why waste good food on a cleaning cloth?'

'Exactly,' Alessandro replied. He turned to Kate with a mischievous grin and she felt herself relax into the moment.

'I suppose I should get myself cleaned up then.'

'Don't worry; I'm sure Alessandro will lick your gravy off too,' Lily said, and the table erupted into fresh merriment. Kate couldn't help but laugh too. Gravy explosions aside, perhaps today wasn't going to be such a disaster after all.

Twenty-seven

There was something poetic in the fact that it had been blazing sunshine the day Alessandro arrived, and the day she had to bid goodbye to him again it was raining. They stood at the entrance to the departure lounge at Manchester airport, Kate stalling for time. Every second she could keep him from going through was precious, even though she knew she would have to let him go, and they had timed it down to the wire. She tried to console herself with the idea that she would only be letting him go for a short while, and she would see him again as soon as she could get organised at home, which would be a lot quicker without him there to distract her. It was scant consolation, though, when already, even before he'd gone through to the part of the airport where she couldn't follow, she felt the void he would leave in his wake open up before her. Nobody had ever made her feel this way before, and the force of the emotion almost overwhelmed her. She'd had no idea she could fall so hard and so quickly, but she had, and now she could barely imagine a life without him in it.

He glanced up at the departure board. 'My flight,' he said, angling his head at the monitor. 'I am sorry.'

'Sorry?'

'I have to leave you now.'

Kate tried to smile, tried to hide the lump that was pushing up into her throat. 'That you came at all is a lovely and unexpected bonus. You have nothing to be sorry for. It's been amazing to see you and I think you might have done wonders with my family too; I think they're secretly big Alessandro fans now, though Anna especially would never say it because she'd have to admit that she was wrong.'

'Good. I am glad they are happy.'

'I think so. It will make things easier when I come to Italy.'

'I hope that is soon now.'

'It will be. . . I'm working on it as best I can.'

He smiled down at her, brushing a stray hair from her face. '*Ti amo troppo.*'

'*Ti amo troppo,*' Kate replied.

He nodded. 'You are learning fast.'

'When it comes to love, yes.'

He bent to kiss her. 'I will be half a man until I see you again.'

Her reply was strangled by the tears that now took her breath.

'Don't cry,' he said. 'It will be soon.'

She nodded. 'Soon,' she whispered.

He gave her one last kiss, and then he was gone.

* * *

The house had never felt so vast and empty and it had never felt less like home. The old rooms she had once loved now felt like prison cells, barriers to her new life and to her reunion with Alessandro. The change in weather hadn't helped, the grey drizzle pressing in at every window, reflecting her mood. She had tried to shake her melancholy in the best way she knew how, by cutting the pieces to start a new dress. Sewing, creating anything, always made her feel peaceful and calm, but today she struggled to keep her mind on any of it. She had a pretty fabric with pastel seaside scenes printed on it, something she had picked up in the closing down sale of a haberdasher's a few months before, and she fetched it from the box that she'd packed it away in to go to the charity shop, when she'd thought she might not have time to make something from it after all.

The first piece she made too small, and then when she cut it again she nicked into the seam allowance. By the time she had decent pieces cut, she'd had enough and no patience to begin sewing and it was lucky there was any fabric left to sew at all. There was certainly no room for error now, and with her brain seemingly elsewhere there was plenty of opportunity for mistakes. With a sigh, she packed everything away and went to get her umbrella.

* * *

'Kate. . .?' Lily opened the door wider as she saw who was on her step. Kate noted with approval that she was dressed and looked tidy, despite her being at home and Joel being back at work now. Less than a week ago she would have stayed in her pyjamas all day and would probably have gone back to bed in the same ones too.

'Have you got time for a miserable cow?'

Lily smiled. 'Always. I haven't got much in the way of snacks, though, so I hope you're not hungry.'

'Oh. . . well, if you need shopping I can go for you—'

Lily shook her head. 'I need an excuse to go out myself. Joel is doing his best but he comes home with all sorts of things that don't go together, so I have to do it sooner or later and if you and Anna and Joel keep shopping for me I'll never go again. Thanks, but when every last crumb is gone I'll psych myself up for the supermarket.'

'We could go together?' Kate said.

'I don't think so.'

Kate took her gently by the arm and began to walk her down the hall. 'You're already dressed, I have my coat on and if I leave you to think about it you won't go. Get your shoes on and we'll go together right now, so neither of us will be backing out. I'm feeling miserable as sin and half an hour fondling marrows in the fresh produce section will cheer me up no end.'

Lily looked set to argue, but then she gave a sigh. 'I suppose I have to go sooner or later.'

'Exactly. And you should make the most of me while I'm still here.'

* * *

'How about some lovely nuts?' Kate asked, holding up a bag of cashews as Lily leaned on the trolley and stared into space. She could have been mesmerised by the tinny music piped in over the sound system, but it was obvious to Kate that her mind was far away from the supermarket.

'Huh?'

'Nuts!' Kate repeated, shaking the bag at her.

'No. . . I don't think so.'

Kate put the bag back onto the display. 'It was actually only a joke,' she said. 'But I can see that my jokes are wasted on you today.' She was beginning to wonder if she'd badly misjudged this shopping trip – perhaps Lily hadn't been ready after all. The shop was hardly busy, but everywhere there were mothers with children. There was one now, just along the display, playing peek-a-boo with a baby in a car seat strapped to the trolley while her companion – perhaps Grandma

– was choosing some oranges. Not exactly what Lily needed to see. 'Do you want to go home?'

'No. . . of course not. Sorry. . . I must be really boring company right now.'

'No more than me going on about how much I miss Alessandro. But if you're not up to this yet I can take you home and come and finish up for you.'

Lily threw her a melancholy smile. 'And then what? That's OK today, but you won't always be here and then what will I do?'

'I don't have to leave yet. . . I can wait until—'

'No you can't and I wouldn't want you to. I have to help myself before anyone else can help me; I know that. I have to go back to work soon and be part of life again, and I have to face all the constant reminders of what I've lost. The world is full of children and mothers and I can't hide away from that fact forever.'

'I know, but nobody says you have to rush it.'

'I say I have to rush it. I'm a burden to everyone like this.'

Kate rubbed her arm. 'No you're not, and you would be there for anyone else if the tables were turned. We all want to help you get through this.'

Lily took a deep breath and forced a smile. 'And keep that Italian stud-muffin waiting for you in Rome? Not on my watch!'

'I think we're at a point now where we're more certain of each other. He knows that even if it takes a little longer, I will go back now for sure.'

'He might, but that doesn't mean you should have to wait if there's no reason.'

'You're a reason. You're my sister, the most important reason. . .'

'And I have a good support network even with you gone so you needn't worry.'

'You and Joel. . .' Kate didn't dare ask, but it was something Lily hadn't mentioned and Kate needed to know. If they were almost back to their old selves, or at least communicating again, Kate was certain that they would pull through together, and that would reassure her more than anything else. If she thought they would be OK, she could leave for Rome happy and guilt free.

'It's tough, but I think we'll get there.'

'But he's not supporting you—'

'I don't need his support. Or at least, if I do, he needs mine too and he's hardly had that over the past couple of weeks.'

'But Anna and I want to support you both.'

'And you do. Even from Rome you could do that. We have these things called telephones now, you know, and they're ever so clever. Besides, Rome is only a couple of hours away and what's to stop me flying over to see you?'

Kate gave a small smile. 'True.'

'So I'll have lots of excuses to go there and I've always wanted to.'

'You'd better – as soon as I'm settled.'

'I might get some apples,' Lily said. 'I haven't had any in ages. Joel doesn't consider fruit to be proper food.'

'You're OK with me going though?' Kate asked as they began to wheel the trolley towards the fruit displays.

'Of course.'

'And you really do like Alessandro?'

'He's wonderful. I think he's the most perfect man. A bit too perfect, actually. I'm thinking there must be some dark secret he's hiding.'

'Really?'

'No, silly! You'll be happy. I'm sad that you couldn't live in England with him but I think he's the man for you. And I can tell by the way he looks at you that he adores you.'

'But you know it's my decision to move to Rome? Alessandro. . . well, he might have come to England if I'd asked him, but I'm not going to.'

'I know. It's a new start for you, and it's a good one. Anna thinks so too.'

'She does?' Kate asked with a bewildered smile.

'Yes, but you know that she'd never say it to you because that would mean she'd have to admit to being wrong about him before she'd met him.'

'We can't expect miracles I suppose,' Kate said, turning her attention to a bag of Granny Smiths.

'Not huge ones. But sometimes tiny ones do happen and if you don't go to Rome and get yours I will be very cross about it.'

* * *

Kate switched off the laptop and squeezed her eyes shut, massaging her temples. No matter how many times she did the sums, setting up in Rome was going to be tougher than she had imagined. The deposit on the apartment she'd chosen was huge for a start, as was the cost of moving even the tiny amount of belongings she had decided to take with her, which, even though expensive, was still cheaper than buying it all again once she got to Italy. Then there was the flight, the money she'd need to live on until she was earning there, the costs of various government permits, selling and legal fees on her house – and she still had to split the profits from that with Matt too. . . The list seemed endless and terrifying now that she saw the whole of it as more than just a distant dream. The date to move had been fixed and plans were in place, but Kate wasn't entirely sure that her odds of success were any good at all. She'd spoken to Alessandro and Lucetta about it all, and they had both assured her that help was at hand whenever she needed it, but she wasn't about to arrive in a foreign country to set up a new life and immediately rely on handouts. This was her venture, and she would succeed or fail by herself.

Her thoughts were interrupted by a knock at the front door. Kate frowned as she looked up at the clock. It had just gone 10 p.m., a bit late for an unannounced visit. She was just wondering whether to ignore it, thinking it could be trouble, when her phone bleeped a text.

I'm outside your house.

It was Anna. Why the late hour and why the surprise visit? Kate pulled her dressing gown tighter and rushed to the front door, pulling the safety chain off and opening up to reveal her sister on the step.

'Is everything OK?'

'Yes. I know it's late, sorry, and I know you weren't expecting me, but I've been asked to go to London for a few days for work and I wanted to catch you before I went.'

'Not that I'm not happy to see you but couldn't it have waited until you got back? I'm not going anywhere for a couple of weeks.'

'I know. But I needed to do this while it was in my mind.'

Kate stepped aside to allow her in and then bolted the front door again.

'I won't stay long,' Anna added.

Kate smiled. 'I don't mind how long you stay. But I expect you've got an early start tomorrow if you're off to London.'

'A bit, yes. I won't beat about the bush. . . it's about our inheritance.'

Kate blinked. 'Dad's money? What's made you think about that after all these years?'

'I was just thinking. And Lily had said you were worrying about money. I know that you ploughed yours into this house when you were buying it with Matt and I suppose he's in no position to ever reimburse you now, so you've lost that money forever.'

'Legally I have no way of getting it back anyway, even if I was going to try – which I wouldn't. It's not fair to ask Matt for that amount of money after all this time, especially when he has a baby on the way.'

'I know you would never ask for it back. It's one of your more admirable and yet frustrating traits.' Anna followed as Kate made her way back to the living room.

'So is there a problem with yours?' Kate asked. 'I thought you'd invested it in some super-duper savings account. It must be something big if it's brought you round at this hour, but if it's financial advice you're hoping for you've definitely come to the wrong place. What does Christian have to say about it? Have you talked it over with him?'

'Sort of. But he agrees that it's money I was given before I met him and so not really his business.'

Kate raised her eyebrows as she gestured for Anna to sit in the space on the sofa she'd just made by moving the laptop. 'Not his business? He doesn't care if there's a problem?'

'None of his business what I choose to do with it. There's no problem. . . Kate. . . I want you to have it.'

Kate stared at her. 'What?'

'You need some start-up money and I have some doing nothing.'

'But—'

'I know you're going to argue, but I also know that Dad always looked out for everyone as best he could. He bypassed Mum and left some of his estate directly with us because he knew that one day we'd need help and Mum wouldn't be able to give it. We all love her to bits but we also know that she's a complete flake when it comes to coping with real life. You need help now and Mum isn't able to give it, just as he'd predicted, and I think he would be happy to know that Lily or I could step in.'

'It's your money; you need it!'

'Not right now I don't. Maybe one day but we're OK, me and Christian. We both have good jobs and we have a bit saved between us. Think of it as a loan if the idea really bothers you, but you know it makes sense to take it.'

Kate shook her head. 'I couldn't possibly. . .'

Anna folded her hands over one another in her lap and held Kate in a frank gaze. 'I thought you'd say that. What are you going to do for money when you get to Rome?'

'I'll work.'

'Immediately? You have a job already. . . one that pays enough for this apartment you're getting?'

'No.'

'So this money will come from thin air?'

'It'll be a struggle but—'

'Why struggle? You deserve some happiness. You have the man so why not have the rest?'

Kate was thoughtful for a moment. Then she broke into a slow smile. 'Are you actually admitting that you like Alessandro?'

'He's alright,' Anna said. 'I have to say that coming to England to put everyone's mind at ease was a lovely thing to do and it shows he must care for you a great deal. Lily adores him now she's met him. Christian liked him too. . .'

'But did you like him? I already know everyone else does – you're the one I want to win over.'

'If you must run off to Italy then I suppose there are worse men to do it with.'

It was as close to an admission as Kate was going to get. She leapt up from the sofa and gave Anna a hug. 'Thank you.'

'I haven't done anything.'

'You've made me feel better about leaving. I would have hated to go knowing you didn't approve.'

'Oh, I still think you're mad. But at least I can see why you're so keen to do it.'

'It's not just Alessandro. You can't imagine how wonderful Rome is until you visit, and I can't wait to make my new life there. Even without him I would want to go.'

'But having him there helps, I imagine. . .'

Kate smiled. 'Of course. It's a very big bonus.'

'Changing the subject will not put me off the scent, though. You need money, and I know you don't have it.'

'I do need it, but I'm not taking yours.'

'Think of it as a loan to make me happy. If I know you have some financial security I won't worry about you as much. Now I don't have to worry about the man, I'll be worrying about how you're feeding yourself if you don't let me help.'

'Alessandro's family will feed me – they love feeding people!'

Anna frowned. 'You know what I mean. I'm talking about your general well-being. I don't think a few lunches will be enough.'

'I'm not taking it.'

'Argh! You can be so infuriating!'

'I think we established that a long time ago.' Anna didn't reply, but glowered at her so severely that Kate couldn't help bursting into laughter. 'If you ever look at Christian like that he must be in a constant state of terror!'

Kate could see that her sister was trying valiantly not to crack, but eventually Anna began to laugh too. 'What am I going to do with you?'

'I have no idea.'

'Me neither.'

'You'll miss me when I'm gone, though.'

'I will – more than you know.' She paused, and her voice was earnest when she spoke again. 'Please take at least some of the money. Not all of it, but something to fall back on. I know you need it and I can't stand the thought that I'm just sitting on what could make a huge difference for you out there. And if you won't let me gift it to you then let me lend it.'

Kate chewed her lip for a moment as she studied her. She could see it meant a lot to her, and she couldn't ignore the idea that this represented Anna finally giving her blessing to her and Alessandro. 'You're not going to let this drop, are you?'

'No. So if you want to shut me up you'd better sit with me now and we'll work out how much you need to make this crazy dream of yours come true.'

Twenty-eight

Summer had turned into autumn, but the change in season served only to intensify the stifling heat as Kate stepped off the plane and hurried across the tarmac of Fiumicino Airport. There was the baggage carousel to get past, of course, and passport control, and all the other travellers to contend with, and she didn't know how she was going to keep her sanity as impatience overwhelmed her. But keep it she must, because the prize waiting for her if she did was worth a thousand frustrating journeys through a thousand packed airports. A new life was just through the arrivals lounge, dazzling and wonderful, and she couldn't wait to get started. The teach-yourself-Italian podcasts had been listened to over and over during the weeks leading up to her flight, which had given her something to do during all those long evenings when she'd had to stay in Anna's spare room to save money once her own house had gone and wanted to keep from being too much of a nuisance to Anna and Christian. The days had been taken up by a temporary job with an agency at a doctor's surgery along with bits of sewing she'd taken in. She'd actually quite enjoyed the change of the surgery, knowing that it wasn't forever and that every bit of cash she earned made a difference to the dream she was constructing, turning it into a reality at last. She'd been reading about Italian property law, immigration policies, and employment and self-employment rules, and had even been to her local bank to talk about small business start-ups in other countries (although the advisor had been a little flustered by the nature of her request and had clearly been out of her depth). Anna, despite giving her blessing and financial help, had done her best to persuade Kate to drag things on at home for as long as possible. Kate knew it was just because parting would be so hard for them, and it proved to be, with tears at the airport on her departure, despite everyone's assertion that she was only a couple of hours away and they would see each other soon for visits. But there would never be the perfect time, and Kate was afraid that if she waited for it, she would never go.

In the arrivals hall now, Kate scanned the crowds, her heart thudding in her chest, almost dizzy with excitement. Alessandro had apologised profusely that he was on shift and unable to meet her from the plane, but that was OK. She would see him later and although Lucetta meeting her from the flight wasn't quite the same, she was just as excited to see her for all that this day represented. They had planned to have lunch with Signora Conti and Abelie first at their home, and then Lucetta would take her to meet her new landlord and get the keys to her apartment. *Her apartment.* It didn't seem possible that this was her life she was talking about. She was getting an apartment in Rome. This incredible, vibrant city was going to be her home from now on.

A hand appeared above the heads of others waiting to greet friends, relatives or simply transfer customers, waving frantically.

'Kate!' she called, and Kate homed in on Lucetta's broad smile. She looked as glamorous and effortlessly stylish as always in a pure white linen dress that virtually no one else could have pulled off, her olive skin glowing and her long dark hair falling in glorious waves around her shoulders. Her husband-to-be was a very lucky man.

Kate broke out into a grin of her own – a grin so wide it threatened to pull free of her face. She began to run, weaving through the crowds, dragging her case behind her. The two women threw themselves into each other's arms like lifelong friends.

'Welcome back to Roma!' Lucetta cried.

'I can't believe I actually made it back!' Kate said. 'I feel sure that if you pinch me now I'll wake up in my house in Manchester.'

Lucetta laughed. 'Then I will not pinch you.' She glanced down at Kate's only suitcase. 'Do you have more luggage?'

'No, just this.'

Lucetta frowned.

'The rest is in the hands of the removal firm,' Kate smiled, guessing Lucetta's next question. 'I wasn't planning on starting a new life on one suitcase, though I don't have a lot more to come if I'm honest. I tried to get rid of a lot of my belongings so that I wouldn't have to move too much here – trying to keep the cost down.'

Lucetta gave a sage nod. 'You can buy things here. I will show you the best places.'

'Thank you!' Kate slipped her arm through Lucetta's. It was strange, but only a few months ago she wouldn't have dreamed of being so familiar with Alessandro's sister. She'd found her unapproachable and rather terrifying, if anything, but now she saw a different side to her. Kate guessed that she had just been looking out for Alessandro, as Anna had been doing for Kate, and she couldn't blame her for that. It made her a good person, and her actions since had confirmed that. 'How's everything at home?' she asked as they walked.

'Good,' Lucetta said. 'Mamma is waiting to meet you later, and she will cook dinner to welcome you back.'

Kate smiled. Signora Conti was still unconvinced that Kate was the right woman for Alessandro, despite her commitment to moving nearby and Alessandro's continued attempts to win her over to the idea. It wasn't personal, though, and her offer to cook for Kate showed that at least she was trying. It would take time, but together they would convince her.

'Alessandro has given her so many flowers this week she does not know where to put them,' Lucetta continued. 'He is trying to make her happy so she will be kind to you, but she will be kind to you anyway because that is Mamma's way.'

'I can just imagine him doing that. He pretends to be a tough policeman but he's really just a softie.'

'Softie?' Lucetta asked. Kate laughed.

'Not as tough as he thinks he is.'

'Ah!' Lucetta joined in with a giggle. 'I will learn your funny English words.'

'I should really be learning funny Italian ones, not teaching you mine. It'd be more useful. My attempts at teaching myself aren't going that well, but I never was good at picking up languages at school. My French teacher despaired of me – said I was unteachable.'

'It will be different living here. You will hear it all the time and you will soon learn.'

'I hope so, because things might get difficult if I don't. Not least talking to your mother.'

'We will help,' Lucetta said. She gave Kate's arm a gentle squeeze. 'Here. . .' she added, stopping at the glass exit doors of the arrivals hall. 'I will get my car and you will wait.'

'Where?' Kate asked, blinking at a wall of white cabs as they stepped out into the sunshine.

But Lucetta didn't reply – she simply grinned at Kate.

'What?' Kate asked. 'What have I done wrong?'

The next moment Kate's eyes were covered by a pair of large hands. Instinctively she spun around, fists flailing, certain she was about to be mugged.

'Kate!' Lucetta squealed. 'Look!'

Kate stopped, hands balled in mid-air in front of her. Not that it would have been much of a punch if she'd thrown it, but she was glad she hadn't. Alessandro stood before her, grinning broadly. 'Oh!' she breathed. And then she threw herself into his arms.

When they had finished kissing, Kate glanced around to see that Lucetta was staring very deliberately at a nearby sign giving parking directions to visitors.

'You are a wildcat,' Alessandro said with that gently mocking smile. 'I was afraid for my life just now.'

'I doubt it,' Kate laughed self-consciously. 'I thought I was being kidnapped. I wasn't expecting you to be here.'

Lucetta smiled. 'We were dishonest with you.'

Kate opened her mouth to reply, but Alessandro spoke first. 'I had to work, but one of my colleagues stepped in when I told him why I wanted to be here today. But I did not know until this morning and I thought it would be a happy surprise.'

'It's that alright. You're making a habit of surprising me. You are allowed to let me have some warning you're going to turn up sometimes, you know.'

Alessandro pulled her close and kissed her again. 'No more surprises.'

'Not no more,' Kate said, smiling up at him. 'Sometimes is OK.'

He leaned in to kiss her again, but mid-kiss Kate felt him jump back sharply. They both looked around to see Lucetta grinning. Alessandro rubbed at his head where his sister had just rapped her knuckles on it.

'Lucetta!' he cried, and she let out a raucous giggle.

'You can kiss later,' she said, wagging a finger at them. 'All of the night. Now we must go to my car.'

Kate smiled as Alessandro took the handle of her suitcase in one hand and reached for her with the other. A feeling of great warmth and contentment spread through her. They say home is where the heart is, but she had never really understood that more than she did right now. Kate's heart was in Rome, and she had the strongest feeling as they walked together behind Lucetta, the sun on their backs, her hand enveloped in Alessandro's, that it always would be.

A Letter From Tilly

I hope you've enjoyed reading *Rome Is Where the Heart Is* as much as I enjoyed writing it. This was a very different book for me; I usually write stories firmly set in England, so it has been an adventure and an excuse to lose myself in another culture. I hope that you've enjoyed getting lost there too with Kate and her new friends. If you liked *Rome Is Where the Heart Is*, the best and most amazing thing you can do to show your appreciation is to tell your friends. Or tell the world with a few words on a social media site, or a review. That would make me smile for at least a week. In fact, hearing that someone loved my story is the main reason I write at all.

If you ever want to catch up with me on social media, you can find me on Twitter @TillyTenWriter or Facebook, but if you don't fancy that, you can sign up to my mailing list and will get all the latest news that way. I promise never to hassle you about anything but my books. The link is below:

www.bookouture.com/tilly-tennant/

So, thank you for reading my little book, and I hope to see you in Rome again soon!

Love, Tilly x

Acknowledgments

The list of people who have offered help and encouragement on my writing journey so far must be truly endless, and it would take a novel in itself to mention them all. However, my thanks goes out to each and every one of you, whose involvement, whether small or large, has been invaluable and appreciated more than I can say.

There are a few people that I must mention. Obviously my family, the people who put up with my whining and self-doubt on a daily basis. My colleagues at the Royal Stoke University Hospital, who have let me lead a double life for far longer than is acceptable and have given me so many ideas for future books! The lecturers at Staffordshire University English and Creative Writing Department, who saw a talent worth nurturing in me and who continue to support me still, long after they finished getting paid for it. They are not only tutors but friends as well. I have to thank the team at Bookouture for their continued support, patience and amazing publishing flair, particularly Kim Nash, Lydia Vassar-Smith and Natasha Hodgson. Their belief and encouragement means the world to me.

As for this book in particular, I must thank my good friend Louise Coquio and her dad, who entered into many Italian lunch-menu debates on my behalf so that Signora Conti could cook the perfect Italian lunch for Kate's visit. I'd also like to thank Simona Elena Schuler for her help with some of the Italian phrases that my poor command of the language failed to produce.

My friend Kath Hickton always gets a mention, and rightly so for putting up with me since primary school. I also have to thank Mel Sherratt and Holly Martin, fellow writers and amazing friends who have both been incredibly supportive over the years and have been my shoulders to cry on in the darker moments. Thanks to Liz Tipping, Emma Davies, Jack Croxall, Dan Thompson and Jaimie Admans: not only brilliant authors in their own right but hugely supportive of others. My Bookouture colleagues are also incredible, of course, unfailing and generous in their support of fellow authors, and I have to thank all the brilliant and dedicated book bloggers and reviewers out there, readers, and anyone else who has championed my work, reviewed it, shared it or simply told me that they liked it. Every one of those actions is priceless and you are all very special people. Some of you I am even proud to call friends now.

Which just leaves my agent, Peta Nightingale at LAW literary agency. She knows that I adore her, but for the record, I'll say it here for everyone to see. She's always there for me, whether it's to celebrate, commiserate, or just to tell me to pick myself up, dust myself off and start again. If it wasn't for her, this book wouldn't exist.